A rap at the front door preceded "Hey, Zoey, it's me," wending from the living room. Hank strode into the kitchen, chafing his hands to warm them. His cop face was still in place. Maybe it was just a trick of light and shadow, but seeing Zoey seemed to have a softening effect on those rigid planes and contours.

"Where's Sergeant Chichester?" she asked, now in possession of a name for the fullback-sized cop she'd dubbed Fat Tire for the brand of draft ale he preferred.

Earlier, she'd watched him cart two pasteboard document boxes out of Charlie's detached workshop and past the breakfast room's sliding glass door. A hyphenated number and FRANCE was block-lettered on each carton in permanent marker.

"He had an errand to take care of." Hank pulled a chair from the table and sat down. On some guys, a day's growth of whiskers was rakish, in a bad-boy sort of way. But he looked like a man one unemployment check away from Dumpster diving for his next meal.

Serving a search warrant on a house nearly as familiar as your childhood home must kindle a depressing sort of déjà vu. Zoey sympathized to a degree.

"I hate this," Hank said.

"Yeah" sounded less confrontational than "Tell me about it, why don't you."

Or so she thought, until he said, "I'm not the enemy, Zoey."

She pondered a moment, then allowed, "Hypothetically, if someone had asked who I'd want to investigate had my dad been arrested for a robbery/homicide, you'd be at the top of the A-list."

SUZANN LEDBETTER

Ahead of the Game

MIRA

MIRA

ISBN 0-7783-2068-5

AHEAD OF THE GAME

Copyright © 2004 by Suzann Ledbetter.

All rights reserved. Except for use in any review, the reproduction or
utilization of this work in whole or in part in any form by any electronic,
mechanical or other means, now known or hereafter invented, including
xerography, photocopying and recording, or in any information storage or
retrieval system, is forbidden without the written permission of the publisher,
MIRA Books, 225 Duncan Mill Road, Don Mills, Ontario, Canada M3B 3K9.

All characters in this book have no existence outside the imagination of the
author and have no relation whatsoever to anyone bearing the same name
or names. They are not even distantly inspired by any individual known or
unknown to the author, and all incidents are pure invention.

MIRA and the Star Colophon are trademarks used under license and registered
in Australia, New Zealand, Philippines, United States Patent and Trademark
Office and in other countries.

www.MIRABooks.com

Printed in U.S.A.

In memory of Smitty, aka Detective Gary M. Smith, Kansas City Crimes Unit, retired.

ACKNOWLEDGMENTS

The numero uno tip of my hat for this tale goes to my editor, Martha Keenan. She's been the invaluable guide and guiding light from our first day working together, but my debt on this title cannot possibly ever be repaid. Or praised nearly enough.

Other instrumental contributors and/or folks that just put up with my peculiar behaviors, questions and plot knots are my cherished husband, Dave Ellingsworth, Paul W. Johns, Susan Fawcett, the forever Smitty to me, Mark A. Elliston, attorney, Elliston Law Offices, Webb City, Missouri; and Mark (he'll know who he is, hopefully), sales associate for Brown Derby International, Springfield, Missouri. Almost last, but not least, the eponymous greyhound characters I adore, J. Robert (Bob) and Freddy Frijole (Fred).

And as always, agent Robin Rue and assistant Emily Sylvan Kim, who are the ne plus ultra antidotes to literary hypertension.

1

Urrt. Urt-urt. Urt.

The distinctive sound of a sofa skidding on the living room's hardwood floors snapped Zoey Jones's eyelids open. Well, the left one, anyway. The right went into spasms.

The digital clock on the bedside table read 6:17. In the morning, she presumed, although darkwise, 6:17 p.m. looked pretty much the same in February in Blytheville, Missouri.

Thump. Rata-rata. Clunk.

That would be, respectively, the coffee table scooting upside the sofa, the floor lamp's shade wobbling, and its weighted base zeroing in for a landing.

Zoey sandwiched her head between two pillows. That muffled the noise, but who, really, could sleep knowing Vesta the Vandal had snuck in the back door again to rearrange the furniture?

Okay, so her mother hadn't exactly snuck. She'd used the key Zoey had given her before realizing the side effects of Vesta's addiction to home decorating programs on cable TV.

Calling her mother a vandal was a bit harsh, too.

The damage Vesta wreaked during her predawn raids was more psychological than actual, except for the time Zoey body-slammed the entertainment center that had been on the other side of the room when she went to bed the night before. And the pratfall over a club chair that had migrated from the picture window to a couple of steps inside the front door.

The latter would have been a minor mishap, had Zoey not been lugging a fifty-pound sack of dog kibble whose string-stitched top required a hacksaw to open, but whose barely glued bottom seam split with one accidental bounce off the floor.

To be fair, when Vesta was in the throes of *While You Were Out*-itis, or *Design on a Dime* dementia, she dusted and polished and whisked all the crumbs from under the sofa cushions—as though any had had the chance to accumulate in the six months since Zoey had moved back to her hometown.

As obsessions went, it could be worse. Getting hooked on *Trauma: Life in the E.R.*, for instance. Zoey shuddered. Impromptu furniture rearrangement paled in comparison to emergency tracheotomy practice, or your basic exploratory brain surgery.

"On the other hand," Zoey muttered as she threw back the blankets, "why can't she just take ceramics classes or beginning decoupage, like a normal, blue-haired, bored-out-of-her-gourd mom?"

Visions of whimsical, painted-plaster elves sitting on whimsical, painted-plaster stumps, and chunks of bad poetry glued on boards and preserved with sixty-two coats of shellac danced in Zoey's head.

If she still lived in the suburbs of Kansas City, they could be hauled out of a closet before her parents arrived for the weekend or holidays. Living a half block away from Vesta and Charlie meant such objets d'art would have to be displayed 24/7. Prominently displayed. Like props from a Disney remake entitled *Snow White and the Nine Thousand, Six Hundred and Forty-two Dwarfs Do Haiku*.

Zoey sighed and raked back the hair from her face. She wasn't quite at the tear-it-out stage, at least.

"Count your blessings," she said, pulling on a brown-and-orange 2X velour robe over her horsey-print flannel pajamas. Cross-dressing wasn't her thing, but neither was hypothermia. Clearance sale men's pj's and robes set new standards for hideous, but their R-factor more than made up for it.

Fuzzy pink bunny slippers completed an ensemble guaranteed to never grace the pages of a Victoria's Secret catalogue. As if she cared. Eighteen years of freezing her heinie off in lingerie hadn't kept passion's flame burning between her and her ex-husband. Best she could remember, they'd started flickering before he proposed.

If she'd learned anything from Stuart abandoning her and their daughter to go find himself in the Caymans, it's that life's too short to sleep in a thong. Or with a shallow, self-absorbed dickhead, even if he happens to be your husband.

Zoey stood, stretched and breathed in the aroma of fresh-brewed coffee. Her mother might be a bubble off-plumb, but she brewed the best cup of coffee in town. Maybe the universe. Sidling between the footboard and the two giant, unoccupied dog pillows crammed between it and the dresser, she followed her nose down the short hallway.

The door to her daughter's bedroom was closed. More than closed, actually. Shut in the typical four-teen-year-old-girl fashion that implied invisible death rays emanating from the jamb and a motion-sensitive booby trap wired to the interior knob.

Claire is a good kid, Zoey mused. An excellent kid. Tough, smart, funny...

Heartbroken. A pretty, auburn-haired, brown-eyed Humpty Dumpty trying too hard to hide the cracks and holes her daddy left. It didn't matter that Stuart had always been a hands-off parent. What had been inevitable and, to be honest, a re-lief for Zoey had devastated her daughter.

Her hand hovered above the doorknob, then dropped. Once upon a time, tiptoeing in to kiss Claire's sleep-warm cheek said *I love you, baby.* Now it was first-degree burglary, felony trespass-ing and, in Claire's opinion, a form of child abuse.

A smile crooked Zoey's lips. *I thought so, too, when I was her age.*

A bona fide burglar, trespasser and, arguably, adult child abuser was bustling about the living room dressed in a NASCAR sweatsuit and low-impact aerobic tennies. The GoreTex tool belt Zoey had given her dad for Christmas rode Vesta's hips, making her look like a gunslinger who did a little carpentry work between shoot-outs.

The furniture stacked in the middle of the room resembled a vertical garage sale. Zoey couldn't de-cide if it was ironic or symbolic. After selling vir-tually everything she owned, including the house, to satisfy creditors after Stuart bought a one-way ticket to paradise (on credit), she had scrounged most of this stuff from garage sales, estate auctions and flea markets.

Her former, thoroughly despised *Architectural Digest* decor had been designed to impress the neighbors, Stuart's clients, his employers, random delivery drivers and anyone else who might have peeked through the entry's carved eight-panel door.

Stuart had had style, she supposed, but she'd felt like a docent in her own home. Even the utility room had had a theme, for cripes' sake. Maybe other working moms yearned for an olde English scullery replete with faux mahogany walls and cabinetry in which to wash, dry and fold their husbands' butt-saggy Jockey shorts.

Zoey Charlene France Jones had not. Ever.

Now nothing matched. The new-to-her castoffs blended in a cozy, hodgepodge collage sort of way. Like my life, she thought. A little nicked and scruffy around the edges, but mine to do with as I please.

Or it will be, as soon as Mom finds a new hobby.

"Interesting traffic flow concept," Zoey said. "The room looks lots bigger with everything jammed in the middle."

Vesta France yelped and went airborne. The plastic sheet she was wrestling floated down around her like a see-through parachute. "What are you doing up at this hour? Get yourself back to bed and stay there."

Grinning, Zoey folded her arms and rested a shoulder against the wall. So much had changed.

Some things never would. "I'm not six years old, Mom, and it isn't Christmas Eve."

Vesta paused, apparently uncertain whether to feign indignation or go the guilt-trip route. The third option was acting as though tearing the hell out of the living room had been planned weeks ago but must have slipped Zoey's mind.

"Oh, this is better than Christmas," she sing-songed, extricating herself from the plastic shroud. "Trust me, sweetheart. It'll be gorgeous when I get through."

When a husband who's also a certified public accountant says "Trust me, sweetheart" he's converting credit limits and marital assets to cash. A used car salesperson who says "Trust me, sweetheart" is making lemonade out of a lemon. Neither struck a tenth as much terror into Zoey as a sweet, moon-faced, titanium-backboned mother who said it with a smile. Not to mention a wad of plastic sheeting clasped to her bosom.

"So what's with the tarp?" Zoey peered around the furniture foothill. "And where are the boys?"

Bob and Fred, her rescue greyhounds, were as sleek and leggy as a pair of tiger-striped Bambis, thus about as hard to overlook as the bus line named for their breed. Usually the boys' basso profundo barks to go out for a morning whiz preempted the alarm clock. The retired racers came equipped with soulful brown eyes and love-at-first-sight personalities, but no snooze buttons.

"They're in the pantry," Vesta said, "chowing down on some leftover spaghetti and soy meatballs."

Not exactly the breakfast of champions—retired or otherwise. "Great," Zoey said. "You can take them home with you, until they stop tooting in Italian."

"Oh, don't be so grumpy. Bob and Fred love people food. Pasta, especially. A treat now and then won't hurt them."

They did and it wouldn't, but that was beside the point. Again, Zoey inquired about the tarp.

Vesta chuckled. "What do you think it's for? I have to cover up the furniture before I can get started."

Zoey's eyes narrowed. Her sleep-deprived brain was slow on the uptake, but she didn't need caffeine to leap from plastic by the acre to its role in her mother's latest urban renewal project. Truth be told, Zoey was amazed that Vesta's inner decorating diva hadn't upped the ante long before this. After all, her mother had told her a few million times already, off-white walls and ceilings were so 1980s.

"No, ma'am. Uh-uh. In other words, forget it. Push the furniture around to your heart's content, but you cannot repaint the living room."

"But—"

Zoey's hands raised and spread in the classic don't-bother-arguing position. "Even if I wanted you to, which I absolutely, positively do not, now or ever, my rental agreement strictly forbids painting anything, indoors or out."

"Hah." Vesta clucked her tongue and snapped the wrinkles from the tarp. "May all your worries be that small."

Something in her tone set off Zoey's radar. Before she could comment, Vesta went on, "I know you've been through hell the past year and pulled yourself up by your bootstraps like a trouper in spite of it, but sweetheart, you've just got to stop taking everything so seriously.

"It's beyond me why your uncle Al made you sign that lease, but he won't hold you to it. I've met some of his previous tenants. Take it from me, Al France should be paying you and Claire to live here, not the other way around."

The contract had frosted Zoey a bit, too, but as Al had explained, business was business. Without one, his insurer and lender would have conniptions, if the property sustained any damage, be it an act of God or not. And he'd knocked fifty bucks a month off the rent, in lieu of the clause requiring tenants' insurance.

Plastic crackled and swooped into position. Vesta shook her head, conveying the love not lost on her brother-in-law of forty years. "I told Charlie, I said, 'Charlie, what that idiot brother of yours is doing is an insult—to Zoey and to us. What's this world coming to when your own kin treats you like a stranger off the street?'"

"It's no big deal, Mom." Absently, Zoey snagged a corner of the tarp and draped it over a bookcase. "Uncle Al is a firm believer in the Turkish proverb, 'Trust in Allah, but tie up your camel.'"

A peculiar expression washed across her mother's face. She flushed and paled at the same time. Zoey wanted to ask what was wrong, but if anyone was treating her like a stranger, she thought it was Vesta.

It was only natural, she admitted, with a twinge of guilt. Yet her mother's habit of confiding in her beauty parlor operator, the shop's regulars and Naomi, the supermarket checker, was a constant irritant.

The two hundred miles that had separated them since Zoey had left Blytheville for college didn't seem like much. From day one, they'd talked on the phone a couple of times a week. Hardly a month had passed without Charlie and Vesta driving up to Kansas City for overnight visits, or later, Zoey, Stuart and Claire heading downstate.

Zoey shrugged, and tore off a strip of masking tape from the roll to tack down a corner of the tarp. Hardly a month was wishful remembering. Over the years, entire seasons had often zipped by between visits. Nobody's fault, really. It just sort of happened that way. One minute, they were all knee-deep in snow, then ziggety-bang, it was Memorial Day weekend.

Her dad's one-doc veterinary practice intruded. Stuart clocked countless evening and weekend hours at the office. So did Zoey, while slogging up the corporate ladder from computer grunt to assistant director of the tech-services department. Claire took dance lessons, violin lessons and gymnastics, played soccer and softball, and every blessed Friday or Saturday night was somebody's birthday party, or a slumber party, or a school-sponsored something-or-other.

When the calendar gods did bestow blank squares on everybody's Day-Runner, you could bet the farm on someone catching the flu or strep throat, or the car going kaflooey.

Or, as Zoey's conscience nagged, she'd sometimes wanted to stay home more than anything, including a winning lottery ticket and a fling with Brad Pitt, and had blamed those no-shows on the flu, strep throat, or the car going kaflooey.

Surely Vesta and Charlie had fibbed a time or two themselves. They had responsibilities. Needs. Lives of their own.

Which was why Zoey felt like a guest in theirs, albeit a welcome one. She hadn't expected everything to be the same. Time marches on and all that crap. She just hadn't expected it to be quite so different. Plenty of those "everything's fine" phone calls and forty-eight-hour reunions had smoke screens on her side, but who knew her parents were faking blue skies and rainbows, too?

She'd had to hear from Walt Nelson, the pharmacist, that Charlie France had shuttered his practice because his heart was failing and he couldn't find a buyer, not because he wanted to retire.

And it was Darla Quinn, Zoey's best friend from high school, who'd told her about Vesta's breast cancer biopsy, five freakin' years ago. In her mother's mind, since the polyp had been benign, she'd spared Zoey a month of unnecessary worry.

And then there was—

"Zoey..."

"What?"

Vesta flinched at Zoey's sharp tone. She perused the blank, vanilla walls, then lowered her eyes. "I guess I can't blame you for being mad at me, but all I'm trying to do is brighten things up for you."

"Yeah, I know, Mom." Zoey sucked in a deep breath, hesitated, then sighed in resignation. Reflex pulled her mouth into a smile. "You always have."

2

Detective-Lieutenant Hank Westlake hunched a shoulder against the wind-driven snow. The distance between the parking lot and the tavern's entrance was maybe ten yards—enough to make him wonder what had possessed him to leave hearth, home and the Mizzou-University of Kansas basketball game on his big-screen TV.

It wasn't thirst. Not with a six-pack of longnecks in the fridge. Hunger hadn't pushed him out the door, either. The jar of salsa and fresh bag of tortilla chips in the cupboard would have curbed his appetite till halftime. Before the third-quarter buzzer, he'd have tucked into a grilled butterfly pork chop and a wilted spinach salad.

So why was he trudging through a vapor-light and neon-tinted blizzard for a beer and a greasy cheeseburger at a bar three miles from his apartment?

The answer was bent over a table, wiping its graffiti-scarred top with a damp rag. In her other hand, she balanced a tray laden with dirty ashtrays, beer mugs and soggy napkins.

My, oh, my. Hank exhaled a long, slow breath.

Something akin to a nearly forgotten, greatest fear realized, hollowed his solar plexus. Zoey France still did justice to a pair of faded blue jeans. Womanly justice, as opposed to the youthful version that had contributed to Hank's lousy grades in world history.

Make that Zoey Jones, he amended. He had been in the service, repaying his country for his college degree, when Zoey returned to Blytheville for her wedding to Stuart Jones.

Hank's mother had meant well when she'd mailed him the newspaper clippings. Unlike those Annie Westlake had sent of other high school classmates' nuptials, accomplishments and felony arrests, the photo of Zoey and her four-eyed groom had been the equivalent of a Dear John letter—although his mother had had no way of knowing that.

Never having had the balls to ask Zoey out when he'd had the chance was a technicality. Hank had darn well intended to, as soon as he was a hundred-and-ten-percent sure she'd say yes. The next thing he knew, he was sweating buckets at boot camp at Fort Hood and Zoey was a freshman at the University of Missouri-Kansas City.

Water under the bridge, Hank thought.

Oh, yeah? said the snide, spidery voice that lived in the back of his mind. Then why are you here? And why'd you screw around for six months, hoping you'd run into her at Wal-Mart, the post office—anywhere but on her own turf?

Without a backward glance, Zoey carried the loaded tray toward the kitchen. She bumped open the bat-wing doors with a hip, then disappeared behind them.

Hank thrust his hands in his overcoat's pockets. The key ring weighting the right one was cool to the touch. He eyed the bar's name written backward in beer-gold enamel on the plate-glass window. Painted below "He Just Left" was an oversized, '40s-style rotary-dial telephone. Its cartoonish, bar-bell-shaped receiver was suspended in midair.

Duct-taped above the streetside door was an EXIT sign. Ambient light lent a two-dimensional brilliance to the reflective orange letters.

A believer in bad juju might be inclined to beat one of those legendary hasty retreats, while the gettin' was still good. Hank was known to read his horoscope in the *Blytheville Bugle,* but he cherry-picked the intriguing predictions and blew off the balance.

His stomach rumbled louder than the Toby Keith song on the jukebox. Screw karmic signage. What he needed in the worst way was food. The vending machine sandwich and chips he'd wolfed down at noon were long gone.

He moved to the brass-railed bar, an L-shaped relic from the same era as the phone painted on the window. The short end angled into the wall was unoccupied, as if reserved for a cop with an aversion to exposing his back to a room.

He put two stools between himself and the customer in a rumpled suit at the corner. The man's stubble was a couple of days old. Clasped in swollen, arthritic fingers was the kind of drink usually served with a miniature parasol and tropical fruit.

Mother Nature had whittled He Just Left's typical Friday night crowd to a dead-dog Tuesday's. Two thirty-something yuppie dudes were playing eight-ball at the table nearest the wall. If the pretty blonde and the brunette chatting tableside were impressed, they hid it behind bored smiles.

A few feet away, a couple sipping white wine had the look and thousand-mile stares common to bad blind dates and parents who'd vowed not to talk about the kids or their jobs. Dispensing with the weather, hopes for an early spring and a quip or two about the latest government boondoggle had reduced them to transcendental meditation.

The three blue-collar guys at the TV end of the bar weren't about to let singlehood, marriage, or Mizzou's lead-assed performance spoil their weekend kickoff celebration. Even when Al France, the bar's owner, called out pro-KU jeers from the kitchen, the gang didn't blink.

From the dearth of vehicles in the bar's side lot, Hank assumed that most of the patrons had walked from the nearby studio apartments and lofts resurrected from the bones of derelict warehouses and hotels.

Downtown had been a second cousin to Disneyland when he was a kid. Beg a ride and a few bucks off the folks and you and a buddy could waste an entire Saturday there. Catch a movie at the Luxe, then loiter on a street corner watching the girls watch the guys in tricked-out cars go by, and count the days till that magic sixteenth birthday wrapped your sweaty mitts around a steering wheel.

Merchants had laughed when local and absen-

tee developers asphalted acres of prime pasture-
land to build Southpark Mall. Months before its
grand opening, Blytheville's commercial hub had
begun to shift two miles off its historic axis. Seemingly overnight, fast-food restaurants, strip shopping centers, office buildings and subdivisions had
sprung up to orbit the mall's perimeter like Sat-
urn's rings. Before Hank entered the police academy, downtown had become a boarded-up,
tumbledown victim of progress.

The deterioration continued until several of the
same developers spearheaded a campaign to res-
urrect the district. Why invest in new construc-
tion, they said, when those blighted old dames
could be face-lifted and repurposed?

Sparing the wrecking ball was a great idea. The
hitch, as colleagues in larger cities had realized,
was that remodeling white elephants for offices required conforming to handicapped-access statutes.
Since those costly rules and regulations don't apply
as stringently to private, single-family dwellings,
lofts and condominiums were carved from upper-
storied spaces that once housed conveyor belts,
coal-fired furnaces and cast-iron machinery.

Hank admitted that the influx of sidewalk-level
artisans, art galleries, cafés, antiques boutiques
and live-music clubs was better than the no-man's
land downtown had become. Sure enough, what
goes down must come up.

There were exceptions, of course. Time, roller-
coaster economics and a succession of owners had
barely nicked the He Just Left. Hank took a lot of

comfort in that and wondered why he'd usually declined invites for an off-duty brew and a burger.

His affinity for nonstop shoptalk had waned, he supposed, and that's what cops did, before, during and after hours. Not that he loved the job any less. It was just that he'd either lived or heard the stories so many times that he was beginning to feel like Methuselah had forged his shield.

"Still snowing?" asked the man with the dainty libation. He looked like the Scotch-rocks type. The roses in his cheeks weren't from windburn.

"Uh-huh." Hank brushed melting flakes from his lapels, then laid the coat on the stool beside him. "Channel nine says two to four inches by morning."

The man jerked a thumb at the muted television bracketed to the ceiling. KU was ahead of Mizzou by seven. "That pretty gal on channel sixteen said one to three. She's a meteorologist, don'tcha know."

So was the forecaster at the competing station. Hank would bet the NBC affiliate won out. Southwest Missouri hadn't seen this much snow since the nineteen-teens and he loved every inch of it. He was as sick of scraping ice off his pickup's windshield as anyone, but crime stats dropped along with the temperature.

"Haven't seen you in here before," the man said, confirming his status as a regular. "Crummy time of year to move to town."

"Yep." Hank let the man's assumption slide. He

focused on the kitchen's bat-wings, willing Zoey to come through them.

They parted with a bang. His pulse kicked up a notch. An elderly waitress emerged with a plastic dish bin propped on one hip. Rumor had it that Gert Massey had been hired on the day Prohibition was repealed and hadn't smiled since Elvis had left the planet.

KU's star forward swished a three-pointer. Hank's groan joined the chorus at the other end of the bar. His new best friend chuckled. "If I was Missouri's coach, I'd be calling the wife to tell her to start packing for a move."

Wishing he'd opted for a nice, private table, Hank eased a menu from between a saltshaker and a bowl of beer nuts. Except for the three-alarm chili, the bill of fare was of the deep-fat-fried, stick-to-your-ribs-and-arteries persuasion.

"Me, I'm in sales," the man went on, as though Hank had inquired. "Restaurant fixtures and equipment. I know. Sounds boring as watching paint dry, but I could tell you some stories that'd curl your hair."

The swizzle stick dredged a five-pointed star in his watery drink. "So, uh, what do you do?"

Bust bar dogs that don't have the sense to know when they're being ignored was the first answer that sprang to mind. Admitting he was a cop would trigger a documentary about every undeserved speeding ticket. "Public relations."

The dodge effected a dubious frown. Nobody knew what public relations was, not even the people who did it.

"Are you ready to order?"

Hank's head jerked up so fast it was a miracle it didn't snap off at the neck. Zoey France Jones squinted at him. Her lips parted in surprise. "Hank Westlake? God, you look the same as you did in high school."

It was intended as a compliment, he was certain, but hard to take as one. For guys, anyhow. Especially former pizza-faced geek guys with three-dollar Beatle haircuts.

Still, the fact that Zoey recognized him at all and remembered his name had Hank grinning. "I'd say you hadn't either, but you're even prettier than you were back then."

"Yeah, right." She flapped a hand. "Nice to hear, though."

The bar dog piped up. "You two went to high school together?" His eyes slanted to Hank. "You told me you just moved here."

"Belated congratulations on the promotion to detective, Detective." Zoey laughed. "What, you're shocked the grapevine stretched clear to K.C.? When it comes to news, my mom puts the Associated Press to shame."

"Public relations." The man shot Hank a dirty look. "That's a good one, bub." He pushed off from the bar stool and shuffled toward the restrooms.

Zoey's gaze followed him. "Poor Rosie. He's really a sweet old guy, when he's not being a pest."

"Every bar has to have at least one mascot. You can't help but feel sorry for them, but strike up a conversation and you're in for a long night."

She removed Rosie's watered-down drink and replaced it with three fingers of Cutty Sark, straight up. "Believe me, I've heard his life story a zillion times. Scary to think that homelessness doesn't always mean not having a place to live."

Hank nodded at the wine sippers' table. "The worst kind of lonely is when you're not alone."

The spider voice said, *Now there's some sparkling repartee, ol' buddy. Order a beer to cry in, why don'tcha.*

Zoey nodded, as though she related all too well. But instead of commiserating, she went for the tease. "Maybe we should sic Rosie on them. Let him do the talking for them."

Her lips pulled back in a grimace. "Shame on me. He's been my human flash card, since I started working here. I'd have quit the first night without him."

Hank arched an eyebrow. "What do you mean?"

She signaled *be right there* to one of the basketball fans. "Let's just say, for a bartender, I'm a fantastic computer programmer, but Rosie's a walking encyclopedia on mixed drinks. Right off the bat, he ordered an Alabama slammer, then rattled out the recipe. Whenever he came in, tested me on a new drink. I thought I was doing great, until we got to *M* for martinis."

She rolled her eyes. "Shaken or stirred isn't the half of it. I just about threw in my apron before I graduated to old-fashioneds, but he gave me an *A* plus tonight on my planter's punch."

With that, she went to answer the summons at the other end of the bar. A moment later, the grate of a blender slushing ice, tequila, Cointreau and lime juice into a professional-grade margarita rose above Sister Hazel's "Out There" playing on the jukebox.

Talk about overqualified, Hank thought. She'd probably earned more in a week at that software company Doc France had bragged about than her uncle paid her in a month.

Computer techs also ranked miles above bartenders on the prestige scale. The Zoey he remembered didn't judge books or people by their titles, but most folks did. Middling towns like Blytheville were notorious for preaching the sky's the limit to their young and then snickering at their falls from grace.

For that reason alone, her decision to leave half a lifetime behind and move home must have been a bitch. Dumping Stuart Four-eyes, or being dumped by him—depending on which whisper on the wind you listened to—might have contributed, but Hank knew there was considerably more to it than that.

The particulars were none of his business. He told himself there were no smoldering old flames to stoke. Even if there were, he wasn't in the market for a relationship. Been there, done that; not only had he saved the canceled checks to the divorce attorneys, he'd framed and hung them on the bathroom wall above the toilet.

The spider voice repeated, *Then why are you here?*

He watched Zoey draw a beer from the tap, then start toward him. Over the past several weeks, her name had bubbled to the surface with increasing frequency. Maybe it was just one of those age things, like a sudden, overwhelming urge to buy a red, T-top Corvette.

Nah. It was because she was Zoey and he was Hank. What they'd always had between them was still there and didn't need a label.

"It's on the house," she said, setting the frosted mug in front of him.

"Thanks." Hank smiled. "Wish you could join me."

"I will, if you'll grab a booth before Rosie comes back and takes you hostage."

Hank dawdled until her back was turned, then poked a folded five-dollar bill into the wine carafe serving as a tip jar. It fell behind a couple of singles. He figured Rosie would add a few more, after he chased his froufrou punch with the shot of Scotch.

In the alcove leading to the restrooms, Hank spotted the old guy punching the pay phone's keypad. His index finger targeted each button with the careful precision of a DUI walking a line with his eyes closed.

Hank hoped he was calling a cab. The Blytheville PD-sponsored Free Ride Home program hadn't won many college-age converts. Regular elbow-benders like Rosie had usually had enough blackouts and near-misses behind the wheel to swallow their pride and let somebody else do the driving.

A few grumbles of protest drew Hank's attention back to the bar, where Al France was taking a remote control from the cash register drawer. Zoey's uncle measured a whisker over five-six in his waffle-soled boots. A food-stained sweatshirt pulled taut at shoulders and biceps hewn from four decades of long-haul trucking.

It was said that, after twenty-seven hours of high-stakes Texas Hold 'Em, the bar's owner bet the keys to the He Just Left on a final, winner-take-all hand. Al threw in the title to his rig, without mentioning the blown engine and stripped transmission he'd hoped to repair with his poker winnings.

The owner verbally conceded his four jacks to Al's four kings, shook his hand, and walked out. A player who'd stood behind him could have sworn the man held four aces, but who was he to argue?

News of the ownership transfer traveled at the speed of light. A slew of lien-holders, tax collectors, lenders and unpaid suppliers descended on Al France, which explained the shadow box nailed above the cash register. It displayed four fanned kings and a brass plaque that read: Sometimes when you win, you lose.

"Bottoms up, sports fans," Al said. ESPN's postgame show flicked to solid black. "We're closing early tonight." A slight dip of his chin offered both a greeting to Hank and an exemption from last call.

In theory, cutting off the booze should have the same effect as a factory's five-o'clock whistle. In practice, those with nowhere they'd rather be paid their tabs, then milked another half hour or so out of their drinks.

The wine enthusiasts stood and lifted their coats from the backs of their chairs like schoolkids bundling up for recess. The blonde, the brunette and a lanky fellow at the bar followed them out into the snow, which had diminished to flurries kiting on the breeze. From the pool table came the crack of a cue ball scattering a new rack.

Hank was digging into a second bowl of beer nuts confiscated from an adjoining booth when Zoey walked up with a cheeseburger and fries in a woven plastic basket, a fresh mug of beer and a coffee for herself. She took a napkin and a handful of ketchup packets from her apron pocket, then slid onto the bench across from him.

The burger was a custom model, piled with coleslaw, tomato, slabs of dill pickle and black olives. Apparently Hank's name wasn't all she remembered. "What'd I do to deserve this?"

Their eyes met and held a moment, then hers flicked to the bar. Hank's gaze traveled from the cash register to Al to Rosie, then doubled back to the empty tip jar.

Message received. A five-dollar tip for the beer she'd treated him to smelled like charity. It would to him, too, if he were in her shoes.

"I gave you the employee's discount on the burger," she said. "And kept the change."

"Fair enough." At first bite, drops of coleslaw dressing and grease rat-tatted on the basket's waxed paper liner. The antacids he'd chase it with later were a small price to pay for heaven on a grill-toasted bun.

Zoey ruffled the hair clinging to the back of her neck, then slouched against the worn vinyl backrest. Her tight-lipped smile was the kind customers received, not old friends. "So, what brought you out on a crappy night like this?"

"You," slipped out, before Hank could jam on the brakes.

Warmth slithered up his neck and he chuckled, as if acknowledging his foolishness made him less of a fool. "Truth be told, I've been asking myself that same question ever since I threw my truck into Park on the lot."

"Really."

"Scout's honor," he said, around a mouthful of food.

"I figured you'd show up, eventually." This time, her eye corners crinkled when she smiled. "Part of me hoped you would."

"Oh, yeah? What about the other part?"

"Well…" She stole a French fry and popped it into her mouth. From the jukebox, Stevie Ray Vaughan's Stratocaster howled primordial riffs that died on the mountaintop with him. "It's just weird coming home after being gone so long. A lot has changed. A lot hasn't."

She squirmed a little. He pretended not to notice.

She shrugged. "I wasn't sure I wanted to find out which category you'd fall into."

He nodded. "What about you? Have you changed?"

"Uh-huh. And hard as I try, I don't fit anywhere anymore."

"Or you do. You just don't want to, particularly."

She winced, as though the coffee she'd sipped had scalded her throat.

"God forbid you'd stayed the same ol' Zoey you'd always been," he continued. "You might as well have stayed put, gone to cosmetology school, married Mickey Schemp, had five kids, found Jesus at the prison chapel on visitors' day and helped Mickey start the All Souls Lost and Awander Church of the Blessed Redeemer in the storeroom of his appliance repair shop."

Snorty laughter wheezed from behind the hands she'd buried her face in. She peeked out between her fingers, lost it again a time or two, then gulped air and knuckled the tears from her eyes. "Westlake, you've always been good for a laugh."

He grunted and knocked back a third of his beer. Brain-freeze stabbed his temple. "I have a couple of ex-wives who'd argue the point. Strenuously."

"A couple?" She whistled backward, as if she'd stubbed a sore toe on the table leg. "Boy, did that ever come out wrong. I didn't mean—that is, Mom told me about the one, but—"

"No sweat." He sighed. "It's tough being a cop's wife. Beverly stuck it out the best she could, but what we had was gone years before things hit the either-or stage. Should have known, I guess, when we didn't have the energy to fight anymore."

Realizing he'd never divulged as much to anyone was like hearing his voice drone from a tape recorder with a broken stop button. "We went to a counselor. Renewed our vows. Talked about starting a family. I took a leave of absence from the department and was negotiating a small business loan for a security service, then..."

His voice trailed off. It was reassuring to feel the

breach in the walls he'd painstakingly erected around himself seal tight again. "Long story short, we'd ridden too far to change horses, by then."

Zoey's thumbnail prodded a cuticle. Shadows thrown by the low-wattage sconces obscured her face. Hank was in the process of giving himself a swift mental kick in the butt for bringing up the subject, when she said, "At least you had a horse to start with." She slanted him a look. "Instead of a jackass."

He laughed, more from relief that he hadn't gouged fresh wounds than from the sarcasm. *Jackass* would be a term of endearment, coming from Mrs. Westlake number two. Gwen would be teasing, but she'd also be right.

As Hank admitted to Zoey, his second stumble down the aisle was too clichéd for a decent soap opera subplot. Boy meets girl in divorce court anteroom. Each confuses sympathizer with soul mate. Loneliness impersonates love at first sight. Seven months later, the judge who'd married them in his chambers pronounced them two-time losers.

Somehow he and Gwen had remained the friends they should have been in the first place, but after ignoring the wisdom of "once burned, twice shy," he'd learned his lesson.

"Then you're not dating anyone?" Zoey asked.

He shook his head, his jaw working fast to dispense with the last bite of cheeseburger. Between swallows, he asked, "You?"

"Nope." She looked down, her fingertip ringing the lip of her coffee cup.

"You will. It just takes a while after a divorce to get over it and get back into the swing of things."

He groaned inwardly, realizing how that sounded. Hank Westlake, postmarital relationship expert.

Eyes focused on a cigarette burn on the tabletop, she spoke, as though she were thinking aloud but unaware of it. "No, I won't. Not because I'm still hurting. Actually, I feel guilty for not hurting—not to mention stupid, for not calling it quits a long time ago. Like before the wedding, when I knew I wasn't having cold feet but convinced myself that was all it was."

A protest hummed in Hank's mind. Before he voiced it, a rippling rush of déjà vu carried him to a muggy summer night on Doc and Vesta France's front porch. Heat lightning pulsed inside clouds as dry as white smoke. He and Zoey sat on the glider, confessing that the wide, wonderful world their class valedictorian had speechified about scared them shitless.

They were more than acquaintances and less than best friends. For hours, they whispered in the dark with the confidence and freedom of seatmates aboard a transcontinental flight. Then the phone rang inside and the lights went on and Doc France came out to tell them that Zoey's grandmother was en route to the hospital after a stroke. Hank shipped out for Texas the day of the funeral.

"The trouble with dating," Zoey went on, "is that it's a down payment on a relationship."

Hank agreed but kept his mouth shut.

"You can't just like somebody and enjoy going out and doing stuff together."

Okay, she was definitely on a roll, but the direction could go south at any moment. He'd be damned if he'd send it that way by saying the wrong thing.

"Me, I'd love one of those 'nowhere' relationships everybody else gripes about."

Hank lied, "Amen to that."

She looked up. Amused skepticism best described her expression. "I mean, what's wrong with two perfectly nice adults catching a movie now and then? Or a concert?"

"Or just hanging out on a Sunday afternoon doing nothing?"

"Yeah." She slapped the table. "Yeah."

"No strings, no expectations."

"None whatsoever." She hesitated, then added, as if it were an afterthought, "And no horizontal boogie."

"Absolutely not."

"Best way I know of to kill a friendship."

Well, his and Gwen's had survived it and a divorce decree, but this was no time to quibble. Not with a full belly and Bob Seger's "Ol' Time Rock 'n Roll" pounding on the jukebox and Zoey's big brown eyes shining back at him.

Toe tapping the chipped linoleum, he pushed the basket and beer mugs aside and went for broke. "So, now that we've squared all that away, you want to go bowling Sunday afternoon?"

3

Zoey's attention strayed from the greyhound's right front paw cradled in her father's palm, to the bluish cast to Charlie France's bulbous fingertips. A slender, wheeled tank fed oxygen through the noose of slender tubing looped over his ears and out the prongs inserted in his nostrils.

Some days, he managed fine without his "scuba gear." On others, his respiration was labored despite it. Many a rally culminated in a slump, and vice versa. Zoey and her mother suspected that he was supposed to breathe oxygen continuously. He insisted it was as needed.

A doctor of veterinary medicine apparently made as lousy a patient as a medical doctor. Of course, males in general weren't adept at accepting the limitations posed by aging and illness.

A white ring gleaming around each of the dog's chocolate brown irises was the sole indication that Fred wasn't as oblivious to the examination as he seemed. Off to one side, Bob squatted on his haunches, his front legs extended, like a fretful version of the Egyptian god Anubis.

Charlie gave the swollen knuckle a final look-see, then pulled away his hand and patted the dog's shoulder. "Good boy, Fred."

"What do you think, Daddy? Is it broken?"

He slowly shook his head. "Oh, I'm afraid the problem's a little more serious than that."

His tone pricked Fred's and Bob's handlebar ears. Zoey felt as if her stomach had shriveled and plunged between her loafers. "What is it? What's wrong?"

Behind his trifocals, the twinkle in the sea-blue eyes Zoey wished she'd inherited belied his somber expression. "Seeing as how I've made an average of two house calls a week since you adopted these guys, my diagnosis is that you're trying too hard to make your old man feel useful."

Using a kitchen chair's seat for leverage, he pushed himself up from the floor. If sarcasm was any indication, the new pharmaceutical cocktail his cardiologist had prescribed seemed to be helping. Zoey just couldn't reconcile the tall, tireless, happy-go-lucky man her father once had been with the wheezing, stoop-shouldered, moody one he'd become.

"Think so, eh?" she said, in the manner of a congenital smart aleck to a recovering one. "Tell me, exactly what part of a ninety-three-pound greyhound horsing around and stepping on his sixty-five-pound buddy's foot can be construed as trying to make you feel useful?"

He availed himself of the chair and took a manila folder from the Gladstone bag on the table. As he opened it, his grin was almost as ornery as ever. "Okay, the bruised toe is legit. Watch it for an increase in the swelling, or inflammation."

Feeling vindicated, at least partially, Zoey moved to the two-gallon jar on the counter and doled out bone-shaped biscuits to the victim and his assailant.

Bob wheeled around and trotted off to munch his treat on his pillow in Zoey's bedroom. Fred gazed up at her, telegraphing naked adoration and the opinion that two treats were the minimum required for proper healing.

It took a certain type of person to just say no to a greyhound. Zoey sighed and dropped another biscuit on the throw rug, as though it had accidentally fallen from her hand.

"However," her father drawled, his finger running down the file notes, "of your forty-seven SOS calls to date, three I'd classify as reasonable, two were borderline and the rest as dumb as the windies you told when you wanted to stay up past your bedtime."

He raised his head, the file closing in his lap. "Not that I'm complaining."

The gurgle of boiling water almost drowned out the crunch of dog biscuits being pulverized. Zoey poured the contents of the teakettle into mismatched china cups. The aroma of decaf Earl Grey was as weak as the brew seeping from the gauzy bags.

"Me and Vesta ran into Cara Flaherty at the Chevy dealership a couple of days ago." Charlie accepted the tea with the alacrity of a lifelong caffeinated coffee addict.

Zoey's lips turned under and flattened. Cara and her husband, Doug, a large animal specialist, had opened their dual-shingled veterinary clinic a few months before Charlie's recurring angina and fatigue had driven him to the family doctor, then a cardiologist.

She dunked the tea bag in her cup. "Are you and mom thinking about buying a new car?"

"Nah. Don't need one. Can't afford it, even if we did." He cleared his throat. "Now, as I was saying—"

"It wouldn't hurt to look, though, would it? Stuart did annual audits for a huge dealership up in Kansas City. This time of year, they all but gave away cars to get them off the inventory."

A grunt signified displeasure at his ex-son-in-law's name intruding on the conversation. "The only thing wrong with ours is it needed a tune-up, and Vesta forgot to get the oil changed and the antifreeze checked last fall. Cold as it's been, it's a wonder it starts of a morning."

How careless of her, Zoey thought. A sick, suddenly retired husband to care for, plus a destitute daughter and granddaughter landing more or less on Vesta's doorstep was no excuse for such an oversight.

"Yes, but you always told me the time to trade cars in was before you needed one."

He blew across the top of his teacup, then sipped from it, his eyes never leaving Zoey's. Returning the cup to its saucer, he smacked his lips, then said, "My bum ticker isn't Cara and Doug Flaherty's fault."

"No…"

"They aren't to blame for me closing my practice, either." An eyebrow crimped as it did when he wasn't finished talking and she'd best settle back and listen.

"You being away for so long, you might not have noticed, but I'm a tad set in my ways. Your mama warned me years ago that I ought to start catering to Fluffy and Fido, instead of livestock. I knew she was right, but being tied down to an office and an appointment book made my neck itch."

He reached back and rubbed his nape, as though the thought of it still did. "I liked working out of my pickup, meandering here to yonder and shooting the breeze with folks over a slice of pie and a cuppa joe. It's all I ever wanted to do. Except it got to where I couldn't make a living at it, long before the Flahertys came to town."

"Maybe so, Daddy, but—"

"There's no maybes or buts about it. Times changed. I didn't. The family farm is dying. Those who are left can't afford to pay for veterinary work they can do themselves."

He grimaced. "Can't afford to baby sick cows, either, when it's cheaper to put them down and go on."

Zoey laid her hand over his. His mottled skin was scaly and as translucent as an onion's. "What hasn't changed is that you're the best vet in the county." She craned her head to see past him. "Isn't he, Fred?"

Paws twitching, deep in dreams of forty-mile-an-hour sprints on packed-dirt tracks, the greyhound snoozing on the throw rug abstained from the vote of confidence.

Charlie splayed his fingers and captured Zoey's between them. "I told Cara to expect a call from you about new patient workups on Bob and Fred."

She tensed, anticipating what he was about to say.

"I can't be their personal vet anymore. Greyhounds aren't barnyard mutts. They're especially sensitive to barbiturates and anesthetic. If there's ever a real emergency, they'll need a doc who's familiar with them and knowledgeable about the breed."

His concerns were valid, as was the advice. The Hippocratic "Do no harm" directive applied equally to veterinarians. Her own inexperience with greyhounds' quirks and anomalies had spiked the house call rate. But what had prompted the discussion? Fred's toe? Or Friday's appointment with the cardiologist?

He squeezed her fingers. "I know what you're thinking and you're wrong. This isn't about me putting my ducks—or your dogs—in a row before I kick the bucket."

His bantering tone and choice of words didn't dispel the knot forming in Zoey's throat.

"This, uh, new course of treatment I'm on is going to give me a new lease on life." Chin buckling, he focused on a spot inches left of her ear. "Things aren't progressing as fast as I'd hoped, but…well, like they say, if there's a will, there's always a way."

The click of the plastic wall clock's second hand dueled with the hiss-and-halt cadence of his oxygen bottle's flow regulator. Disquiet squirmed behind Zoey's breastbone. She leaned sideways into his line of sight. "By course of treatment, do you mean the doctor put you on a different medication or something?"

His hand jerked from hers and wrapped around the teacup. Peering into it as he raised it to his mouth, he muttered, "You and your mama are two peas in a pod."

"Why? Because we love you?" Zoey couldn't quite extinguish a flash of anger. "Or because we resent being shut out? You won't even let Mom in the same room with Doctor Amanpour."

"Aw, baloney." He batted the air. "Vesta can't savvy half what the man says, and I haven't needed a woman to lead me into an exam room since I was six years old."

Footsteps drummed on the utility porch. The balky back door shuddered in its frame. Startled, Zoey wrenched around in her chair. Fred scrambled up from the rug a second before Bob's toenails clacked down the hallway. Claire rushed into the kitchen, breathing hard, her cheeks rosy from the cold.

"Hey, there, beauty," Charlie said, visibly relieved by the interruption. "Where's the fire?"

The greyhounds jockeyed around her like rockstar groupies, Claire said, "Gram told me to tell you that lunch is ready."

"What, the phone's out of order?" Zoey snapped, transferring her frustration to an innocent party.

Her daughter's face squinched into the "Cute, Mom" sneer hard-wired into every teenager's DNA. "Hazel Lou Murray called an hour ago, about a Heart Association fund-raiser on Valentine's Day, and Gram can't get her off the phone."

Charlie scooted back from the table. "Knowing Hazel, your grandma could've hung up and that chatterbox wouldn't have hushed long enough to hear the dial tone."

He fished a key ring from his trousers pocket. Zoey knew it galled him to drive around the block, instead of cutting through yards, as Claire had, but cold and exertion could trigger an angina attack. Or worse.

"Let's get crackin', girls. The recipes that nutritionist gave Vesta don't make your taste buds rear up and whistle 'Dixie' straight from the stove."

He lobbed the keys to Claire. "Want to warm up the car while I put on my coat?"

"Dad." Zoey lunged, but she bungled the interception. "She can't even apply for a learner's permit for months."

"Like I need one to sit in the car in the driveway."

"Yeah, smooth out, Zoey." Jaw slanted upward, he did a shoulder-rolling, shadow-boxing maneuver. "Grip it on that other level."

"You go, Grandpa." The greyhounds wriggled out the door ahead of Claire, then it closed on her pealing laughter.

Holy freakin' Moses. Grandfatherly indulgence was one thing. Being double-teamed was another. Too much was her straight-arrow, seriously uncool father talking jive and doing gangsta moves.

A car engine fired at full throttle; the noise resonated through the walls and the linoleum-tiled floor. The gas gauge's needle probably dipped a quarter inch before Claire let up on the accelerator.

Zoey groaned. "I don't want to think about her bumping the gearshift out of Park."

"Then don't." He pulled on the wool-lined, canvas barn coat he'd worn every winter in her memory. Now the fabric tented around his waist and the sleeves' frayed hems hung to his knuckles. "Even if she did, ten'll get you twenty that her feet are on the brake pedal, the way I showed her."

"And me." Zoey took down her hooded parka from the hook beside the door. "About a hundred years ago."

"It doesn't seem that long ago to me, sugar." Pinning the oxygen tubes with each ear, he tugged down the lumpy black-and-gold sock hat Claire had knitted him for Christmas. "Maybe I shouldn't tell you this, for fear you'll think my chain's slipped a cog, but sometimes, a certain look comes into Claire's eyes, or she'll smile that goofy, crooked smile, and for a minute, it's like having my little girl back again."

He returned the file folder to his medical bag, followed by the tools of his former trade he'd scattered on the table. "I expect I've called her by your name as often as I have by her own, but instead of giving me what-for, you know what she told me?"

The question didn't require an answer. Just as well. Zoey was biting the edge of her lip too hard to speak.

"First off, Claire asked what me and Vesta were thinking when we stuck a name like Zoey on a sweet little baby." He chuckled. "I told her we were so far back in the name book before we found one we agreed on, you were lucky we didn't call you Index."

Zoey had heard that France family chestnut approximately eight million times, but smiled, imagining Claire laughing at the punch line.

"Then she said I should quit apologizing for the mix-ups." He looked at Zoey. "Because if I confused her with you so much, then she must be pretty special."

He lifted his Gladstone off the table and draped his other arm around her shoulders. "Yeah, she's a teenager. Having had some experience with the species, I know there's a chance she was blowing sunshine up Grandpa's pant leg and, by association, yours." To her amazement, he voiced her thoughts precisely.

"But you don't think so."

"Not for a second." He smooched her temple. "I also know you can't pretend her troubles up in K.C. never happened."

No, she couldn't. Blaming Stuart's defection had enormous valid appeal, but excuses were just verbal Band-Aids.

"What you can do," Charlie went on, "is show Claire the credit and trust she's due. I'll wager she'll surprise you the right way more often than she disappoints you."

She already had. It was just easier to take the positive for granted and pounce on the negative. Zoey swiped at her nose with a mittened hand. "Oh, yeah? And when did you get so smart?"

He stood back to let Bob and Fred in the door, then held it for her. "About twenty-five years too late to do you any good."

Of two things Zoey was certain during the brief,

nail-biting ride to her parents' house. Her father had again evaded specifics about his heart condition and treatment. He had also decided to immediately test her and trust in Claire by telling the kid she could drive, then drawling, "That is, if it's okay with your mother."

Retribution was lame but swift. As they trooped into the Frances' postwar, vinyl-sided time capsule, Zoey said, "Jeepers, look at the slush we're tracking in all over Mom's clean carpet. Why didn't you have Claire pull the car into the garage, instead of leaving it in the driveway?"

Vesta, whose hearing hadn't failed one decibel since birth, hollered from the kitchen, "Charles Herman France, you'd better not be letting that child drive my car."

Zoey whispered, "Hear that? Do it again and I'll rat you both out."

Claire grinned. "You've gotta catch us, first."

While Charlie shambled off to the den, she and Claire cut through the living room to the kitchen. Though he tried to hide it, his strength was flagging. Once he disconnected the portable oxygen cylinder, he'd tether himself to the stationary electric oxygen concentrator and crank back in his recliner till bedtime.

Vesta was spooning melon balls into clear glass punch cups when Zoey and Claire entered the kitchen. Alongside the stove were four dessert plates with servings of peppered tuna steak on beds of lettuce, steamed broccoli and carrots and a whole wheat dinner roll.

The classic dieter's trick of using pint-size

dishes to make portions appear larger was like wearing black to look svelte. Such illusions might work, if everybody and his sister Sue wasn't already wise to them.

"How's Fred's toe?"

"Dad doesn't think it's broken, but he told me to keep an eye on it."

A local supermarket commercial's voice-over blared from the den. Vesta frowned. "Gallivanting around town always wears him out, but he's never too pooped to work the remote."

How visiting Zoey constituted gallivanting around town, she didn't know, but she reserved comment. Charlie's illness and retirement had isolated her mother, too. Activities as innocuous as going to Wal-Mart—let alone having her hair done, playing bridge or attending garden club meetings—had ominous implications.

Distance from home and the span of time Vesta felt comfortable leaving him alone was a perpetual crapshoot. Zoey and Claire being nearby, or in attendance to keep Charlie company didn't assuage it. If that euphemistic "something" happened while Vesta was gone, she'd never forgive herself, whereas his forays out into the world showed the type of all-American do-or-die spirit that won wars and football games.

Of course, her mother wouldn't forgive herself if "something" happened when Charlie went out, either.

She fit the punch cups into circular depressions in the plates and handed two of them to Claire. "Tell Grandpa to turn off the TV." Reading her granddaughter's face like a Gypsy does tea leaves, she said, "Off meaning off, missy. Not just turning down the sound."

Claire rolled her eyes and heaved the sigh of the eternally oppressed. "Ohh-kayyy."

When she was out of earshot, Vesta wrenched on the sink faucet and rinsed her hands. "I know, I know. I shouldn't be so bossy."

"You weren't—"

"Charlie can't help being sick. It's silly for him to haul that portable oxygen tank, just so we can sit down together at the table." She ripped a paper towel from the roll, dried her hands, then tossed it in the trash. "But God, how I hate eating in the den with that damned TV blasting away. You can't talk. You can't even think. I—I just hate it."

Zoey gently turned her mother away from the sink and tucked her into her arms. Age had softened muscles once toned by meticulous housekeeping and work as her husband's unpaid assistant. A vague fishy note mingled with the scent of beauty-shop hair spray and the Jergens lotion faithfully applied after every bath.

Vesta neither sagged nor stiffened, but rested against her daughter as if taking comfort in Zoey's touch without surrendering to it. Give in too much or too often, and emotional muscles lose their tone as well.

The TV went silent in the midst of a Tuesday-only sale on choice cuts of grade-A beef. Charlie blustered, "Tuna steak, my sweet asparagus. Until fish drag up on dry land and sprout legs, tails and horns, there's no such a-thing." To which Claire said, "Yeah, and if you'd eaten more of this kind, instead of the other, maybe your heart wouldn't be so screwed up."

"You'd better watch your mouth, kiddo."

"And you'd better start filling yours, before Gram and Mom come in here."

Vesta's shoulders were shaking before she eased back from Zoey's embrace. "That child…"

"Ought to have her braces welded shut," Zoey finished.

"Don't you dare. She doesn't take an ounce of guff off of your daddy and it's the best medicine there is for him."

Zoey's brows knitted. "What happened to respecting your elders? If I'd ever popped off to him like that, he'd have sent me to my room for, oh, probably a year. Maybe two."

"That's because you're his daughter."

"So?"

"Parents never stop raising their kids, no matter how old they are. Grandparents just sit back and watch them grow." Vesta handed her a plate. "Charlie clips her wings when they need it—don't think for a minute he doesn't."

An unspoken "sure he does" must have shone through, for Vesta teased, "Not that he had a lot of practice trimming yours. Law, you were born too big for your britches and it was me that pared you down to size most of the time."

"Funny, but that isn't the way I remember it."

"Of course you don't. I'm your mother. Everything I said went in one ear and out the other side.

That's why, on those rare occasions when Charlie lowered the boom, you sat up and took notice."

"Stood up and took notice," Zoey amended. Sitting down was out, until the sting from the dreaded forsythia switch wore off.

Ninety-nine times out of a hundred, all her dad had to do was eyeball the twig atop the fridge and Zoey became the epitome of the sugar, spice and everything nice little girls were made of. Once, maybe twice, the transition had been a smidgen slow.

Vesta started for the den, saying, "Remember when you were Claire's age and I told you I hoped you had *six* kids as spoiled, ornery and smart-mouthed as you were?"

Zoey did, along with her youthful opinion that civilization would benefit from a half-dozen exact replicas of her brilliant, erudite, insightful self.

"Well, sweetheart, like my wise ol' mama said when you were little, raising an only child doesn't necessarily mean you're five kids shy of a wish come true."

4

"You're still on the pill, right?"

The sweater bag on the closet's top shelf tumbled off and whacked Zoey upside the head. Without further ado, it fell down the narrow chute between the double row of jam-packed clothing and landed at her feet.

Zoey gawked at Claire, hunched over on the end of the bed, painting her toenails an exquisite shade of algae green. No sooner had she removed the cap from the bottle of polish than Bob and Fred had whiffed the fumes, sneezed violently and decamped to the living-room rug.

"If you're asking what I think you're asking," Zoey said, "Hank Westlake and I have known each other since eighth grade. We're just friends."

Claire gave her a skeptical look.

"We're going bowling, for Pete's sake."

The brush slimed the next little piggy. "Bowling can be a date."

Groaning, Zoey bent over and picked up the sweater bag.

Her camisole's spaghetti strap slipped off her shoulder, pinning an arm to her ribs. Jerking it back in place, she elbowed her way out of a closet only a hobbit could love. "Yes, bowling could be a date," she allowed, plopping the bag on top of the dresser, "but in this case, it isn't." The zipper's metal teeth unclenched, exhaling a lemony gasp from the sachet tucked in a corner of the bag. "And by the way, if you'd even started on your homework for tomorrow, I'd invite you to go with us."

"Spare me very much." Polish swooped wide of its mark when Claire cackled at the unintended pun.

Grateful the subject had ended on an up note, Zoey perused the folded sweaters she'd deemed too dressy, expensive, or bulky to wear to the He Just Left. Bowling wasn't a night at the Lyric Opera, but it deserved something nicer than work clothes.

As she rummaged through the bag, anything trimmed in sequins or beads scored an automatic no. The rust-red angora would be snazzy with her pleated khaki slacks and leather boots, but it itched like a hives attack after a couple of hours' wear. By the second game, she'd be roasting in the cream-and-navy cashmere. Ditto the wool fisherman's knit.

She was examining a lavender floral twinset, wondering what in God's name she'd been thinking, when Claire said, "If this really isn't a date, how come you've changed clothes four times already?"

"I have…" The "not" died in Zoey's throat at the mirrored reflection of the rejects strewn across the bed pillows, nightstand and a ladder-back chair. The mess made four changes seem like a conservative estimate.

Wadding the twinset into a ball, she stuffed it back in the bag with the other discards. "For the last time, this is not a date," she said, as much to herself as to Claire. "There's nothing wrong with wanting to wear something besides jeans and a sweatshirt once in a while."

She moved from the dresser to the chair and shook out the wrinkles from a white knit top. Pairing it with the moss shadow-stripe blazer on the bed would do just fine. Casual. Comfortable. Neutral.

The last gave her pause. Neutral might apply to this outfit, but it didn't describe her wardrobe as a whole. The sardine-can condition of the closet notwithstanding, before the move to Blytheville, a women's shelter had received ninety percent of her shamefully huge wardrobe. Until now, she hadn't realized that what she'd kept had memories attached, like care tags stitched in the seams that pricked her subconscious instead of her skin.

Not that all of them chafed. The outfit she'd worn to Claire's debut as Sandy in her school's production of *Grease*, for instance. The plum silk designer suit she'd splurged on after her promotion to assistant director of information technology. A sense of failure clung to the jersey sweater dress and matching duster she'd worn to divorce court. So did feelings of deliverance, liberation and confidence.

Whether the memories were sweet, sour, or in-between, the closet rods bowed with clothing that belonged to someone else. The khakis, the green blazer and the cotton T-shirt were unquestionably hers, even though she'd bought them at The Secondhand Rose on Main Street.

The mirror declared the shirt a perfect fit, though Vesta would say it was a fraction snug at the bustline. Her girls wouldn't send Cher to a plastic surgeon for a silicone booster shot, but at least they were in pretty much the same place they'd always been.

She turned sideways. Scowled. Sucked in her stomach. Not good, but better. If she didn't breathe much, eat or drink anything—or God forbid, sneeze—the pleats in her pants had a slimming effect. Now, if she could just suck in her ass....

Claire fell back spread-eagled on the bed to let the polish dry. Ankles flexing, her feet did a soft-shoe on air, the cotton balls jiggling between her toes. "That's what you're wearing on your non-date, huh?"

Zoey nodded and began gathering the rejects for near-future consignment to the resale shop. Her eyes roved her daughter's heart-shaped face. There were no discernable signs of distress, but that could mean Claire's mind was humming a copacetic tune, or her face was masking an internal, emotional volcano.

Zoey swiveled around and sat down on the bed. Her daughter's sidelong glance imparted the normal adolescent melange of wariness and boredom. "What?"

"Oh, nothing." Zoey plucked at the tunic crushed in her lap. "I was just wondering...I mean, Hank asking me to go bowling really isn't a date. If it was, or even if I thought he thought it was, I'd have turned him down flat."

"Okay."

"Not that I dislike him. He's a nice guy. Always has been. We've been friends forever, but never anything more than that."

"Okay."

On his part anyway, Zoey thought, recalling the tiny, completely unrequited crush that had materialized whenever she'd been between boyfriends or he'd been between girlfriends, which never extended beyond a lunch hour.

She'd almost dropped the tray she was holding when he walked into the He Just Left, Friday night. She truly had expected him to drop by the bar, sooner or later. It was feeling the same old electric zing shoot through her at the sight of him that took her by surprise.

Playing it cool was a pipe dream. Scuttling to the bar's kitchen seemed a more appropriate reaction than hurling the tray to the floor and herself at an adolescent heartthrob, who'd seriously improved with age.

As if Hank needed to. He wasn't the handsomest guy to stride Blytheville High's hallways, but he'd always had...presence, was the imperfect word for that indefinable something that made a girl—or a woman's—belly tingle.

Stuart Jones didn't have it. Couldn't have strummed Zoey's solar plexus with a Taser. And with her new life in the baby-steps stage, how smart was it to let herself anywhere near a man who always had?

"Look," she said, "even if this bowling thing is nothing besides a couple of old high school buddies hanging out together for an evening, I can't help but wonder how you'd feel if it was an honest-to-God date."

Claire lay motionless a moment, made a half growling, half laughing sound, then sat up. One leg winged horizontally and the other rose vertically to prop up her chin. "What you're asking is, even though you and Daddy never got along and now you're divorced and he's living large, screwing some slut not a whole lot older than me on a beach somewhere, would I totally freak out if a dude you haven't seen since high school asked you out on a date?"

Zoey's mental synapses flickered, not unlike a power grid approaching brownout. The random vowels and consonants that emerged eventually formed a drawling, "Uh-huh."

Head tipping to one side, Claire traced her instep's fine bones and swales. A glossy green fingernail followed a valley upward to her big toe, bulldozed a cotton ball, then burrowed into the next. "I dunno."

The response dumbfounded Zoey more than the earlier one had. She swallowed an impulsive *What do you mean, you don't know?* an instant before it slipped out.

A less confrontational substitute had yet to present itself when Claire said, "I'm not stupid enough to believe Da—to think my father—is ever going to, you know, like ring the doorbell someday, then we'll all cry and group-hug and everything'll be the way it used to be, only better."

She looked up. "I really don't, Mom. The way it was sucked."

Zoey struggled to keep the pain twisting her insides from showing on the outside.

"School still does and I hate this cliquey little town, except for Gram and Grandpa." She shrugged. "It isn't like I care if you go out with somebody. It's just kinda weird, thinking about it."

"Weird, how?" Zoey asked, tentatively.

The alarm clock's digital display advanced a minute. Fluffy globes of cotton dotted the comforter like a meteor shower. "I dunno."

"Claire—"

"Gawd, will you give me a freakin' break?" She scooped up the polish bottle and her pedicure kit and flounced off the bed. "I was just kidding you about changing clothes. Do you have to make an issue out of everything?"

Seconds later, the door slammed across the hall. A rap song's backbeat pummeled the walls like giant fists. Zoey stared at the floor. A drop-down menu of valid reactions listed anger, denial, regret, derision. She highlighted each in turn, then segued to the childish, shameful wish that she could ship the child she loved more than anything in the world to some remote outpost that specialized in turning teenagers into human beings.

She took the phone book from the nightstand's drawer. Its tissue-thin pages rustled as she turned to the residential section and advanced to the Ws. Allen, Clinton, Gwendolyn, K. G., William and Yolanda Westlake were present and accounted for. Hank was not.

Absent also was Beverly Westlake, for whatever that was worth, which was essentially zip. Nothing short of Armageddon erupting in Zoey's backyard would incite a call to Gwendolyn, presumably ex-wife number two. Or to the Blytheville PD. Whoever answered the PD's phone might pass on a message, but wouldn't divulge Hank's unlisted phone number.

The doorbell bonged. Bob and Fred scrambled up from the living-room rug and hit the hardwood in a single bound, their tails whacking the back of the sofa. Across the hall, the musical temper tantrum ceased, the door flew open and Claire yelled, "I'll get it!"

Claire had a firm grip on Bob's and Fred's collars and was opening the front door when Zoey charged into the room. The image of her tropically tanned, penitent ex-husband standing on the stoop clanged in her mind. But no, it was only good ol' Hank, grinning at the one-girl, two-dog welcoming committee.

"I seem to recall you always wanted a pony," he said, stepping inside. "It appears you went whole hog and got yourself a pair of them." Claire introduced Bob and Fred, then Zoey introduced her daughter. Hank stuck out a hand. "Pleasure to meet you."

They shook on it, Claire obviously surprised and delighted by the courtesy. It was then that Zoey noticed her daughter had exchanged her favorite grubby sweatshirt for a chenille turtleneck. And brushed her hair. Ye gods, the child was even wearing shoes.

Claire's mouth quirked at the corners. "Okay, so go ahead and say it."

"Say what?"

"How I look just like Mom when she was my age."

Hank kneaded the dogs' ears, as they snuffled at the legs of his jeans and leather coat. "Do you know the school maintenance man? Tall, gray-haired fella, walks with a limp?"

"Yeah," Claire said, stringing it out a couple of extra syllables.

"Well, if you don't mention how much I look like him, I won't say a word about you resembling your mother."

Comprehension widened Claire's eyes. She shrieked, "Omigod, you do look..." Then she clapped a hand over her mouth.

The ka-ching of brownie points racking up in Hank's favor was almost audible.

So was his reaction to the living room's spanking new decor. Vesta's vision for it centered on a retro Miami Beach motif she'd seen on *Trading Spaces* last week. Not bad, Zoey admitted, but not quite her, either, even if the paint color her mother had swooned over was the same shade of turquoise as the Plymouth Belvedere they'd brought her home from the hospital in.

When Vesta said, in her own defense, "I was just trying to think outside the plain white box," something had snapped inside Zoey's head.

Possibly my sanity, she thought, surveying the results as a visitor might. Such as the somewhat stupefied Hank Westlake.

The woodwork was gloss white. The walls and ceiling were a lush satin black, except for a border of the original flat white they'd taped off to create a coved effect.

Yards of snow-white sheers gathered on rods above the windows "popped," as Vesta crowed in HGTV-speak. So did the bronzed metal ironing board lowered to coffee-table height. Zoey's rebelliously mismatched yellow vinyl-upholstered sofa and red velvet easy chairs were anchored by an oval braided rag rug borrowed from her parents' attic.

Black spray paint rendered the cheesy, fake-wood entertainment center virtually invisible. Furniture polish and sock-footed buffing had coaxed a semblance of shine from the exposed hardwood floors.

On what had been a bare wall was Vesta's pièce de résistance: a white bedsheet stapled to a simple wood frame, at which she, Claire and Zoey had hurled gobs of primary-colored poster paint. It was doubtful that Sotheby's would call anytime soon to appraise their masterpiece, but Zoey wouldn't part with it for a million bucks.

Bohemian chic, Vesta had declared. Claire called it sick, this week's synonym for awwwesome. The color-blind greyhounds loved the rug. That morning, Charlie had hated the whole thing at first glimpse, hence his defection to the kitchen to examine Fred, talk in circles and sip heart-healthy tea.

Hank's lips puckered around a low wolf whistle. Directed at the room, rather than a female, implied two interpretations: "Fantastic" or "Call an ambulance, quick."

Zoey preferred the former but didn't really care

whether he liked it or not. His dislike of it might come in handy. If she ever moved, or wanted a change, he'd be easier to coerce into rolling on the ten coats of primer necessary to blot out the black.

"I always wanted to paint a room black," Hank mused. "I figured it'd make the walls close in more than they already do, once in a while." He smiled at Zoey. "Instead, they kind of disappear, don't they?"

Claire chuffed. "Don't let Grandpa hear you say that. He calls it a womb with a view."

"Good to know Doc hasn't lost his sense of humor," Hank said, laughing. "As I recall, he was quite the practical joker, too."

How dull the Elks' Lodge and Legion Hall meetings must be without him. Charlie France's pranks had escalated from sealing toilet bowls with food wrap—a never-fail classic—to sending an open house invitation to every Elk in three counties, except the host, due home that evening from a two-week business trip.

"If you're sure it's okay," Claire was saying to Hank, when Zoey mentally rejoined the conversation.

"What's okay?"

"For me to go bowling with you guys." She gestured like a defense attorney rebutting the prosecution. "Yes, I told you I had a ton of homework, but I just said that so you wouldn't make me go with you."

"Uh-huh." Zoey crossed her arms at her chest. "Then after we get home, or tomorrow morning, you'll be in a purple panic over an assignment you thought you finished or forgot all about."

"No, I won't. I did everything over at Gram's last night while you were at work." Pause. Switch on whipped-puppy look. "Call her, if you don't believe me."

Hank ducked his head a moment too late to hide a grin. Zoey struggled to keep a straight face. Hearing the same bushwah you told your parents repeated back at you was the essence of child-raising. Well, half of it, anyway. The other half was repeating your parents' bushwah to your own kid.

"All right, you can go, but if I find out later that you do have homework, you're in deep trouble, my dear."

"You won't," Claire insisted, just as Zoey had, when the reward for lying and getting away with it was worth burrowing under the bedcovers to finish assignments by flashlight.

Twilight was falling as Zoey jiggled the door and her house key to engage the dead bolt. Locking up combined basic physics and body English. Uncle Al was a peach of a landlord, other than his fanatical faith that WD-40, duct tape, or baling wire were the answers to any minor repair.

Zoey trailed her daughter and Hank down the fractured concrete driveway. Vapor streamed from her nostrils like a peevish dragon's breath, yet compared to midday, the air felt almost balmy.

Crocker Avenue was devoid of traffic, both pedestrian and vehicular. Friday night's accumulated snow had melted off the streets and sidewalks, but was refreezing in crusty patches on the asphalt and lawns.

Claire scooped a handful of snow from the boxwoods fencing the neighbor's yard and threw it at Hank. It whizzed past his ear, but his retaliatory shot nailed Claire's shoulder and splattered Zoey's neck. Icy slush trickled down her collarbone and into her bra. "Hey, I'm an innocent bystander."

"What's the matter, tomboy?" Hank taunted, deflecting Claire's second attempt. "Lose your arm, up yonder in the big city?"

The double handful Zoey scraped from the hedge caught him in the jaw and the chest. Claire nailed him with a bull's-eye to his forehead. He staggered backward against his car. "Okay, okay," he said, signaling for a truce. "You two oughta try out for the Royals."

"Mom was my softball team's pitching coach. We went to state three years in a row."

"Hustled me, didja?" He unlocked a dark-blue sedan's passenger door and pressed the armrest button to release the back door. "No more Mister Nice Guy. Retribution will be mine at the bowling alley."

Claire laughed. "In your dreams."

He apologized for the notebooks, paperwork and paraphernalia heaped on the back seat. "I'm technically off-duty, but I am on call till midnight." The rosy splotches on Claire's cheeks were paling even before he added, "Ever ride in a police car before?"

She looked at Zoey over the window frame. Her eyes projected alarm and loathing. "Mom never said you were a cop."

You didn't ask, Zoey thought. *Knowing how you'd react, I chose not to rock an already rickety boat.*

A silver minivan cruised by, the driver taking his share of the street out of the center. Hank's head moved with it as it passed. "Everybody's got to be something. It just happens, I'm a detective with the homicide unit."

Claire peered up at him for a long moment, her expression stony. A vaporous whorl billowed from her mouth. "Great. If any of the kids at school see me with you, they'll think I'm a narc."

"Oh, yeah." Hank motioned her inside the car. "On Sunday nights, the Bowl-A-Rama draws teenagers like a Kenny Rogers concert."

"Who's Kenny Rogers?" A slight buckle of her upper lip telegraphed "Oh. I get it."

True to his prediction, the bowling alley's patrons were few, several lanes between, and largely eligible for the senior citizen's discount. Alongside the far wall were two families whose children barely outweighed the featherlight bowling balls they heaved between their legs. The farther the balls thudded down the alley before careening into the gutter, the louder the parents cheered.

A lanky fellow with Buddy-Holly-style glasses was practicing his hook shot. He stomped and mumbled to himself when the head pin or the corners defied him, as if glued to the boards. Two stout, gray-haired women in Bubba's Bar-B-Q shirts sympathized from afar.

Claire said the hangarlike building smelled like feet. To Zoey, it smelled like Monday nights when she'd sat tailor-fashion on the counter atop the ball racks slurping a cherry ice from a soggy paper cone. Her father's teammates called her

Princess, rubbed her curly mop for luck, gave her quarters for the pinball machine and told jokes she didn't understand but laughed at as though she did.

She'd never been much of a bowler and hadn't tried in ages. Claire threw a natural Brooklyn, but like the bespectacled wanna-go-pro was plagued by 7-10 splits and sleepers. Hank added hers and Zoey's scores together and still won three straight games.

"Tell you what," he said, clearing the electronic scoreboard, "I'll throw left-handed this time."

Zoey massaged her aching shoulder. "Are you nuts? I'll be lucky to raise my arm enough to feed myself for the next couple of days."

"Puts a whole different spin on sore loser, doesn't it?" He neatly dodged a kick to his shin. "How about you, kid? I'll even spot you, say, thirty pins."

Claire flopped down on the molded fiberglass bench. "Gawd, isn't anybody starving besides me? All I've had since lunch is some chips and a candy bar and two sodas."

Zoey visualized the contents of her refrigerator. Tomorrow was grocery day. Unless Hank was a breakfast for dinner kind of a guy, grilled cheese sandwiches and canned tomato soup was all she could offer.

"Supper's on me," Hank said before she could speak. "I'll turn our shoes in and meet y'all in the Spare Room."

For Claire's edification, he added, "That's the bar and grill on the other side of the restrooms."

She looked over her shoulder at Zoey. Chin

aloft, she swallowed like a patient recovering from a tonsillectomy. "Uh, I'm not—you know—gonna faint from hunger. We can go someplace else, if you want."

"And break with tradition?" He shook his head. "You being a first-timer and all, we've got to eat here. Never let it be said that Hank Westlake cheated you out of the full bowling alley experience."

When they walked into the Spare Room, an elderly black woman, doing triple-duty as the cook, waitress and bartender, greeted Hank by name. Her birdlike eyes shuttled to Zoey, then widened. "Land o' Goshen, what do we have here? The Princess of France? Is that truly you?"

Zoey glanced up at Hank, grinning from ear to ear, then ran around the counter and into Jamesina Glick's spindly arms. "I can't believe you remember me."

"You're a mite taller and filled out where a gal ought to, but I'd know that face anywhere." She chucked Zoey under the chin. "Wouldn't have had to squint if you'd had a cherry-red mustache and dribblins down your shirtfront like you used to did."

Zoey introduced her daughter. "Pretty name, Claire," Jamesina said. "Means 'bright,' as I recollect. 'Course I'd've guessed the girl was kin, her being the spittin' image of you at that age."

Looks were exchanged, then the three of them burst out laughing, Claire loudest of all. Miracle of miracles, Hank's remarks at the house had changed an irritant into an inside joke.

Unfortunately, it was lost on Jamesina, who hadn't suffered fools gladly thirty years ago and wasn't amused by the trio's snickers. She informed Hank that he could either order or pay rent, and she didn't much care which.

Zoey was savoring her corn dog, curly cheese fries and a thick, real-strawberry shake when Hank's pager buzzed. Checking the readout, he excused himself and retreated several paces, thumb already working his cell phone's keypad.

"Westlake. Whatcha got?" The transformation from Hank to homicide detective was evident in his voice.

Jamesina clucked her tongue and pulled the pencil from behind her ear. She licked the lead tip and started adding up their check.

"At the Bowl-a-Rama," Hank said. "I'm aware of that. Where's Chichester? Jesus. Look, I've got two civilians with me and—"

Zoey looked at Claire, who was already wrapping her food in paper napkins. Smart kid. Swiveling on the counter stool, she stacked Hank's paper tray on top of hers and reached for his drink cup. Jamesina doled out lids and brown paper sacks.

"Yeah. Okay. I'm en route. Tell Chichester to meet me there, ASAP."

Two strides closed the distance to the counter, where Zoey and Claire were pulling on their coats. "I reckon I don't have to ask, if you overheard."

"Pretty hard not to."

He took out his wallet. "The convenience store two blocks down was just robbed. The clerk's in a bad way. At the moment, I'm the closest available."

A twenty-dollar bill skated across the counter. "Keep the change, Jamesina."

"Mind you keep your head down, boy. Hear?"

"Yes, ma'am." Simultaneously walking and talking, he said, "There's no time to take y'all home. I'm hoping when we get there, a uniform can give you a ride."

"We could call a cab," Zoey suggested.

"I'd rather you didn't. Not from here."

The surrounding neighborhood had never ranked among Blytheville's best and hadn't improved over time. Daytime shabbiness became sinister after dark.

Loath as Zoey was to admit it, darkness bothered her everywhere these days, not just in questionable neighborhoods. The older she got, the more childhood games of hide-and-go-seek and tag under the streetlights felt like figments of her imagination, not memories.

Al always walked her to her car after work, but oftentimes, the shadowed space between her car and the back door of the house loomed like an assault waiting to happen. She didn't miss Stuart, the corporate rat race, the gridlocked commute, or the second-mortgaged Tudor at the end of the cul-de-sac, but oh, what she wouldn't give for her attached garage in K.C. with its remote-controlled door.

Once inside Hank's unmarked car, it seemed as though he'd sprouted four extra hands. He keyed the ignition. Cranked the police radio's volume knob. Flipped on the headlights, grill lights, siren. Dropped the gearshift into Drive and wrenched the steering wheel.

The sedan wheeled from the parking lot and into the street. The tires whined, churning slush in wide arcs. Disembodied voices, male and female, blared from the radio, like a dozen talk shows broadcasting at once.

His face grim in the dashboard's chartreuse glow, he said, "You will stay in the car. Windows up. Doors locked. Got that?"

"Absolutely," Zoey said.

His eyes flicked to the rearview mirror. "Claire?"

"Yes, sir."

He swerved around an officer blocking traffic at the corner. Ahead, the strobing red, blue, amber and white lights of emergency vehicles flooded the pavement and storefronts. Hank double-parked the sedan beside a cruiser. The siren halted in midhowl; the radio went off. He popped the trunk release, then squeezed Zoey's shoulder and glanced back at Claire. "Sorry about this. I promise, I'll get you a ride, soon as I can."

The door slammed behind him before Zoey could utter a word. Bangs and rustling noises seeped inside from the trunk. A silver metal case in one hand and bulging duffel bags slung over his back, Hank jogged past the front bumper and disappeared from view.

Banners, posters, beer and cigarette advertisements, and the backs of a row of gondolas obscured the bottom two-thirds of the Jiffy Stop's plate windows. Above them, fluorescent fixtures chained to the ceiling cast a blinding band of light that diluted the beams from the security lamps bolted to the exterior awnings.

Uniformed officers milled about outside, gesturing, pointing, making notes on the small tablets cupped in their palms. An EMT sprinted around them and climbed into the cab of a waiting ambulance.

Claire unlatched her seat belt and winged her arms between the headrests. "You okay, Mom?"

"I'm fine. My heart's just pounding about ninety miles an hour, is all." She reached back and patted Claire's hand. Her fingers were clammy and ice-cold. "How about you?"

"Kind of scared." Claire chuckled nervously. "I probably shouldn't be but, you know, it's kind of exciting, too. In a creepy sort of way."

Zoey agreed, adding surreal to the description. "I feel like I'm watching a drive-in movie, but I know I'm not."

"Uh-huh. I wish we could hear what everybody's saying, though." She fidgeted against the seat. "Hey, if you want, I know which button'll turn on the radio."

"I don't want."

More fidgeting. "I'll bet Hank meant to leave it on."

Zoey thought, *I'll bet you'd fit in the trunk with all his stuff out of it, too.*

Two paramedics exited the store with a gurney. Blood smeared the upper edge of the wheeled stretcher's mattress and streaked the sheet-draped form strapped to it.

Claire whispered, "Oh, shit."

Zoey said nothing, her gaze locked on the pointy-toed cowboy boots projecting from the gurney's far end. The heels bounced and the soles swayed then tapped together, as though engaged in a hideous two-step. A third EMT helped the paramedics load the gurney into the back of the ambulance. All three emergency workers leaped inside and yanked the bay doors shut. Siren wailing, the cumbersome vehicle roared down the street.

"The clerk," Claire murmured. "Hank said he was in a bad way. Do you think the robber shot him, or something?"

Zoey removed her seat belt and scooted closer to the windshield. A van-sized ambulance had been parked alongside the larger one. Two policemen and a female paramedic were huddled around a figure seated on the curb. The man was leaned forward, his arms behind his back. Something dark stained the sleeve of his canvas coat.

"Mom? Hey. What's the matter?"

A raw, bilious taste spilled into Zoey's mouth. She jerked a glove from her pocket to scrub the condensation from the glass.

The EMT turned to speak to the taller of the two officers. The man on the curb looked toward them. An oxygen mask covered his mouth and nose.

"Oh, God. No…no."

Zoey fumbled for the door latch. Hammered the lock mechanism. Shoulder jammed against the side window glass, she hurtled out the door. Arms pumping, she dodged parked vehicles, eluded officers lunging to grab her, screaming, "Dad-dy. Da-deeee…"

5

The average human body contains approximately eleven and a half pints of blood. Hank examined the dark red pool coagulating on the storeroom's concrete floor. If he didn't know better, he'd swear several gallons must have seeped out of the clerk's fractured skull.

The man had been alive when the ambulance hauled ass for the hospital. It'd be a miracle if he was on arrival. No one could lose that much blood and survive.

Hank tuned out the racket drifting in from the sidewalk in front of the Jiffy Stop. More uniforms had responded than necessary or desired, but they'd isolated and secured the scene to his satisfaction.

The storeroom's steel-reinforced rear door couldn't be opened from the outside. With the exception of Detective Lonnie Chichester, nobody else would enter the building until Hank gave the all clear.

Counting himself, seven already had. Under the circumstances, it couldn't be helped, but each individual's entry and exit altered the scene. Something was carried in, most commonly on the soles of shoes. Something else was transferred out. Convictions had been lost due to that fundamental law of physics.

A by-the-book investigator would have already popped the latches on the equipment case and warmed up the camera's flash attachment. When feasible, Hank paused first to give free rein to his mind and senses. Investigative technique was a science, but also an art.

Blood-smeared shoe prints resembled the paper guides those of the two-left-feet persuasion used for do-it-themselves dance lessons. Which pairs belonged to the paramedics was fairly obvious by their proximity and relation to the gurney's wheel tracks leading from the room. He'd take comparison prints for elimination purposes.

Another set, unique in the soles, zigzag pattern, arced and swerved like a macabre question mark. They delineated the shape of the victim's head and right side of his upper torso. That set also trailed out the doorway.

Interspersed were faint smudges and melted slush left by Peter Dunleavy, the first officer to respond to the 911 robbery-in-progress call. Dunleavy's backup, Eve Ash, had contributed a few muddy, ladies' size-seven tracks.

The hammer lying a yard from where the clerk had crumpled to the floor told the tale. It was a steel-handled model with a perforated rubber grip. Strands of hair, brain matter and blood clung to the head.

Reasonable to assume—for now, anyway—the assailant had taken it from the open toolbox on a plywood shelving unit to Hank's left. The hammer's presence didn't necessarily mean the perp wasn't armed when he entered the store. Guns are noisy. Caving in a skull with a metal hammer is as quiet as the plop of a cantaloupe rolling off a produce bin and onto the floor.

Every time Hank thought he'd seen it all—witnessed the aftermath of the most senseless, savage acts a person could perpetrate on another—the bar jacked up a notch.

When he'd come on the scene, the cash register's drawer had been sticking out like a broad slotted tongue. The coins appeared untouched, but the bills were gone.

An average convenience-store robbery took ninety seconds. Few netted more than fifty dollars. Regardless of the amount, what a thief wanted most was to get away. Adrenaline and flight instinct were as volatile as nitroglycerine. Robbers had been known to rip an entire cash register off the counter when clerks failed to open the till fast enough to suit them.

Scenarios ticked through Hank's mind. If the clerk surrendered the night's take, why escort him to the storeroom and bludgeon him with a hammer? If the clerk was already in the back when the thief walked in, why not just punch "no sale," grab the swag and run like hell?

Maybe the drawer had been locked. Maybe the clerk had been that conscientious one in a hundred who kept the keys in his jeans pocket, instead of leaving them dangling in the lock. So…what? The robber hustled him to the storeroom, bashed in his head and took the keys? Or took the keys, then clocked him?

"For thirty-seven bucks." Hank's thigh muscles burned from squatting on his heels. Rising to his feet was out of the question. The urge to kick the mop bucket through the back wall was too great.

Knowing a suspect was in custody eased the pounding at his temples. Not much, but a little. Dunleavy had caught the old bastard dead to rights, bent over the clerk's body, his clothing soaked with blood. A zip-top sandwich bag with the cash and—get this—a friggin' stick-on label with Jiffy Stop written on it was in his coat pocket.

The rest of the particulars—the perp's name, age, date of birth, address—likely a homeless shelter—and bullshit assertions of innocence could wait. Collecting and preserving the evidence was job one. He glanced at his watch. If God smiled, after Hank processed the scene, there might be time to shower and shave at his apartment before Monday officially started.

The clerk died at 11:07 p.m.

Name, Joe Donny Marlowe. Five-ten. A hundred and sixty pounds. Black hair, hazel eyes. No outstanding wants or warrants.

Cited for DUI and excessive speed twice. A failure-to-yield resulted in a non-injury fender-bender. He'd dropped out of high school his senior year, eventually wised up and passed the test for a GED. Come May, he'd have earned technical school certification as a heating and air-conditioning specialist.

He was twenty-six years old.

* * *

It was 6:35 a.m. when the elevator doors at the hospital rolled open onto the fourth floor's Cardiac Care Unit. Hank's eyes slid from the glowing indicator light downward to the lobby button on the control panel. His thumb chafed the side of his index finger, then his hand folded into a fist.

Sometimes he hated his job. Never more than he did right now. Shit—not even close.

Other than the truck stop out on Highway 65, Sanford Memorial Hospital was the busiest place in town this time of the morning. Doctors on rounds, nurses taking vitals and doling out meds, food service personnel delivering breakfast trays, patients being jitneyed to surgery or to other floors for tests.

Breathing deeper and faster than normal entitled Hank to a full complement of smells associated with sickness and the treatment thereof. Disinfectants and air fresheners thickened the stew but didn't improve it.

He reached the corridor's T intersection and turned left. The narrower hallway dead-ended at a sealed, tinted-glass window hung with vertical blinds. Outside the door to the last room on the right, Sergeant Eve Ash was slouched in a plastic bucket chair. Her crossed knee propped a section of the newspaper. In one hand was a half-eaten health bar, its wrapper peeled like a banana. The other held a foam cup of coffee.

Vesta France and Zoey Jones were seated in those disproportionately high-backed lounge chairs that converted to cots for family members who stayed the night with a loved one. Beside them on a cushioned bench, Claire Jones was asleep, her arms and knees tucked like a praying mantis.

Seeing Hank, the women brightened, their shoulders rising and pulling back. Then their half-formed smiles froze and faltered, as if what he represented had superceded who he was.

A hometown boy straddling the barbed wire between friend and law enforcement officer wasn't a rare situation, but it was never comfortable. Some folks expected special treatment. Others' humiliation was pitiful to witness. A belligerent minority got in Hank's face, calling him everything but an American, as though it was his goal in life to heap misery on theirs.

He didn't expect any of those reactions, yet he wasn't prepared for the trembling, age-spotted hand that reached out for his. Vesta's palm was satiny cool. Its gentle pressure radiated up his arm and banded his throat. "It's so good to see you, Hank."

"You, too, Mrs. France."

Exhaustion rived her face and bloodshot, hooded eyes. Somehow, he suspected it predated the night's sleep she'd lost sitting a vigil. He wondered how long it had been since her head had hit the pillow and stayed there for eight uninterrupted hours.

If he asked, she'd tell him to tend to his own knitting.

The outfit Zoey had worn last night was creased and somehow seemed a size too large. Coffee rings and drips splotched her khakis above the bend of

her knee. Her expression was guarded and a touch
defiant, but not hostile. Not yet, anyway.

Hank tipped his head toward the door embla-
zoned with an orange Oxygen In Use; No Visitors
sign. "How's Charlie doing?"

"He's critical but stable," Zoey said. "The morphine drip to ease the angina zonked him out."

Her tone implied his status was patient, not
prisoner.

She must know he had been arrested and Mirandized before his transport to the E.R. Could
she have convinced herself that Charlie was an
innocent bystander? A wrong-time, wrong-place
victim of circumstance?

Yes, she could. He was her father. That our sons
may be as plants grown up in their youth; that our
daughters may be as cornerstones. Whether or not
Zoey recognized the quote, she exemplified it.

"If you'll excuse me a minute," he said to her
and Vesta, "I need to have a word with Sergeant
Ash. Then we'll talk."

As he backtracked down the hall a few yards,
Eve Ash disposed of the newspaper, cup and
empty wrapper. In her midnight-blue uniform and
Sam Browne belt, she resembled a chunky, middle-
aged third-grade schoolteacher.

Many a fleeing felon, not to mention fellow officers, had learned how much appearances could
deceive. Ash jogged five miles a day and could
bench-press two-eighty without breaking a sweat.
She only perspired when playing the harp in her
chamber quartet.

Hank made a show of checking his watch. "Correct me if I'm wrong, but shouldn't your shift have ended about seven hours ago?"

She grinned. "Always a pleasure to see you, too, Loot." Anchoring the heels of her hands on her holster and the belt's magazine pouches, she stretched the kinks from her spine. "Since I was already here and third shift was thin, the watch commander worked a trade-out."

A soft groan escaped, then her arms dropped to her sides. "Whoever designed that chair oughta be locked up for life, plus twenty-five."

"Uh-huh. I'll bet moseying down to the canteen for coffee felt pretty good."

"Nice try, Westlake. You know better than that."

He did. Her duty log would note every second she had been away from her post for restroom breaks, along with the name, employee number and probably the blood type of security staffers who covered for her. Also recorded would be the name, rank and serial number of every person who'd entered France's room, the purpose and the time elapsed.

"There's another granola bar in my jacket, if you're hungry," she said, "and a coffeemaker in the nurses' station. They brought us our coffee. If you want some, go down there and tell 'em Eve sent ya."

"Umm, how about you just fill me in on what's happened since you rode along with Marlowe in the ambulance."

She shook her head and sighed. "No dying declarations, that's for sure."

"He didn't regain consciousness?"

"That poor kid was so far gone, the paramedics had to jolt him with the defibrillator paddles before we got to the E.R." She grimaced. "In my nonmedical opinion, he was dead an hour before the docs gave up and pronounced him."

Eve had a son and a daughter around Marlowe's age. Civilians had no idea how often a cop's prayer for the injured and dying included giving thanks for sparing their own kids. This time.

Eve continued, her voice conveying the detached quality noncops often mistook for callousness, rather than a survival skill. "I bagged the vic's hands before he was sent to the morgue, then notified the medical examiner. Marlowe's clothing and personal effects were turned over to Lonnie Chichester, along with the list of E.R. personnel and treatment records. Lonnie took a statement, then I proceeded to the cubicle where the suspect was receiving treatment and followed him up here to his room."

"Did France say anything?"

"No." She frowned. "He responded to the doctors and nurses, but it was gibberish to me with that oxygen mask strapped over his face."

Hank nodded. "Good job, Eve."

"All in a day's…" She ran her fingers through her cap of salt-and-pepper hair. "I don't mind telling you, this one's got me bummed, big time. I mean, c'mon. Doc France knocking off a convenience store is crazy enough, but beating the clerk to death with a hammer? It's—it's—"

"Incomprehensible," Hank finished for her, as if a word—or a dictionary full of them—could describe the emotional impact.

Zoey's father being suspected of serial jaywalking barely tipped the scale of believable. That he'd been found at the scene on his knees beside Joe Donny Marlowe, his hands and clothing bloody and the money from the register in his pocket, was simply not possible.

Except evidence was impartial. Every piece Hank had gathered, photographed and sketched at the Jiffy Stop implicated Doctor Charles H. France for robbery and second-degree homicide. If proven that the hammer belonged to him, premeditation would up the charge to first-degree murder.

"We've known each other a long time, haven't we, Hank?"

Nothing good ever followed that intro. It was a forerunner to salary freezes, loan denials, medical and theological sermons, tax audits and divorce petitions.

"I don't have the rank or the right to say this," Eve went on, "but I think you'd be wise to back off and let Lonnie handle this one."

He started. His temper flared. "No, Sergeant. You don't have—"

"Everybody at the scene—including the media—saw Ms. Jones and her daughter bail out of your car and run to Dr. France. It doesn't matter a damn how they happened to be with you when you got the call. If it had been Chichester, you'd yank him off the case in a nanosecond."

Hank stanched a knee-jerk response, allowing his brain a moment to clear and, perhaps, function objectively.

Barring a family member's involvement, cases didn't come more personal than this one, but criminal investigators weren't judges. They didn't have the luxury of recusing themselves.

Bias didn't necessarily defang the proverbial fine-toothed comb. The truth was, Zoey's father had put himself in a box so airtight, torching the evidence lockers wouldn't save him. If there were any gaps, Hank would bust his chops to find them. If not, he'd know in his gut and his heart that Charlie France was guilty beyond a reasonable doubt. A *shadow* of doubt, if it was humanly possible to determine.

"I respect your opinion, Eve, and I appreciate you giving it. But no, if Chichester were in my shoes, I'd trust him to do his job."

Her lips puckered, then smacked apart. "Okay, sir. Anything I can do, let me know." A shoulder roll disguised a surreptitious backward glance. "Makes you sick at your stomach, though, doesn't it? Those gals' whole world has been turned inside out and the man who did it is in there sound asleep, snug as a bug in a rug."

"Which is where you ought to be." Hank clapped her elbow. "Go on, now. Tell dispatch you're ten-seven and scram. Whoever's next in the rotation will be here before I'm ready to leave."

He picked up her chair and moved it in front of Vesta and Zoey. Claire was awake, but groggy. Her mouth contorted into an ugly sneer. "If you're here to tell us how sorry you are, save your fuckin' breath."

The look Vesta leveled at her granddaughter

would have melted corrosion off battery cables. Her tone cut syllables like a serrated blade when she said, "I'm madder at your grandpa than you'll ever be, missy. Taking it out on Hank shows how much growing up you need to do. Apologize to him. Now."

Tears welled in the girl's eyes, already swollen from crying. Claire bowed her head and muttered, "Sorry," through clenched teeth.

Zoey's crossed arms tightened. One hand chafed her jacket sleeve, as if warding off a chill or an outburst. The tension rippling between the three of them would set a cat's fur on end.

He ought to separate them. Speak with each individually, beginning with Vesta. Dunleavy and Chichester had taken their statements last night, but they'd had hours since to discuss, speculate and conjecture.

Hank, the reluctant Trojan horse, would repeat many of the same questions, paying closer attention to their reactions than to their answers.

A nurse carrying an IV bag padded by and pushed open the door to Charlie's room. Hank pulled a notebook from his pocket and paged through it to a clean sheet. He jotted the time and drew a circle beside it to fill in later with her name.

Sedation was by legal definition a form of impairment. Even if Charlie France was alert enough to respond to questions, he couldn't be held accountable for anything he said. The rule of law extended to comments made to or overheard by medical personnel.

Once the dosage was curtailed, the officer on

guard would accompany all hospital personnel, and anyone else, into the room and monitor verbal exchanges. Consultations with an attorney were the sole exception.

Zoey said, "The policewoman told us we aren't allowed in Daddy's room, on your orders."

"In accordance with procedure." His voice was gentle but firm. For all intents, her father's hospital room was a jail cell and subject to the same restrictions.

"This is an active investigation, Zoey. For the time being, only medical personnel are allowed inside." To Vesta, he added, "And legal counsel, if you've retained an attorney on his behalf."

"Not yet, but we've known Gavin Van Meter for years. He helped us when Charlie closed the practice and with our wills and…" She slumped, as if a yoke had dropped from the ceiling onto her shoulders. "Gavin's not the kind of attorney you mean, is he?"

Zoey clasped her wrist. "It's too early to worry about that now. Office hours don't start for another couple of hours. We'll make some calls then. Okay?"

Looking somewhat relieved, Vesta said, "And to the bank, too. The first thing a lawyer wants to know is whether you can borrow enough money to pay him."

Hank said, "I'm guessing Charlie's retirement hurt y'all a little, financially. Was he worried about money?"

"Are you implying that my father robbed the Jiffy Stop to pay the electric bill?"

The remark lingered, as sharp as ozone, until

Vesta said, "Charlie has been irritable off and on, the past month or so. No, since around Christmastime. I never dreamed the bills had anything to do with it."

"Mother!"

"Be quiet, Zoey. We can either answer Hank's questions here, or he can haul us down to the police station's interrogation room."

Humor was at a premium, but Hank had to squelch a smile. Vesta was apparently a fan of *Law & Order*, along with home decorating shows.

"Charlie made a good living," she continued, "but veterinarians don't earn the kind of money folks think they do. Especially old softies like Charlie. He'd let the charges stack up, even though he knew the feed store was getting paid Johnny-on-the-spot.

"We were getting by all right on Social Security, before he got sick. We couldn't afford to keep our private insurance—the premiums went up every time we turned around. Medicare is a godsend, but it doesn't pay for the medicine Charlie has to have. The cheapest prescription he takes is forty-some dollars a month."

She turned to Zoey. "That's why I have to be there with him, when it's time for this pill or that one. If I'm gone, he'll skip taking them, thinking he'll stretch the prescriptions out longer."

Claire said, "He tried to fake me out last week. He pretended he'd swallowed it, then it fell out of his hand, when he spilled the water." She rolled her eyes. "If I tried that, he'd stick it down my throat, like a cow or something."

"Why am I just now hearing about this?" Zoey demanded.

"I didn't want to worry you, sweetheart. No sense in it, now that we're wise to your father's tricks."

The answer didn't mollify her daughter one iota. Hank sympathized with Zoey. Annie Westlake's latest antiworry scam had been telling Hank and his dad that she'd misplaced her billfold, not that it was snatched from her purse during choir practice.

When it and her fib were discovered, her reasoning was that she hadn't seen who took it and had canceled the credit cards and notified the bank, so why raise a fuss?

He said, "I'll need a list of the medications and dosages Charlie was on, as well as any over-the-counters he took."

Vesta reached into her purse for a small spiral notebook similar to Hank's. "Everything's in there. Lord knows, somebody has to keep track."

Hank thanked her and slid it into his pocket. Interviewing the pharmacist would supply details on side effects and possible interactions, particularly if they weren't ingested as prescribed.

"What's the nature of his heart condition, exactly?"

Vesta and Zoey exchanged glances, then looked away, as if embarrassed. Zoey answered, "His heart is enlarged. He has palpitations, angina—severe at times."

Vesta chimed in, "He went to the doctor because he loves to putz around in his workshop, but it got so he was tired all the time. He's not well now, by any means, but the medicine is helping. Some days, he can go quite a while without his oxygen."

Hank frowned as he added the information to his notes. What they'd mentioned were symptoms, not the cause. Odd, as most family members could rattle off multi-syllabic Latin terms like a second language.

His knowledge of coronary diseases was limited, but he asked, "Was the diagnosis atherosclerosis, or uh, maybe endocarditis...?"

Again, they consulted visually. Zoey's features tightened with annoyance. "The truth is, Hank, we don't know a precise diagnosis. Dad blows his stack if we pester him with questions."

"What about his doctor? Surely he'd tell you, if you asked."

"Oh, no, he won't. Congress passed this idiotic thing called the Health Insurance Portability and Accountability Act. Dr. Amanpour says if he tells me anything without Charlie's permission, the government could fine him a quarter of a million dollars."

"Amanpour's overreacting," Zoey said, "but the law is a huge mishmash nobody understands and the fines are too high to take any chances."

Amanpour didn't need a federal boondoggle to stonewall Hank. Doctor-patient privilege would be the answer to any question Hank asked.

Claire said, "The store repossessed our computer before we moved, so I went online at school and looked at a ton of medical Web sites. Type symptoms into their search engines and they match them with diseases. All I found out was that about everybody with heart trouble has angina and palpitations and stuff.

"Then I tried Googling the names of Grandpa's medicines. That was about worthless, too. Most of them aren't prescribed just for heart diseases."

Judging by Zoey's and Vesta's expressions, this was all news to them. In particular, her mother was staring at her in amazement. "I went to the library and did exactly the same thing."

"Oh, yeah? Well, gee, thanks for telling me. I skipped lunch for a whole week and wasted a bunch of study halls for nothing."

Zoey shook her head, a slight tremble in her chin. "No, you didn't, baby. I'm proud of you for trying."

"I had to do *something.* Nobody tells anyone anything in this family. Like it's a big secret that we don't have any money and that Grandpa's sick. Get real, why don'tcha? Everybody in this crummy town knows that."

"Why don't you yell a little louder?" Zoey shot back. "Somebody out in the parking lot might not have heard you."

"Hush, the both of you, and I don't mean maybe."

Hank cleared his throat. "Just one more thing for now, then I'll be on my way." He looked at Vesta. "Where did Charlie say he was going when he left the house last night?"

"Well…" She fiddled with the purse in her lap. "We had a nice dinner. Broiled chicken and steamed asparagus and the gelatin salad with pineapple chunks he's 'specially fond of."

Hank nodded to prompt her along.

"After I cleaned up the kitchen, he was watching TV and had the sound turned up so loud I couldn't concentrate on the book I was reading. To get away from it, I went into the bedroom and…I, uh, I must have dozed off for a bit."

"Then you don't know when he left."

"No, I can't say as I do."

"What was he watching on TV when you went into the bedroom?"

Her thumb worried the purse's strap. "A car race? Maybe that motorcycle show. The one where that man and his son holler at each other constantly."

"Do you have any idea how long you might have slept?"

She shook her head. "I'm sure it was just a catnap. I had to give Charlie his meds and—oh, I almost forgot, I wasn't finished in the kitchen when Zoey phoned from the bowling alley to tell me Claire had gone with you."

Hank smiled. She was trying to help, but that didn't narrow the time frame much.

"The next thing I knew, the girls were beside the bed, shaking me awake."

"Was the television still on?"

"Why, yes. As a matter of fact, it was. Loud as ever, too."

That would have absorbed the sound of the garage door opening and the car backing out. But what if Vesta had wakened while he was gone? "Was he in the habit of leaving the house of an evening? Going out for a drive or anything?"

Her eyes narrowed. "Absolutely not."

No pause for thought and emphasis to boot. As honest and straightforward as she'd been, Vesta France had looked Hank straight in the eye...and lied.

6

The latest issues of *AARP Magazine* and the *Journal of the American Veterinary Medical Association* arrived with the Frances' Monday mail. Zoey sat at their breakfast-room table, idly flipping pages. She skimmed photos, their captions and the article titles. Her attention span wasn't short. It was nonexistent.

The phone rang, as it did every five or ten freakin' minutes. She took up the pencil beside a ruled tablet. Silly, she supposed, to screen calls with the answering machine, eavesdrop on the audio portion, and write down the caller's name and gist of the message.

Few of them would be returned. None, if Vesta heeded Zoey's advice.

When she'd let herself into the house, the machine's indicator light had been blinking, as if its tiny electronic mind was about to blow from an unprecedented number of messages. Al France had called twice last night, before Zoey reached him from the emergency room. Local television and newspaper reporters asked for, begged for, demanded interviews. Reverend Harris was organizing a prayer chain. A notorious ambulance-chaser had tendered his services, flouting the law against direct solicitation. Friends, neighbors and former veterinary clients offered support, casseroles, condolences and companionship, as though Charlie had passed away.

This morning's callers included Darla Quinn, reminding Vesta of her perm appointment on Thursday, then urging her to sue the police, the prosecutor and most of the population for libel—or was it slander? Darla could never keep straight which was which.

An oddly succinct Hazel Lou Murray said the Valentine's Day fund-raising committee thought it best that Pearl Sears replace Vesta as co-chair. MasterCard expressed concern about a late payment. The Chevy dealership's customer service manager inquired whether the Frances were completely satisfied, satisfied, somewhat satisfied, or unsatisfied with the recent repairs to their car.

For the sheer hell of it, Zoey was tempted to call him back to say she'd let him know, as soon as the homicide squad released her parents' car from the impound lot.

Pencil poised to add another entry to the list, she tensed, as the ring sequence halted. *Don't let it be the hospital, or Mom, or Claire,* she chanted to herself, as if a mantra warded off heart failure.

Two words into the machine's outgoing message, the caller hung up. Hallelujah.

The clatter of the pencil on the table blended with the creak of the aluminum storm door. "Hey Zoe, it's me," Hank called from the living room.

He strode into the kitchen, chafing his hands to warm them. The cuff of a latex glove dangled from his overcoat's pocket. His cop-face, as Claire aptly described it, was still in place. Maybe it was just a trick of light and shadow, but those rigid planes and contours seemed to soften when he looked at her.

"Where's Sergeant Chichester?" she asked, now in possession of a name for the fullback-sized cop she'd dubbed Fat Tire for the brand of draft ale he preferred.

Earlier, she'd watched him cart two pasteboard document boxes out of Charlie's detached workshop and past the breakfast room's sliding glass door. A hyphenated number and FRANCE were written on each carton in permanent marker.

"He had an errand to take care of." Hank pulled a chair from the table and sat down. On some guys, a day's growth of whiskers was rakish, in a bad-boy sort of way. He looked like a man one unemployment check away from Dumpster diving for his next meal.

Serving a search warrant on a house nearly as familiar as your childhood home must kindle a depressing sort of déjà vu. Zoey sympathized to a degree. It wasn't exactly rhapsodic to be here sparing her mother the humiliation of watching two burglars with badges pawing through everything from her underwear drawer to the Christmas decorations in the attic.

"I hate this," Hank said.

"Yeah." That sounded less confrontational than *Tell me about it, why don't you.*

Or so she thought, until he said, "I'm not the enemy, Zoey."

She pondered a moment, then allowed, "Hypothetically, if someone had asked me who'd I want as an investigator if my dad were arrested for a robbery/homicide, you'd be at the top of the A-list."

His lips curled inward, a grimace merging with a feeble smile.

"Except this is real. He's old and sick and in solitary confinement in a hospital room and I need an enemy. Somebody I can blame and despise and curse for this…this…" She gestured futilely. "*Nightmare* is the obvious choice, but that's not even in the ballpark. Those, you wake up from. This just keeps going and going and getting worse."

The phone rang. She jumped as if a bomb had detonated. Pushing up from the table, she reached across the counter and unclipped the line from the jack. The ringer on the extension in the family room had been switched off months ago. Distance muted the other one in Vesta and Charlie's bedroom to a palatable cheep.

Retaking her chair, she blew the hair out of her face and glared at Hank, daring him to criticize or rebuke her. Or refer her to a therapist.

Too bad that an objective person to vent to wasn't in the budget. She felt as brittle as the icicles clinging to the patio's awning. Divorce stress, job stress, no-job stress, moving stress and single-parent stress now felt like petty irritations.

"You're my rock," her mother had told her that morning at the hospital. "I don't know what I'd do if you weren't here."

Zoey's mind had screamed, "I don't want to be your rock. I'm not that strong. How about somebody being my rock, for once? And dear God, what I wouldn't give to be anywhere but here right now."

A mental image of running down the corridor, shooting down to the lobby in the elevator, bursting out the brass-framed glass doors and driving hellbent for the highway—any highway, any direction—had been so vivid that when it evanesced, she had been surprised to find herself clenching the chair's cushioned armrests instead of a steering wheel.

The emotional crush had relented enough for to natter something inane like, "Don't worry. Everything's going to be okay." That had been a ridiculous lie, not only to her mother, but also to herself. The apparent comfort Vesta had derived from it centered on the assurance that whatever the outcome, she wasn't alone.

Lie like that to me, Zoey thought, looking at Hank. *I won't believe it. I won't hold you to it. Just hearing it might chase away the helplessness, until I can figure out who to fight and how.*

Aloud, she said, "You believe Daddy murdered Joe Donny Marlowe, don't you?"

He blinked as though taken aback, yet she sensed the question was not unexpected. Over the course of his career, he'd likely been dared to admit or deny bias countless times.

She wasn't merely a suspect's relative, though. Nor a unit commander, a reporter, a defense attorney, or your basic snoop-on-the-street. And his name hadn't been picked from a roster to investigate the case.

"This is going to sound like canned dialogue from every cop show on TV," he said, "but what I do or don't believe is immaterial."

"It isn't to me."

He looked behind Zoey, probably staring at the pair of gaudy ceramic roosters squared off to spar. "If that's the criteria for enemy versus friend, then feel free to hate me for being a cop."

His gaze shifted to her. "Evidence is what I believe in. Sure, pieces have been misinterpreted, especially when we don't have much to go on, but they never lie."

Zoey sniffed. "But people sometimes do."

"Not sometimes. Constantly. Well-intentioned ones outnumber the bald-face, save-your-ass type, but if folks kept a daily tally, like they do for calories and fat grams, the total would knock their socks off."

Picking up the pencil, she began doodling a sinuous question mark. "So what you're really telling me is, whether you personally believe it or not, the evidence says my father is a thief and killer."

"It's preliminary...." He rubbed a spot above his eyebrow. "All right. Yes. I'm sorry, but it does."

"And the search?" Eyes, fangs and a forked tongue were colored in at the tip of the mark. She glanced up. "I'm assuming the boxes I saw Lonnie Chichester carry away weren't empty."

"Nope."

She gored the sheet of tablet paper with the pencil lead. "Then it's a slam dunk. A done effing deal. All over but the plea bargaining."

Again, he broke eye contact. "I wouldn't say that."

Of course he wouldn't. The investigation was less than a day old. Her father's side of the story had yet to be heard. Even though she'd gleaned all her knowledge of investigative procedure from Nancy Drew novels, select movies and *NYPD Blue*, she knew perpetrators weren't arrested, tried and convicted within hours of committing a crime.

More like weeks. Hah, Ms. Ever-the-Optimist, try months. Years. She didn't need to be a cardiologist to know Charlie France didn't have years to devote to proving his innocence. Neither did her mother.

And what about Claire? She was just a kid. Oh, she worked overtime trying to act twenty-five, street-smart and world-wise. In some respects, she was more mature than Zoey had been when she *was* twenty-five. Yet behind that closed bedroom door lived a girl known to drag out her Barbies from beneath the bed and whose secret favorite movie was *The Little Mermaid*.

Tears swam in Zoey's eyes, hot and briny. Four lives were being torn apart because a retired veterinarian with a failing heart drove across town to a convenience store at the worst possible time.

Why, she had no idea. Figuring out what had happened next was a matter of deductive reasoning. Charlie had walked into the store and spied the Baggie with the cash on the floor—accidentally dropped by the panicked killer when he ran out. Charlie probably hollered for the clerk. When no one answered, he'd pocketed the money for safekeeping and found Joe Donny Marlowe unconscious and bleeding on the storeroom floor.

Between shock, excruciating chest pain and breathlessness, it was a miracle her father had lived long enough to be admitted to the hospital.

The truth will out. His faith was solidly vested in that adage. Since he'd said it an average of once a week throughout her lifetime, hers should be, as well.

"Don't worry," she'd told her mother. "Everything's going to be okay."

A lie? Obsessing on the cops' version of the crime had made it taste like one, but evidence-schmevidence. Charlie France wasn't a thief. If he wasn't a thief, he damn sure wasn't a murderer.

Moments before he'd entered the Jiffy Stop, somebody had rifled the cash register. That same somebody had attacked Joe Donny Marlowe with a hammer. Her father might well have seen the real killer and would soon be able to identify him.

"Penny for your thoughts," Hank said.

Zoey arched her eyebrows. "Save your money. Mine have occurred to you, if you're half the detective I know you are."

"Meaning…"

Positing her alternative modus operandi like that eureka moment when a computer program compiles without a glitch. Hank's reaction was typical cop-style stoicism. "Interviewing your dad should clarify a lot of things."

"Oh, it will. I guarantee it." Also on the agenda was medical clarification from his doctor, if Zoey had to shake Amanpour till his stethoscope's ear gizmos clanked like castanets. "After you talk to Daddy, we'll be allowed to visit him, won't we?"

"First things first. Like you catching up on some sleep." Hank's chair stuttered backward on the linoleum. "How about if I walk you home? Sunshine and fresh air will do us both good."

He knew Vesta and Claire had borrowed Zoey's car for the appointment with an attorney. He'd probably guessed she'd have walked over to unlock the house for him and Chichester, regardless.

"Why am I getting a vibe that you told Chichester to pick you up at my house, when he finished his errand?"

"Beats me. I told him to check here first. If I wasn't out front, to try your place."

She tore the list of messages from the tablet and stuck them in her purse, then reconnected the telephone line. "Nothing like hedging your bets."

"Transportation was the least of my worries." He unhitched her coat from the back of the chair and held it for her. "I figured it was fifty-fifty, whether you'd kick me out and throw the dead bolt."

Turning, she looked up at him, expecting a grin, not his melancholy smile. "I could never do that to you, Hank."

He snorted. "My mama told me 'never' is the most edible word in the English language."

Maybe so, but Zoey had never seen a friend more in need of a hug. He'd spent the night at the crime scene. Her father being the prime suspect had Hank walking a wire between private citizen and public servant. The strain showed and it hurt to see it.

Her fingers hooked his jacket lapels. "Aw, c'mere." Pulling him closer, she said, "I'm declaring a sixty-second truce. Me, same ol' Zoey. You, plain ol' Hank."

"I don't think that's..." trailed off as her arms slipped around his waist. He sighed "Oh, hell," and buried his face in her hair.

Nestled against his chest, ignoring the shoulder holster inches from her nose, she inhaled the rich scent of leather, a faint note of cologne and an indescribable aroma unique to him.

Listening to his heartbeat quicken, she realized he wasn't the skinny boy she'd hugged goodbye so many summers ago, then cried herself to sleep over; yet he was, in ways she'd missed and no one else ever matched. The familiar entwined with the unexplored whisked away the dust from an old, enduring attraction.

Tipping back her head, her cheek grazed his stubbled jaw. Their mouths were a whisper apart and she was eighteen again and silently begging him to kiss her, just once, just to know the taste and feel of his lips.

Eyes hooded, his palms brushed her back, then his fingers closed gently around her upper arms. He eased from her embrace. "I don't know about you, but things are getting a little too friendly for me."

Robbed of the wondrous warmth of his body pressed to hers, the air space dividing them cooled and condensed, as though she'd thrown open a door and rushed outside.

Rejection felt like amputation with a plastic knife. Had it been bona fide, she could have accepted it. God knew, she'd had plenty of practice.

But he'd wanted to kiss her, to hold her, to stop time and shut out the world and everything in it as much as she had. He still did. His expression, the eyes that refused to meet hers, betrayed him. "Too…friendly?"

He stroked her arms, then his hands fell to his sides. "It's my fault. I was afraid this would happen." He sighed. "Who am I trying to kid? I hoped it would."

Zoey stared at him, her mind a whirl of confusion, anger and resurrected wounds.

"That's why it took me six months to hie down to the bar. I realized that yesterday, when I changed shirts three times to go bowling with you. We can't be just friends, darlin', and we can't be anything more. Not with six kinds of shit hittin' the fan and more on the way."

He started from the kitchen.

"Hank, will you—" Zoey lunged and snagged his sleeve. "Don't you dare walk out on me again."

He halted in midstride and looked back at her.

"*We* can't this. *We* can't that. Funny, but I don't recall my opinion being asked."

"You know I'm right, Zoe."

"Oh, so not only can you speak for me, you're a mind reader, too? Well, here's a news flash, old friend. I don't have a clue what you're talking about."

Her hands balled into fists. "Unless it's that I've always been handy to have around for laughs, or when you need somebody to tell your troubles to, but not nearly good enough to mean anything else to the great and powerful Hank Westlake."

Head shaking, he gazed up at the ceiling. His teeth champed a corner of his lip. "Yeah, that's it." A chortle pulsed his throat. "You've got me pegged. I am one fair-weather, sly dog, son of a bitch."

His hands cupped her face. His kiss was as tender as it was brief. "And I've been crazy about you since the day you walked into Spanish One in that flowery sundress with the lace around the pockets."

A couple of minutes, perhaps as many as five, ticked past before Zoey moved from the spot where he'd left her. Then the argument commenced, the one with herself that she couldn't win. Analyzing what he'd said, what he hadn't, what it all meant and how she felt was like trying to catch soap bubbles in a breeze.

As though she'd been teleported, she found herself at her own front stoop. Her keys were in her hand, but she had no memory of leaving her parents' house or walking home.

Exhaustion hit her like a wall of water. A high-pitched whine in her ears muffled Bob's and Fred's boisterous greeting. After shedding her coat and purse, she let the dogs out, at once wishing Vesta and Claire had returned from the attorney's office but grateful to have the house to herself.

The extra few dollars a month she paid for an unlisted telephone number now seemed more prescient than indulgent. Being a Jones instead of a France added a layer of insulation as well, though its R-value would be temporary. The media adage "If it bleeds, it leads" usurped Fourth Amendment rights to privacy.

She opened the door for the dogs. The mud Bob and Fred tracked in would be there when she mustered the energy to clean it up. As she sank down on the couch, the dogs stood shoulder-to-shoulder, staring at her as if the woman who'd rescued them had turned into a cyborg. A zombie was nearer the truth.

She should go to the hospital. Couldn't, without a car. She should call the hospital. And would, as soon as her legs and equilibrium were equal to the hundred-mile hike to the phone in the kitchen.

The furnace's fan was like a one-note lullaby. Its hum drowned out street noise, panting dogs, somersaulting thoughts and sorrows. Zoey laid back her head and closed her eyes. The sofa's vinyl upholstery cradled her neck like a cool, steady hand. That sensation and the bolster cushioning the small of her back were achingly similar to the feeling of her father buoying her six-year-old self in a deadman's float in the shallow end of the pool.

"Just relax," he'd say. "Breathe in...breathe out. That's the ticket."

Gradually, she'd succumb to the rocking motion, relishing the tiny waves lapping at her cheek and the sides of her legs. Then his hands would slip away and she'd feel as weightless as a leaf for a blissful sweet second before the water always closed over her, pulling her down...into the waiting arms of the man who'd let her go, but never, not even once, let her fall.

7

"Shh," Claire whispered. "Mom's trying to sleep."

"How can she, with the racket you're making?" Vesta whispered back. "Girl, can't you get a spoon out of the drawer without rattling everything in it?"

"*You* dropped the coffee canister."

"*You* let the blankety-blank storm door bang shut when we came in."

Fred and Bob commenced an agitato, snoot-to-booty shakedown. Their collar tags clinked like dimes in a tin dishpan.

Claire and Vesta's dual "Shh" would have sent a snake charmer running for dear life.

A few yards away in the living room, Zoey's eye roll squinched into a yawn. An infallible cosmic law ordained that the harder people tried to be quiet, the noisier they were.

She couldn't have slept long but she felt recharged, as though her brain had cranked through the four NREM cycles and proceeded straight to dreamless REMs. Good thing. A glance at her watch warned her that she had to clock in at the He Just Left in an hour.

Her daughter's and mother's backs were turned when Zoey entered the kitchen. Flanking them, the greyhounds counter-surfed for edibles within range of their needle noses. Given proper incentive, extending their giraffelike necks added a good six inches to their reach.

Bob, the taller, craftier and faster of the two, had mastered the art of snatching a sandwich in that split second when its maker was screwing on a pickle jar's lid. Or unscrewing the jelly jar's lid. He preferred his peanut butter sandwiches plain, thank you very much.

The illusion of normalcy was so pervasive that, had Zoey not known better, she'd think she truly had just awakened from a nightmare. Sort of *It's A Wonderful Life* meets *Groundhog Day*, directed by the Coen brothers. Bizarre as it was, she wasn't eager to break the spell.

Vesta's maternal radar must have blipped, for she said, "Have a nice nap, sweetheart?"

Claire started, looked back at Zoey, then gawked at her grandmother. "How did you—" She shuddered. "I hope you know, it seriously creeps me out when you do that."

"Do what?"

Zoey crossed to the cupboard for a coffee mug. "She used to tell me she had eyes in the back of her head."

Claire made a face. "Oh, guh-ross."

Vesta put the finishing touches on a plate of thick, deli roast beef and cheese sandwiches. A jumbo bag of chips, French onion dip and store-baked brownies were on the table. Seeing Zoey's smirk, she said, "That's right. If your daddy was here, there isn't a thing he could eat and I bought every damned bit of it on purpose."

"Shame on you, Mom." Zoey draped an arm over her shoulder. "I hope you picked up some vanilla ice cream and hot fudge topping for the brownies."

"Not much comfort in one without the others, is there?" Setting the sandwich plate on the table, she motioned for everyone to sit down and dig in. Bob and Fred received a "get lost" glare. A verbal vamoose seldom worked for Zoey, but the greys slunk into the living room, their tails at half-mast, as though resigned to imminent starvation.

Vesta asked for and Zoey provided a selective report on the house search and the phone messages. "Nobody from the hospital called there, or here. It's stupid, I know, but I went with no news being good news and talked myself out of calling them."

Vesta favored her with a "you're getting more like me every day" smile. "They wouldn't have told you anything, if you had. 'Resting comfortably' means 'the patient was still breathing, last we looked.'

"That's why Claire and I swung by there before we went to the supermarket. Do you remember Agnes June White? She and her sister had that goat farm out on Rosedale Road. Pygmies, they were. Cute little things."

Zoey assumed it was the goats, not Ms. White or her sibling, that were of the cute pygmy persuasion. What connection they had to the hospital visit was marginally clarified when Vesta said, "I forgot that Agnes June's son, Hugh Wayne, is a police officer."

Isn't everyone's? Zoey thought, scooping potato chips from the bag. Maybe Blytheville High should start holding class reunions at the station house.

"It's a wonder Hugh Wayne amounted to anything," Vesta went on, "what with him being born on the wrong side of the blanket and his aunt being tetched in the head and all."

"She is not," Claire said, around a mouthful of sandwich.

"You think it's normal for a woman to tote her dead husband's ashes around in a sugar canister? The poor man passed over ten years ago, for heaven's sake."

"It doesn't mean she's crazy." Claire nudged a spoonful of dip onto her plate, then licked her finger. "We think it's incredibly romantic. Euell had a major sweet tooth, which was bad, on account of him being diabetic, but he was the love of Bella Donna's life and they promised they'd be together forever."

She passed the dip carton. "Besides, she always puts Euell in the back seat when we're in the car."

"Who's we?" Zoey demanded. "What car?"

"Hel-lo." Claire's tone implied that her mother must have short-term memory issues. "That would be like, you know, Laura Peters? My best friend?"

Zoey bit deeply into her sandwich, which in the pantomime language of mothers and daughters warned that Claire's head might be next, if the girl didn't lose the attitude.

In a somewhat milder tone, Claire said, "Bella Donna Sewell is Laura's mom's cleaning lady. She picks us up from school sometimes 'cause Mrs. Peters is too busy with Laura's bratty little brothers and her dad's out of town a lot."

Zoey was aware the housekeeper had carpooled Claire and her best friend on occasion. No, she shouldn't have let the Cleaning Lady suffice as identification, yet it never occurred to her to inquire whether additional passengers might include a deceased diabetic's cremains.

"It's no big deal, Mom. Mr. and Mrs. Peters are cool with it, especially now that Bella Donna taped the lid shut after Euell fell off the seat that time."

Vesta coughed and clasped her bosom. "Oh, my Lord."

As a wad of roast beef got stuck in midswallow, Zoey made a mental note to have a chat with Thena Peters, then immediately scratched it. What right did Zoey have to question a cleaning lady's sanity, when her father was a homicide suspect?

Every right, actually. But at the moment, Claire's continuing friendship with Bella Donna Sewell wasn't a top priority.

"Meanwhile," she prompted, "back at the hospital…"

"That Hugh Wayne guy—the new cop outside Grandpa's room—let me and Gran peek in at him for a minute."

"Tick-a-lock," Vesta said to Zoey. "Not a word about it to Hank. Promise?"

Also no big deal. Sometime between walking home and wakening on the couch, Zoey had permanently archived the idea of any relationship with Hank Westlake beyond professional.

The past, what there was of it, was…well, past. A litany of what-ifs and if-onlys aside, they didn't have a present, let alone a future.

"Grandpa was asleep," Claire said, pulling Zoey from her reverie, "and his skin was this awful gray color, but the nurse told us he's much better than he was last night."

"Thank God," Zoey said, choosing the nurse's secondhand opinion over her daughter's physical description. Again, she wished she had gone to the hospital and seen for herself, but hindsight just added another "what if" to the bone pile.

"They're weaning Charlie off the morphine." Anxiety creased Vesta's brow. "If he stays flat on his back too long, they're afraid he'll retain fluid in his lungs and develop pneumonia."

The scourge of the elderly, including those with healthy hearts. Super-antibiotics had lowered the casualty rate, but the odds of a recovery were slim for a man with a preexisting heart condition.

"Daddy's tough," Zoey said, to convince herself as much as her mother and daughter. "And cutting back on painkillers is a definite sign of improvement."

"Physically, yes. Legally…" Vesta gestured *comme çi, comme ça.* "The attorney Gavin Van Meter recommended was a lot less excited about Charlie's progress."

Claire chimed in, "I told Gram she ought to hire somebody else. I mean, what kind of a name is Osbert Schlomo? And he looks like that guy on *De-*

signing for the Sexes, only with a pouffy comb-over instead of bald."

Peculiar names tended to be memorable. Zoey recalled Schlomo's in regard to a change-of-venue homicide trial that had dominated the *Kansas City Star*'s front page for weeks. The attorney's unorthodox tactics had incensed the judge and the prosecution, but the jury had acquitted the accused—who, in Zoey's opinion, had murdered his wife as surely as her life insurance policy had a double-indemnity clause.

Defending an innocent man shouldn't ruffle a strand of Schlomo's carefully arranged hairdo.

Vesta continued, "Mr. Schlomo says all the police could do last night was a partial booking. They took Charlie's fingerprints before the ambulance took him to the E.R., but they can't question him until he's clearheaded enough for his answers to be admissible in court. Then, even if he has to use a wheelchair, he'll have to appear in person before the judge at the arraignment hearing."

A moment to digest the information didn't generate the apprehension her mother's tone implied. "If I understand you correctly, if Daddy continues to improve, the police could interview him tomorrow, or maybe the next day."

"Exactly."

"What's so bad about that? No doubt, Schlomo wants to drag out this mess to keep the bill-meter running. The sooner Daddy explains what really happened, the sooner he's in the clear."

"It's not that simple. We know your father is innocent. He'll tell them himself, by and by, but it won't end there. The prosecutor told Mr. Schlomo that if Charlie went to trial today, there's already enough evidence against him to convict him of second-degree murder."

"Bullshit. He's bluffing."

"No, he isn't. When Charlie's discharged from the hospital, the police will take him straight to jail. There's nothing the attorney can do to slow them down, much less stop them."

A queasy sensation roiled Zoey's stomach. She felt the blood drain from her face, yet her skin suffused with heat.

"Bail," she stammered. "We'll post bail."

Forcing out a term that until now she had connected only with famous, greedy financiers and human monsters unleashed a torrent. "Daddy'll plead not guilty at the arraignment, then the judge will set bail. It can't be that much. It's not like he's a flight risk—he's too old and sick. Whatever it is, all we have to give a bondsman is ten percent and we can bring Daddy home, and—"

Vesta gripped her wrist. Her voice was low and strained but inordinately calm, as people's often are when on the verge of losing control. For Zoey, it was more chilling than a scream. "Ten percent of nothing is nothing, Zoey. I barely scraped the money together to pay Schlomo's retainer."

Tears swelled in her eyes and spilled over. "The police will find the real killer. I know they will. But what if it's too late? That sweet, gentle man I love with all my heart could die in jail for a crime he didn't commit."

"No, he won't." It sounded like a platitude, one

of those threadbare phrases as involuntary as a sneeze spoken at times of crisis without thought or substance.

Zoey pulled back her shoulders. Breathe in...breathe out. That's the ticket. She looked at Claire. "No." Then at Vesta. "He won't."

Her daughter recoiled, contemptuous of another empty, feel-better promise. Zoey was as guilty of feeding those to her as Vesta had always been. Claire hesitated, still wary, but then she began to nod, each lowering of her chin a trifle less resentful and a trifle more trusting. "We won't let him."

"Not without a fight, we won't."

Hope glinted in Vesta's eyes. She reached for a napkin to wipe them dry, only to throw the makeup-blotched paper on the table with a sigh. "I know you mean well, but saying it doesn't make it so. In a way, it makes it worse."

"I don't mean well at all, Mom. The road to hell is paved with good intentions."

Vesta blanched.

Zoey's fingertips slashed across her throat. "I've had it up to here already with being helpless and afraid. With bending over and waiting for the next kick in the ass."

"And just what do you propose to do? Turn back the clock a day? Short of that, there's nothing you or anyone else can do, other than make matters worse."

Which, of course, they could be. Well, then, damn the damned torpedoes. Twenty-some years of the put up, put out, shut up and be nice routine had taught Zoey that sometimes you're the *Titanic* and sometimes you're the iceberg.

"Listen to me, Mom. This is a chess game for the police, the prosecutor and the judge. I wouldn't call Daddy a pawn. That's an insult to all concerned, but they play by rules, procedures and evidence. To paraphrase Hank, if it walks like a duck and quacks like a duck…"

"It ain't a polar bear." Claire dunked a potato chip in the dip, then popped it into her mouth. "To quote the juvie officer who busted me for shoplifting."

The incident in Kansas City. Claire's trouble. That problem up yonder. Her daughter's introduction to the legal system had begotten more euphemisms than the Civil War. Claire had coined her own batch. A few were unrepeatable. Others were comical—or would have been on a sitcom. Code-speak and street slang predominated.

Until two seconds ago, "shoplifting" had been excised from the France and Jones families' vocabulary. Its resurrection was as startling as an obscenity.

A social worker's input wasn't necessary to know that a kid with twelve dollars and change in her purse who tried to boost a five-dollar pair of flip-flops—sized too small for her, at that—was lashing out at her father for leaving her.

Emotional trigonometry held that good girls aren't flicked away as casually as a cigarette butt, therefore Claire must be a bad girl and, if so, bad was what she'd be.

Thank God she was prodigiously lousy at it.

Getting cuffed and stuffed into a patrol car, lectured by a juvenile officer and a judge, then sentenced to counseling and fifty hours of community service had scared her straight.

Too straight, Zoey prayed, for her grandfather's arrest to kick her to the curb again.

Vesta moaned. "What if the police find out about Claire's trouble?" That conclusion jumped to, "What if a reporter does? They'll drag Charlie through the mud as it is, the vultures. Think they'll balk at taking her down with him?"

Before the alarms blasting in Zoey's mind subsided, Claire said, "It's not like it's a big hairy secret or anything. Everybody at school already knows." She peeled a strip of beef from her sandwich. "Let 'em write about me. I am a minor, you know. We'll sue their pants off and use the money to get Grandpa out of jail."

Zoey waved both hands, palms out. "Whoa, whoa, back it up a second. What do you mean, everybody at school already knows? Those records were supposed to be sealed."

Claire slouched in the chair and loosed her here-we-go-with-the-fifth-degree sigh. "I didn't mean everybody everybody. My Comp One teacher, mostly."

She made a face. "Mrs. Postema assigned an essay about our worst-ever day. Mine had to be the best one, 'cause she grades on the curve and she knocked off twenty points when I turned in the one on Martin Luther King, Jr., a couple of days late."

"Oh? And that would be because…"

"It wasn't my fault. Laura was totally freaked

about this algebra test and I promised to help her, then her mom ordered pizza and reruns of *Buffy the Vampire Slayer* were back-to-back on TV and...well, I just forgot.

"Anyway, half the class was writing about divorces, the single-parent thing, the stepparent thing. Then there was stupid stuff, like Evan Christopher whining about missing a free throw in a basketball tournament. So to be different from everybody else, I wrote about the Winona Ryder thing."

Okay, Zoey thought, saying the dreaded S-word must have been a slip of the tongue. "The Winona Ryder thing" was Claire's favorite synonym for shoplifting.

Vesta frowned. "The country singer?"

"That's Wynona Judd, Gram. Winona Ryder's a movie star. You know, dark hair? Huge brown eyes? She was in *Beetlejuice* and *Girl, Interrupted*." Claire gestured fuhgeddaboudit. "She got arrested for ripping off tons of clothes and junk from some stores on Rodeo Drive."

There was a pause for effect. "That's in Beverly Hills."

The comparison implied that a celebrity's upscale lapse in judgment condoned a mere adolescent mortal's. Zoey didn't want her daughter to don a hair shirt for the rest of her life, but shoplifting in word and deed becoming passé wasn't the object lesson she had in mind.

Claire said, "I thought Dr. Phil was whacked when he told this woman on his show that worrying about somebody finding out a secret is usually worse than the secret."

Her grandmother couldn't have agreed less. It was as plain as the defensive jut of her jaw. Claire, sneaking bits of sandwich to Fred under the table, didn't notice. Zoey remembered a similar reaction to one of Hank's questions at the hospital that morning.

"I still think cops are jerks—except for Hank and maybe that Hugh Wayne dude—but Dr. Phil and that shrink the judge made me talk to were right. Owning up to a mistake is better than letting it own you."

She grinned. "Especially if you get an A and twenty-five bonus points out of it."

"Oh, sweetheart." Vesta appealed to Zoey, as though at a loss to explain those instances where honesty wasn't the best policy without sounding like a hypocrite.

It was an impossible task. Any halfway decent, loving parent was a solid gold, do as I say, not as I do-er. Present company most assuredly included.

"To heck with the grade and the points," Zoey said. "You could have pulled those no matter what you wrote about. I'm proud—very proud—of you for having the guts to tell the truth."

Claire smiled but was too cool to say thanks. "Yeah, well, an essay for school isn't like, you know, rocket science."

"Whether it is or isn't, it's time for your grandmother to be honest, too."

"To be—" Vesta pursed her lips, obviously insulted and not a little hurt. "What on earth are you talking about?"

Zoey's resolve faltered. She didn't want to be

devil's advocate—to harass her mother just because she'd intuited an off-note. But her suspicion had nettled her like a mental hangnail all day. How lovely it would be if a point-blank question would squelch it.

"A few minutes ago, you said you trusted the police to find the real killer."

"Of course I do."

"I don't. Not enough to stake Daddy's life on it Assuming the case against him is as strong as the prosecutor says, the police aren't going to devote much effort toward proving themselves wrong."

"Hank Westlake will."

"Maybe. But even if he goes the extra mile, it's my father, not his, under armed guard in that hospital room."

"Butting in won't change that. Hank doesn't for one instant believe that Charlie is capable of what they're accusing him of. Mind your own business and let Hank do his job."

Zoey leaned on her forearms. "If you have that much faith in him, why'd you nearly jump out of the chair this morning when he asked if Dad was in the habit of going out at night?"

"Because—" Vesta darted a glance at Claire and back again. "I did no such thing."

"Fine." Zoey shook her head. "My mistake. Sorry I asked."

"Don't you take that tone with me." Her gaze again strayed to her granddaughter. She tipped her head toward the door as if to excuse Claire from the room. A hydraulic winch couldn't have separated Claire from her seat.

"If," Vesta began, "and I do mean *if* I reacted at all, it's because I didn't appreciate the insinuation that my husband tomcats around. That's what Hank was really asking and it made me madder than hops. Even before he got sick, Charlie has always been home with me, where he belongs."

She looked Zoey in the eye. "I'd swear it on the Good Book to Hank Westlake, to you, or anybody else, if it comes to that."

8

There wasn't a palm tree in sight, other than on the labels on bottles of Malibu rum and Blue Hawaiian schnapps. The only sand was spiked with cigarette butts in tall canisters near the pool tables. To portray some of the customers as exotic, instead of a few noodles short of a casserole, required a sizeable thesaurus and stretch of the imagination.

Deep-fried fat, spilled beer and secondhand smoke flavored the air, not the sea's salty tang, but for Zoey Jones, the He Just Left was as welcoming as a tropical island. The fabled port in a storm. A blessed refuge from Bizarro World.

The fantasy lasted long enough for the door to close behind her. Al France looked up from the drink he was mixing at the bar, then did a double take. "What are you doing here?"

"Same thing I've done every Monday for six months." A generic smile encompassed patrons chalking cue sticks, seated at tables, in booths and bellied up to the bar. "Clocking in for work."

He followed her into the combined kitchen, storeroom, employee's lounge and office. "When

I talked to Vesta this afternoon, she said you were too worn out to come in tonight."

Zoey flung her coat over a case of toilet tissue. "She was wrong."

The vaultlike cooler door swung open. Gert Massey emerged, hugging a gallon-sized jar of chicken wing marinade. Al fancied himself the Colonel Sanders of chicken wings. The ingredients of his concoction were secret, but relied heavily on cayenne, lime juice and red clover honey.

"Hey, kid," she said. "How's your old man doin'?" Everyone was Hey, kid to Gert, except for Al, who was consistently addressed as Hey, you.

"Better, thanks," Zoey said.

"Hmmph." The waitress's rheumy eyes did an up-and-down. "You look like somebody dragged you through a knothole backward."

From anyone else, the observation would be insulting. Gert's bluntness was an acquired taste. Zoey had actively despised the woman for weeks, then realized that beneath that skeletal exterior and pruned skin resided a soul as guileless as a child's.

A raspy male voice hollered from the bar, "Fer Chrissake, whaddaya gotta do to get a beer 'round here?"

"Stand on it, Gert," Al said. "I need to talk to Zoey a few."

He shook an unfiltered Camel from the pack on the prep table. The inner knuckle of his thumb was callused from decades of flipping open a black-and-red enameled Zippo and snapping the striker wheel.

In deference to Zoey, he turned his head away

and exhaled a stream of smoke. "I wouldn't have called in Gert to cover for you, if I'd known you'd be here."

"I'd have called you if I couldn't make it."

"Vesta said you were out like Lottie's eye, when I talked to her on the phone a while ago."

"I took a nap." She extricated her hair from the apron's neck strap. Folding the material upward by the waist strings adjusted the length from calf-long to midthigh. "I might have taken a longer one, except my hard-ass landlord has a thing about the rent being paid on time."

Al chuckled, shifting his weight from one bandy leg to the other. Why veteran long-haul drivers were often as bow-legged as cowboys was a mystery to Zoey. Charlie was fond of saying his older brother couldn't stop a pig in a ditch with his knees roped together. "It will be, lest you fritter away your check on geegaws. Your hard-ass boss done gave you a week's paid vacation."

"I don't want it." Zoey winced at the stridence in her tone. "Hey, I love you to pieces and I know you're trying to help, but time off is the last thing I need right now."

Along with losing a week's worth of tips. On paper, they weren't factored into her monthly budget. In reality, she'd already used tips to pay for a new car battery, a Siberian winter's triple-digit gas bill, money for school activities, advances on Claire's allowance, doctor's visits, prescriptions, and video rentals and late fees.

Earmarking tips as a rainy day fund was a

swell, fiscally responsible idea. Her fund just had a tendency to leak like a sieve.

Al drawled, "Pretendin' there ain't more on your plate than you can say grace over don't scrape it clean."

"Brooding about it doesn't, either." Her hands slid into the back pockets of her jeans. "This is just between me and you, okay?"

A drag on his cigarette indicated agreement. He'd smoked two-plus packs a day for fifty-some years and drank red beer for breakfast. Grease was a lifelong major food group, the flight of stairs up to his bachelor pad his sole source of exercise, and his heart was none the worse for it.

"Mom is staying at my house with Claire. Partly because the phone's ringing off the hook at hers. Mostly to keep each other company."

"Uh-huh." Moving nearer his unholy mess of a desk, Al flipped ashes in an upturned Oldsmobile hubcap. Smoking in the kitchen violated health department regulations. Last month's unannounced inspection had at least cured him of using the floor for an ashtray.

To the inspector's astonishment, it was the only infraction cited. The He Just Left fit the description of a hole-in-the-wall, but was as clean as bleach, degreasers and relentless scrubbing could make it.

"Mom does have cab fare, if…well, if the hospital should call. Otherwise, she's pretty much stranded."

He grunted. "The cops impounding her car's kindee a blessing. Holding down a chair at the hospital all night won't fix what's ailing Charlie. He'd fret about her, frettin' about him."

Zoey nodded, feeling traitorous, then admitted, "You know what they say about three's a crowd, though."

Al slanted her a look as he stubbed out the cigarette. "You gonna pedal the metal, or do I hafta tow ya, 'cause if'n I do, I might as well fetch a brewski whilst you're in Georgia overdrive."

She rolled her eyes at the trucker-speak for neutral gear. Beyond the bat-wing doors, the drone of casual conversation, throaty laughter and Brooks and Dunn's boot-scootin' tune on the jukebox mocked her.

"Bottom line, then. I'm tired, scared, my nerves are raw and I'm pissed at the whole world. Odd mood to desperately want to sling drinks and talk to strangers, but it beats hell out of being shut up inside that tiny house."

"With your mama."

"Yes. No. All right, yes. She'd say the same about me, only she wouldn't because she seldom has a bad word to say about anybody."

"Vesta's a fine woman, hon. None finer and I've known plenty enough to judge, but that's stretching it a mite." He shoved aside a mound of invoices, receipts and unopened mail and hiked a hip on his desk. "She's looked down her nose at me since the day she dumped me for my baby brother."

"You? And Mom?"

"Yes-sir-ree Bob." Head atilt, he regarded the stamped-tin ceiling as though a projector screen was mounted there. Whatever images flashed behind his eyes brought a wan smile to his face.

"Them were the days. Law, she was prettier than a speckled pup under a red wagon and danced like a house a-fire. I wasn't no Fred Astaire, but when we hit the pavilion's floor, ever'body else scootched back against the railing to watch."

As surely as the dogwoods and redbuds burst into bloom, each spring her mother reminisced about the free band concerts on Sunday afternoons at the park. How she'd loved the music—blues and Dixieland jazz, especially. Not once had she mentioned dancing, with or without Al France.

He sucked his teeth. "She was awful young—too young for a rascal like me, but we had a barrel of fun till her and Charlie locked eyeballs. I'll tell you for true, what that spunky little thing saw in him, I never featured. Now Charlie's got an ornery streak. Always could take a joke as easy as tell one, but bookish as the day is long."

Zoey rocked on her heels, trying to picture her mother as Ginger Rogers, her and Al as a couple—ye gods, her and Al in the same room for more than an hour without annoying the crap out of each other. It didn't parse.

"Opposites attract, I guess," she said, thinking of Stuart, then others whose magnetic pull gradually turned to push.

"That they do. 'Course those three miscarriages afore the stork brought you took a lot of the jitterbug out of your mama." He scowled. "You didn't know about that, either?"

"No."

"Hurt too much to talk about, I'd guess. No sense in it, with a sweet baby girl like you to love."

Zoey blurted, "That's the real story behind my name, isn't it? They'd already chosen three and were afraid to pick another one until I was born."

"Yes'm. They was so gun-shy, they didn't buy diapers till you arrived safe and sound. You slept in a dresser drawer for a couple of days, whilst me and your daddy got a nursery fixed up."

"Jesus H. Christ." Zoey paced the floor. Secrets. Stupid secrets at that. So what if Vesta and Al were an item a million years ago? What damned difference did it make if she resulted from her mother's fourth pregnancy, not her first? Tragic for them at the time and probably painful to recall, but hardly a skeleton worth sealing in a closet.

Al grumbled, "I shoulda kept my trap shut."

"Wrong. You should have opened it two or three decades ago." She planted her hands on her hips. "What else don't I know about? That's what infuriates me. Top that with the fact whatever caused Mom's miscarriages might have affected me, when I was pregnant with Claire."

He fished for another cigarette. "Didn't appear to—"

"That's no excuse. Daddy's a doctor, for God's sake. Veterinarian or M.D., he knew obstetric complications can be inherited."

She tuned out his reply. Why bother? It was undoubtedly another example of her parents' reluctance to worry her. Until, of course, there was something to worry about. The end, a smooth, full-term pregnancy and healthy baby, justified the means.

A thought suddenly reverberated amid the clamor in her brain. *Old habits die hard.*

Jerking loose her apron strings, she said, "I'm taking that vacation after all."

Al pushed off the desk. "Simmer down, hon. You're riled and I don't blame you, but this ain't no time to give your mama Billy Ned for stuff that happened forty years ago."

"Thirty-eight." And she didn't plan to. Oh, those moldy family skeletons would jitterbug like a house afire, if she had to lock Charlie, Vesta and Al in a closet, until flames licked out from under the door.

First things first. Whatever sins of omission her father was guilty of, he wasn't a thief or a murderer. Problem-solving was her forte. She'd made a career of it, hadn't she? Debugging software and exonerating her father seemed like apples to cauliflower, except for mathematical progression.

The universe and virtually everything in it operated by mathematics in some form or fashion. Coincidence repudiated the concept, if you believed in coincidence. Zoey did not. Events don't happen, or fail to happen, by rolls of the cosmic dice.

Mathematical progression applied to police investigations, too. Crime + evidence = perpetrator. Zoey had a week to find the variables missing from that equation.

Other than divorced, Darla Quinn was everything Zoey was not. Childless. Tall. Blond. Willow-thin. Sloe-eyed. Big-boobed.

Big-mouthed, too, without respect to a tiny assist from a collagen injection. The boobs, damn her, were real.

She was waxing her hair salon's checkerboard floor when Zoey knocked on the leaded glass door. A no-peek wave answered, "It's Monday. We're closed. Go away."

In the era before labor unions, barbers and beauticians worked seven days a week, late into the evening and at least half days on holidays. How they must have rejoiced when the trade-wide Sundays and Mondays off idea was hatched.

It seemed appropriate to tap out shave-and-a-haircut, two-bits. Darla's exasperated snarl pulled into a grin at Zoey's face smashed against the glass.

The lock clacked and the door swung wide. "Get yourself in here. No, not there, I just waxed that side. Where the heck have you been? I've called umpteen times. Is Charlie okay? How's Vesta doing? And Claire—why that poor child must be devastated."

Zoey held up her hands to halt the barrage. Darla slapped the mop handle in one of them. "Hold this." Over the cheep-clap of four-inch leather espadrilles making tracks on the linoleum, she said, "I've got just what you need in the back room."

Unless a homicidal convenience store robber was bound and gagged in the supply closet, Zoey doubted it. She leaned the mop against a vintage Coke machine and sat down in a sink station's chair.

Darla had named her place of business for herself on the premise that anyone who asked customers who so expertly had cut, curled, or colored their hair would say, "Darla" or, at most, "Darla

Quinn." Calling her shop The Cutting Edge, Hair Affairs, or the Clip 'n Curl would have confused the issue. One look in the phone book and Darla's would ring the asker's bell.

After several interior conversions from glossy black and silver-foiled disco fever to jungle-themed to Barbie-Dream-House pink to minimalist chic, Darla had realized retro appealed to trend-conscious teens and was delightfully nostalgic to their mothers and grandmothers.

The decor was a bright, chrome-intensive funky '50s, right down to the reproduction beehive hair-dryer hoods. Poodle skirts curtained wheeled equipment carts. Salvaged venetian blinds hung at the windows. Wall art included letter jackets, saddle oxfords, pennants, pom-poms, yearbook photos and two ghastly ruffled nylon net prom dresses.

The proprietor clumped back through the beaded curtain with a schooner of wine in each hand. "I know white is your favorite, but I'm fresh out. You'll just have to make do with Velvet Red."

Eying the enormous glass, Zoey said, "Why didn't you just bring me the bottle?"

"Thought about it." Darla plunked down in the adjacent swivel chair. "Couldn't find a long-enough straw." She crossed a slim black Spandex-clad leg at the knee of the other. "Chug about half of that, then start talking."

The wine was ice-cold, very sweet and yes, exactly what Zoey needed. Almost as much as a trusted childhood friend. A trusted female childhood friend.

Between sips, she answered all Darla's questions and synopsized the latest developments. It was Vesta's choice whether to divulge the house search and Zoey's to skip over the interlude afterward with Hank.

"Claire seems to be coping. Better than me and Mom, in some respects. Her response to going back to school tomorrow was her usual 'Whatever.'"

Darla hiked a shoulder. "Wisdom for the millennium—never let 'em see you sweat. Moms especially."

"That isn't healthy."

"What is? Hiding in her room? Hanging down her head in shame? Knocking the snot out of the first kid who looks at her cockeyed?"

"No, but—"

"Let Claire handle this the same way you and Vesta will. The best she can. If she needs help, give it. If she doesn't, leave her alone."

"She's only fourteen."

"Ew, dear." Darla's arm swooped theatrically. "Well, in that case, tell her how to act and what to say and when to shut up and she'll do fine."

Fighting words, each a bare-knuckle wallop below the belt line. Someone far wiser than Zoey once said the best mirror is an old friend. "I hate you."

Darla examined her blunt coral nails. "Whatever."

Dashing wine in her smug, gorgeous face was tempting, but jeez, she'd just cleaned the floors. Also, she'd let fly with hers and there might not be another bottle in the back.

Waste not, want not.

"Here's a whatever for you. Whatever happened to innocent until proven guilty? While I was at the bar, a reporter came in, asking for Al. I had to sneak out through the alley."

"Nothin's happened to it. It's like Rhett Butler. Never existed, except on paper."

Gone With the Wind was Darla's favorite book. Quite possibly, the only one she ever read. "When did you become such a cynic?"

"I date, therefore I am." The phone rang. She glanced in its direction but made no move to answer it. "You were smart to duck out, but I don't think the media's wise to you yet. Nobody's mentioned your dad's name." She angled her glass like a microphone. "Authorities have not identified the suspect, pending formal charges."

Thank God for small favors. Zoey assumed that meant he'd have to be arraigned before the feeding frenzy officially began. At the rate the word was zipping over the grapevine, the indictment would be old news by then.

"I saw the report on TV last night," Darla said. "The shot of Charlie hunkered on the curb was shadowy, and if I didn't know Claire, I wouldn't have recognized you."

Zoey blocked a mental replay of the scene. Earlier flashbacks were disjointed and distorted. Someone—a cop, maybe a paramedic, a burly bystander, for all she knew—had bundled her into his arms and held her, flailing and screaming, until her father was loaded into the ambulance. Claire was likewise restrained.

The patrol car ride to her mother's, then on to

the hospital and the emergency room melee, was a blur. Better that way, she supposed.

"Want to know why I didn't recognize you on TV?" Darla inquired.

Her tone suggested the question was rhetorical. Coming from her, it was also unavoidable, but Zoey tried. "No, not really."

"Because your hair looked like shit. Like a fright wig in a wind tunnel." Darla held up a hand to halt Zoey's retort. "Yeah, least of your worries then. This is now. Take it from a professional hair-apist. You look good outside, you feel better inside. Guaranteed."

Zoey faked a smile. "I know you're trying to take my mind off what happened—"

"The hell. Your hair's looked like you comb it with a weed whacker for months. I'm beginning to take it personally."

"*You* are?"

Darla pointed at the windows. "See those cars going by? Probably some of the drivers are customers. Those that aren't, could be, by and by. You walk outta here as stray dog-scraggly as you came in and business will suffer, sure as cows give milk."

Zoey laughed in spite of herself. "I came here to let my hair down, not get a free haircut."

"Who said anything about free?" She toed an equipment cart alongside the chair and rifled the drawers. "Shoot. Must have put my hedge clippers in the other one."

A plastic drape appeared out of nowhere and covered Zoey from neck to tennis shoes. Liberating the wineglass not a moment too soon, she said,

"Will you give it up? Mom thinks I'm at work. How am I going to explain my hair when I get home?"

"Same way you explained the empties in your dad's car, graduation night." The chair wheeled a one-eighty to face the mirror. "Lie, then run for the bathroom and throw up."

She fluffed Zoey's hair, scrunched it, let it fall, then finger-combed it backward from the crown. The sides were asymmetrical, the ends frayed and brittle-looking. More silver-gray strands—lots more—gleamed in the suspended funnel lights than under her low-wattage ceiling fixture at home.

Zoey grimaced. "It is pretty bad, huh?"

"Lucky for you, I love a challenge."

The wineglass was plucked from her hand, then the chair spun around again and the back lowered. The sink's porcelain cradled Zoey's nape like an upside-down guillotine, but she moaned as sheets of silky warm water flowed over her scalp.

Eyes closed, she surrendered to the simple luxury of Darla's fingertips massaging coconut-scented shampoo into a lathery meringue, then rinsing, slathering on conditioner and another rinse, the water a few tingly degrees warmer.

No wonder her mother was religious about her weekly beauty shop appointments. Then again, she had time to pamper herself. Corporate Zoey had shoehorned dry cuts into lunch hours, along with dental appointments, doctor appointments, gift buying and sundry other errands, and even an honest-to-God meal every blue moon or so.

Upright again, her swimmy head turbaned in a thick towel, she clung to the chair's arms to keep from slithering off the seat. "Don't take this wrong, but that was better than sex."

Darla cackled. "With a pencil-dick account-ant, maybe. It isn't if it's done right with the right guy."

Her mind closed to speculations with a partic-ular name attached, Zoey rattled off haircut in-structions as tangles relented to a wide-toothed comb. Shorter, but not too short. Layered on top, just not too much or they'd stick out like warped shingles. Feathered at the sides, not shagged. Bangs at the arch of the eyebrows.

"Here, Goldilocks." Darla handed her the half-full glass of wine. "Drink up, sit still and keep your lip zipped."

Zoey took a deep drink, then replaced the glass on a shelf so it wouldn't get filled with hair.

Scissors blades snipped a salsa rhythm. Wavy wisps strewed the vinyl drape and ringed the chair like a moat. Her back was to the mirror. The 45-rec-ords and album covers tacked to the opposite wall didn't reflect worth a hoot. Absent the visual dis-traction, her thoughts refocused on the original purpose for the visit.

"Those news reports you heard. Did they men-tion the convenience store clerk's name?"

"Joe Donny Marlowe." Curls dappled the cape like fat, frightened wooly worms. "He's Trudy King's boyfriend. Her mom's neighbor's cousin-in-law owns the coffee shop next door."

Snip. Snip. "Rumor is, Trudy's ex-husband smacked her around on days ending in Y."

Zoey supposed she meant Ms. King's ex, not the

coffee shop owner. Like her mother, most other Blytheville natives were conversationally dyslexic.

"When the son of a bitch started in on the kids, she finally got the gumption to kick him out for good."

Darla moved in for a frontal assault on Zoey's bangs.

"When was that?"

"What? Oh. Don't ask me. Never met her."

The admission deleted Trudy, her mother, the neighbor and shirttail kin from Darla's client list. Had any of them patronized the shop regularly, the font of information wouldn't have sputtered to a halt.

"Best guess, Trudy sent him packing last spring," Darla murmured, intent on amending Zoey's most recent sewing-scissor trim job. "Around Easter, the coffee shop room had a—will you keep your eyes closed?—had a Victorian fashion show. I did the models' hair."

Two-beat pause. "Sausage curls are a pain in the ass. How our great-grannies pulled 'em off before hot rollers and electric curling irons were invented is beyond me."

Tiny bits of hair sprinkled Zoey's cheeks and tickled her nose. "So, uh, was Trudy one of the models?"

She realized her mistake a second too late. Darla had already said they'd never met.

The scissors hovered in midair. "Okay. What's with the questions, all of a sudden?"

Zoey peeked through her lashes. "Nothing."

"Uh-huh. Then why's your face turning redder than the Coke machine?"

Answering truthfully was out if Zoey wanted to do some investigating on her own in secret. Oh, Darla would swear on her daddy's grave not to tell a soul. And wouldn't, save one, possibly two absolutely trustworthy exceptions. Who'd consequently swear on their ancestors, and thus-and-so, until few occupants of Maple Park Cemetery were innocent of conspiracy.

The dodger Zoey chose soured the wine in her stomach. "Because the girl thinks my father robbed and murdered her boyfriend."

9

A strip of red cellophane tape sealed four clear plastic evidence bags lined up on the desk blotter. An evidence tag bore Hank Westlake's initials, the case number, the item number, its description and date and the time and location of the recovery.

Inside each bag was a zip-top sandwich bag. The cash it contained ranged from forty-seven to eighty-three dollars. Fingerprint powder smudged the bags' outer surfaces. Overlapping patterns of latent arches, whorls and loops resembled a surveyor's topographical map.

Hank leaned back and folded his arms behind his head. His cockeyed view of the display wasn't entirely the fault of a gimpy swivel chair inherited from its former, three-hundred-and-twenty-pound owner.

Criminals with IQs a notch above a cinder block watch enough cop dramas on their stolen TVs to know better than to commit bare-handed robberies. Fortunately for the good guys, a significant percentage failed to grasp the concept of wearing gloves to prevent fingerprint identification. For law enforcement, such distinct and damning sets of latents as those lifted from the money bags were the equivalent of El Dorado.

Oh, Hank wanted to like them. To love them. Being wrapped in tamper-resistant packaging instead of ribbons and bows didn't make them any less of a gift. That's what had a nerve in his jawbone stuttering. The phrase "an embarrassment of riches," seldom applied to homicide investigations.

Thumbs to pinkies, every latent on every bag matched a rolled impression on Charles Herman France's print card. The stash in his coat pocket Sunday night at the Jiffy Stop was red-handed prima facie evidence. Yesterday afternoon, the additional three bags were discovered in an old coffee can full of odd screws, nuts and bolts in Doc's workshop.

At the time, had Hank paused for thought, would he have snapped on the lid before Chichester saw them? *No* was the automatic answer—the one befitting a cop who'd worked his tail off to earn every stripe and promotion. Who'd put the job—the calling—ahead of two wives and another serious relationship that tanked when she'd realized his gold shield might as well be pinned to his skin.

Except easy answers don't pertain to crises of conscience, especially in retrospect. If Hank had resealed the coffee can and returned it to the shelf, he wouldn't have felt like his chest was bound in barbed wire when Zoey explained how the Jiffy Stop bag might have migrated into her father's pocket.

She was right. Hank had considered that alternate scenario. Despite some gaping holes in it, he hadn't expected the house search to net much besides a far-too-intimate knowledge of the Frances' personal lives.

He swiveled around to stare out the window, as if turning his back on the truth nullified its existence. On the pavement three stories below, frozen mounds and mountains of bituminous snow hogged a dozen parking spaces. Person or persons unknown had sculpted an ice obelisk and staked a sign beside it that read In Memory of Our Fallen Officers, to honor those who'd shoved their tailbones up between their ears skating from their cars to the station's main entrance.

Two patrol units roved the lot in vain. Hank looked past them, his mind casting images on the wall of the adjacent Miner's Bank building. He saw himself set that rusty Pandora's box with Maxwell House electroplated on its face back on the shelf above Doc's workbench. Acting as frustrated as Chichester when their search came up empty. Taking Zoey in his arms and kissing her, the way he'd fantasized a thousand times, instead of pushing her away, keeping her at arm's length.

What was integrity, a reputation for never cutting corners or compromising? Hank whirled around and glared at the four bags on his desk. They mocked him, each dirty crease bowed upward like a fuck-you smile.

Woulda. Coulda. Shoulda. *Didn't*. An honest cop's epitaph, if ever there was one.

"Hey, Loot." Lonnie Chichester didn't just enter a room, he raided it. "You are not gonna believe this."

Three robberies' case folders sailed into Hank's lap. The Pump 'N Go had been robbed on December 28. Jerry's Quik Mart on January 13. Chang's Market, ten days later. Add their report on the Jiffy Stop heist and you had a mini crime spree totaling two hundred and forty-seven bucks.

"Great work, Sherlock." Hank jerked a thumb at the recovered cash on his desk. The information on the files' tabs corresponded to the times, dates and locations handwritten on the sandwich bags' stickers. "How did you ever guess which files to pull?"

Lonnie splayed his feet and crossed his arms at his chest. "Check out the witness descriptions."

Hank scanned the pertinent pages. The twitchy jaw nerve joined forces with a cluster behind his temple. No wonder the robbery detail hadn't connected the dots. On only one point did the three other clerks agree: the thief who cleaned out their cash drawers was male.

"Any video surveillance tapes to go with these?" he asked.

Lonnie shook his head. "The Jiffy Stop's and the Pump 'N Go's indoor/outdoor cameras are dummies. Like it's the thought that counts. The film from Jerry's was excellent, if you've got a floor fetish. Once upon a time, somebody banged the camera mount with a ladder or something, then kind of forgot to reposition it."

Same shit, different day, Hank grumbled to himself. Chances were, the tapes weren't changed until they disintegrated, anyway, if then. A million-dollar security system wasn't worth squat, if multiple recordings stretched the tape, or degraded the resolution to continuous, staticky bands shimmering from the top of the screen to the bottom.

Lonnie went on, "I ought to send the cartridge from Chang's to a funniest-video show. What it lacks in suspect footage, it almost makes up for with shots of Chang's son, Jimmy, having a foodie triathlon. He mowed down beer bottles with a coconut, then shot some hoops with the hydroponic tomatoes. The grand finale was kickboxing the crap out of the paper towel and toilet paper displays."

"Seems that his old man had gotten curious as to why the inventory didn't jibe with sales. The day before the store was hit, Chang Senior adjusted the camera angle to pan the aisles, instead of the counter."

"Hence, no robbery footage."

"Not a frame stars anyone but Jimmy Chang."

Much as Hank would like to fault retailers for bollixing surveillance, their employees were more effective thieves than the ski-masked type. Store owners lost an average of a thousand dollars per clerk, per year to damaged and stolen merchandise, vanishing lottery tickets and underrung sales.

Not my problem, Hank thought, refocusing on the witness descriptions. "You've got home addresses for these clowns, too?"

Lonnie delivered the "gimme a break" look Hank deserved. Chichester was young but a crackerjack investigator. Most importantly, he wasn't wrestling demons and dreams to maintain objectivity.

"Okay, then let's roll." He moved to the coat tree where his topcoat shared hook space with jettisoned ties, ball caps, windbreakers, laundered shirts and a shaving kit. "I can hardly wait to hear Clerk Number Two explain how he confused a seventy-three-year-old Caucasian with Shaquille O'Neal."

Lonnie boxed the money bags for their return to the evidence locker. "Assuming he did."

"Well, if he didn't, you'll be explaining to me why Shaq stashed his swag in Charlie France's workshop."

"Without leaving any prints on it."

"Yep." Hank ran a finger under his shirt collar. It didn't alleviate the noose effect. If he'd kept his mitts off that damned coffee can, they'd have never linked the prior three robberies to Zoey's dad.

"Senseless" modified "crime" in more references than not, except crimes weren't often senseless. Morally, yes. The tablets Moses toted down from the mountain didn't quibble on killing, stealing, lying, coveting and such. Neither did the *Koran*, the *I Ching*, the *Talmud*, *Torah*, *Book of Mormon*, *Dianetics*, *Popol Vuh*, or *Dhammapada*.

Hank scowled as he dug in his slacks pocket for his keys. In his experience, atheists weren't philosophically in favor of anarchy, either.

Morality aside, on the surface, to rot in prison for five or ten years for stealing a load of microwaves and stereos wasn't logical, but it wasn't senseless. The majority of crimes were perpetrated for gain, monetary being the most common. Personal gain also included revenge, racial motivations and removal of perceived obstructions to life, liberty and happiness.

Hank's fingers drummed the steering wheel. He stifled an urge to flip on the siren and goose the delivery van chugging along in front of him. Like cops and cameras, there was never a "How's My Driving?" decal on a vehicle when you needed one.

Speed killed; getting caught behind Slow Joe just made you want to.

Lonnie said, "We've gotta make a right up on Washington Avenue."

"Uh-huh." Taillights flickered. Hank's foot kneaded the brake pedal. "Why would Charlie France knock off four convenience stores over a five-week period to steal less than two hundred and fifty bucks?"

Lonnie grinned. "Willie Sutton."

In response to a reporter asking Sutton why he robbed banks, the famed and remorseless thief had replied, "Because that's where the money is."

Hank stopped for a traffic light. "Him and Vesta could've held a one-day garage sale and made more than that."

"In February?"

A snide look from his commanding officer brought a "What's bugging you about this one? Besides having the hots for the suspect's daughter."

The car's interior temperature jumped fifty degrees. "Sport, if I were you, I wouldn't say that again in this life."

"Hey, I was just—" Lonnie coughed and sat up straighter in the seat. "Sorry, sir."

After a punitive moment of silence, Hank said,

"Senior citizens resorting to shoplifting food from a grocery store I understand. Ditto slipping prescriptions off the counter and trying to walk out because they don't have the money to pay for them. It shouldn't happen in the U.S. of A., but that's a whole other subject."

The direction blinker's tick metered his words. "An old gent with money enough to get by on jacking convenience stores? That I don't understand."

Chichester's expression said he didn't have to. Their responsibility was nailing down the who, what, when, where and how aspects of the case. Whether the why of it was clear, obscure, or unknowable, it wasn't mandatory.

"Inquiring minds want to know," he muttered.

Washington Avenue Apartments wasn't what you'd call an asset to the neighborhood. The developer's request for rezoning from single-family to multiple had flown under the home-owners' radar until after the city council's unanimous approval.

Each of the complex's two-story buildings was subdivided into eight apartments accessed by a central breezeway/staircase. At ground level, patio doors opened onto concrete slabs large enough for a kettle grill and a lawn chair. Directly above were wooden decks where second-floor tenants could breathe in charcoal smoke and lighter fluid while flames licked the planking beneath their feet. Snow swagged the foundations and capped cotoneaster bushes along the concrete walks.

A baby's wails were audible before Hank and Lonnie climbed the stairs to apartment 224. The door was opened by a bare-chested young man in low-rise jeans. A stench of baby puke, dirty diapers and scalded formula rolled out from behind him.

"Are you Michael Vincent?"

"Yeah." He looked as though he'd swap his identity with Hank or Lonnie in a heartbeat, no questions asked.

Hank introduced himself, Chichester and the purpose of their visit.

"You want to come in?" Vincent glanced over his shoulder, then grimaced. "The place is kind of a mess. My little girl's sick and my girlfriend's with her...."

Hank and presumably Lonnie had detected the hint of marijuana riding the putrid air. Busting the kid for dope wasn't the order of the day and wouldn't abet his cooperation. They'd have to, though, if it or any drug paraphernalia were lying around in plain sight.

"How about you grab a coat and some shoes and meet us over there by the swing set." Hank's tone implied it wouldn't be smart to keep them waiting.

Vincent added a knitted hat, a cigarette and a travel mug of coffee to the suggested ensemble and still rejoined them before they reached the play yard.

"Damn," he muttered, wiping drops of spilled coffee from the back of his hand. "I should've asked you guys if you wanted some."

Hank gestured thanks, but not necessary. "I'd appreciate it if you'd read over the description you gave of the man who robbed the Pump 'N Go last December and tell me if it's accurate."

The clerk scanned the photocopied report's highlighted passages. Two sentences, two drags on his cigarette. "Sounds right to me."

He handed back the paper, his eyes rising no higher than the knot in Hank's tie.

"Male, wearing a ski mask, no age, height, or weight estimates," Hank said.

Vincent nodded. "It happened so fast, I didn't get a good look at the guy."

Hank pulled a card from the file he carried. Known as a mug shot 10, it held photographs arranged in two rows, similar to a high-school yearbook page. "Let's see if any of these jog your memory."

The clerk studied each in turn. The one of Charles France differed from the rest, as it was taken at the scene rather than during a routine booking process. Was that why Vincent homed in on it and repeatedly returned to it?

Twenty bucks said no.

He regarded Chichester, then Hank. A hound dog with a thorn in its paw would look happier than he did.

Chichester warned, "It's against the law to give false statements to the police. It might even be cause for an obstruction of justice charge."

Hank said, "Vague as you were, Mike, that ski mask you mentioned... Well, could you describe it? Like they say, the devil's in the details."

He preferred not to divulge that the Pump 'N Go robbery had escalated to a homicide investigation. No sense bringing a cannon to a squirt-gun fight. He had a feeling he knew the reason for Vincent's reluctance. In this instance, adding murder to the equation might clamp his jaw tighter.

The clerk's cigarette had burned down to the filter. It fell from his fingers into the sallow grass. The ball of his boot screwed it into the spongy ground. "Okay. I'm still not believing it myself, even after all this time, but it was Doctor France that came into the store that night."

His mouth quirked at a corner. "Wasn't wearing a ski mask, either. Hell, he didn't do anything to disguise himself. Just walked up to the register and said, 'Gimme the money.'"

Not a direct quote, Hank assumed. "Was he armed?"

"No, sir."

"Did he say he was?"

"Uh-uh." Vincent shook his head. "I shouldn't have lied, but I couldn't snitch on a nice ol' fella like him. 'Specially, being so hard up for money to pull a stunt like that." He shrugged. "Besides, he didn't get more than forty-some bucks and the store's insured."

It took a fair amount of arm-twisting for the clerk at Jerry's Quik Mart whose original description had called up images of the Shaq-meister to pick France's picture from the photo lineup.

The clerk had never met the retired veterinarian and hadn't lied out of compassion. Blaming a black man and a huge one at that was easier than admitting he'd offered no resistance when an unarmed geezer cleaned out the cash drawer.

Besides, the store was insured.

Jimmy Chang didn't know Doc France, either.

"I didn't want to get involved," was his excuse. "I go to college days and work at Pop's store nights. Man, I don't have time to take a dump, much less give depositions, then testify against the dude in court. And—"

Hank's hand shot up. "Besides, your dad has insurance."

"Yeah." Chang smirked. "Might as well get his money's worth, right?"

Zoey wheeled into the crescent drive outside the school's main entrance. A few bikes were chained in racks alongside the imposing double doors. A woman's silhouette glided past in an upper-story window near the corner of the building. Parked in a red-painted fire lane was a soft-drink delivery truck.

"Are you sure you don't want me to go in with you and explain that you're late because I overslept?"

"Nah." Claire flipped down the mirrored sun visor, as though the arduous, ten-minute journey from home might have wreaked havoc on her appearance. "I've got your note in my backpack."

"I really am sorry, sweetheart," Zoey said, hoping the tardy excuse was sufficient to offset a detention. Schools' zero tolerance policies were boon or bane, depending on your point of view. "I should have put the alarm clock in the living room."

By her reflected sidelong look, Claire was primed for, "And you should have switched on yours before you went to bed."

True, but Rule Five of the mother's manual was, "Why say it, if the kid's already thinking it?"

Claire and her grandmother had been sound asleep when Zoey arrived home from Darla's salon. After rounding up a couple of blankets and the pillow her mother wasn't using, she'd crashed on the couch, assuming Vesta or the dogs would waken her in plenty of time to take Claire to school.

Naturally, between the wine and pure exhaustion, she'd have snoozed through Mount St. Helens erupting in the middle of the living room. Bob and Fred had eventually barked her awake. She'd greeted the sunlight blazing through the sheers with an exuberant, "Aw, shit."

According to the note Vesta had left on the kitchen table, she'd tiptoed out at the crack of dawn, walked home to shower and change clothes, then taken a cab to the hospital. Charlie was doing fine, she'd assured Zoey, but her place was by his side—or as close as the law allowed.

"Your hair looks great," Claire said. "Darla's kind of a ditz, but she knows what she's doing."

Exception could be taken to the ditz part, but Darla wouldn't, so Zoey let it go. "Thanks. I'll tell her you said so."

The visor thumped upright. "It's okay if I go to Laura's after school, isn't it? She asked me last night, when she brought my biology book and assignments and stuff."

Whew boy. Bella Donna and her deceased dearly beloved would undoubtedly provide the ride. Then again, the Peters family not ostracizing Claire for the supposed sins of her grandfather was gratifying.

"Sure. I'll call you there later, for a pickup time."

"They'll probably invite me to stay for dinner, too."

"Um…well, let's leave that at 'we'll see.'" Leaning over to kiss her daughter's cheek, she spied a corner of the morning newspaper protruding from her bulging Trapper Keeper.

Vesta had fetched it from the lawn and left it open on the table beside her note. While Claire had been showering, Zoey had read the article about the Jiffy Stop robbery. Darla had been right. The suspect in custody wasn't named.

Joe Donny Marlowe's obituary was in the second section.

Trudy King wasn't mentioned, as significant others often were. There was no phone book listing for her, either.

When Claire had come down the hall, Zoey had cast about for a hiding place, then crammed the newspaper under a place mat. Later, it was nowhere to be found.

"Is that today's paper?" she asked, as one might ask, "Is that an oak tree?"

"Uh-huh. Laura said I had to bring one for Comp class. We've gotta do something dorky like diagram sentences or circle the action verbs."

The teacher often solicited articles from national magazines and the newspaper as exemplars. Failure to provide cost grade points. Just their luck, today's edition was required.

"Don't worry, Mom. I'm okay with it." She grinned and finger-waved, then strode up the walk to the door.

Zoey waved back, then watched until she disappeared into the interior gloom. Funny how her daughter was nearly as tall as she was, but looked as small and fragile as she had on her first day of kindergarten.

10

For forty-three years, Nelson's Pharmacy had been located in the middle of a strip shopping center across the street from Sanford Memorial. Like his father before him, Walt Nelson was known to traipse to the store in the wee hours to refill a critical prescription. Unlike his father, Walt charged desperate, after-hours customers ten bucks a pop for the service.

"Odd choice for lunch," Lonnie said, as the unmarked's front tires bumped a concrete curb stop. He'd offered to buy after they left Chang's Market—partly, Hank suspected, because he ate like an All-Conference nose tackle and partly to atone for his earlier remark about Zoey.

"I want to check something out," Hank said. "Won't take a minute."

The pharmacist was putting on his coat to leave for lunch himself when an assistant ushered Hank and Lonnie into Nelson's office. The windowless room measured sixteen by twenty and was carpeted in the ultrasoft pile that skewed visitors' equilibrium. Bookshelves, museum-quality artifacts and oil paintings covered the mahogany paneled walls, along with about six dozen framed certificates of achievement.

Nelson had been a licensed pharmacist for thirty years, but also held degrees in biochemistry and, of all things, Egyptology. Two of the three fields of expertise interested Hank.

"We won't keep you long, Walt." He laid a list typed from Vesta's notebook on a desk countless teak trees had given their lives for. "What I need to know is the expected side effects of these medicines—individually and in combination."

Nelson looked down at the paper, then up again. "Charlie France, I presume?"

"Yes, sir."

He harrumphed and switched on the computer monitor on the credenza. A few keystrokes brought up a document file. Two more taps engaged the printer. "I had a feeling I'd better save the information. I guess I should have printed another copy, while I was at it."

Hank repeated, "Another copy?"

"A young lady from Osbert Schlomo's office was waiting for me when I arrived this morning." His tone implied amusement at her getting the drop on the police. "She asked for the same information about Charlie's medications."

So Vesta had hired Schlomo to defend her husband. Blytheville's pick of the legal litter didn't come cheap. He'd taken cases pro bono, but it was doubtful that France's was high-profile enough for a free ride.

The three pages of bulleted text Nelson handed him were still warm. It appeared he'd scanned the pertinent sections from package inserts, then cut-and-pasted them into a document file. A quick-and-dirty method, but it supplied half the answers Hank sought.

"These side effects and interactions pertain to full doses taken at the prescribed intervals, right?"

"Correct."

"What if they weren't? What if he took half a dose? Or skipped a day, either regularly or on occasion?"

Nelson smiled. "Which he did, the stubborn old cuss. Vesta's consulted me several times, terribly upset after she'd found capsules hidden under a chair cushion or caught Charlie palming them."

Hank nodded, not so much in agreement as to prompt a more specific answer.

"I'll tell you the same thing I did Schlomo's paralegal. What effect that might have had is impossible to know. It depends entirely on which medicines he skimped on, when, and for how long. I daresay going off his oxygen treatment when it suited him may also have had an effect. Whether it did and to what extent, again, I can't say."

"Could a doctor?"

Nelson stiffened as though insulted. "Quite frankly, I'd be skeptical of any determination, whether the findings were indicative or contraindicative."

The hat he settled over his thinning hair was a subtle reminder that his lunch was being delayed. "How it could be ascertained in hindsight, I can't imagine, especially with no idea of how much and when each medication was ingested."

Common sense had already drawn that conclusion for Hank. He thanked the pharmacist for his time and bid him a good day.

Walking back to the car, Lonnie said, "Care to tell me what that was all about?"

"Being thorough." That was about as lame as a three-legged mule. The extent and effects of Charlie France's pharmaceutical treatment weren't germane to their investigation. "Want to grab some soup and a sandwich at Panera's?"

"That'll work." Hardly missing a beat, Lonnie added, "It never hurts to know what the opposition's up to."

"You aren't gonna let this go, are you, kid?"

"If I was in your shoes..." Lonnie waved away that approach. "Mrs. France is a sweet lady. Almost as much a victim in all this as Marlowe, if you ask me. How's she going to feel if she figures out the shyster she's paying thinks her husband is as guilty as we do?"

Defense attorneys didn't necessarily care about their client's innocence or guilt. For all intents, clients didn't stand trial, anyway. Evidence did. And that evidence had to convince a jury beyond reasonable doubt that the individual charged with the crime was the only one who possessed the means, opportunity and motive to have committed it.

"You think Schlomo's angling to have France plead not guilty by reason of diminished capacity?"

Hank shifted the car into Reverse. "Sounds like he's fishing that pond, yeah."

The strategy called into question whether a defendant was, due to a mental disorder, incapable of resisting or controlling the impulse to commit a criminal act.

Defense attorneys had stretched the definition of a mental disorder to include chronic alcoholism and drug addiction—sometimes successfully. Precedents had also been established to include Alzheimer's disease.

Hank wasn't aware of any diminished capacity cases where prescription medications were blamed for inducing dementia-like side effects, but hell. There's a first time for everything. Judges who disallowed evidence of that nature could be accused of bias against the mentally ill, regardless of cause.

Lonnie said, "Giving the prosecutor a heads-up can't hurt."

"It won't help much, either, if Walt Nelson's right."

"Why not? Forewarned is—"

"The defense can't prove diminished capacity, but the prosecutor can't disprove it, either."

"Oh, great." Lonnie sneered. "Bet my gang of expert witnesses can whip your expert witnesses."

With Vesta France paying through the nose for every shrink and geriatric specialist Schlomo called to the witness stand.

"It's gonna be ugly," Lonnie said. "Man, I just love cooling my jets at the courthouse waiting to testify at a trial."

Hank agreed, then much as he hated to admit it, added, "Schlomo's good, but I don't think Clarence Darrow himself could pull off a diminished capacity defense in this case."

His grip tightened on the steering wheel. "Not when there's three convenience store clerks who'll swear Doc France robbed them over a six-week period prior to taking a hammer to Joe Donny Marlowe's skull."

Zoey washed down two extra-strength aspirin with a swig of diet cola. The only reason she preferred white wine to red was that it didn't kick up a dull, morning-after headache.

Giving the pain relievers a chance to do their analgesic thing, she paged through the newspaper she'd bought from the machine in the fast-food joint's drive-through lane.

As memory served, Joe Donny Marlowe's obituary appeared on page 4D. The inch-square photo accompanying it looked like a yearbook picture. His hair was flat on top, but scraggly around his face and ears, as though he'd wet a comb in the boy's restroom for a last-minute stab at making himself presentable.

His mouth crooked in a Bogart leer that didn't jibe with his deep-set, long-lashed eyes. Genetic typecasting, she thought. Try as they might, the Opie Taylors of the world just couldn't play a convincing bad-ass.

"Damn it." She jerked up her head, blinking away an onslaught of tears. God, he was so young. Older than the photo, but only twenty-six.

Leaning back against the headrest, she gazed out the fishbowl of a windshield. Four lanes of traffic sped by, as if divine missions were taking them in opposite directions. Across the street, a store employee in a ski jacket wielded a grab-it pole to rearrange letters on a signboard. Couriers delivered parcels. Small brave birds cuddled on power lines.

A ragged sigh escaped her lips. Life wasn't fair. Never would be. It just went on.

She swiped at her nose with the back of her hand and filled her mouth with sweet, icy soda. The aspirin was healing her headache There were no fast, easy cures for heartache.

With the tip of a pen, she razored the obituary's text from the page. She didn't need a blurred black-and-white image to remember Joe Donny Marlowe by.

Turning to the classifieds, she jotted on a small sticky note the names, addresses and phone numbers of a few businesses seeking part-time, minimum-wage employees. Next, the address and office phone number of a low-rent apartment complex. Perusing the real estate ads, she memorized an agent's first name, combined with another's last.

She eased the car beside a trash can. The reek of moldering burgers and rancid ketchup gusted out as she pushed the rest of the newspaper through the hinged plastic flap. Disposal alleviated the need to explain to Claire or her mother why she'd bought a second copy, much less the jagged hole in the Local section.

Lunch-hour traffic almost doubled the travel time across town. She watched for Hank's unmarked sedan, but unless he'd been among the bozos careening out of parking lots in front of her, or swooping upside in the merge lane, the odds of spotting him were nil.

She might have cruised past the Jiffy Stop if not for the towering standard and flashing sign out front. In sunlight and without police cars, ambulances, uniformed officers and paramedics, the store looked shabbier and more benign than she remembered.

She parked at the opposite end of the sidewalk apron from where her father had sat, his hands cuffed behind him and coat sleeve drenched in blood. That mental picture was unforgettable, too.

An orange-and-black HELP WANTED sign was taped to the right-hand door's inside glass. Business went on, too, she thought as she opened the door. Someone had affixed a tiny yellow ribbon to one corner. It softened the sign's harshness…a little.

Behind the counter was a neon-pink-haired girl too young to ring up a customer's twelve-pack. Two teenagers slouched behind waiting to pay for snacks and sodas. In a center aisle a woman Zoey's age deliberated a candy bar versus a SnackWell's for dessert. Almond Joy won the toss.

Waiting for the line to disperse, Zoey wandered about, wondering for the hundredth time why her father had driven past who knew how many other stores nearer the house to come here. Nothing special about it, the merchandise, or the prices.

Unless…her gaze moved to the counter. Could he have known Joe Donny Marlowe from somewhere? Maybe heard he was working here, and too bored and restless to watch TV, took a notion to drive over and say hello?

Possible. Likely, even. Charlie France's practice had taken him all over the county. When she was growing up, a day seldom went by without a stranger saying, "You're Doc's daughter, aren't you?" The recognition factor had put the quietus to plenty of downright brilliant pranks.

"You gonna buy something, lady?" the clerk asked.

"No, I—uh, I saw your sign in the window. Are you the manager?"

She turned and hollered, "'Ey, George. Lady wants to talk to you up front." The narrow-eyed look she shot Zoey branded her a ghoul.

If only she knew…

A perspiring, obese man of about forty lumbered from the rear of the store. Jiffy Stop was embroidered in red thread on a patch above his shirt pocket. The plastic nameplate pinned below said George Santini, Owner/Manager.

He had a wide nice-guy smile. She'd hoped for a jerk. You could almost forgive yourself for conning a jerk. "Afternoon, miss. What can I do for you?"

Zoey introduced herself as Brenda Cummins. "I'm here about the job. That is, if it's still available."

Santini sobered instantly. "Truth is, I've got three openings to fill. Can't say as I blame them, but a couple of my people up and quit yesterday morning." He reached under the counter for a clipboard with application forms attached. "I suppose you heard about the trouble we had, Sunday night."

Understatements didn't come much larger. Zoey nodded and said, "It was on the news." According to Darla Quinn, anyway.

Pink Hair mumbled, "Real sweet of you to wait a day to come after Joe Donny's job."

Santini scowled, but reserved comment. He probably couldn't afford to lose another clerk. Pink Hair looked the type to take an advantage and squeeze it till it squealed.

Motioning with the clipboard, he said, "Let's go to the back and you can fill this out."

Zoey faltered, assuming he meant the storeroom where Marlowe was attacked. About to wheel and run for the exit, she realized he was heading for the opposite corner, near the coolers.

Judging by several light-colored rectangles on the linoleum floor, gondolas and freestanding displays had been moved to allow room for a six-drawer metal desk and office chair. Heavyduty extension cords stretched from under the storeroom's door along the breadth of the refrigerated cases to power an iMac computer and printer.

The manager fetched a folding chair for her, then sat down behind the desk. His obvious exile from the crime scene was like putting butter on a third-degree burn.

"I am sorry for your loss, Mr. Santini."

"'Preciate you saying that. Marlowe was a good fella. A good worker, too." He tapped a temple. "A mite slow, but as dependable as daybreak."

"It must be awful for his family." Zoey knew from the obituary that a brother, his parents and grandparents preceded him in death. Two sisters, one listed as a California resident and the other, address unknown, survived him, along with a cousin—presumably on his mother's side, as his surname differed.

"For what's left of it, I guess." Santini shook his head. "You know what they say about if not for bad luck, a guy'd have no luck at all? That fit Joe Donny to a T."

A chuff enlarged to a chuckle, as it did when a fleeting thought jogged a memory. "A while back, it was all over the news that this asteroid was barreling toward earth. In the end, the thing wasn't within twenty thousand miles or light-years, or however they measure it, but ol' Joe Donny, he said if a chunk ever crashed down, they were sure to find him under it, squashed flatter 'n a flitter."

Zoey laughed with him. She couldn't help herself—it was the Rodney Dangerfield meets Jeff Foxworthy effect. But adding dimension to a name, photograph and fate also induced a more personal sense of loss.

"Yeah, Joe Donny was a good fella," Santini said. "Happy as a clam, too, the last month or so. It's hard to say which he was more excited about—the engagement ring he bought to give his girlfriend on Valentine's Day, or finishing technical school and hiring on with a big heating-and-cooling outfit down in Springfield. Crazy kid went so far as to put money down on a house there for him, his bride and her kids."

He sighed, muttered, "Jesus," and clucked his tongue. "I don't mind telling you, I hope they hang the old bastard they've got locked up. Life in prison's too good for what he did to Joe Donny."

Agreement would be the natural response. Zoey couldn't think it, much less voice it.

Anguish must have shown in her expression. Santini apologized for rambling and passed her the clipboard and a pen from a coffee cup with an amputated handle. "Look, uh—Brenda, wasn't it? I don't mean to scare you off. We've never had anywhere near that kind of trouble here before."

His tone implied a fluke. What "anywhere near" might constitute, he chose not to elaborate.

Surreptitious peeks at the crib note crumpled in her palm supplied Brenda Cummins's apartment address and an employment history cadged from the classified ads.

Fudging her own birth date and transposing her home telephone and Social Security numbers filled those respective blanks. If Santini checked Ms. Cummins's references, which prospective employers seldom did, the bogus information wouldn't cost him more than a few minutes' telephone time.

The application's bottom line required a signature attesting to the veracity of the information provided. Zoey balked, as though signing a fictitious name was more deceptive than printing it.

She repressed a sigh. She hadn't learned much about Joe Donny Marlowe, but that conversational window had closed. A slick way of reopening it without arousing Santini's suspicion escaped her.

"Finished?" His hand extended for the clipboard.

"Almost." Zoey's thumbnail separated the top sheet from the one below it. "I should have asked sooner, I know, but those three openings you mentioned. Are they for day shifts or nights?"

His eyes telegraphed, *Don't tell me, let me guess.* "You don't want to work nights."

"Actually, I can't. I already have a night job. My schedule varies some, but..." She slid the application from under the holder. "Not enough, I'm afraid."

Santini looked disappointed, not angry. He stood and shook her hand. "Pleasure meeting you all the same, Brenda. Drop by sometime. I'll treat you to a soda, or a cup of coffee."

"Thanks. I'll do that," she said, adding another lie to the day's total.

Practice, she rationalized, for tonight's marathon event.

11

The restroom stall's metal wall was as cold as an igloo against Zoey's panty-clad butt. She sucked air through clenched teeth and curled her toes to keep from falling off her shoes.

Thumbs hooking the waistband of a pair of panty hose that looked too small for a Bratz doll, she realized why superheroes wore their leotards and tights under their street clothes. Leaping a tall building in a single bound was a freakin' snap. Try doing the nearly naked mambo balanced on tennis shoes in a greasy spoon's public restroom to avoid barefooted contact with a beau-nasty ceramic tile floor.

Not that she could have crammed her black wool suit, silk blouse and a slip into her jeans and polo shirt for an emergency phone-booth striptease. For one, she hadn't seen a four-walled phone booth since *Psycho* last aired on the Turner Classic Movies channel. Secondly, layering such diverse ensembles required foresight. She might have given double-dressing a shot, had she known when she took Claire to school that she'd be attending the funeral home's visitation for Joe Donny Marlowe.

The idea developed after she left the Jiffy Stop. No disrespect for the dead or grieving was intended. What she hoped to gain was obscure. Initiative was tolerable. Inertia was not.

From the convenience store, she'd proceeded to the hospital. Officer Hugh Wayne White, again guarding the room, allowed her to wave, whisper "I love you" and blow kisses from the doorway. The feeble, dopey grin her father returned was at once encouraging and heartrending.

It also erased any lingering doubts that doing something trumped doing nothing. Putting the plan in action without her mother or Claire finding out was going to be the trick.

She'd been mulling viable excuses for going AWOL in an outfit appropriate for the visitation when her mother was paged to the nurses' station and told the police had released the car. The news seemed like cosmic intervention. Zoey drove her to the impound lot, confident that she could beat Vesta to the house, let out the dogs, grab some clothes, dash off a note about meeting Darla for dinner and asking Vesta to pick up Claire at Laura's, let in the dogs, and be gone before her mother puttered across town.

And she would have, if two nimrods hadn't plowed into each other at an intersection, snarling traffic for blocks. By the time Zoey got home, her mother was reorganizing the pantry, à la *Clean Sweep*.

Desperation inspired an alternative. Zoey congratulated herself for not mentioning her paid vacation, while she stuffed the suit and accessories in a duffel bag, chucked it out the bedroom window, relayed the pick-up-Claire request to Vesta and pretended to go to work, as usual.

Actually, the ladies' at the He Just Left would have been a good place to change clothes, except for loitering reporters and Gert Massey. In a nanosecond, she'd guess where Zoey was bound and tattle to Al, who'd consequently speed-dial Vesta.

Taking refuge with Darla, the soul of indiscretion, would reap a similar result. Simply whipping around the block to her parents' empty house didn't occur to Zoey until her butt was to the freezing-cold metal wall.

Now shivering as she struggled to pull on the hyperpetite panty hose, Zoey sniffed once, twice, and identified the aroma permeating the stall as Eau de Dogshit. Well, of course, the duffel bag had dropped from the window into Bob and Fred's primary dump site. Mothers sat at the left hand of God, so He could use His right to smack down their sneaky, conniving daughters. The merciful factor was that the bag was lined in vinyl. The poop-smear on the bottom hadn't seeped in and perfumed her suit. Plus, there was a bicycle tire-sized toilet paper dispenser to wipe off the glop and a commode to put it in. Cleanup and dress-up completed, Zoey moved to the sink. Nobody in Blytheville had seen her in anything except jeans since who-knew-when, but as disguises went, a severe black suit, hose and pumps was pretty thin.

The restroom's doorknob rattled. A fist banged the flimsy wood. Zoey called out, "Just a minute…"

The disembodied reply sounded threatening.

Tap water, paper towels and liquid soap disintegrated every trace of makeup. On went enough mousse to flatten her wavy hair and skim it back into a bun at her nape. She wouldn't win a beauty contest on the best hair day of her life, but without the bangs she'd had virtually since birth, and with a drugstore pair of nerdy, nonprescription glasses, she looked ten years older and perfectly hideous.

The woman waiting outside the door gave Zoey the up-and-down, then flinched. Her expression and tone contrite, she said, "Beg pardon, Sister."

Zoey prescribed five Hail Marys and managed to keep a straight face all the way to her car.

A bookstore across the street from the funeral home provided an observation post, until Zoey judged it time to join those paying their respects to Joe Donny Marlowe. The attendance was higher than anticipated, especially for a young man whose immediate family consisted of two estranged sisters—an assumption Zoey drew from the obituary referring to one as a California resident and the other with no known address.

The turnout might also be due to the fact that no traditional funeral was scheduled—just the visitation, followed by a graveside service on Wednesday afternoon.

Head lowered, Zoey scanned the room, alert for familiar faces that might recognize hers. She paid special attention to the men. As a rule, women look pretty much the same, whether they're going casual or in their Sunday best. Stick Joe Blow in a suit and tie, lose the ball cap and run a razor over his cheeks and chin, and he'll resemble a corporate middle manager.

In lieu of canned Muzak hymns lilting from the chapel's sound system, Garth Brooks sang a muted ode to friends in low places. Between the back wall and rows of upholstered chairs, people clustered together, murmuring, nodding and occasionally glancing toward the front of the room.

Now and again, like an ice floe breaking free of a glacier, a couple or a group drifted down the center aisle.

Zoey sidled from behind a tall woman in a faux-fur coat, then halted, her breath catching in her throat.

Floral arrangements on wire stands backdropped a casket resting on a skirted bier. A spray of red carnations fanned across the foot of the casket.

A young woman with corn-silk hair to her waist sat in the front row, acknowledging the well-wishers who passed by. An introduction wasn't needed for Zoey to identify Trudy King, the girlfriend Joe Donny would have proposed to on Valentine's Day.

Cuddled to her were two little blondes of perhaps four and six, the hems of their dresses and socks trimmed in lace. The four-year-old was crying, but judging by her wails, more from frustration at being restrained than from sorrow. A stout older woman scooped up the little girl and carried her, patting her back and crooning, to the other side of the room.

"I never dreamed the casket would be open," a low female voice drawled in Zoey's ear.

The speaker shuddered and hugged yards of

synthetic fox to her chest. "Not after...I mean... well, did you?"

Zoey confirmed she hadn't.

Another woman passing by chimed in, "Oh, the funeral director's wife is fantastic with makeup. My mother-in-law looked ten years younger and healthy as a horse after they fixed her up."

Zoey excused herself and was turning away when Fox Fur grasped her elbow. "Listen, you're alone, too, aren't you? No husband or significant other out parking the car?"

"Uh, well—"

"I don't know about you, but going down there to see Joe Donny and talk to Tru all by myself is just..." Her eyes, rimmed in heavy black liner, flicked to the front of the chapel. "We both have to, sooner or later, though, so how about we go together and get it over with?"

"No." Zoey backed up a step. "I—I can't do that. Sorry, no offense to you, but...I just can't."

The woman's expression turned glacial. "What do you mean, you can't? If you didn't come to tell him goodbye, or say something to Tru and the kids, why're you here?"

Good question. For which leaving—now—was the only answer.

Arguably deserving of the "funeral junkie" Fox Fur muttered at her back, Zoey froze when she spotted George Santini holding the outer door for a couple to precede him inside.

Trapped between Fox Fur and the convenience store manager, Zoey spun to her right and merged with the human barricade. She must hide within it until the convenience store manager started down the aisle to pay his respects to Ms. King, then scurry outside like the rat she was.

Chin lowered, she breached perfume vapor-trails and fragmented conversations, her field of vision a melange of shoulders, sleeves and shoes.

"The old vet? Nah, Elmo's got his ear to the wrong keyhole. I'm not buying that for a second."

"Are you serious? Jason's hooked up with Alesha Twain? Since when?"

"And then you drizzle the chocolate syrup over the pudding layer..."

"Poor Trudy. Out of the frying pan, into the fire."

"That's not funny, Helen. Not one bit."

"Funny? I wasn't trying to...oh, Lord, I forgot all about that."

"Ten bucks says Duke makes the Final Four."

"Twenty says they clutch before the Sweet Sixteen." A groan, then, "Holy shit, will you look who...what's W.C. doin' here?"

Zoey paused and looked up. The thirtyish man who'd spoken stared toward the front of the chapel. His huskier friend said, "Dunno, but it's a lead-pipe cinch, the last person Trudy wants to see tonight is her ex."

Necks craned. One by one, nearby voices stilled, the silence slithering like a draft.

The two men beside Zoey and three others, including George Santini, edged toward the center aisle. Swaggering down it was a lean, broad-shouldered man in paint-streaked coveralls. A jet-black ponytail hung to his shoulder blades and a Fu Manchu mustache framed his bulldog jaw.

"Daddy!" The little girl wriggled in the older woman's embrace, demanding to be put down, then ran to him, her bow-tied sash flapping like ribbon wings.

Her sister leapt from her chair and wrapped her arms around his waist. Her joyful smile exposed a vacancy two baby teeth had recently filled.

"If W.C. thinks he can just waltz out of here with those kids," an observer said, "he's got another think coming."

A teenager about Claire's age said, "That's low, man. Even for W.C."

With a daughter riding each hip, his forearms supporting their bottoms, he knelt down in front of Trudy King. George Santini and the other four paused at the third row down. By the glances exchanged, they'd agreed that for now, watch and wait was the wisest course of action.

Presently, W. C. King gained his feet as though unsaddled with an extra seventy-five pounds. Trudy stood to help her daughters into their coats. She rose up on tiptoes to kiss them, then briefly, their father.

The five incredulous guardians parted to let him through, as did those blocking the exit.

"Did you see that?"

"What in blue blazes...?"

Then Zoey heard a louder, familiar-sounding, "I had a feeling I'd find you here."

Zoey whirled around. The expression on Hank Westlake's face wasn't cop-rigid, but it wasn't particularly friendly, either. "Your mom and Claire think you're at work. Al told me he gave you the week off. Darla said she hadn't seen you since yesterday evening."

"Then how—"

"I'm a detective, remember? And I know how you think." His mouth tucked at a corner. "That Marion the Librarian getup is a hoot. Lame, but a hoot."

Mustering the tiniest speck of outrage, she said, "Who do you think you are, checking up on me?"

"C'mon, Zoe." He curled an index finger. "We need to talk." It was a command, not a suggestion.

"Fine. I was about to leave, anyway."

His palm pressed the small of her back as though glued there. They fell in behind others moving toward the door. Just inside it, Hank extended his hand to a dark-haired man in a three-piece pinstriped suit. A black armband encircled his sleeve. Bereavement, sleeplessness and the tight-harnessed emotions a funeral imposes compromised his handsome features.

"I'm sorry for your loss, Andrew."

He nodded. "Thank you for coming, Hank."

As they walked outside into the frigid night air, Zoey said, "Andrew Kelly, I presume?"

"Uh-huh." Hank delivered a sidelong look. "Guess you understand why I skipped the introductions."

She did. "Why didn't you tell me Joe Donny's cousin was a friend of yours?"

"How did you know they were cousins?"

It was rude to answer a question with a question, but this wasn't a good time to quibble about etiquette. "From the obituary in today's paper."

She pointed left. "My car's over there."

"I know. I'll bring you back to it later."

"Back from where?"

"My place. Like I said, we need to talk. In private."

His brusqueness dispelled any thought of an ulterior motive, as well as the compulsion to ask what they'd talk about. In general, her father. The specifics she'd learn soon enough.

"Before we go, do you mind if I get the bag with my jeans and stuff out of the car?"

He shook his head. "I'll meet you there," he said over his shoulder as he headed toward his own vehicle.

His truck pulled alongside her car just as she relocked the piece-of-crapmobile's finicky passenger door. Honestly, she didn't know why she bothered. No self-respecting thief would steal it, if she left the keys in the ignition and taped a big red bow to the roof.

Four-wheel-drive pickups, even those equipped with chrome running boards, are not designed for passengers wearing pencil skirts. Zoey resorted to a butt-first scoot onto the leather seat, then dug a heel into the floor mat to swivel around.

As they queued up behind other vehicles leaving the funeral home, she said, "So why didn't you tell me you were friends with Joe Donny's cousin?"

"Because I'm not. Kelly's vice president of the loan department at the Bank of Blytheville. He's the one I talked to when I was looking to start up the security business."

"Oh." Resting a forearm on the window ledge,

she sighed, then said, "All right, I shouldn't have come here tonight. Believe it or not, I realized that about two seconds after I walked in."

"No harm done. Leastwise, none that I noticed." An oncoming car slowed to let them out. The pickup's rear tires grated the pavement as they wheeled into traffic. "Care to tell me what you hoped to accomplish?"

"At the moment, I'm not sure I know." Her knuckles rapped the ledge's cold vinyl surface. "Maybe in the back of my mind was this Perry Mason-style fantasy. That the guy who did rob the store and kill Marlowe would be compelled to come, then be so overwhelmed by guilt and remorse that he'd shout out a confession."

To her everlasting gratitude, Hank smiled, but he didn't laugh. "Yeah, well, thinking along those lines is how I figured out where you were. If I wasn't a cop and the situation was the same, doing something would feel a far sight better than sitting around doing nothing."

"Even if it's wrong."

He made a face. "I wouldn't call it wrong, as much as wrongheaded. Now if you'd set out to cause a ruckus, that would have been wrong."

The tiniest of semantic loopholes. Hank knew as well as she did that had someone recognized her, it would surely have set off a ruckus.

"Your reason for being there was iffy," he went on, "but you did have one. Truth be told, a goodly number of those folks were there out of curiosity."

Zoey turtled her neck. "Thanks, but that doesn't exactly exclude me."

Seemingly opposite thoughts suddenly came together. No, it wasn't hope of a television-inspired denouement or simple curiosity that had propelled her to the visitation. Not entirely, anyway.

"It wasn't until quite a while after I moved back home that I realized how estranged I'd become from my parents."

Hank glanced at her. "What do you mean, estranged?"

"Okay, not estranged. Distanced from them. Not intentionally and not because we don't love each other to pieces. It was more like a gradual, benign neglect—the kind that phone calls and weekend get-togethers seem to make up for, but don't. Not really."

"No," Hank said, "but you don't have to move to another city for distance to creep in and take hold."

The allusion to his failed marriage—the first, more so than the second—was clear. So was the residual guilt for allowing it to happen.

"As you pointed out, though," she said, "distance and estrangement aren't synonyms. I think there's been a subtle undercurrent of 'There but for the grace of God go I' nagging at me, ever since I read Marlowe's obituary.

"No, I was nowhere near being estranged from my folks, but I can't help wondering how Joe Donny became so alienated from his sisters that whoever wrote his obituary didn't know where they lived."

A parallel explanation presented itself. "Or was it just designed to look as though they cared so little for their brother that they didn't bother to stay in touch?"

"Some of both would be my guess."

"But why?"

The truck slowed, then turned into a driveway flanked by fieldrock retaining walls. Hank pulled under the carport at the far end, shut off the headlights and ignition, and turned toward her.

"When Marlowe was thirteen or fourteen years old, his parents and younger brother were killed in one of those freak accidents you hear about happening somewhere almost every winter. Propane was leaking from the furnace, the stove—could have been the water heater. There wasn't enough left of the house to determine where the gas came from or what ignited it."

Zoey recalled George Santini saying if Joe Donny didn't have bad luck, he'd have no luck at all.

"I think he'd have accepted their deaths a little easier, if they'd been killed in a car wreck. I'm told he never forgave himself for being out carousing with his friends that night. Like he should've been there to save them. Or died with them."

Hank exited the truck and walked around to help Zoey down from the seat. As a precaution, she'd put the fragrant duffel bag in the bed. He retrieved it and motioned for her to precede him up the railroad-tie steps to the door.

"Did Joe Donny get that idea on his own?" she asked. "Or from his sisters?"

"Depends on who you ask. Tammy and Renée were married and gone from the house when it happened, but a tragedy can do peculiar things to a family. Sometimes it brings one together. Others, it tears apart."

Zoey pondered that while he unlocked the door. "Wouldn't you think they'd feel sorry for him? He was just a kid—the same age as Claire, for God's sake."

"Whether they did or didn't, they packed up and left town shortly after Joe Donny went to live with his grandmother."

Questions still percolating in Zoey's brain evaporated as she passed by Hank into the living room. The walls were a creamy mocha. Underfoot was sculptured-pile carpet in a rich chocolate brown. No bachelor's domain would be complete without a leather recliner and big-screen TV, but guests could choose between the cushy, ultrasuede couch or one of the matching armchairs.

Floor-to-ceiling bookshelves held an extensive collection of hardcovers, paperbacks and hand-thrown pottery.

Lamps crafted from petrified wood rested on glass-topped rattan trunks. A towering banana palm thrived alongside a sliding glass door to the deck.

"Ye gods." She surveyed the adjacent dining room's pub table and upholstered, barrel-back chairs. A gallery of matted black-and-white photographs covered the walls. "What happened to the landfill with a bed in the middle?"

"So I used to be a slob," he said, chuckling. "Took a couple of decades, but I reformed."

"I'll say." She peeked around into the galley kitchen.

Stainless-steel appliances. Ceramic tile counters and floor. Raised panel cabinetry. Ceiling-hung pot rack, replete with copper-bottom cookware.

Not so much as a saltshaker out of place. "And then some."

Astonishment seemed to please him more than verbal compliments. "You hungry? I can stir-fry some steak and veggies, while you're changing clothes."

Stir-fry? The Hank Westlake she remembered couldn't heat a can of SpaghettiOs without scorching them. "Thanks, but I had a sandwich for dinner."

"In that case, how about a beer? Wine? Coffee?"

Their eyes met. His issued a gentle reminder of why she was there.

"Beer," she decided. "Then coffee."

12

Hank leaned against the kitchen counter, one ankle crossed over the other, staring at the stream of brewed coffee filling the carafe and second-guessing the wisdom of bringing Zoey to his apartment.

Privacy had been the impetus, but this wasn't the scenario he'd envisioned countless times. In those mental meanderings, a candlelight dinner led to snuggling on the sofa, a kiss, then another, a gradual escalation to that wondrous, whirling only-two-in-the-world feeling and he'd carry her to his bed, then taste and touch and make love to every inch of her, until their bodies screamed for release.

Sweat beaded Hank's forehead. Lust wasn't the cause. A slimy, sweltering wretchedness seeped from his pores and leached into his mouth. Fingers curled around the countertop's polished edge, he raised his gaze to the wall, as if he could see through it and into the bathroom where Marion the Librarian was turning back into the woman he'd loved his entire life.

No, he thought, it wasn't supposed to happen this way. After they talked—after what he knew to be true devoured every shred of faith she had in her father's innocence—Hank's home would usurp the Jiffy Stop in Zoey's mind as the place where nightmares grind your guts into fine powder and cast them into the wind.

He could have told her at her house. Sat Zoey, Vesta and Claire down at the table and torn them apart all at once. He could have avoided it entirely. His job didn't oblige him to tell a suspect's family Jack-diddly about the investigation. Just the opposite.

"I helped myself to your shampoo and a towel."

Startled, he lurched away from the counter, the jolt from deep thought to reality giving his brain the bends. "Wha-what?"

Zoey smiled. "The gunk in my hair wouldn't brush out. I had to wash it in the sink." She fluffed the shining, towel-dried cowlicks and waves skimming her shoulders. "And you, being a guy, don't own a blow-dryer."

Actually, he did. It was in a bottom drawer of his dresser, along with other remnants of a life poorly lived. But 'fessing up would rob him of that precious, fresh-scrubbed face surrounded by a wild, wonderful water-darkened mop of curls.

"Are you warm enough? Be glad to loan you a sweater, or a hoodie or something, until your hair's dry."

"I'm fine." She pulled out a bar stool, sat down and rested her elbows on the counter. "I'm ready for that beer, though."

So was he, but he warned himself to stick with coffee.

He took a long-neck from the fridge, popped the cap and set it in front of her. He gestured for her to wait, then backtracked for a glass beer stein from the freezer.

The cabinet beside the sink yielded a wooden serving bowl. From another, left of the range, he snagged a bag of potato chips. He'd poured the latter into the former and was perusing the refrigerator for dip, when Zoey said, "Hank..."

"Yeah?"

"You're stalling." She patted the adjacent bar stool. "I have a feeling that whatever you brought me here to say won't go down any easier with a snack."

He drew in a breath and let it out slowly. The refrigerator door reclosed with a somber hush. Retrieving his coffee, he nixed the invitation to sit beside her and wedged a hip into the kitchen side of the L-shaped counter.

Zoey looked up at him, her expression placid. The knuckles hooked around the beer stein's handle were bone-white.

"We have reason to believe—" Oh, for Christ's sake. Ditch the Detective Sipowicz routine. He cleared his throat and started again. "When we searched your dad's workshop, I found three bags full of cash identical to the one in his pocket at the Jiffy Stop. The dates and store names on their labels corresponded to robbery reports at those locations."

Zoey's lips parted a fraction, as if sipping his words from the air made them easier to comprehend.

"Chichester and I reinterviewed the clerks. Each of them identified Charlie France as the robber."

She snorted. "What did you do? Hand him Daddy's picture and say, 'Is this the guy?'"

"They were shown a layout of ten photographs. The only clerk who balked at first had given the vaguest description possible, the night of the robbery. Turns out he knew Charlie. He didn't want to ID him, until he realized protecting your dad could result in an obstruction of justice charge."

Creases tined above her nose suggested she thought he'd applied strong-arm tactics. He refused to honor that with a reply. "We fingerprinted all the bags, inside and out. No one had touched them except Charlie."

"How about the money inside?"

"We didn't test it. Paper is a great medium for prints, but it has to be fumed, or sprayed with ninhydrin. Bills pass through too many hands to waste the chemicals and lab time."

Plenty of people, irrespective of gender, would shout denials. Cuss, spit in Hank's face, or leap off the chair, fists cocked and ready. Not Zoey Jones. Her eyes dulled to a thousand-mile stare. Thumb grazing the frost from the side of the glass, she forced emotion aside to weigh, dissect and analyze what she'd heard.

Damned if he wouldn't take a screaming, spitting hissy fit any day.

"Okay if I ask a few questions?"

"Fire away."

"When was the first robbery?"

"December twenty-eighth."

Her chin bobbed, as though confirming the

date. "The three bags you found still had the money in them."

"Yes. Each jibed with the cash register's tally of the amount stolen."

Her head tilted. "You don't think that's a little odd?"

"In what way?"

"Well, if my dad was desperate enough for money to steal it, and he robbed the first store seven weeks ago, why didn't he spend any of it?"

Hank took a swallow of coffee. "That I can't answer."

Seeing her nostrils flare, he added, "I said can't, not won't. I don't know why he didn't."

"Don't thieves usually spend the loot as fast as they steal it?"

"Faster, more times than not."

She fell silent again, hoisting the glass, drinking from it, then lowering it, like one of those mechanical dolls in a department store's window at Christmas time.

"And the clerks were positive the robber was Daddy."

"I'm sorry, but yes, they were."

"I don't believe it." A smile whisked the pall from her eyes. "I said don't. Not can't."

"Zoey—"

"Oh, I believe he robbed the stores. The Jiffy Stop, too. I'd be an idiot not to."

She slipped off the bar stool and carried the beer stein to the sink. "Why he did it— Well, when you get right down to it, that doesn't make much difference, does it?"

Opening a cupboard door, she helped herself to a coffee mug and filled it. Grasping the carafe's handle, she came toward Hank. "What I don't believe is that he killed Joe Donny Marlowe."

She poured steaming coffee into Hank's mug. Tipping the pot level again, she looked him straight in the eye. "Not by accident. Not intentionally."

Returning the carafe to its warming plate, she cradled her mug in both hands. That smile appeared again, almost feral, yet as enigmatic as the Mona Lisa's. "And despite all that irrefutable evidence you've collected and the people you've talked to and all your years of experience, neither do you."

They stared at each other, not moving, Hank scarcely breathing, for what seemed like a quarter hour. He knew her certainty wasn't a loyalty test. What he'd thought would shatter her from the inside out had welded her resolve, crystallized her gut-level belief in what her father was capable of and what he was not.

And if he read her right, she didn't give a flying fuck whether he admitted a doubt or two or choked on them.

Her hand shot up as he started to speak. "Save the replay of the doesn't-matter-what-I-believe speech, okay? Here's the deal. My friend Hank shares what he knows about the murder itself, or Detective Westlake takes me back to my car and I find out on my own."

He mulled the proposition over. Bandied the pros and cons on either side of the line. The inescapable conclusion was that she'd dynamite his office, if necessary, to get what she wanted.

"Anything I tell you from here on out doesn't leave this room."

"Promise."

"Too quick. I mean, no slips of the tongue to Vesta, Darla, Uncle Al and, so help me God, not within ten miles of Osbert Schlomo. Not even a whisper in Bob's or Fred's ears."

Her mouth crimped in deliberation. "I have to tell Mom about the earlier robberies. It's just as cruel to let her hear it from someone else or read about in the paper."

Precisely the reasons Hank had divulged the information to her, as well she knew. "If you'd rather I talked to her, I will."

"Uh-uh. My not-so-little pitcher has big ears. Claire will have to be told, but I'll decide when, where and how."

"That has to be the extent of it, though," he said.

Her chuckle conveyed no humor whatsoever. "I haven't been one for a while, but scout's honor."

Ignoring the free-fall-down-a-black-hole sensation engulfing him, he said, "Okay, but I'm not going to show you the crime scene photos. They're gruesome and there's no point."

He paused to munch a few chips and wash them down with coffee. "To be honest, now that I think about it, there really isn't a whole lot to tell."

"What? God Almighty damn, Hank. You just—"

"Hey, hey, hey. All I meant was, you already know most of it. And nitties to gritties, all I can think of that you don't is that we confirmed the hammer came from the toolbox in the storeroom, and we've yet to locate the witness who called 911 to report a robbery in progress."

Setting aside the coffee mug, she dug her hands in her jeans pockets. "So there's somebody running around somewhere who saw what happened? Could describe whoever else was in the store, besides Daddy and Joe Donny?" She tensed. "There had to be somebody else. Good grief, maybe the caller went there with him to hassle Joe Donny about something, then chickened out and dialed 911 to end the fight before it began."

The phone rang, interrupting Hank's bubble-bursting response. Lonnie Chichester's cell phone number materialized on the cordless handset's caller-ID screen. He keyed the talk button and pressed the unit to his ear. "Westlake."

"'Ey, what's it feel like to have the night off?"

"I wouldn't know, Chichester. I'll make notes when I get one." To Zoey, Hank signed, *This won't take long.*

"At least you're home. Last time I saw my place, the neighbor's tulips were blooming."

Hank rolled his eyes. With Lonnie, not talking advanced a conversation faster than talking.

"I just heard the other homeless guy didn't make it. The fire marshal's ruled it arson. Deliberate, not from the barrel fire they had going to keep warm."

Firemen answering a two-alarm at a downtown building undergoing renovation had discovered two homeless men unconscious in a stairwell. One was DOA at the scene.

"Any identifications yet?" Hank asked.

"Nothing besides nicknames, but we're working on it."

"I'll be here for a while. Keep me posted."

"One other thing. Thought you'd want to know, the lab couldn't raise an identifiable print off the hammer from the Jiffy Stop. The grip was rubber and those perforations did a slice 'n dice on points of similarity. Like you scribbled all over a print card with a marking pen."

The news wasn't a surprise. At the scene, Hank had observed that the grip was cracked and peeling from age, weathering and use.

"Later, dude. Got another call," Lonnie said, and hung up.

Had Zoey's face been a billboard, *What was that about?* would have been plastered on it in big, flashing letters.

Hank said, "Before you fall in love with the tangent you were on when the phone rang, to inject one, nine, or a couple dozen people into the scenario and fabricate a motive for them, is like stirring chickpeas into a pot of chili. There's no basis for it, they don't belong in the mix and they'll force you to add a bunch more stuff to try and make it palatable."

"Oh, yeah?" Her head ticktocked. "Ever try putting chickpeas in chili?"

He grinned. "Do you know what chickpeas are?"

A screw-you look sufficed as an answer. "It's a fact that somebody called 911. What are you doing to find him?"

"Questioned everyone at the scene. Canvassed the neighborhood. Lonnie checked with the cab companies, in the event a driver was in the area at the time."

"Nothing, huh?"

"Dispatch receives lots of calls from this individual. His name is I Don't Want To Get Involved."

"But he was, Hank, the instant he dialed the phone."

His rang again, as if on cue. "It's a matter of degree," he said, frowning at the readout: Number Unavailable. "Plugging a cord into a socket doesn't make you an electrician, either."

Expecting a telemarketer, he said, "Westlake" with a thumb poised on the disconnect button.

"Detective Westlake? This is Osbert Schlomo, attorney for Mr. Charles France."

Hank's pulse tripped. "Yes, Mr.—" His eyes flicked to Zoey. "Yes, sir."

"Sergeant Chichester preferred I call you directly, rather than leave a message with him, in regard to scheduling an interview tomorrow with my client."

Struggling for nonchalance and a reply that wouldn't sound inane to Schlomo or tip off Zoey, Hank settled for, "The sooner the better."

"Yes, well, do bear in mind, this meeting is at my client's insistence, counter to both his primary physician's and my advice."

Hank focused on a cabinet knob. "I understand that."

"As I told Mr. France, I'll be in court until early afternoon. So shall we say 3:00 p.m.?" Schlomo paused. A smile altered his voice, when he added, "Unless, of course, something changes between now and then."

Such as you talk Charlie out of it, Hank thought. Or you persuade his doctor to order some midafternoon tests. Or you just string your court case out so long, the poor old guy's too worn out to answer questions.

"I'll be there," Hank said and disconnected the call.

This time, Zoey didn't hint. She came right out and asked, "Who was that?"

Hank shrugged. "Lonnie. What looked like an accidental, two fatality fire just graduated to arson and either homicide or manslaughter."

"At the old moving and storage building downtown?"

"Yep." Exhaling in relieved, millimeter increments, he docked the handset in its charger. "Two homeless men were the victims."

"I hope he can find out who they were, for their families' sake."

"So do I."

A warning, then a curse, tolled in his mind, a second before she said, "Though considering that you outrank Lonnie, why in the world would you call him 'sir'?"

Zoey pulled into her driveway behind Vesta's car, hesitated, then groaned and shifted into Reverse. Parking the piece-of-crapmobile on the street all night invited a hit-and-run sideswipe—as if she'd notice any new dents, scrapes, or dings.

The drive home from Hank's had assuaged much of her anger. Partly because the heater was just beginning to wheeze warm air out the vents.

Mostly because temper required fuel and she was just too tired to keep feeding it.

Stifling it as well, was the feeling evoked just by being around him. An emotional form of modern jazz—a disjointed, off-key, off-tempo sensation constantly ricocheting from happy to melancholy, hopeful to hopeless, infatuated to infuriated and, okay, horny to...hornier.

The bastard. He'd welched on their deal, as surely as she'd been standing there, when he lied about Chichester being on the other end of that second phone call.

When he'd left the kitchen to fetch her coat, she activated the caller-ID memory function. Unavailable Number, it snickered. There wasn't time to press redial and see who answered. Later, doubling back and following him after he dropped her at her car was a sucker punch. He'd been a hundred-percent truthful about going to his office.

As Zoey stepped through the front door, the vestiges of anger directed at her mother drained away. Vesta was dozing in the chair, her socked feet crossed on top of the coffee table and her head tilted to one side and forward. The TV's remote was clasped to her bosom like a child's teddy bear.

Claire had gone to bed early or was hibernating in her room. Maternal sensors detected a batch of homemade oatmeal cookies lurking in the kitchen, but no subsonic turmoil, past or current.

Bob and Fred, lying on their sides on the rug, each had one eye open and an ear aloft, either too comfy or too full of kibble and table scraps to get vertical.

Zoey eased the door shut, then shouldered it the mandatory three-eighths of an inch to secure the dead bolt.

"Al must have let you off early tonight."

An elephant stampede down Crocker Avenue, a UFO landing on the roof, a drum and bugle corps marching down the hallway—those, her mother would sleep through. An immediate family member's virtually inaudible egress, or ingress? Never. A quirk Zoey should have remembered sooner.

"I don't have to go back until next week. Al gave me a few days' vacation."

Vesta harrumped. "One less paycheck to write."

"Uh-uh." The short walk to the kitchen to dispense with her purse and coat and a forced smile stemmed a twinge of irritation. "I haven't taken a paid vacation since Bill Clinton's first term."

"Well." Her mother swung her legs off the table and sat up straighter. "You had a few phone calls. There's a list by the phone. Darla said to call her back, no matter how late."

"Yeah, well, she always says that." Whew, boy. She'd have to invent an explanation for where she'd been and why Hank was looking for her, before begging a favor.

"Hank stopped by, too, wanting to talk to you." Vesta's eyebrow arched. "Strange he'd come here, instead of the bar."

Kneeling to pet the boys gave Zoey's hands something to do besides curl, as if encircling a particular homicide detective's throat. "Hank doesn't know my work schedule." She chuffed. "I don't know my work schedule from one week to the next."

"That boy's crazy about you. Always has been." A wistful sigh prompted a dreamy expression. "The other night at dinner—law, it seems like months ago, now—Charlie and I talked about you and Hank going bowling and that maybe, after all these years, you two would finally get together."

Her thumbnail worried the crease in her slacks. "Your daddy frets about you, being alone and with a child to raise. And that you'll latch on to some dimwit like Stuart again."

Moving to the sofa, Zoey chuckled at her mother's fate-worse-than-death tone. "Gimme some credit, okay? I couldn't be that stupid twice."

"Plenty have been. Why, just the other day, I heard that Mitch Fairfax and Cindy Leigh Lamott are getting married in June." Vesta splayed her hands. "How many gold-digging little hussies take Mitch to the cleaners before he learns his lesson?"

Zoey thought, *Until he starts thinking with the organ between his jug ears.* "Not to change the subject, but is Claire asleep?"

Vesta nodded. "She finished her makeup work and homework at Laura's. School must have been tolerable today. I didn't pry or anything. She'd have clammed up if I'd tried, but she's been a perfect angel all evening."

The description didn't sound like Claire. Then again, it came from her grandmother.

Balancing the remote on the armrest, Vesta bent over and felt around for her crepe-soled shoes. "Seeing as how I have my car back and Claire doesn't need baby-sitting any more than I do, I believe I'll go home and sleep in my own bed tonight."

"I wish you wouldn't," Zoey said. "It's cold and it's getting late and walking into a dark, empty house alone isn't a very good idea."

Vesta smiled. "As if you ever listened when I told you that."

"Take it from me, stubbornness doesn't cure the goose-pimpled, bug-eyed creeps."

"Oh, for heaven's—"

"C'mon, Mom, half the town knows Daddy's in the hospital. I'm not trying to scare you, but this isn't the best time to rattle around over there all by yourself."

Vesta gnawed her lower lip. "I have thought about that." The shoes dropped to the rug. "Silly, I guess, to venture out at this hour."

Relief didn't lessen the tension cording the muscles in Zoey's neck. "And there is something I have to tell you."

The facts of the three earlier thefts were related Hank-style: in a calm, objective voice, leaving no room for debate. Kinder, Zoey realized in hindsight, than giving doubt a niche to burrow into.

Tears shimmered in her mother's eyes, then trickled from the corners. "Of all the things…" Her head fell back, rocking slowly from side to side. "I've conjured a thousand excuses…reasons…explanations for why one minute, he'd be reading the paper or watching TV and the next, he'd just be…gone. I'd run around, inside and out, frantic with worry, then he'd come dragging in, gasping for breath, and collapse in that damned recliner with not so much as a word to me."

Mouth agape, she made a gurgling sound that

was not as wrenching as sobs and too raw for laughter. "Of all the things I thought he was doing—accused him of, dared him to admit to me—never once in my wildest imaginings did it occur to me that he was out robbing convenience stores."

Dazed and bewildered, Zoey just sat there, as insentient as a throw pillow, while her mother began to chuckle, then burst out laughing.

Dabbing at her eyes with her knuckles, she stammered, "I know, it's not funny. Not a bit. It's terrible…ought to be ashamed of myself. But…for weeks…I thought Charlie…I thought he was having an affair."

"What? Oh, for God's sake—"

"I did, Zoey. Why else would a man just up and vanish like that, time and time again?"

"Because…" Zoey gestured concession. "Hell, I don't know, but thinking Daddy was out screwing around is about as goofy as it gets. Jeez Louise, he has a heart condition, he's on oxygen, there's been days when it's been all he could do to make it to the bathroom."

"I'm not talking about a sexual affair." Vesta fished out a tissue from her pocket. "The emotional kind is far worse. And who could blame him? I'm not his wife anymore. I'm a bossy old battle-ax of a nurse."

Wrinkling her nose, she singsonged, "Take this pill. Finish your dinner. Did you have a bowel movement? Time for a nap. Here, drink your juice, like a good boy."

Fresh tears rimmed her eyes. She wiped them

away with the tissue. "Charlie France loves me more than life itself, but why wouldn't he run to anyone in a skirt who treated him like a man instead of a sick child?"

Like a confession masquerading as a song, the lyrics from Sister Hazel's "Killing Me Too" wended through Zoey's mind. "Oh, Mom. I had no idea—" She stopped herself. "That isn't true. I'd have to be blind, deaf and stupid not to notice how hard Daddy's illness has been on you."

Vesta tut-tutted. "Now, don't you go to feeling sorry for me. I knew the 'in sickness and in health' part of the wedding vows didn't mean just a head cold or a toothache.

"As for the other—well, if Charlie was being any kind of unfaithful to me, that was my concern and no one else's. For all I knew, the other woman worked at the Jiffy Stop or met Charlie there on the sly."

Reluctant as Zoey was to admit it, a thread of logic shone through the tangled assumptions. "And if he was, you didn't want Hank to find out about it."

"Absolutely not."

"Well, you know, I can understand that. You couldn't stop Hank from nosing around on his own, but why put him on the trail?"

"That's right. My thoughts exactly."

"But what I do *not* understand," Zoey said, "is why you lied and kept on lying to me."

Vesta recoiled. "Not telling isn't the same as lying."

"Since when?"

"Listen here, Miss High-and-Mighty. How much of what Stuart did—or was accused of doing—have you told your daughter? Not a jot more than necessary. Why? Because jackass or not, he's still her father.

"I was wrong about Charlie. I pray Jesus he'll be with me long enough to laugh about it someday, but it wasn't till five minutes ago, when you said he'd robbed those other stores, that I knew he wasn't out carousing with some hussy."

All right, already. Checkmate. End game. Zoey groaned. She was about to bow to her mother's goofball wisdom when a tickle like spider feet tiptoed up her nape. Bob and Fred reposed on the rug, as though Velcroed to it. A petulant, defensive Vesta glared at her expectantly.

Gaze sliding to the hallway, Zoey's peripheral vision swept the narrow space for movement or shadows. Finding none, and hearing not a single sound, meant one of two things.

Her sixth sense needed defragging. Or practice had perfected Claire's eavesdropping skills.

13

"Mr. Schlomo." Hank shook the attorney's smooth, dry hand. "This is my partner, Lonnie Chichester."

"Chichester." The watch on Schlomo's wrist would have made a couple of Hank's truck payments. "I daresay, I didn't expect you quite yet. It is only half-past two."

Hank's eyebrows arched. "Since it appears that court must have finished early, looks to me like we're right on time."

No offense taken, no advantage won. Just the usual song and dance. Schlomo enjoyed it as much as Hank did.

The uniform posted at the door stood as rigid as one of those muff-hatted sentries outside Windsor Castle. Hank gave him leave for a cup of coffee and a piece of cafeteria pie. Skinny as the kid was, Hank hoped he sprang for a scoop of ice cream on it.

A lumpy tote bag with knitting needles forked out the top occupied the chair across the corridor. Hank supposed Vesta France had ventured downstairs for a snack herself. Or she could be picking up Claire after school.

Telephone calls to Zoey's house had gone unanswered. Probably, she was ducking him. Fair enough, but if Chichester hadn't been riding shotgun, Hank would have acted on the urge to cruise by the cemetery where Marlowe's graveside service was being held.

He didn't truly believe she'd attend. The visitation last night had shaken her to her shoes. Except necessity was the mother of a helluva lot more than invention.

"Shall we proceed?" Schlomo said.

"After you, counselor."

The hospital room smelled as musty and medicinal as any Hank had entered, but chillier than most. On the TV bracketed to the wall, Alabama was routing Arkansas in an ESPN Classic rebroadcast from 1981. Roll Tide had been more of a prayer than a victory cry since Bear Bryant went to that locker room in the sky.

Doc France was semireclined on the hospital bed. White whiskers burred his gaunt face. His hair was an Einstein tangle of kinks. Tubes and wires tethered him to machines, monitors and IV trees. Liver spots, scarlet splotches and distended veins limned the backs of his hands and forearms.

The wide grin he flashed and the sparkle in his eyes belied the straits he was in, medically and legally. "Hank Westlake. God, it's good to see you, son. I used to run into your dad, now and then, but this bum ticker of mine's kept me housebound for quite a spell."

Schlomo looked from his client to Hank. "I wondered why Mr. France demanded to speak with you specifically."

"Because he's in charge of my case," Charlie said. "Nothing wrong with wanting the best cop on the force to hold your feet to the fire." Charlie nodded at Chichester. "No insult meant."

Hank hadn't known what to expect, but a prodigal-son-style welcome confused the bejesus out of him. Zoey's father was nobody's fool.

Procedure, Hank thought. Make this one so by-the-book that the roadkill plastered across Schlomo's skull will jump up and cry "Uncle."

He removed a portable tape recorder from his pocket and was clearing space for it on the bedside table when Charlie said, "Take all the notes you care to, but no tapes."

A backup recorder in Lonnie's coat pocket had been running since they entered the room. Hank's glance at Schlomo said, *Hey, you're raking in the big bucks by the hour. You tell him.*

"The police are permitted to record the interview, with or without your knowledge or consent." Schlomo spread his hands. "It's for your protection as much as theirs."

Charlie scowled and fumbled for the television's remote, obviously tempted to amp the volume a notch or ten. He thumbed the off button instead—grudgingly.

"Charles France, do you understand that you are in police custody?"

He nodded.

Hank cleared his throat and pointed at the recorder.

"All right, yes, I understand I'm in police custody. Can we just get on with it?"

Although any cop could recite the Miranda warning in his sleep and probably did on occasion, Hank took out a laminated card and read every blessed word aloud. "Do you understand these rights, as they have been presented to you?"

"Yes."

Hank then turned over the card and read the waiver printed on the back. By itself, the Miranda recitation didn't comply with the Supreme Court ruling. Suspects must also voluntarily and intentionally waive their Fifth Amendment rights.

"That part about not wanting an attorney present," Charlie said. "Does that mean I have the right to talk to you in private?"

Startled, Hank said, "Yes, it does." He jammed his teeth together before he blurted, *But with a homicide charge against you, you'd be crazy to show your attorney the door.*

"Then Mr. Schlomo, I reckon you and Sergeant Chichester can keep each other company outside while we do."

The attorney's conniption went on for several minutes. He railed, cajoled, ranted, pleaded and swore he'd quit, but failed to dissuade his client. Before he stormed out, Hank provided Charlie with a printed waiver for his signature. It wasn't required. It just kept things nice and unquestionably legal.

Subtle gestures relayed to Lonnie that he—and his concealed tape recorder—must abide by Doc's wishes. The kid would learn that, sometimes, the best way to take control of a situation was by appearing to relinquish it.

Shirt now stuck to his back like a field hand's, Hank shed his overcoat and moved to pull a chair beside the bed. "Hike it up here, son," Charlie said, patting the mattress. "No sense shouting across the room at one another."

Exertion had already taken a toll. His breathing was shallower, the respirations labored. Lips pressed together, he inhaled pure oxygen, compensating for the thinner air he'd drawn in through his mouth.

Hank eased onto the bed, a shoe braced on the lowered side rail. Notebook balanced on his thigh, he was paging to a blank sheet when Charlie rasped, "Tell me, son. How are my girls doing?"

"Doc, uh, this isn't a social call."

"I know, I know. We'll get to the other, by and by. I just can't rest for worrying about them."

"They're holding up all right." Hank hesitated. "But I've gotta say, this has been damned hard on them."

"Couldn't be helped." He winced and pushed the oxygen tube's prongs deeper into his nostrils. "You tell them for me, everything's going to be fine. May be a while, but I'll be good as new, real soon."

It sounded like wishful thinking, a verbal palliative the dying espouse to comfort the living. And there was no doubt that Charlie France wasn't long for this world.

"Vesta always said there's more money in poodles than polled Herefords. Once I'm back on my feet, I'm starting up a mobile pet clinic. Dogs, cats—sick hamsters, if it pays the bills. Tell her and Zoey and Claire, I love them more'n anything and I'm gonna take care of them."

Hank's fingers closed into a tight fist. Relaxed. Tightened again. *Can't let this get to me*, he thought. *Snap out of it, or turn it over to Lonnie.*

"Oh, before I forget," Charlie said. "You've got the money from the Jiffy Stop. When we're done, you need to go by the house. There's a coffee can in my workshop. Maxwell House—second shelf, right of the workbench. The money I stole from three other stores is in it."

Stunned didn't begin to describe Hank's reaction. "Do you realize you just confessed to four convenience store robberies?"

"Of course I do. I'd've stopped at one, if the cops had got off their duffs a tad quicker." He sucked his teeth. "Nah, I can't fault the police. Poor planning was to blame. Took three tries to get my timing right."

Hank sighed and rubbed his brow, struggling to comprehend what he was hearing. Was the morphine Charlie had received still impairing his judgment? Legally, it didn't matter. He'd waived his rights. His statements were voluntary. His confession couldn't be voided on a technicality.

"That's why Sunday night, I went out to the pay phone and dialed 911 first."

Hank's head jerked up. "You called in the robbery-in-progress?"

"Had to. The cops weren't ever gonna catch me unless I gave 'em a headstart."

"Doc..." Hank glanced at the tape recorder. The

cassette's dual hubs spun in relentless circles. "Let's start over, from when you arrived at the Jiffy Stop."

Nodding, his gaze ratcheted upward to the ceiling. "I went inside. Nobody was behind the counter. I wandered around a minute, thinking the clerk must be out back, smoking a cigarette."

"Was anyone else in the store?"

"No."

"Any other vehicles on the lot?"

"Maybe." Charlie frowned. "Seems like there was an SUV way down toward the ice machine. I can't say for sure."

Before he dismissed it entirely, Hank said, "What color was the SUV?"

"Dark, I guess." His lips pursed. "For all the attention I was paying, it could've been the Dumpster."

"So you went inside the store," Hank prompted, "and were looking around for the clerk."

"That's when I got the idea to call 911. I went back out to the pay phone and—"

"Was the SUV still there?"

"I—c'mon, Hank. Already said I can't swear there was any kind of car out yonder." A coughing spasm bathed Charlie's face with sweat. Heels of his hands digging into the mattress, he pushed himself higher on the bed. "Didn't do this...just to...die from pneumonia."

"That's enough for today, Doc. I'll come back another time."

"No. Time I don't have, son. Gotta finish my confession now." Fear, not pain, contorted his features.

He wasn't a Catholic and Hank darned sure wasn't a priest. What Charlie France was afraid of—why telling it was worth torturing himself—Hank couldn't imagine, but reluctantly, he sat back down.

Gratitude shone in Charlie's watery eyes. "Good man."

At the moment, Hank couldn't have agreed less.

"Sorry if this messed up things between you and Zoey."

Hank shook his head. "Nothing to mess up, Doc. We're friends. Always have been, always will be."

"Being blind and stupid when you're kids is one thing. Staying blind and stupid your whole life is another." He snorted. "The only way to get what you want most is to go after it."

Warmth suffused Hank's neck and seeped upward. "Yeah, well, I'll keep that in mind."

Doc shot him a disgusted look. "Where was I, before wasting my breath on you?"

"The 911 call, from the pay phone."

"I hung up and went back inside. Still no clerk. Dawdled a mite, then decided, hell with it. I'd best take the money from the register before the police came."

"So you could get away."

"No, no, no. Because they weren't about to arrest me for thinking about robbing the place."

"You wanted to—"

"I hit the no-sale button," Charlie went on. "Took the cash, put it in the bag I brought from home. Now I'm getting irritated. No clerk. No cops, either. I can't just stand there waiting, so I walk back to the storeroom."

Eyelids fluttering, he let his head fall back on the pillow. "Gruesome. Horrible. That poor boy... Lord, I thought he was dead. No pulse at his wrist—felt a thready one at the carotid. Massive hemorrhaging from his skull. I applied arterial pressure where I could, but..."

He looked at Hank. "Funny, but I never heard any sirens. Next thing I knew, a policeman was there yelling into his shoulder mic for an ambulance."

As if he'd forget a word of the oddest interrogation he'd ever conducted, Hank caught up on his note-taking. Asterisks flagged margin notations.

"Let's go over this again, Doc. You admit to opening the Jiffy Stop's register and stealing money from the drawer."

"Yes."

"Do you know how much you took?"

"Wasn't much in there. Fifty, sixty dollars, I s'pose."

Thirty-seven was in the sandwich bag confiscated from Doc's coat pocket. Six singles and a ten were in his billfold. He wouldn't have divvied the swag and shorted himself in the process, so he didn't count the stolen money before he bagged it.

Which meant...squat.

"You're aware that the clerk died."

"Yes." Charlie sighed. "I'm an animal doctor, not a physician. Didn't need to be, to know that with as much blood as he was losing, there wasn't much hope."

Hank looked him in the eye. "Did you kill him, Doc?"

"No, sir. He was unconscious on the floor when I found him."

"After you robbed the cash register."

"Yes."

"Which is what you set out to do, when you entered the store."

"Yes."

"Did the clerk try to stop you?"

"No. First I saw of him, he was on the floor in the back."

Hank's pen tapped in cadence with the heart monitor. From the outset, he'd watched it and other devices tracking Charlie's respiration and blood pressure.

The coughing jag had triggered the strongest physical reaction. Second place coincided with Hank entering the room. Schlomo's hissy fit scored a distant third. None of Hank's questions and none of Charlie's responses had caused noticeable elevations.

Which also meant squat. Bona fide lie detector tests administered by experts were too unreliable for admission in court. Credence lent to similar machinery hooked up to an old man with a "bum ticker" was lousy science and worse detective work.

"You don't believe me, do you?"

"I swear, Doc, it's tough to swallow much of anything you've said."

"Every bit's the God's honest truth."

"Maybe. Maybe you're guilty as original sin. Your lawyer's famous for showboating. Maybe his whole performance was for my benefit. Groundwork for an innocent by reason of diminished capacity plea."

Hank slid off the bed. Felt ten feet tall staring down at the sick old man whose eyes were riveted on him. "You confessed to the robberies. What's the problem with admitting you killed Marlowe? Schlomo'll plead you down to a stretch in a mental hospital and I can close the file on this one."

Charlie chuckled, a harsh phlegmy rasp that seemed to emanate from his chest, not his throat. "All I was trying to do was get ahead of the game."

"Ahead of *what* game?"

"Know what they say about a cop never being there when you need one?" Charlie smiled. "It's true. If I'd been smart enough to call in the robbery at the Pump 'N Go, before I ever left the house, I'd have a new heart by now and everything would've been fine."

He clasped his hands together on his distended belly. "I hear the arraignment's set for Friday. Schlomo doesn't know it yet, but I have to plead guilty."

Hank cursed and threw the notebook on the table. "So now you're saying you did kill Marlowe?"

"No, but I've got no choice but tell the judge I did."

"Why?" Hank bellowed.

"If I don't go to prison, I'm a dead man," he said. "I have a family to take care of. A granddaughter to help raise. Her daddy failed her. Damned if I will."

As though speaking to the blank television screen, he continued, "When Doctor Amanpour told me a transplant was the only hope, I thought my veteran's benefits would take care of it. Uh-uh.

Private insurance? No dice, even if I had some. Heart transplants are cash only and up front, just to get your name on the list."

He looked at Hank. "Unless you're in prison."

The enormity of what he'd said had Hank groping for the chair.

"I read about it in a news magazine I subscribe to. 'Twas clear as day, what my choices were. I could die, a law-abiding, God-fearing man. Or I could rob a store, plead guilty as charged, get a new heart courtesy of the state prison and be around to take care of my girls a few years longer."

Hank slouched down in the chair and crossed an ankle over his knee. Of one thing he was certain. Doc France would do anything for his wife, his daughter and his granddaughter. If his heart was sound and any of them needed a new one, she could have his. No hesitation, no regrets.

His plan, if true, wasn't entirely far-fetched. Almost thirty years ago, the Supreme Court had ruled that denying an inmate the same medical care available to the general public—including organ transplants—violated the Eighth Amendment's protection against cruel and unusual punishment.

In theory, Charles Manson could receive a taxpayer-funded heart transplant, while Charlie France went begging for lack of money to pay for it. The phrase "same medical care available to the general public" was the ongoing tilt in what was intended to level the playing field.

That was what Doc France meant by trying to get ahead of the game. Available and free-of-charge isn't the same as available if you can afford it.

"Have you told Osbert Schlomo any of this?"

"Nah. He thinks I'm pleading innocent at the arraignment."

"Listen to me, Doc. If you didn't kill Marlowe, you can't plead guilty to second-degree homicide."

"*You're* the one that's not listening. I *have* to."

"Do that and the minimum the judge will sentence you to is twenty-five years. With or without a new heart, you can't take care of your family if you're in prison for the rest of your life."

Charlie's fingers crabbed over the bedcovers toward the edge of the mattress. He reached out a palsied hand to Hank. "I won't be, son. This isn't the way I wanted things to turn out, but I'm counting on you to catch whoever beat that poor young man to death."

14

If anything's happened to Darla...

In the living room, Bob and Fred goalposted the sofa. Hunkered on all fours, their snouts wedged between their front paws and brown marble eyes riveted on the kitchen, they resembled crocodiles surveying a swamp.

Fingers splayed at the small of her back, Zoey retraced her steps from the sink to the table. Floor joists squawked. Gnats circled the bowl of decomposing bananas. Her mouth tasted metallic, as though her fillings had dissolved.

Joe Donny Marlowe's graveside service had ended an hour and a half ago. Two at the outside. Darla could have walked from the cemetery to the house by now. On her knees, for cripe's sake.

Calls to the shop transferred to voice mail on the second ring. Ditto Darla's home number. Her cell phone's provider reported that the customer sought was unavailable—robotspeak for "the phone is turned off, or its nimrod owner forgot to charge it again."

Zoey told the dogs, "Fifteen minutes, then I'm calling Hank."

Neither twitched a whisker. They'd heard it all before. Twice.

I should have gone myself, she thought. *Wrong.* Intruding once on the bereaved's privacy was one time too many. Twice—even by proxy—was reprehensible.

Gripping the chair's back, she looked at the clock, the front door, the wall phone that refused to ring. How soon was too soon to call Hank? How long was too late? As surely as she hit the streets herself, they'd miss each other, leaving Darla wondering where Zoey had disappeared to.

Unless Darla herself had already disappeared. A man who'd killed in a fit of jealous rage wouldn't balk at committing a second murder to cover his tracks.

The water heater cycled. To hypersensitive ears, the sound mimicked a car's engine droning outside. Fool me once, shame on you. Fool me nine times already and the hell with you.

In perfect tandem, the greyhounds lifted their heads. Necks craned, they listened a moment, then sprang to their feet to peer out the front window.

"Thank God." Zoey ran to the door, throwing it open, just as Claire pulled back on the storm door.

They both yelped, jumped backward, blurted, "You scared the crap out of me."

It took a second for Zoey's brain to register her daughter's face, instead of her best friend's. "Oh—uh, hi, sweetie."

Vesta bustled up behind Claire. "Get a move on, child. I don't have all day."

They trooped inside, Bob and Fred nuzzling

and hopping and essentially herding Claire to the kitchen for their daily after-school treats. Halting just past the doorway, Vesta glared at Claire's back. "I swan, that girl wouldn't know *hurry* if it tapped her on the shoulder."

"What's wrong?"

"Six of one thing, half-dozen of another." She heaved a sigh. "Not five minutes after the nurse relayed your message to pick up Claire, Osbert Schlomo came down the hall, saying he was meeting Hank there in a while to question Charlie.

"I had to leave before Hank showed up, then I had trouble finding my car out in the lot, then when I got to the school, there was no sign of Claire. I waited and waited and was trudging up the sidewalk when she and Laura Peters ran around the corner of the building and then I had to drop off Laura at her house and…"

Breathless, her arms flapped the universal semaphore for days when a tiny glitch triggers an avalanche. "Well, hang it all, if you're here, why'd I have to pick up Claire in the first place?"

Uh-oh. Zoey clenched the doorknob. "My car. It wouldn't start."

"Again? Well, c'mon, then. Get your coat and take me back to the hospital and you can have mine."

"No, no. It's okay now. Just flooded the engine, I guess."

"Not hard to do, this time of year." Her mother's eyes narrowed. "If you're sure that's what it was."

Nodding, Zoey peered out the storm door's foggy glass, willing Darla to pull up at the curb. No such luck. "I'm sorry I had to draft you for carpool duty."

Vesta chuffed. "Oh, no need to apologize. If I hadn't left when I did, I'd have gnawed my fingernails to my wrists by now, wondering what Charlie's telling Hank."

A hairline to shoestring description of Joe Donny Marlowe's killer, Zoey hoped. And a reasonable explanation for robbing four convenience stores and hoarding the money.

Vesta started out the door, then paused, turning to look at Zoey. "Is something bothering you, sweetheart?"

"Kind of a dumb question, these days." Zoey pecked her cheek. "You will call and let me know what's up at the hospital, won't you?"

"Yes...but why don't you and Claire just come with me? Hear it firsthand?"

"I can't, Mom." Floundering for another excuse, Zoey settled for the truth—or what she prayed was true. "Darla will be by any minute."

"Oh. Well, tell her I said hello."

When Zoey entered the kitchen, her daughter's coat was on the table, gloves and sock hat on the floor, and gaping Trapper Keeper on the counter. Their owner was gobbling a cold, double-decker hot dog sandwich. On either side was a greyhound, his entire being focused on telekinetically swiping her snack.

"Good grief, kid. Didn't you eat lunch today?"

"No time."

Chances were, she was saving her lunch money for a new CD. The lunacy of starving herself to fatten a mega-millionaire rapster's income was an old argument unworthy of revival.

Moving the coat and accessories to the hook beside the back door, Zoey said, "Tell me you didn't leave your books and backpack in Mom's car again."

"Nope. No homework." Claire's tongue probed the corner of her mouth for a stray gob of ketchup. "Except we have to go to the library."

Disregarding the don't-talk-with-your-mouth-full rule, she added, "Research paper. The library at school sucks."

"When is the paper due?"

"Tomorrow. When's Darla supposed to be here?"

"Two hours ago. You don't have homework, but you have a paper due tomorrow."

"Uh-huh. Me and Laura are working on it together. How come Darla's not at the shop?"

"Laura and I," Zoey corrected. "She closed at noon to do an errand."

"Sheesh. What kind of an errand takes from noon till—"

"Hey—knock, knock."

"Darla!" Zoey spun around, instantly joyous and fire-breathing mad as her friend came through the front door. "Where in the hell have you been all afternoon?"

Darla butted the door shut. "Well, that's a fuckin' fine howdy-do for your spy coming in from the cold."

Zoey singsonged, "Claire is in the kitchen."

"Ohmigod. That poor, innocent baby's never heard the f-word before." Laying her fleece-lined robe-coat over the sofa, Darla reached to pet the boys, started, then looked at Zoey and mouthed, *Oops.*

The odds of *your spy* meaning anything to Claire were zilch. "Think before you speak" would just be a lovely attribute for Darla to develop. Then again, if she did, she wouldn't be Darla.

"Just watch it, okay?" Zoey said, a dual, implicit warning in her tone. "I'll fix hot chocolate while you tell me about that new styling salon you scoped out."

"The wha—er, uh, yeah. That new salon. Tacky, tacky, tacky. Wouldn't take my dog there."

Claire hugged Darla, scooped up her Trapper Keeper and said she'd use the phone in Zoey's bedroom to call Laura. "You can take us to the library, can't you?"

Zoey nodded. "Tell her we'll pick her up in an hour or so."

"Cool. Thanks, Mom."

Darla propped an elbow against the refrigerator to watch tap water and powdered mix alchemize into foamy mud. "That girl's prettier every time I see her." She chuckled. "Are you sure the dickhead is her daddy?"

"Unfortunately, yes." Zoey set the mugs in the microwave and set the timer. Hearing the bedroom door shut, she pressed the start button. "Now, where the hell have you been?" Glancing downward, she added, "And please, tell me you didn't wear painted-on leather jeans to a graveside service."

"These old things? Heavens, no. I wore pasties, a thong and a smile." She cuffed Zoey's shoulder. "Or maybe a long black skirt and a sweater."

"Do you have a clue how worried I was?" Zoey flapped a hand. "No, you don't, because instead of coming straight here afterward, like you promised, you went home, ignored the forty-seven messages I left on your machine, changed clothes and, for all I know, had a freakin' tea party first."

"Sheesh, Zoe." Darla backed up a step. "I'm sorry. I should have known you'd be watching the clock. But I was in and back out of the house in five minutes, max, I swear. And I didn't call, because…well, by the time I did, I could've driven over here."

The microwave dinged. "It's me that should apologize. To say I'm a little edgy these days is like saying this cocoa's going to be slightly gross."

Carrying the mugs to the table, Zoey flopped down in a chair, groaned, then pushed herself up again to check the hallway for James Bond, Jr.

"Coast clear?" Darla asked.

"For now." Zoey grinned. "I keep intending to loosen some flooring, so they'll squeak on the approach."

"Teach Bob and Fred to follow her around."

"They do. With their eyes."

Claire rounded the corner into the kitchen, startling the conspirators. "Laura says she'll be ready whenever we are." She thumped her Trapper Keeper back onto the table as she passed by. Seconds later, a soda in one hand and cookies in the other, she waltzed into the living room and turned on the TV. Loud.

Zoey hollered, "You forgot your notebook."

"Get it in a minute."

Zoey and Darla traded sly smiles. James Bond, Jr. was in their crosshairs and no way could she hear them over *The Simpsons* reruns. Couldn't have planned it better themselves.

"Go for it," Zoey said. "From the top."

"It was a nice service. Sad, but nice. Closed casket, but thanks for the warning. Just as you thought, W. C. King was there. Suit, tie, braided ponytail, the works."

Darla settled back in her chair. "He hovered around Trudy—near enough for a show of support, far enough back for propriety's sake. She was a wreck. Tried to hold it in, but anyone could see that the fact that Joe Donny was gone was sinking in."

Zoey fought the images forming in her mind. "Were there a lot of people?"

"Twenty or thirty. I kept my head down. Stayed outside the tent, afraid of getting spotted by one of my customers or something, but it was mostly men. Young ones, about his age."

Darla sipped her cocoa and made a "not bad" face. "I sort of panicked when everybody started going back to their cars. Trudy rode in the limo with her mother and a couple of other women. W.C. was talking to one of the pallbearers, but I couldn't walk up and strike up a conversation."

"So, uh, what did you do?"

"First, I asked myself what Katie Scarlett O'Hara would do."

Fiddle-dee-dee. Myriad possibilities, not a few of them scary. Zoey held her breath.

"Then I faked a twisted ankle." Darla's wicked smile was a poor second to Vivien Leigh's. "Even a woman-hating creep like W.C. can't resist damsels in distress."

"Woman-hating?"

"Oh, yeah. The only difference between him and Stuart is hairstyle and education, which makes W.C. a more honest asshole, if you ask me. What you see is what he is, but that's flame to female moths set on taming bad boys. Your ex was an asshole disguised as a good boy. Just as controlling but way sneakier about it."

Zoey agreed. Stuart had seemed like the kind of guy you're proud to take home to mama. Vesta, however, immediately pegged him for a jerk, but trusted her daughter would wise up before the wedding.

Darla continued, "After W.C. helped po' li'l ol' me to the car, he suggested a beer to ease my pain." She rolled her eyes. "We went to this dive a few blocks from the cemetery. Long story short, he definitely has an 'If I can't have her, nobody can' attitude about Trudy. Now that Joe Donny is out of the picture, he's hell-bent to get her and his daughters back."

The phone rang. Before Zoey made a move to answer it, Claire hollered, "I'll get it," and ran down the hall to Zoey's bedroom.

She glanced at the clock. "Probably Laura again. God forbid those two go fifteen minutes without talking to each other."

Darla laughed. "Brings back memories, eh?"

"Uh-huh. Except Claire thinks my refusing to get her a cell phone is child abuse. Like I can afford a kazillion minutes a month for her and Laura to watch TV together in separate houses."

Keeping one eye on the sofa for her daughter's reappearance, Zoey said, "Bottom line, do you think W.C. hated Joe Donny enough to kill him?"

"No doubt about it." Darla hiked a shoulder. "Except he didn't."

Zoey scowled. "You sound awfully sure—"

"I am. The cops arrested him for drunk and disorderly at a party Sunday afternoon. He spent the night in jail with five or six of his closest friends."

"Shit." Zoey sat back and folded her arms. "That screws up everything. Unless…what if W.C. hired somebody to take Joe Donny out? Getting arrested would be a humdinger of an alibi."

"Not a chance."

"Why not?"

"Because housepainters don't hire hit men. Hit men don't use hammers. W.C. isn't smart enough to give himself an alibi in advance and if he wanted to off somebody, he'd do it himself. With a gun. Or a knife." Darla grimaced. "Maybe a power tool, but c'mon. A hammer?"

Yeah, well, everything else fit, Zoey thought. Snake-eyed ex-husband murders rival for ex-wife's affection, before ex-wife becomes rival's wife. Crime of passion meets crime of opportunity.

Except it wasn't Valentine's Day yet. Joe Donny had confided his intentions to George Santini but planned to surprise Trudy. As if she would have been. More female significant others are surprised—not to mention pissed—when The Question *isn't* popped on V-Day.

Except Darla was right. If W.C. thought Trudy was about to be lost to him forever, he'd have shot Joe Donny in cold, premeditated blood.

"The ring," Zoey blurted. "Trudy's ring. And

the house. Santini said Joe Donny put money down on a house in Springfield. Betcha five bucks, he was going to tell her about it when he asked her to marry him."

Darla waved a time-out. "I'm only a mind reader on weekends. What ring? What house?"

Zoey looked toward the living room. The top of Claire's auburn head was visible above the back of the couch. Still, Zoey leaned forward, elbows scooting across the table until the edge pressed her ribs. "Never mind the whats. Where does a technical school student and convenience store clerk get the money to buy an engagement ring and a house?"

"Saved it?"

"At eight, nine bucks an hour? Minus tuition? Not. Yeah, he had a great job lined up, but that was months away. All he had to come up with was earnest money to hold his love nest, but thirty days is standard for closing the contract. Then we're talking a lump sum ten or fifteen percent of the purchase price, incidental fees, maybe a share or all the closing costs—lots of moolah."

Darla repeated, "Thirty days."

"From when his offer was accepted," Zoey reminded her. "Santini didn't say and I couldn't ask."

"And if he'd hit the lottery, why was he still working at the Jiffy Stop?"

"Bingo."

"Well, you know what that leaves." Darla hesitated, as though testing her idea for validity before voicing it. "And it fits, too. Especially if Joe Donny wasn't sure Trudy would say yes. A ring and a house miles from W.C. would be tougher to turn down."

"And the supposedly easiest way to lay hands on a chunk of cash in a hurry?"

"Drugs. Buy low, sell high." Darla chuckled. "Literally."

"A drug deal gone sour is a fast way to get dead, too."

"Yeah, but…Joe Donny was a nice guy. Not that his radio wasn't short a few frequencies, but drugs?"

Zoey sat back, the idea's brilliance suddenly losing some wattage, but nothing else jumped up waving its little filaments, either.

"Follow the money," she said. "Wish I had a dollar for every time I've read that in a crime novel."

"Okay. But how? Especially if you don't know where it came from."

"I know where it went," Zoey said. "It'd cost a fortune to call every real estate company in Springfield to check out the house Joe Donny bought, but the ring? There aren't that many jewelry stores in Blytheville."

"You lost me, kid." Darla squinted at the clock on the microwave. "And I'd better get lost, so you can take the girls to the library."

And while Claire was safely out of sight and mind researching her little fingers to the bone, Zoey would find out how much Joe Donny Marlowe paid for Trudy's engagement ring.

A chip diamond? Par for his assumed net worth. A rock that'd make her heart go pitty-pat? Even Hank might find that a wee bit suspicious.

15

Hank swept the lighted magnifying glass from the fingerprint on the left to the one on the right. The former was complete and sharply defined on the card in black ink. The latter—a partial, middle-right index finger—was a damn fine tape lift, if he did say so himself. Just slightly less than perfect—no thanks to the outline of the number 9 impressed behind it, among other things.

Blinking didn't stanch eyestrain's burn or dryness. Occupational hazard of comparing miniscule loops and lines for going on thirty minutes. Confirming points of distinction was akin to balancing a checkbook. Run through once and you're a penny short. Repeat the process and you're two cents long.

Between both prints, four points were deadbang definite. The fifth Hank wouldn't stake his life on. Usually, he wasn't content with less than seven, but four was good enough to corroborate the dispatch log.

He switched off the magnifier and pushed away from the desk. Bowing his back, he rolled his shoulders, arms winged, then gradually, painfully, pulled them back, as though the Lord intended a man's elbows to touch behind him. Pops and snaps and muscle cramps had Hank moaning, groaning, then snarling like his grandpa used to every morning, sitting up on the side of the bed.

Nothing a workout at the gym wouldn't cure, he thought. A mental note was made to do just that, as soon as he had the time.

Time I don't have, Doc France had told him at the hospital. He'd given Hank precious little of it to redirect the investigation, too. A shade under forty-eight hours to save a man from himself wasn't much, but it was all Hank had before Doc pleaded guilty to a murder he didn't commit.

Might not have committed.

Additional prints lifted at the scene from the alley door now seemed like a loose end rather than a dead end. The one-way door's metal surface was like a vertical garbage can. From floor level to approximately shoulder height were months' worth of caked-on grease, mud, tar, mop-bucket sludge, food smears—grime of every kind human hands could transfer.

None of the prints belonged to Doc France. Marlowe's prints, and those of other store employees and Santini, the manager, were excluded as non-suspect latents. None of the remainder scored a hit on the Automated Fingerprint Identification System database.

All that told Hank was whoever they belonged to—anyone from delivery drivers to significant others sneaking out the back when the boss arrived unexpectedly—did not have an arrest record.

In the desk lamp's pyramid-shaped beam, a four-inch stack of crime scene photos posed like a car dealership's bargain of the month. Hank palmed half of them to deal into two categories: review and extraneous.

"Got a minute?" Chichester straddled the threshold. A can of diet soda was in one hand, a Chubby's Cheeseburger sack in the other.

"Yeah, sure." Open door policies weren't all they were cracked up to be. Hank glanced at the comparison prints. But there was always room for a second opinion. "Pull up a chair, kid."

The sack yielded a foil-wrapped burger, a sleeve of French fries and an invisible cloud of airborne cholesterol. "You said you weren't hungry, but there's plenty here to split."

"No, thanks. Food might dilute the caffeine I'm living on these days." Hank finished shuffling the photos and pushed the extraneous stack to one side. "How was the interview with the building owner?"

Lonnie motioned *okay* with his cheeseburger. "Big as you are on trusting your instincts, mine say he's not our arsonist."

"Why not?"

"The building was underinsured by about fifty grand, for one thing. Unusual to torch something you'll lose a serious chunk of change on. According to the fire marshal, gasoline was the accelerant—common, but crude. Especially since there was paint thinner, muriatic acid and other flammables on site."

Hank's thumbs tapped a riff on the blotter.

"Umm, my jury's still out. Insurance is the typical money motive, but not the only one. A fire that spreads fast enough to trap people inside makes me hinky."

Lonnie nodded, his cheeks bulging like those of a squirrel anticipating a long, cold winter. "Gonna poke around the scene again in the morning."

The statement presumed Hank would also be donning chest waders, rubber boots and a hard hat. Well, not if he could help it. He and Lonnie were partners but not joined at the hip. Their caseload was too heavy to follow each other around all day.

To the front edge of the desk he moved the two fingerprints he'd gone bleary-eyed examining, along with the magnifier. "Give those a gander, will ya?"

Still chewing, Lonnie wiped the grease off his hands with a napkin and leaned forward. Noting the name on the print card, he shot Hank a quizzical look, then started comparing it to the unidentified tape lift beside it.

Rather than watch Lonnie's eyeballs ping-pong from one to the other, Hank studied the photos, arranging them by location and chronology. Some had been taken when the cops arrived at the store, others after they'd examined the crime scene proper.

The sandwich and most of the French fries had been deposited in the vast, bottomless cavern that was Lonnie's stomach before he said, "Yeah. I'd call 'em a match."

"So did I."

"Where'd you get it?" Lonnie indicated the tape lift.

"Off the pay phone at the Jiffy Stop."

"When?"

"After the interview with France."

"No way." Lonnie killed the last of the diet soda in one gulp. "A public pay phone? Uh-uh. Not after this much time."

Hank shrugged. A reminder that their suspect had been in custody since the homicide, thus couldn't have planted the print after the fact would be an insult to Lonnie's intelligence.

"I'll admit," he said, "the odds were lousy, except for a few tips in France's favor."

"Such as?"

"There's no nine in Blytheville's prefix. The one on the phone's keypad was a mess. So were the zero and the five. But anybody who's used that phone since the homicide had a one-in-ten chance of punching the nine.

"Now factor in that damn near everyone in creation has a cell phone. The phone company's jerked out pay phones by the thousands nationwide. It's costing more to maintain them than they're bringing in."

By Lonnie's expression, the argument was persuasive but a quart shy of convincing. Apparently, he hadn't tried to find a pay phone lately, when his cell crapped out.

"Dispatch reconfirmed that the 911 call came from that pay phone," Hank said. "A robbery-in-progress report. Louise remembered it, because she thought it was weird that the caller was cool as a cucumber. 'Like he was ordering a pizza' is how she described it. That pretty much negates the theory that France panicked after the assault."

"Not necessarily," Lonnie said.

"Panic presumes a fit of remorse."

"So?"

"Then why did France calmly report a robbery-in-progress, instead of screaming for an ambulance?" Hank paused to let that sink in. "He's a veterinarian. If he went loony-tunes and attacked Marlowe with the hammer, the presumed fit of remorse would have anybody with medical training calling for EMTs, stat."

Anyone with eyes who took one look at Marlowe would have called an ambulance—and probably not from the pay phone, either. People do goofy things in an emergency, but the store had a phone on the counter and an extension in the storeroom. Running outside to the pay phone defied logic.

Hank crooked a finger, beckoning Lonnie to come around the desk to look at the photos. "See these footprints leading out of the store?"

"Uh-huh. Zigzag sole pattern."

Meaning they were made by Doc France's tennis shoes. "One set."

"Gotcha." Lonnie's tone suggested the obvious was…well, obvious.

"Riddle me this, Batman. If France bludgeoned Marlowe, then went to the pay phone, then went back to the storeroom, where Dunleavy found him crouched over the body, how come there's only one set of his prints between the storeroom and the front door?"

Lonnie scratched his jaw. Moved to peer over Hank's other shoulder. Reached for the magnifier and scrutinized several shots from varied angles. Returning to the chair, he sat down and glared at Hank. "Shit."

"Yeah."

"How we missed the footprint pattern from the get-go blows my mind." Lonnie grunted. "Missed it, hell. I never looked that close."

"No reason to, when we thought an unlocatable witness called 911. If so, a single set of prints was all there should have been. Other than a hinky feeling about the choreography from the start, the evidence pointed at France as the robber and the killer."

"Back up a sec. What do you mean, the choreography?"

"Marlowe getting his skull cracked in the back room." Hank watered the spindly philodendron on his desk with cold coffee, then refilled the cup from a thermos. "If he was behind the counter, why'd the robber hustle him into the storeroom? Why'd Marlowe go, for that matter?

"If Marlowe was there when the robber entered the store, why'd the perp seek Marlowe out, much less attack him? The only M.O. that made sense was if the register was locked and Marlowe had the keys on him."

"But it wasn't," Lonnie said. "And the keys were on a shelf under the counter." Elbow propped on the chair arm, he rested his chin on his fist. "You never mentioned this choreography thing before."

"We had a suspect in custody with the money from the register in his pocket. How the dance went down wasn't critical." Lofting his cup, Hank added, "Until Doc's statement sang a slightly different tune."

The coffee he swallowed was, at most, ten degrees hotter than the stuff he'd dumped on the plant. Like everything else, they just didn't make insulated bottles like they used to.

"That's why I dusted the pay phone for prints. Without one, we'd have the same interpretation of the same evidence. The print doesn't change everything, but it sure puts a kink in what we thought we knew."

Lonnie agreed. "It's unlikely that France could go out to the phone and come in again without tracking blood, but not impossible."

"Highly unlikely. But no, not a hundred-percent impossible."

Hank had also swabbed the pay phone's 9 button for blood. Not a molecule, even though Doc's hands were soaked to the wrists when he was arrested. None on the money, either, which also alluded to its removal before the attack, not after.

A commercial-sized Dumpster was stationed at the far side of the lot, opposite the pay phone. Did Charlie see it, or a dark-colored SUV? God only knew and he wasn't telling.

"Okay," Lonnie said, "so shit is what the prosecuting attorney's gonna do when he hears this. Our sweet, airtight case springing a leak will not make his day."

"Not with a signed confession." Hank shook his head. "If the case was going before a jury, yeah.

It ain't gonna matter a damn, if France pleads guilty to all counts at the arraignment."

"Schlomo may talk him out of it."

"He doesn't know about it and there's no way for him to find out. Doc won't tell him. We can't tell him. Can't put a bug in Zoey's or Vesta's ear, either."

Lonnie glanced at the open door, as though one, the other, or Schlomo himself might be lurking outside. "Prosecution has to provide defense with a copy of the interview transcript, though. Sticky-note saying 'Read it and weep' attached, optional."

"Provide, yeah, but I guarantee, on the off chance it's a trick, Schlomo's copy will be lost in the Wewoka switch until after the hearing."

"Huh? The We...what?" Lonnie grinned. "Whooee, Loot, I jes' luv hit when you tawk Ozarks. Don' make a lick o' sense, but hit shore is cullerful."

Damn fool kid. Hank ought to bust his chops for insubordination. Hard to be a disciplinarian when you're laughing your butt off for the first time all day.

Presently, he informed Mr. American History Minor that during the 1920s oil boom, Wewoka, Oklahoma, the switching point for the Choctaw & Gulf Railroad, went from processing a handful of freight shipments to hundreds of trainloads.

Lost shipments with paper trails ending at the Wewoka depot became so commonplace that the Rock Island Railroad had a rubber stamp made that read: Search the Wewoka Switch.

"Before long," Hank said, "instead of describing somebody as being between a rock and a hard place, folks said he was 'lost in the Wewoka Switch.'"

Lonnie chuffed. "Are you pulling my leg?"

"I kid you not."

"Blind sows and acorns. Suck-egg hounds. Yeah, the Wewoka Switch is another for the file." He wadded the empty food sack and three-pointed the trash can. "Guess you could say Charlie France is lost there, too, huh?"

So am I, Hank thought. *Between now and Friday, if I prove he's innocent and get the charges dropped, he'll die of heart failure. If I can't, he'll go to prison for the rest of his life.*

Even if Marlowe's killer was later apprehended, a year could pass before the case went to trial. With Doc already serving time on a guilty plea, persuading a jury to convict the real perp would be a prosecutorial mountain climb. If by some miracle the jury did, convincing a judge to release Doc despite the guilty plea would be miracle number two.

Sympathetic as the court might be to Doc's motivation, committing a crime for the express purpose of receiving medical treatment isn't a precedent any judge would be eager to set.

Hank had explained it all to Doc. Did his level best to make the stubborn old man understand that guilty or not, once you're in the system, it's the devil's own to get out.

"You were never convinced France killed Marlowe, were you?" Lonnie asked.

"Believe it or not, I'm still not entirely convinced he didn't." Hank stood and pushed the shirt cuff back from his watch. "And all we have is a click under forty-two hours to prove it, one way or the other."

The plump woman behind the jewelry counter wore a brass badge with Patsy O. etched in Olde English script and a crestfallen expression. "I just came back from a trade show in St. Louis last night. I overheard an employee talking with a customer about a clerk being killed at the Jiffy Stop. It never dawned on me that the victim could be Mr. Marlowe."

Excitement zinged through Zoey. Meerschaum's was the ninth jewelry store she'd visited since dropping Claire and Laura at the library. At about the third, a gremlin in her head whispered that Marlowe might have bought the ring in Springfield, too. Or found it at the bottom of a box of freakin' Crackerjacks.

"Such a sweet young man," Patsy O. said. "I simply can't imagine…."

"It was a shock to lots of people," Zoey said. "No place seems safe anymore. Not even good ol' Blytheville."

"You're from here?" She studied Zoey's face, like a bouncer presented with an out-of-state ID.

Leaving a lasting impression was not the plan. "Well, I was born here, but I lived in Kansas City for years."

"I see. And why are you inquiring about the engagement ring Joe Donny purchased?"

Zoey aimed a rueful glance at her jeans and sweater. "I realize I don't look much like a bank vice-president's executive assistant, but my statute of limitations on high heels ends with regular office hours."

"Oh, honey. I can sympathize with that. Some days, it's all I can do to hobble to my car."

Lowering her voice, Zoey said. "Just between us, my boss, Mr. Kelly, would be furious if he knew I was dressed like this, even though I'm doing him a favor, not on official business."

"Andrew Kelly? At the Bank of Blytheville? Why, he and his wife are two of my best customers." She smiled, adding, "I doubt if that man owns a pair of jeans, more's the pity. I guess you have to be a workaholic to become the bank's youngest vice president."

"Which is why I probably won't ever be one." Zoey pulled back her shoulders and raised her chin a fraction. She hoped Patsy would catch the body language cue that the conversation was shifting gears. "Often as Mr. Kelly urged his cousin to make a will, Joe Donny passed away intestate—"

"Joe Donny and Andrew were cousins?" Patsy O. pressed a hand to her chest. "Gracious, I had no idea. Different as day and night, those two."

"Yes, well, knowing Mr. Kelly as you do, I'm sure you understand his desire to put Joe Donny's accounts in order. No easy task, believe me, especially under the circumstances. That's why I volunteered to help."

By the woman's pursed mouth, Zoey feared she'd said too much, or not enough. Or that her cover story was as transparent as the excuse for her outfit.

Changing clothes would have fostered questions from Claire. There hadn't been time to zoom back home. And by now, the suit still in the trunk probably did smell like dog poop. Even if it didn't, Zoey lacked the wherewithal for another rest-room stall makeover.

Patsy O.'s caramel-pink fingernail tapped the glass. "Being Mr. Kelly's assistant, you must have received one of those for Christmas."

Velvet-boxed pen and pencil sets gleamed in the lighted display case. The one Patsy O. indicated was a gorgeous Montblanc Boheme Noir fountain pen and ballpoint. Not every woman went drooly over fancy writing instruments, but Zoey had yearned for a Montblanc since college.

"I suppose it isn't telling tales out of school to tell you that his account needs tending to. You're his assistant, after all." Chin rumpling, she stiffened, as though smelling a foul odor. "But now that I think about it, you aren't the lady he sent to pick the pens up."

Converting a strangled cough into a haughty chuckle, Zoey said, "Not hardly. *My* assistant does those types of errands."

Patsy O. flinched. "Forgive me, please. It's been a trying day and—"

"Better to err on the side of caution."

"Yes." Relief beamed from her moon-round face. "Yes, it most certainly is." Turning from the case, she said, "Now, if you'll excuse me, I'll have that information for you in just a moment."

While she was in the office, Zoey moved to the white satin-festooned cases where engagement rings, wedding sets and bands were displayed on stumpy faux fingers. By their number, diamonds remained the most popular, but star sapphires, jade, emeralds, rubies and lesser gemstones were holding their own.

If she had it to do over again, she'd hold out for the platinum mounted pear-cut solitaire. *Bling-bling* wasn't her thing, but in retrospect, she could have hocked that headlamp for much bigger bucks than she'd got for the cheesy set Stuart had bought on sale at the mall.

"There you are." The twinkle in Patsy O.'s eyes was cherubic. "If you see anything you like, I'd be happy to let you try it on."

"Oh, no." Zoey waved her hands. "Thank you, but I'm not in the market for a husband."

"Pshaw. When the right man comes along, one who loves you exactly as you are, you'll fall head over heels."

"I hope not. My health insurance has a thousand-dollar deductible."

Patsy O. clucked her tongue and slid a photocopied sales receipt across the counter. Under her breath, Zoey wheezed, "Holy Moses."

Joe Donny's cash down payment had barely offset the sales tax. A handwritten note said, *Gift wrap—purple foil, silver bow. Customer to pick up 2/12 @ 4 p.m. Balance due in full.*

"Tell Mr. Kelly it's against store policy to refund a deposit. We usually charge a ten percent restocking fee, but if he'll instruct us in writing to return the ring to inventory, we won't file a probate claim against Mr. Marlowe's estate for the balance."

Zoey frowned, then realized she was. "I'm sorry. This is all new to me. I didn't know creditors could do that." Catching her gaffe, she added, "Obviously, I've never worked in the bank's estate or trust department."

"Well, I'm old enough to remember when the only departments banks had were for savings and for loans." Her gaze strayed to a couple entering the store. "My, uh, other salesperson is at dinner. Is there anything else you need?"

Smiling, Zoey said, "No, but thank you so much for your help. This is exactly what I was looking for."

16

Hank left the cop shop bound for nowhere in particular. His belly was empty, but he had no appetite. His mind was full to bursting. Questions, speculations, contradictions writhed like fishing worms in a bait bucket. He could have stayed at the office. Sifted through the evidence. Reread the reports, his notes, the doodled hieroglyphics on the desk blotter. Brainstormed with Chichester awhile. Listened to the interview tape. Again.

Therein lies madness, he thought. And the reason Isaac Newton didn't discover gravity hunkered down behind his desk.

The fruits of inspiration were fickle little bastards. Seldom can they be forced.

Hank envisioned ol' Isaac, frustrated and exhausted from a marathon brood in his dungeon laboratory, throwing up his hands and hollering "Fuck it, I'm outta here." No sooner had he cranked back against a tree to soak up some rays, than the fabled apple conked him on the head.

But in February in southwest Missouri, with a ten-knot north wind and temperatures hovering in the teens, all Hank stood to gain from sitting in the dark under an apple tree was a flash-frozen ass.

Cruising around town in a cluttered, rank-smelling unmarked vehicle to effect a degree of mental detachment might prove less than inspiring, but at least the heater worked.

Christmas lights and electric icicles still rimmed a few residential rooftops, as though the home owners figured as long as it was too cold to take them down, they might as well let them twinkle. At a tiny municipal park, mesh netting fastened to the fence behind the tennis courts flapped like phantom players practicing lobs and backswings.

A supermarket's lot held fewer cars than shopping carts abandoned by customers too cold and eager to get home to push them twenty feet to the courtesy corral.

Farther on, an elderly woman in a long wool coat, knitted hat and snow boots trudged the sidewalk pulling her groceries home in a two-wheeled cart.

Hank pulled alongside the curb, displayed his badge and offered her a ride. She smiled, thanked him, said her house was just around the corner and that if he wanted to see eighty-two, he should use his legs the way the good Lord intended.

Still grinning as he braked for a yellow light, he checked her progress in the rearview mirror. Sure enough, she'd turned the corner and was plodding up a gingerbread cottage's flagstone walkway. Sconce porch lights beamed a welcome, as did a lamp in the front window shining through parted white lace curtains. He could almost hear a teakettle whistling on the stove and a fat tabby cat meowing for its supper.

Eeep. Eeep. Hank's head jerked left, expecting to see a Chihuahua in respiratory distress. In the sedan beside him, Zoey Jones waved a sheet of paper as though it were the map to the legendary treasure trove buried in Old Spanish Cave.

I have to talk to you, she mouthed.

Before he'd left her father's bedside, Hank had vowed to keep his distance until the arraignment hearing. He shook his head. *Can't.* He spread his hands. *Sorry.*

Please? Her fingers steepled like a roof, then she pointed at him. *Okay?* she mouthed. A tiny space between her thumb and forefinger signed, *Just for a minute?*

She wanted to go to his apartment. They weren't far from it. She probably thought he was headed home already. In the same instant that his hand moved to switch on the dashboard gumball and pretend he had a call, he realized he was nodding like a bobblehead doll.

Tires chirruped on the pavement. She rabbited through the now green light. Her taillights were narrowing to scarlet hyphens before his unmarked rolled through the yellow-painted crosswalk across the street.

Nice goin', sport. You stuck to your guns for a whole two, three seconds. He changed lanes, then popped up the turn signal lever. Just keep your mouth shut, listen to whatever she has to tell you, then say you're late for a suspect interview on that arson/homicide.

When he wheeled into the driveway behind his pickup, Zoey was already out of her car and waiting at the door. Under her smile, her chin trembled. The tip of her nose and her cheeks were rosy pink. Hair whipping over, then back from her face created an illusion of shape-shifting from the girl she once was, to the woman she'd become.

"Hi."

Hank inserted the key in the lock. "Hi, yourself."

Rushing inside to escape the wind, she spun around and said, "I promise I won't keep you."

He knew what she meant. He just didn't like hearing it.

"What's up?"

"This." She thrust the paper she'd waved in the car into his hand.

He scanned the photocopied receipt twice, wondering where she'd obtained it and how. He wasn't about to ask questions he'd be happier not knowing the answers to.

"Okay." Judging by her expression, his reaction was disappointing, aggravating and ignorant. "Marlowe bought an engagement ring a couple of weeks ago."

"A four-thousand-dollar engagement ring."

He looked down at the paper. "Dang-near forty-one hundred. Not counting sales tax."

"Jeez, Westlake. He worked at the Jiffy Stop. The deposit was three-fifty in cash. How'd he plan to scrape up the balance by February twelfth?"

Hank shrugged. "Put it on plastic. At twenty

bucks a month, he'd have it paid off a tad before his pension checks started rolling in."

"Oh." Deflation slumped her shoulders for maybe a nanosecond. "Why make a cash deposit on January twenty-sixth, if you're going to charge thousands on February twelfth?"

"To hold the ring till the card issuer upped his credit limit. Or until he could glom on to another handful to divvy the tab."

Her head was shaking before he finished speaking. "I might agree, if he hadn't also signed a contract to buy a house in Springfield. I'm not sure when, but the deal would have closed within a month. Six weeks at the outside."

Hank curried his mustache, not as intrigued by the information as by her agile mind. He'd always known she was smart, but intelligence alone did not a natural-born sleuth make. For a computer programmer turned bartender, she was a pretty fair amateur detective.

And it worried the hell out of him.

He folded the paper in half, then fourths, then doubled it again. "Cozied up to Trudy King, did you?"

"No. Even if I was that crass, she didn't know about the ring or the house. They were surprises for Valentine's Day."

Easy to imagine Marlowe fantasizing about that dreams-come-true moment, when he would solve all Trudy's problems.

Trudy's first husband, W.C., aka Winston Curtis King, had evaded a statutory rape charge by marrying his pregnant fifteen-year-old girlfriend.

By all accounts, the dirtbag loved his children, just not enough to stop drinking, drugging, screwing around and beating their mother.

Before the case against Doc France ever sprang a leak, Hank had pulled up King's docket on the computer and found a D&D arrest hours prior to the Jiffy Stop homicide.

The devil, as they say, takes care of his own.

"Who's your source of information?" he asked.

"Reliable."

He blew out a raspberry. "Darla Quinn."

"Gorgeous, funny, loyal. Not reliable. Well, info-wise, anyway." Zoey glanced at the door. "I have to pick up Claire and her friend at the library in a few minutes. There isn't time to grill me about how I found out about Joe Donny's spending spree. Besides, it doesn't matter.

"It's obvious he didn't have much money but was expecting to hit a serious jackpot within days. Not wishing on a star. Expecting. Could be he already had, and that's what got him killed."

"Four grand isn't chicken feed," Hank said, "but it's not exactly a jackpot."

"What about the house?" An upraised finger preempted him. "Ah, you ask, what about those no down, no closing-cost deals? Well, read the fine print. Those costs aren't waived, they're folded into the mortgage. Over the life of a loan, they compound into major money. Ditto equity insurance in lieu of a down payment—kind of a loan within a loan equaling fifteen percent of the purchase price. Put 'em together and they spell way-higher monthly payments, before tacking on prorated home-owner's insurance and property taxes."

Hank laughed. "Darlin', when you answer a question with a question, you really let 'er rip."

"Yeah, well, much as I love going home from work smelling like beer, burgers and cigarette smoke, I may enroll in real estate school this spring."

Now there was a relief. Tapping brewskis at the He Just Left wasn't the worst job in the world, but the hours were awful, the pay couldn't be great, and secure it wasn't. "You'd be good at it. You've always been good at anything you set your mind to."

"With a couple of notable exceptions."

He grinned at her. "Such as accepting a compliment instead of picking at it."

"I'll add that to my list of New Year's resolutions. Now back to the convenience store clerk and part-time trade-school student who could suddenly afford a honking diamond ring, house payments, a wife and two stepdaughters. Care to offer an explanation for that?"

"Not particularly."

"Fine. Here's *mine*. Joe Donny had the inside scoop on a lotto winner, or the sister without an address is actually deceased and he was a beneficiary. Or he was dealing drugs, about to pull a bank heist or a kidnapping, or was blackmailing somebody."

Hank opened his coat and slid the folded paper into an interior pocket. "I'll have to get back to you on that."

"Ha! It's blackmail, isn't it? Marlowe knew something on somebody who decided it was cheaper to silence him permanently."

The theory smacked of whodunits and approximately every third episode on cop TV, but it did happen, on occasion. For Hank, it was an escape hatch. "Darlin', much as I appreciate the help, promise me you'll take care of Vesta and Claire and leave the thinking and poking around to me from here on out."

"Excellent idea." The Cheshire cat with a canary in its mitts had nothing on Zoey's smile. "Your cop-face is slipping, Westlake."

"Beg pardon?"

"Aw, c'mon. Give it up. Mom told me you went to the hospital to interview Daddy this afternoon. Yes, I should have been up there visiting him, not checking up on Joe Donny, but wait'll Claire hears that's where we're going after we drop off Laura Peters."

Her eyes searched his face. Her smile faded, then rekindled, as though his silence must be a twinge of disappointment at having good news for once and she'd guessed it, before he could tell her.

"I'm sorry, Zoe, but the interview didn't change anything. Charlie's still in police custody."

"Oh—well, yeah, because of the robberies, but—" she started. "You mean with a guard at the door?"

Hank nodded. "That's the way it has to be, until he's arraigned."

"What? But that's— How can nothing have changed, if Daddy told you what happened?" Her hands flew to her mouth. "Oh, Hank. Oh, dear God."

He pulled her into his arms and held her, stroking her hair. She wasn't crying, but she was shak-

ing so hard she clenched her teeth to halt the quaver in her voice. "I didn't believe he robbed those
stores, either, did I? But he did. You proved it. Already proved that nothing—nothing—is impossible...."

If a white lie is a kindness, Hank thought, why
not a white truth? What if, say, it had been Joe
Smith stretched out on that hospital bed this afternoon? Never met the man, didn't know his family, but the story he told me was identical. "During
the interview," he said, "I asked Doc point-blank
if he killed Joe Donny Marlowe."

Slowly, Zoey's head turned and she looked up
at him.

"He swore he didn't."

Maybe paraphrasing the exchange cheated ethics like invisible strings up a magician's sleeve
cheated the eye.

It probably wouldn't be an issue if Joe Smith's
daughter was clawing for a thread of hope to hold
on to. Zoey was no less deserving of a chance to
decide whether her father had proclaimed his
innocence or denied guilt.

"What else did he say?" She turned, flattening
her palms on his lapels, gripping the edges.
"Please, Hank. I'm not asking you to tell me everything. You can't. I understand. I respect that and
you, for being as straight with me as you can."

Hank looked away, loosening the embrace, but
unable, unwilling, to let her go. Had she tried to
parlay their friendship to her advantage, even
hinted at doing so, he could have stepped back, literally and emotionally.

"Just tell me why Daddy robbed those stores. Why he was so desperate for money and for what. The rest can wait till the arraignment."

A few hours ago, Doc said he was dying of hypertropic cardiomyopathy. The disease had shut down blood flow to the left side of his heart and was gradually destroying the right. Drugs and oxygen eased the symptoms. Without a transplant, heart failure was inevitable.

His family's right to know had commenced with France's first appointment with the cardiologist. Refusing to tell them wasn't an act of love. It was unconscionable, an indictment that included his doctor. And a part of Hank hated them both for making him an accomplice.

The diagnosis and prognosis linked four robberies and a homicide to a presumed guilty plea. That's why Hank couldn't answer what Zoey thought was a simple, reasonable question. He was cowering behind a gold shield, just as France's cardiologist was using privacy statutes.

The hell. If he were, he'd wrap his badge and service weapon in a letter of resignation and lay them on the chief's desk.

The realization staggered him. It also armorplated his resolve. Shifting the burden of truth onto Zoey solved nothing, changed nothing. She couldn't confront her father.

Couldn't stop Charlie, either. Expecting Schlomo to intervene invited court-ordered psychiatric testing and evaluations, delays and a legal Gordian knot. Dying of heart failure in a mental hospital was a poor substitute for dying of it in prison.

Hank cradled Zoey's face in his hands. "I can't tell you. The reasons are so convoluted and twisted and paradoxical, I'm not sure I should trust my gut, much less how I can ask you to do the same. But darlin', for now, that's what I have to do."

He sighed. "Damned if I can explain the why of that, either."

Her gaze locked on his, searching, questioning, challenging, as if she could somehow absorb what she ached to know. On her face, he could see an agonizing battle raging between her impulse to despise him and her instinct to trust him.

The conclusion was visible before her lips pressed together, as though uncertain her instincts weren't deceiving her. "I always have trusted you. Until a few days ago, you ranked right up there with my father." Blinking away tears, she added. "I guess, now, that makes you the one and only."

"Oh, Zoey. Don't—"

"I love my dad with all my heart," she went on. "But no, after all he's put us through in the last few days, I don't trust him the way I once did."

Stepping back, she took Hank's hands in hers, signalling a need to stand alone and a reluctance to let go. "That doesn't mean I believe he grabbed a hammer and hit Joe Donny Marlowe hard enough to kill him."

Hank cleared his throat. "Neither do I."

She smiled. "News to you, maybe. Not to me."

"At least, thanks to you, I have a lead to look into."

Her smile widened. "Is that a round-the-barn

way of saying I'm right? You think Joe Donny was blackmailing somebody?"

"Well…how about that I'm real curious about where the money for his spending spree was coming from."

"The expectation of money," she corrected.

"Yes, dear." He mentally reviewed what she'd said about the ring and the house. Bad enough that restarting at square one and following a financial paper trail was going to be tedious and time-consuming. Other than interviewing Trudy King, which he doubted would be worth the phone call, he was stonewalled until businesses opened tomorrow morning. By then, Lonnie Chichester would be tied up with the arson/homicide case. Hank couldn't draft an investigator from another unit to assist, either. With a guilty plea in the offing, the France case was all but closed.

"Remember what I said about leaving the poking around to me?"

"Yes, and don't worry, I'm more than happy to bow out."

"Then I reckon bowing back in with me at the courthouse tomorrow morning isn't going to happen."

For a medium-sized female with small-to-medium-sized hands, she had one helluva grip. "What time?"

"Eleven sharp. In the lobby."

"You got it." She turned his wrist and squinted at his watch. "Holy crap. I should've been at the library fifteen minutes ago."

"Speed limit or below, hot rod." He kissed her brow. "See you in the morning."

"See ya." She opened the door, started out, then turned on a heel. Her expression equal parts frown and bafflement, she said, "Westlake, are you ever going to kiss me like a man, instead of a seventeen-year-old kid?"

Hank pulled her back inside and bumped the door shut with his knee. One arm slipped under her coat and around her waist. He smoothed back the hair from her face, then his fingers dove into those wild, messy waves and cupped the back of her head. "Now, okay with you?"

If she answered, he didn't hear it. From the moment their lips touched, he was lost. Mindlessly, irrevocably submersed in her scent, the taste of her, the whirling, swirling magic of a dream coming true.

When they parted, breathless, he gazed down at her fluttering eyelids and her mouth, slightly open as if in twilight sleep. Aching to kiss her again, he resisted, knowing that if he did, he couldn't stop, and that rushing would cheat them both.

"I don't want to be just friends," he said. "Never did."

"Neither do I."

"I want strings. Dozens of 'em."

She looked up at him, nodding. "Me, too."

"A somewhere relationship. Expectations."

"Yeah." She grinned. "Yeah."

"But no horizontal boogie."

Her head tilted, as people's do when a momentary hearing loss is suspected. "No?"

"Uh-uh."

"But—"

"Someday, after we've tortured ourselves awhile and the time is right and there's no ticking clock in our ears, I want to make love to you. With you. All night long and into the next day and then sleep in each other's arms."

"Perfect." She smooched the tip of his nose. "And then we'll grab a pizza and go bowling. Just the two of us."

He blinked...chuckled...threw back his head and laughed till he almost choked. "Deal."

17

Zoey caught herself humming as she folded the morning's second load of laundry. Not a song—at least, not one she recognized. More like a ditty. Yeah, well, it was probably a jingle for a feminine hygiene product, but who cared?

She'd wakened smiling. Treated Bob and Fred to doggy biscuits before their breakfast. Didn't say a word to Claire about the earrings and sweater she hadn't asked to borrow.

In the time usually allotted to carpooling, Zoey luxuriated in a long, hot bath, while Bella Donna Sewell and, presumably, Euell, delivered Claire and Laura Peters to the halls of higher learning.

Now, burying her face in a warm, wildflower-scented towel, she couldn't remember when she'd last felt so alive. So happy. So happy to be alive. And, she admitted, guilty, too, for her Ms. Merry Sunshine outlook. Her father's heart condition had stabilized, but his arraignment was tomorrow afternoon.

"Unless," she told a stack of washcloths, "Hank and I dig up something that puts him in hot pursuit of the real killer."

Could be Hank already had. Before Zoey had left his apartment last night, he'd said he hoped to squeeze in some phone calls between checking Lonnie's progress at the burned-out building and follow-ups on other open cases.

Unspoken was an agreement to put their relationship on hold until Charlie France's criminal proceedings were done. A neat trick, perhaps, but Hank understood. It wasn't a matter of priorities. Life was a juggling act. Just because the object was to keep all the balls in the air, sometimes one or two fell and had to roll around on the floor a bit before they could be picked up again.

Laundry being a part of life, especially with a teenager in residence, the metaphor also applied to the fingertips-to-chin-high stack of bath linens Zoey carted up from the basement. She was midway across the kitchen when the phone rang. Unloading the towels on the table guaranteed they'd remain upright just long enough for her to answer the phone, then topple to a floor muddy with greyhound tracks. Zoey leveraged the bottom towel against the end of the counter. With one arm stabilizing them and her chin clamped down on the washcloths, she snatched the receiver from its cradle.

"'E'lo?"

"Zoey? Is that you?"

"Oh—'i, Mahm." Tilting her head didn't alleviate her voice's adenoidal Ernestine the Telephone Operator quality. The stack, however, bulged ominously in the middle.

"Why do you sound so funny? Are you sick?"

"Ne, ne, I'yem fine. Godda aremlud ov ta'els."

"Can't you— Never mind. I'm just calling to see if you'd meet me at Osbert Schlomo's office at four. He wants to discuss strategy for the arraignment tomorrow. Now, if you have other plans, something more important you need to do, that's perfectly fine with me. I'd feel more comfortable with you there, but if you're busy, I can certainly manage all by myself."

Zoey stifled a groan. Couldn't her mother ever ask for help without wrapping it in concertina wire? Utter a simple yes or no question without barbs like *other plans*, *more important* and *busy*.

Umm, that would be no.

According to Claire, Bella Donna couldn't pick up the girls at school today or tomorrow, thus was taking them on both days—a schedule approved by the passengers, not Zoey, who'd hoped for dibs on mornings.

How she'd manage Friday afternoon if school ended before the arraignment did, she'd figure out later. As for this afternoon, she'd pick up her daughter before going to the lawyer's office. Claire's smarts and objectivity would be an asset to the pro-am investigation team.

So much for that, she thought. "Sure, Mahm. I'yel be dere."

Chuckling, Vesta thanked her and rang off.

"Well, hell," Zoey told the greyhounds, snoozing on their pillows beside a floor register. "Claire seeing Hank's detective side working for her grandpa would've been great."

Bob snuffled and cocked an ear.

"Yeah, you're right. Common cause or not, a homicide investigation isn't a bonding activity. The less Claire knows and the less she's involved, the better."

Other than the outburst at the hospital, if Claire held a grudge against Hank, it wasn't apparent. She had, in fact, asked about him several times—in a casual, offhand manner, like she did Darla and her great-uncle Al.

So far, she seemed to be handling the situation very well. Too well, perhaps, from a still-waters-run-deep perspective. Except Zoey sensed that Laura had been a true-blue sounding board whenever Claire needed to vent, or cry, or be told to get her shit together and quit whining. Her Darla, as it were.

And, after all, Zoey hadn't shared many feelings and fears with Vesta, and vice versa. Being strong for each other bucked them up individually. No weak links allowed in their chain, by God.

Stuffing towels in the bathroom's tiny under-sink cabinet, Zoey sucked in her lower lip, biting down to stop its trembling. Her little girl was growing up.

No, she amended. *She's outgrowing me.*

When had telling her to stand on her own two feet, to think for herself, to for Pete's sake *grow up,* switched from carping to a fait accompli?

Nurture was supposed to lose out to nature eventually. Just not quite yet. Claire was only...

Zoey stood and stared at the mind-boggled woman reflected in the mirror. "Four years from graduating from high school?"

She counted on her fingers. Scowled. Picked up a brush and yanked it through her hair. "Unless she flunks a couple of times. The little sneak. It'd serve her right, jumping from a car seat to Driver's Ed behind my back."

Thirty minutes later, images of Claire in a collegiate cap and gown, a wedding dress, pushing a stroller and visiting Zoey in the nursing home evaporated at the sight of Hank leaning against a wall in the courthouse's lobby.

The man had style. Subtle, undefinable, yet a definite notch above average. Pairing a black dress shirt and black sweater-vest with charcoal slacks wasn't revolutionary, except guys seldom had shirts and slacks tailored to fit them, rather than make do with clothes manufactured for the multitudes who were more-or-less their size.

His signature, calf-length topcoat probably cost him more than his second divorce. Worth every nickel, too, in Zoey's opinion. Veddy Pierce Brosnan with elements of Darth Vader.

"Am I late?" she asked.

"Nope." He reached for her hand, then jerked his away. "Right on time."

Zoey realized the risk he'd assumed by asking for her help. Being observed fraternizing with a homicide suspect's daughter would beg questions he'd be hard-pressed to answer. Particularly any directed by his superiors, the prosecuting attorney's office, or heaven forbid, the press.

"Low profile," she murmured.

"That's my girl." If noticed at all, his wink could be mistaken for a tic. "Couple of things to note before we go upstairs. Mainly, that I haven't made much progress."

Narrowed, slightly bloodshot eyes conveyed it hadn't been for lack of effort or caffeine.

"Marlowe's account at Miner's Bank didn't reflect any peculiar transactions—deposits or expenditures. It does appear, though, that the down payment on that ring put him behind on his car payment."

"Could you tell whether he usually paid his bills on time?"

"Looked like it."

"Okay, then doesn't that sound like he was expecting money?" Zoey added, "Applying for a mortgage is a dumb time to screw up your credit rating."

Hank agreed, "But the timing's too tight to know whether he'd have used the next paycheck to make up the difference, plus the late fee."

From personal experience, Zoey doubted it. Getting a little behind invited the salary gods to trash your transmission. "For sure he couldn't have paid off the balance due at Meershaum's Jewelry Store."

"No, but checks were written to a credit card company every month. The balance and limit on it, I didn't have time to find out. I can't get ahold of Trudy King, either. When I couldn't get her by phone, I blew an hour going to her house, then her work address. Seems she left town yesterday shortly after the graveside service."

"Oh, really?"

"Lower the antennae, Nancy Drew. It's been a

rough few days for her. I was told that Trudy and her mother went to a friend's cabin up at Lake of the Ozarks for some recreational shopping at the outlet malls up there."

"Away from W. C. King, too, I'll bet. An asshole being Prince Charming is scarier than an asshole being an asshole."

By his expression, Hank surmised the remark wasn't secondhand and would enjoy pummeling its source. "Trudy's co-workers insinuated that, yes. I got a phone number for the cabin, but nobody's answering. Story of my morning, pretty much."

"What are we after here?" Zoey asked.

"Process of elimination. Marlowe's name didn't ring bells with the drug enforcement officer I talked to. No history doesn't exclude the possibility, but if he was dealing, there'd be whispers on the wind."

Before she could comment, he said, "Nobody gets rich on a single score. You have to be in the life awhile before anybody'll trust you're legit."

"Meaning not an undercover narc."

"Which brings us to your inheritance angle. To give you fair warning, I'm skeptical. From what I gather, Marlowe's family couldn't rub noses with the Rockefeller's garbage man."

Zoey snorted. "Blackmail still has my vote. Yes, I'm hung up on the expectation thing, but there aren't many ways to anticipate a windfall with enough certainty to spend some of it in advance."

Frowning, Hank motioned at the antique Regulator on the wall between the elevator cars. "Might oughta watch what you wish for, darlin'."

The hand Zoey pressed to her belly didn't halt the sinking sensation within. *Tomorrow* beguiled the mind—its vagueness sounding abstract and blithely futuristic. Not until then would a circuit court judge read the charges imposed by the State of Missouri against Charles Herman France.

The clock compressed tomorrow to immutable, finite numbers. Twenty-five hours and forty-three minutes. And counting—backward.

"We've gotta find something, Hank. We can't let Daddy die in jail waiting to be tried for a crime he didn't commit."

"That isn't—" Jaw clamped, his thumb gouged the elevator button. "If there's something to be found, we will."

Refusing to dwell on what that *if* implied, Zoey wandered about, as normal people do when trying to mask impatience with nonchalance.

Modernizing the block-granite, antebellum courthouse, while preserving its original splendor, was an eternal architectural and engineering challenge. As imposing as the three-story building appeared on the outside, broad corridors, cavernous ceilings and a soaring central cupola reduced the square footage earmarked for office space.

Progressing from privies on the lawn to indoor restrooms, and from telegraphs to satellite communications and equipment undreamt-of in the late 1800s had advanced shoehorning to an art form.

Exempt from the twentieth century, let alone the twenty-first, was the elevator system's human element. A gnomelike octogenarian at the helm bid Hank and Zoey good morning and cautioned them to watch their step.

After closing the brass accordion gate, he slid the control lever. The car whisked them to the third floor at the breakneck pace of an inch per second.

The circuit court's probate division was on the right near the end of the hallway. At one glance, Zoey deemed it an anal-retentive filing clerk's hell on earth. Computerization notwithstanding, manila folders in piles and cartons layered every horizontal surface, particularly the floor. A gazillion trees had been sacrificed to build a paper mountain range.

The hushed, pervasive noise of clacking keyboards, ringing telephones, muted conversations and file shuffling defined the phrase *hive of activity*. Drones were at a premium, though.

"Can I help you with something?" A lanky young man approached the raised-panel counter, as though Hank and Zoey were contagious.

Hank scanned the other clerk seated at a desk, actively ignoring their entrance. "I'm looking for Susan Fawcett. 'Preciate it, if you'd tell her Hank Westlake's in need of another favor."

"Susan called in sick this morning. Her son has the stomach flu that's going around." The clerk's tone suggested, *a likely excuse.* Gracing them with a "better luck next time" smirk, he turned from the counter.

"*Yo.*" Hank opened his coat to display the wallet shield in the inside pocket and, consequently, the shoulder-holstered pistol strapped to his chest. "And what might your name be?"

"Oh. Oh. It's uh—uh, Raymond, sir. Raymond Junge. I didn't know you—"

"Well, now, Ray. Seeing as how Ms. Fawcett isn't available, I do hope it won't strain your milk to assist us in a records search."

"No—I mean, yes, sir. I'd be happy to." His glance extended the magnanimity to Zoey.

Hank slid a computer-printed reproduction of a newspaper obituary across the counter. "The dispensation of Ms. Thelma Thomason's estate is what I need. According to this, she died about fifteen months ago."

The clerk took the paper. "That gives me a time frame to find the case number and files. If you can come back later this afternoon, or in the—"

"Actually, Ray, I need a copy of those files, like, yesterday."

He blanched as though his life—or the workload parked on his desk—was passing before his eyes. "I'll get right on it."

When he'd retreated out of earshot, Zoey whispered, "Who's Thelma Thomason?"

"The only deceased relative unaccounted for in Marlowe's family tree. His grandparents—both sides—died years ago. The surname doesn't jibe, but by Thomason's age, I'm guessing she was a great-aunt."

Zoey recalled her conversation with George Santini. "I was told Joe Donny lived with his grandmother after his parents died in a fire."

"He did. She passed when he was twenty, twenty-one."

Anticipating the next question, Hank added,

"No estate there to speak of. A stroke left Thelma paralyzed on one side. The nursing home drained what assets she had."

Skeptical? A fiberglass pole and a running start wouldn't hurdle Zoey an inch higher than dubious. The odds of a wild, golden goose in Joe Donny's family tree seemed too slim to chase. Of course, Hank wasn't especially forthcoming with rhymes and reasons.

"How'd you find out about Ms. Thomason?"

"Spent half the night at the office on the computer." A yawn overwhelmed his attempt to contain it. Excusing himself, he went on, "A search engine finally popped a newspaper archive within a genealogy site. Marlowe's name was in her obit."

"There are shortcuts for those types of searches," Zoey said. "If I'd known, I could have saved us a ton of time."

"Yeah, well, for the record, I'm no slouch at the computer. I just didn't become a cop to practice my typing skills."

A courier walked by lugging a binful of mailers curtailed an equally snide response. Zoey was angry at Hank and furious with herself. For four freakin' days, she'd ditzed around town, not once thinking to do an Internet search. Ye gods, during last night's jewelry store pilgrimage, Claire and Laura could have done it for her at the library.

Not every Tom, Dick or Joe Donny entered into a search engine scored comprehensive results. The pedigree gleaned from his obituary—date and place of birth, high school attended, father's and

siblings' names and mother's maiden name—
would have widened and winnowed the search.

The courier waved an electronic wand over the
parcels' coded labels with the precision of a guy
five minutes shy of his lunch hour. Hank turned
his back on him. "Sorry, Zo. I shouldn't have
sniped at you like that."

"No sweat. I started it." Observing Raymond
Junge's bumblebee flight from file drawers to floor
cartons frazzled what few of her nerves remained.
"So what do they use their PCs for? Paperweights?"

"The system crashed between Christmas and
New Year's. They're having fits keeping up day-to-
day. No telling when they'll restore the older files."

"Restore? Well, that shouldn't take… Oh,
please. Don't tell me they weren't backed up."

A clerk craned her neck and fired Zoey a nasty
look. Her head whipped in the opposite direction
when Raymond balanced the files on her desk on
his thigh to flip through the tabs.

Monotone words were exchanged. Ms. Cheer-
ful flounced to a file cabinet and yanked open the
drawer. Both ignored the courier's departing, "See
ya in the morning."

After a moment she slammed the drawer shut
again, snatched up her coat and purse and stalked
through the door to an adjacent hall.

Raymond's blush scalded his pale complexion.
"Poor ol' Aggie gets tetchy when she's hungry.
Don't worry, though. Misfiled isn't the same as lost."

Zoey raked her hair back with her fingernails.
A lacerated scalp seemed preferable to leaping the
counter and throttling the clerk.

Hank's cell phone twittered. He stepped into the main corridor. "Not Trudy King," he said, when he returned. Neither were the other four he received before Raymond ripped a thick folder from a desktop stack—his desk, the last place he'd looked—and held it aloft.

Eyeing the hulking, single-page copier in the corner, Hank tapped the countertop. "Lay it on me, Ray. If I need a dupe, I'll let you know."

Raymond handed over the file.

Riffling through the stapled sheaves, Hank muttered, "Damn it. These ought to be in chronological order, by hearing date."

"We should be so lucky."

Accepting a half share of the documents, Zoey noticed the date atop a certificate and order of probate of last will and testament of self-proved will. "Wait a sec. Isn't probate a six-month process? If Ms. Thomason died fifteen months ago, the court would have distributed the estate last spring."

"Six months, barring complications. There are always complications. The heft of her file tells me this one wasn't smooth sailing."

Intervals of silent speed-reading were punctuated by remarks on points of interest.

"Joe Donny was Thomason's executor," Hank said. "Pretty much a form cosigner, though, since her lawyer had power of attorney."

Embezzling from an estate was a good motive for blackmail. Perish the thought—for now.

"Ms. Thomason never married," she said. "Hence, no children."

"Explains why there aren't any surviving and

few predeceased relatives in her obit. She wasn't Marlowe's blood kin."

"Unless he was illegitimate."

Hank grimaced. "Sixty-one is a mite late in life for a fling."

"Excellent. Almost two hours gone and we smack into a big fat dead end."

"Patience is a virtue, Zo. Have some."

Hearings had been scheduled, then postponed for weeks or months. The cause of the delays was unstipulated.

Minutes later, her finger paused midway down a page. "Hey. Here's an address list. Joe Donny, his long-lost sisters and cousin Andrew."

"Heirs, apparently." Hank copied the information into his notebook. "Maybe of the two hundred acres I came across. From the legal description, the parcel's about fifteen miles southeast of town."

"Even split four ways, that'd be a chunk of change, wouldn't it?"

"Quarter of a mil, at least."

"Could be Joe Donny sold his, but the deal hadn't closed yet."

The next page blew that theory to smithereens. "Here's your stupid complication." She waved a motion entitled Objection To Sale Of Real Property. "Thelma Thomason bequeathed her land to the Humane Society."

"Yep." Hank held up a quarter-inch stack of documents. "Joe Donny's sisters took serious exception, too. Tried to prove Thelma was mentally incompetent when the will was drawn up."

Glaring at the unexamined pile, Zoey said, "What

right did they have, if they weren't related? Better question, why would she leave anything to them?"

"Dollars to doughnuts—no pun intended— Thelma was a dear friend of Joe Donny's grandma's. Kind of adopted the grandkids as her own."

The supposition proved accurate when Hank unearthed an inventory of the estate's assets. Included was a savings bond issued in 1986 in the names of each of the Marlowe siblings and Andrew Kelly. With interest accrued, the value was just over twenty-five thousand dollars apiece.

"And here's the kicker," he said. "Judge Kritz's final order of distribution, dated last Friday."

"So, the bonds would be in the mail?"

"Depends on how fast the lawyer dictated cover letters and his legal secretary addressed the envelopes. The end of this week at the outside."

Zoey slumped against the counter. Joe Donny Marlowe died Sunday night. Being right about him expecting a windfall was no comfort. A savings bond was non-transferable. Only the designated recipient could convert it to cash.

A living designated recipient.

18

The eighth floor of the Bank of Blytheville resembled a palatial living room dotted with potted palm trees and islands of tasteful office furniture. Sofas and side chairs hugged mahogany coffee and side tables. Porcelain lamps shed redundant light on figurines and coasters painted with Asian water-garden scenes. *Banking Today, Entrepreneur, Inc.* and *Business Week* were fanned on a console alongside today's pristine edition of *The Wall Street Journal*.

A receptionist directed Hank to a secretary, who led him to an assistant assistant's desk, who offered him coffee and invited him to take a seat while she ascertained whether Andrew Kelly was in or out of the office—in other words, receiving.

Hank declined the coffee, the chair and, by association, the illusion of hospitality bestowed on plebeians. The keys to timely cooperation were a gold-plated badge and the louder-than-library-appropriate words *homicide investigation*.

The vice president's left-of-the-corner office was wide and long enough to necessitate a fair stretch of the legs to reach his oak table-style desk. Sage-green walls mimicked the ink-shading on currency, just as the carpet color matched its unprinted background.

Hank didn't share Vesta France's addiction to home decorating shows, but had watched a few when the sports networks were showing golf tournaments and skateboard competitions. He assumed Kelly's decorator had chosen the oil paintings because their ruddy daubs and dashes were analogous to the upholstered pieces' oxblood leather.

Silhouetted by floor-to-ceiling windows, the banker rose from his desk like a slo-mo paper target at a firing range. "Come on in, Hank. Sit down, sit down."

Andrew hesitated. "I, uh, hope you'll forgive me for not shaking hands. I'm feeling a little under the weather today."

On closer examination, that unseasonal tan did seem to stand away from his face an inch or three. "No problem. In fact, I appreciate the warning. There's a lot of stuff going around and I don't have time to get sick."

"Oh, I hear you on that." Andrew chuckled. "I'm already in the doghouse for not flying to L.A. this morning with my wife and daughter."

A silver-framed glamour shot of a pretty, blue-eyed blond teenager was turned toward Hank. "Tiffany's auditioning for some commercials— maybe a walk-on in a movie. I'm behind her a hundred-and-ten percent, but plane tickets don't grow on trees."

"Your daughter wants to be an actress, eh?"

"She is, actually. Several commercials on her résumé." Andrew coughed into his fist. "Last weekend, at a pageant in St. Louis, a director scouting locations for a TV pilot took me aside to ask if Tiff might be interested in testing for the daughter's role."

Small-town beauty queen goes Hollywood. Hank hoped he looked impressed. "I'm told folks jam those pageants like bull-ride night at the county fair."

"They do. Except ninety-eight percent of them are female. Babies to great-grandmothers. It's a madhouse."

"Could be that's where you caught your cold. How long were you up there?"

Andrew tensed slightly and steepled his fingers. "As I told the officer, until Sunday. We arrived in St. Louis on Friday around noon and didn't leave until…well after four…on Sunday."

A violent sneeze intervened. Apologizing as he wiped his nose and watery eyes with a tissue, the banker could nail a starring role in an antihistamine ad. "I really do feel like hell warmed over. What's this all about?"

"Just tying up a few loose ends—which I could have done by phone, if you'd returned my calls."

Muttering under his breath, Andrew thumbed through the pink message slips lying beside the phone. "Nothing here." Watery, red-rimmed eyes glared in the direction of the outer office. "What can I say? Other than I'm truly sorry for the inconvenience."

Hank smiled. "If I had a dollar for every message I didn't receive, I'd be your largest depositor."

"Any regrets about not going into business for yourself?" Andrew perked up, blinking the dull glaze from his eyes. "The rate on small business loans is lower than it was before. Ridiculously low, if you ask me. We've also bundled some new services that I'm sure you'd find of interest."

"No, I think I'll stay where I am till the retirement party."

Andrew assumed the banker's stance: leaning back, an ankle crossed on his knee, elbows on the chair arms. "It'll be here before you know it. Consider your position. You're young, no dependents. Now's the time to channel your investments toward that—"

"Speaking of time," Hank said, "I don't want to take more of yours than necessary. Do you happen to know whether Joe Donny had a will?"

"Did you when you were twenty-six?" His brow furrowed. "Why do you ask?"

"Ms. Thelma Thomason wasn't blood kin to you or the Marlowe kids, right?"

Andrew's face expressed an "Aha," then shut down entirely. "Much as I resent the intrusion, your thoroughness is impressive."

Hank stifled a retaliatory remark. Want thorough and intrusive? Try applying for a loan sometime, man.

"We called her Aunt Thel, but no, she wasn't related. My grandmother joked about them being twins, but said Thel was better than a real sister."

"You and Joe Donny weren't party to the motion his sisters filed, questioning Ms. Thomason's competency at the time her will was written."

Andrew snorted in disgust. "Heavens, no. If I had, Grandma wouldn't have rolled over in her grave. She'd have climbed out to haunt me like Jacob Marley did Ebenezer Scrooge. Thel was eccentric and reclusive, not senile. She was taking in stray dogs and cats and finding them homes years before the county had a humane society."

Shaking his head, he added, "Tighter than Dick's hatband, too. I had no idea she had the money to buy those bonds, much less that she did, until she passed away."

Hank asked, "What was her cause of death?"

"The certificate says heart failure. Her doctor said she died in her sleep of old age."

"We should all be so lucky." *Unless*, Hank thought, *your heart fails you by inches, like Charlie France's.*

"Amen to that. Thel was ninety-three, but true to form, she canned twelve pints of pumpkin butter before she went to bed that night."

"Odd, though, you being older and a banker, for her to designate Joe Donny as executor. And to grant her lawyer power of attorney."

"Not really. Not for Aunt Thel." Andrew stared off, as though reminiscing about happier times. "She swore she'd live to be a hundred and fifty. I think we all halfway believed it, too. As for the power of attorney—well, I'm sure she had her reasons. What they were, I have no idea. Her lawyer might."

Another as-yet unreturned phone call. Hank presumed the lawyer would cite attorney-client privilege, anyway. It wasn't a loose end, truth be told. More like a greasy straw he was clutching.

"The newbie probate court clerk I spoke with earlier doesn't know his butt from a hole in the ground. I'm curious what'll happen to the savings bond Thomason left Joe Donny."

"I'm told, since he died intestate and without direct heirs—a spouse, children—the probate court will divide it and any other assets between his sisters."

"What about you?"

"I'm just a cousin."

Hank figured it would revert to Thomason's estate and be divided three ways. Even so, a third share of twenty-five large was a negligible motive for murder.

"Greedy little sluts," Andrew added. "The irony is that what money they receive from Joe Donny's estate probably won't cover attorney's fees for the motion they filed against Aunt Thel's."

Score one for Zoey. Hank needn't ask whether the sisters' bare mention in their brother's obit was a subtle up-yours from Cousin Andrew. Propriety precluded ignoring their existence. The sisters would also pocket Marlowe's deposits on the engagement ring and house, if either was refundable. Andrew must not know about them. Hank wasn't obliged to tell him.

Andrew sneezed again, then poured orange juice from a thermal carafe into a lead-crystal glass. Nodding at a bar cabinet along the wall, he said, "Too much talking dries out the pipes. Help yourself to coffee, a soda—there's a pitcher of iced tea in the minifridge, too."

"I'm fine, thanks." Pausing until the banker had

quenched his thirst, Hank said, "Since Joe Donny didn't have a will, I'm guessing he didn't have any life insurance."

"None that I know of."

"So who paid for the funeral?"

From Andrew's frown, it was clear that the question wasn't appreciated. Hazard of the job. *Tacky* was an investigator's middle name.

"His girlfriend insisted on buying the casket. How she'll manage the payments, I can't imagine. Marge and I will take care of the rest."

He returned the glass to the tray, then folded his hands on the desk. A feverish sheen glistened on his forehead. Hank wished the desk was a couple of acres wider.

"Come on, Hank. Level with me. What is this all about? If I didn't know Charles France was under arrest for murdering my cousin, I'd think you were desperate for a suspect."

Hank started. The media had ID'd Doc at the scene, but hadn't named him—couldn't, legally, until he was arraigned. Cops arrest; judges mete out formal charges. If a suspect was named but never charged, a libel suit could result. Gagging the rumor mill was impossible, but its range was limited.

"Care to tell me where you heard that?"

"Osbert Schlomo's law partner plays racquetball with the head of our legal department." A sigh gusted from his lips. "I couldn't believe it, at first. Never met the man, but I understand he's a salt-of-the-earth type. Good grief, my daughter and his granddaughter are in the same grade at school."

Hank wondered if Zoey was aware of that.

Probably not, or she'd have mentioned it. His already high estimation of Claire rose several notches. Like her mother, she wasn't as tough a cookie as she wanted everyone to believe, but handling that kind of notoriety at the sausage factory known as middle school took guts.

"France isn't long for this world, anyway, is he?" Andrew asked. "Cancer? Or was it a heart condition?" He gestured dismissively. "Doesn't matter. I cannot let myself feel sorry for him."

Hank almost reminded him of the "innocent until proven guilty" principle. Doc France's subterfuge fouled the words, made them grate the back of his throat.

In a thinking-aloud tone, Andrew went on, "I don't feel right about the girlfriend paying for Joe Donny's casket. A lovely gesture, but with those two little girls to support…"

He looked at Hank. "Do you think she'd be insulted if I went ahead and settled that account with the funeral home?"

Hank pushed up from the chair. Chances were, when grief subsided a bit and judgment returned, Trudy would be relieved. "That's for the two of you to decide."

"Joe Donny and I weren't as close as we could have been. Should have been. Just too big an age difference and very little in common, I guess."

In lieu of a departing handshake, Hank rapped his knuckles on the desk. "I appreciate the help. Take care of yourself, now, hear?"

Nodding, Andrew leaned back in his chair again, as though the spirit was willing to stand but the body was not. "A good night's sleep would do wonders." A flicker of a smile. "Whether it does or doesn't, there's a board of directors meeting at nine sharp tomorrow morning."

Hank strode across the carpet. A sudden tautness below his eyes felt ominous. Kelly's sniffling, sneezing misery could turn a lamppost into a hypochondriac.

Hand poised on the door handle, a thought hit him. He turned and asked, "What kind of vehicles do you and your wife drive?"

"Beg pardon? I can't imagine why..." He coughed and snapped a tissue from the box. "Marge drove a Lexus until a few months ago. She talked me into trading it for another Escalade."

Hank's grip tightened. Escalades were the Queen Marys of the SUV market. "What color?"

"Color? Well, Marge's is white diamond. They're both white diamond. You know, his-and-hers."

Zoey arrived at Claire's school fifteen minutes late and fifty bucks poorer.

That was the going rate Thelma Thomason's lawyer charged for answering a simple question. After, of course, Zoey had cooled her jets in his crummy waiting room for over an hour.

Had Joe Donny Marlowe died within sixty days of Ms. Thomason's death, the bond would have reverted to her estate. Since he didn't, after all debts and fees were subtracted, his sisters would receive the change.

Life wasn't fair. Death could really screw you over.

Zoey's eyes scanned cliques and solitary students loitering on the low walls near the steps, clustered under winter-denuded trees and straying to the parking lot.

No Claire. No Laura Peters.

Rolling down the window and calling out an inquiry was verboten. Such a transgression would necessitate a midnight move to Tunisia, though it was only a matter of time before teenaged Tunisians got wind of it and shunned Claire accordingly.

Exiting the car to look for her was worse. Vesta was sort of exempt. Being a grandmother, she wasn't expected to know the anti-dorkhood rules, let alone abide by them.

To the west, a storm cloud flotilla along the horizon resembled an atmospheric bruise. The cold seeping through the floorboards was destined to get colder—as if anyone recalled what warm felt like by comparison.

Waiting was not Zoey's favorite pastime. It seemed she'd done nothing else all day—to scant effect and her cumulative aggravation.

Damn it. The kid used to hurtle out the door while the echo of the final bell was still reverberating in the hallway. Maybe Bella Donna Sewell tolerated dawdling; Zoey France Jones did not.

Patience, said Hank, in her head. Have some.

"Stick it, Westlake," she said to the dashboard. "Where the sun don't shine." Pivoting in the seat to look out the back, she yelped when a flushed, grinning face pressed the glass.

Panting for breath, Claire expertly performed the kick-push-pull-up maneuver required to open the passenger door. She threw herself on the seat, as if deposited there by a tornado. "Sorry I'm late."

Not good enough. "Where's Laura?"

"Cramps. Big time." The seat belt's buckle clacked. "She went home fifth hour."

Zoey started the car but didn't shift it into gear.

Presently, Claire fidgeted and heaved a groan. "Come on, Mom. Everybody's staring at us. I said I was sorry."

"Apology appreciated and accepted. Why you were late yesterday and today, I'm waiting to hear."

"Okay, okay. I'll tell you, but can't we just go?"

Zoey was braking for the stop sign at the corner when Claire said, "Promise you won't get mad?"

"No."

"Am I gonna get grounded?"

"Yes, if you don't start talking."

Squirms. Mouth noises. Trapper Keeper hugged like flotsam from a shipwreck. A protracted stare out the side window, similar to Bob and Fred's when their backyard bathroom was a dark, cold, drizzly place.

"I've been in detention and I've been late 'cause I can't leave the room until a teacher signs me out, 'cause if I do, I'll get suspended."

An internal tirade of obscenities, incomplete questions and disparagements imploded to a doleful, "Oh, Claire."

Detention explained her chronically absent backpack. Zoey's inquiries about the dearth of homework allowed a technically truthful answer. Claire had completed assignments while in solitary confinement.

"I should have told you, okay? And I would have, except with Grandpa and everything... Well, like you needed something else to be upset about, you know?"

Zoey glanced sideward. "Sweetheart, upset before, upset now. Same thing, different day. Get it?"

"Yeah." Claire hooked her fingers over the notebook. "I am sorry." She switched on the radio.

Zoey switched it off. Deeming a reflexive "What did you do this time?" as harsh and judgmental, she amended it to, "Why are you in detention?"

"Because—hey, how come you didn't turn back there?"

"I don't have time to drop you at home." Glaring into the rearview mirror at a tailgater, Zoey prompted, "Because..."

"The tardy note you gave me Tuesday didn't fly. So where are we going?"

"Schlomo's office to meet your grandmother. What do you mean, it didn't fly?"

"The assistant principal said I had too many tardies already." Voice recalibrated to a kindergarten wheedle, she said, "Do I have to go with you? I can hang out at Laura's, or at the mall, or—"

Zoey couldn't resist saying, "Yes, you could have, had I known about the detention and warned Gram that I might be a few minutes late."

The sulk of champions ensued—a muffled huff and puff and blow-your-house-down hissy, culminating in, "I hate you."

"Spare me, okay?" With one eye on traffic, Zoey devoted the other to counting off block numbers on buildings, many of which were absent. "I've had a lousy day, *I'd* rather hang out at Laura's than another freakin' attorney's office and it pi—uh, it irks me to no end that notes from a parent don't fly with your stupid assistant principal."

She veered into the left-turn lane. "Which I'll be delighted to discuss with him, first thing tomorrow morning."

The seat belt prevented Claire's bolt upright from becoming a head-butt against the roof. "No, Mom. Please don't call him. It's okay. Tomorrow's Friday. Just let it go."

Eyes riveted on two lanes of oncoming vehicles, seeing a gap so she could make a left turn, Zoey realized that she never reacted in a daughter-approved manner.

"What do you mean, another attorney's office?" Claire asked.

Uh-oh, Zoey thought. *Did I say that? Yes, I most certainly did, when my temper overrode my brain.*

If all else fails, the mother's unwritten handbook advised, play deaf and/or incapable of talking and driving simultaneously.

Claire's tone brightened. "Cool enuff. Gram's going to fire that dweeb Schlomo, isn't she? That's why she wants you there. For backup."

The car's springs heehawed over the bump between the street and parking lot's apron. "No-o-o." The truth was unavoidable. "He wants to talk to her—to us—about the arraignment tomorrow."

Two slots were available near the door. The first was designated handicapped. The other was Zoey's. Claire said, "Gram ought to fire him."

"Honey—"

"She really should, Mom. See, if Grandpa doesn't have a lawyer, they can't do the arraignment. It's, like, in the Constitution. Or maybe it was the Bill of Rights."

Zoey looked at her as she cut the ignition. "Who told you that?"

"I saw it on this show about the Menendez brothers. They kept ditching lawyers, so the judge had to postpone the trial, over and over again."

Zoey's expression must have betrayed her dubiousness, for Claire added, "It was on PBS."

Smiling despite the welling pressure in her chest, she cradled her daughter's chin, wishing she had the power to promise blue skies and rainbows ahead; that her grandfather hadn't deserted her, too, though it surely must feel like it; that everything would be fine again soon.

"I love you, baby."

"Love you, too, Mom." Easing away, Claire pulled up on the door handle. "We'd better go in. Gram gets flustered when you're late."

The law offices of Schlomo, Parks, Chilton & Hong were neither flashy, nor as fusty as the dreary strip center Thelma Thomason's attorney shared with a print shop and a floor covering store.

Minimalist plumbing wholesaler was Zoey's take on the decor. Vesta beckoned from a hallway leading from the reception area. She looked at once exasperated, happy, apprehensive and hopeful, as only mothers past a certain age can.

"How's Daddy?" Zoey asked.

"Feeling cooped up and restless, I'm told. Walking around the room, sitting up in the chair to take a gander out the window."

"I wanted to come by to check on you and him. Time got away from me. Again."

"I'm just so glad you're here now. The girl at the desk just told me Mr. Schlomo would be with us directly." She hugged Claire's shoulders. "You don't mind waiting out here, do you?"

"Yes."

"That's my girl," Vesta said, oblivious to Claire's reply. "Just find yourself a magazine to read and we'll be back before you know it."

Claire's eyes smoldered with resentment at the demotion from participant on Monday to tagalong today. Like a general happy to defer to the commander-in-chief, Zoey tipped her head a fraction toward Vesta and mouthed an apology.

Claire whirled and strode into the anteroom. Farther down the hall, a door slammed. A bearded man in dudgeon miles higher than Claire's pushed between Vesta and Zoey.

"Of all the nerve." Vesta tottered back a step, sputtering, "I swan, it's been one thing after the other, this entire livelong day."

"Tell me about it."

"Well, first off," she said, starting down the hall, "I don't know what that mechanic did to my car, but I had to stop for gas this morning—twice in one week, I'll have you know. Then my hair appointment completely slipped my mind and when I called, Darla couldn't fit me in, because she just up and took the afternoon off yesterday—can you believe that?—and rescheduled those appointments for today."

Vesta paused to peer around a doorjamb, then marched into the office. "Now here we are, but Mr. Schlomo isn't."

The visitors' chairs were chrome-and-leather slinglike affairs well back from a boomerang-shaped birch and bottle-glass desk. With a matching credenza, hutch and bookcases, ebony plank floor and silved-globed lamps and torchieres, the room was as warm and inviting as the He Just Left's walk-in cooler.

Vesta sniffed. "You'd think as much as he charges, he could afford a rug and nicer furniture."

Unwilling to educate her on the outlandish cost of industrial ugly, Zoey said, "Before he graces us with his presence, Cl—er, somebody told me that if you fired him, the judge would have to postpone the arraignment."

Vesta's arms encircled the purse on her lap, as though they were at a bus stop. Her coat, she left on. So did her daughter. "Fire him? Why would I want to do that?"

"How about to keep Daddy out of jail? And give the police more time to find Marlowe's killer."

An indulgent smile softened the creases bracketing her mother's mouth. She didn't say, "There, there sweetheart," or "You'll understand when you grow up," but she might as well have shouted it. "Even if Mr. Schlomo wasn't the best defense attorney in town, lawyers don't refund their retainers. I can't afford him, much less someone else."

That fact qualified the adage, "Money can't buy

happiness." Having it by the vault-load financed revolving representation. Granted, in celebrity cases such as the Menendez brothers' and O.J. Simpson's, judges set bail at megamillions or refused it altogether, but the rich and not-so-famous seldom spent a night behind bars.

Those who did, Zoey thought, didn't share cells, mess hall meals and showers with homicidal thugs and gangbangers, either.

"The prosecutor is after Charlie's doctors to discharge him," Vesta continued, "but he's just making noise. I'm told it'll be Monday at the earliest, if taking him to court and back tomorrow doesn't cause a setback."

"But—"

"Lest you forget, prosecuting attorneys are elected by popular vote. Regardless of what Charlie's accused of, how would it look if a sick old man was discharged too soon, then took a turn for the worse?"

"Politics?" Zoey's voice slid up an octave. "You're relying on an election next fall to keep Daddy out of jail?"

"Being locked up in a hospital room is worse than jail. We can't visit him. Can't talk to him on the phone. Can't write him letters, telling him how much we love him and believe in him."

Vesta opened her purse and took out a framed snapshot. It was taken in the backyard on a sun-drenched afternoon, likely on impulse—perhaps by a friend or neighbor with a new camera, or to burn the last couple of frames on a roll of film. She and Charlie were looking at each other laughing, his arm around her waist, her head against his shoulder.

"You miss your daddy. Claire misses her grandpa." Vesta's thumbs stroked up and down the frame's metal sides.

"I miss the love of my life. My best friend. My husband." Her breath hitched, but she swallowed down the heartache before it engulfed her. "In all our years together, I haven't passed a day without talking to him, at least on the phone. There've been less than a handful without seeing that grin, hearing him laugh, or saying 'I love you.'"

Eyes slanting to Zoey, she said, "The time will come when all I'll have of those things I cherish are pictures and memories. If I had a million dollars in my pocketbook and ten under the mattress, I wouldn't spend a red cent to keep him where he is now."

Vesta hugged the photograph to her chest again, either as a poor but tangible substitute for the man it portrayed, or a shield against her daughter's reaction.

In light of the circumstances, she might have been surprised, even angered, to hear the selfish thought drumming in Zoey's mind. *I want to love somebody like that. To miss his grin, his laugh, his voice so much I'd choose a bulletproof-glass shield between us on visitors' day over an impenetrable wooden door.*

She wasn't aware Osbert Schlomo had entered the office until he sat down behind the desk. His vanity hairstyle and wiry build were less impressive than in newspaper photos and impromptu TV interviews on the courthouse steps. Neither captured the intensity of a childhood underdog turned intellectual bully.

He said he was glad to make Zoey's acquaintance, inquired after Claire, then leaned his forearms on his desk. "The reason for this meeting is to ask for your help. As I told you at the outset, Mrs. France, your husband's position has not been favorable. New, and I daresay compelling, evidence supporting the fact that the Jiffy Stop robbery was Mr. France's fourth, not the first, has strengthened the charges against him."

"Whether it was four or forty," Vesta said, "Charlie didn't hurt that young man."

Zoey laid a staying hand on her mother's arm. "Go ahead, Mr. Schlomo."

"Numerous conversations with my client, including a consultation earlier this afternoon, have been virtually one-sided, other than his adamant refusal to enter the plea I recommend."

Schlomo paused, his shrewd hazel eyes shifting from Vesta to Zoey. "In my opinion, considering Mr. France's age, serious health issues and treatments he's undergone as a result, I sincerely believe pleading innocent due to diminished capacity is the only course of action available to us."

"Diminished capacity?" Zoey repeated, an icy sensation flooding through her. "Meaning what, exactly? That my father is insane?"

"Not insane, Ms. Jones. That his faculties are impaired as a result of his heart condition and side effects of the medications prescribed to treat it."

The attorney smiled and rested a hand atop a foot-tall stack of files on the corner of his desk. "I've become rather an overnight expert on cardiac medications and oxygen therapy. Forgive my bluntness, but it's a wonder your father could summon the mental acuity to dress himself in the morning."

"Some days he couldn't," Vesta allowed, quietly.

Schlomo nodded. "My recommendation, distressing as it may sound in legal terminology, is an excellent compromise. If the judge agrees, instead of a trial, Mr. France—"

"It's Doctor France," Zoey said, acid lacing her tone. The attorney's calculating gamesmanship was off-putting.

"Sorry," he said to Vesta, visually excluding Zoey from the apology. "The court will require competency examinations—basically, a series of questions and simple tests that can be administered in his hospital room. The results will be reviewed and if our plea is substantiated, the judge will remand Doctor France to a psychiatric facility."

Schlomo sat back in the chair, as if awaiting kudos for a particularly splendid gift. "Bottom line? He will be spared the experience of awaiting trial in jail for an indeterminate period. And we'll certainly alleviate the risk of imprisonment by verdict."

Vesta said, "Would we be allowed to visit him there?"

"Absolutely. The psychiatric community believes interaction with family members is critical to a patient's treatment and recovery."

She gasped, her expression suffused with hope. "How long would he have to stay there? Where would he go afterward?"

"I daren't predict the first, though if the sentence seems inordinately harsh, we'll appeal. Upon his release, he would be allowed to come home, where he'd meet periodically with a court-assigned therapist."

Vesta whirled in the chair, her purse toppling to the floor. "Did you hear that, sweetheart?" She clutched Zoey's arm, her fingers like steel bands. "It's an answer to our prayers. Everything is going to be all right."

"No, Mom. It's not that simple. Listen between the lines. Diminished capacity, insanity—who cares what you call it? It's legalese for 'the devil made me do it.'"

Vesta recoiled. "What's wrong with you? A few minutes ago, you wanted me to fire Mr. Schlomo to delay your daddy going to jail. Now he doesn't have to—"

"That's right. Except his get-out-of-jail-free card is telling the judge he robbed those stores and murdered Joe Donny Marlowe. It's a guilty plea with an excuse attached."

Zoey glared at Schlomo. "That's why you need our help, isn't it? To convince Daddy to go along with it. I'll bet there's a secretary standing by the intercom waiting for us to dictate a statement to that effect to cover your ass and give you more ammo when you talk to my father again."

Vesta said, "Is that true?"

"Mrs. France, I—"

"Answer me. Yes, or no."

"Well, yes, a member of my staff is available—"

"Fine." Vesta took a deep breath, her eyes defiant and unwavering. "Send her in."

19

The last time Zoey's doorbell had rung at 7:13 a.m., a guy in navy coveralls had informed her that he was repossessing Stuart's car and hers at the behest of the leasing agency.

It was too early for Bella Donna to fetch Claire, who was in the shower, actively emptying the hot water tank. Vesta's invasions were through the back door. Barring a tornado or Armageddon, Darla was still hammering her snooze alarm at fifteen-minute intervals.

Bob and Fred were on point, panting and doing the greyhound version of the Hustle. Look at the doorknob, look back at Zoey. Doorknob, Zoey, doorknob, Zoey, their eyes telegraphing, "If we only had opposable thumbs, we wouldn't need you, slowpoke."

Shutting one eye and squinting the other gave a peephole view of four knuckles clenching the top of a small paper sack. Written on it in black marker was, Got Coffee?

A rueful downward glance at her flannel men's pj's, the beloved brown-and-orange robe and her pink bunny slippers didn't transform them into a silky lace peignoir and stiletto mules.

With a shrug, she pulled open the door and said, "Trick or treat."

There was some comfort in Hank looking almost as ratty and disheveled as she did, albeit more color-coordinated. A five o'clock shadow was fourteen hours old. Yesterday's sweater-vest was untucked, his shirt rumpled and his slacks stained and baggy.

"I'll swap two breakfast sandwiches for a cup of coffee." He waggled the bag. "Hash browns on the side."

Zoey sniffed bacon, fried eggs and cheese congealing on toasted English muffins. "Deal."

While he waded dogs as eager to snatch the sack as they were to be petted, she turned off the stove burner under a simmering pan of cinnamon milk no longer destined to become oatmeal.

Taking a mug from the cupboard, she filled it from the carafe and set it on the table. "Okay, that's it. Go away."

Hank paused, a sandwich in hand and a befuddled expression on his face.

"Not you," Zoey said, laughing. "The four-legged people-food addicts." Pointing at Bob, she added, "He's the one you have to watch. Elbows on the table here are mandatory. It's the only defense against high-speed plate-pickers."

"I'll keep that in mind." Motioning at a tumbler of apple juice, he said, "Claire hasn't left for school, has she? I brought enough for all of us."

The predicted, dreaded battle to attend the arraignment hadn't materialized. No doubt, as the assistant principal had rejected Zoey's "family emergency" excuse, Claire presumed leaving early would prompt a suspension.

"She'll be out in a minute," Zoey said. The pipes under the house juddered in response to the faucets shutting off in the bathroom. "I'd better warn her there's a man in the house, though."

Hank caught her arm and kissed her till her bones rattled louder than the plumbing. "Good morning, darlin'."

Staggering backward, lashes fluttering as though glued together, Zoey grabbed a chair back for balance. Her inner slut, which she'd never known existed until Hank had kissed her at his apartment, whispered, "Do me. Do anything you want to me, right here, right now, on the floor."

When her eyeballs rolled forward again and her vision cleared, his grin suggested she might have said it aloud and though he wasn't appalled by the idea, he preferred the slow, sensual seduction plan he'd outlined Wednesday night.

Body aflame with more than embarrassment, she hastened from the kitchen and knocked on the bathroom door.

"I *am* hurrying, Mom."

Finding the knob locked—huge surprise, that—Zoey said, "Hank's here. He brought breakfast."

A two-beat silence. "Yeah, okay, that's cool. Don't let the boys get mine. I'm, like, *starving*."

Returning to the kitchen, she found Hank about to sneak a chunk of hash brown patty to Bob. Fred the Timid stood behind, salivating copiously.

"Ah-ah-ah. No potatoes for them. Greyhounds don't digest them, or onions, very well."

"Sorry, guys. You heard her." Transferring the bite to his own mouth, Hank swallowed, then said, "I've bet on a few races but never been around greyhounds before. Any other rules I ought to know about?"

"Never, ever let them out the front door, unless they're leashed. If they bull through and escape, run *from* them, don't chase them, or the race is on. Otherwise, just relax and let 'em steal your heart, which shouldn't take more than about five minutes."

"Too late for that." He extended his elbows to protect the rest of his food. "I gave mine away before I was old enough to shave regularly."

A sensation, like lightning captured in a bottle, fluttered in her solar plexus. Determined not to let the effect show on the outside, she simpered, "Why, Lieutenant Westlake, you do say the sweetest things."

Unwrapping his sandwich, he held it aloft, gazing upon it as Midas would a gold bar. "It's true. I wasn't more'n a coupla years older than Claire, the first time I sank my teeth into one of these babies. Been hooked on 'em ever since."

"Smart-ass."

"Takes one to know one," Claire said from the doorway.

She was dressed in a U.S. Open souvenir T-shirt of her father's, holey acid-washed jeans and the scuffed, outgrown Doc Martens Zoey thought she'd pitched before the move.

"Nice outfit."

"Yours, too. Goes great with the monster hair."

"Funny. It's twenty-seven degrees outside, not

seventy-seven, and the weatherman's predicting sleet."

"The school's a hundred-and-seven. I've got a coat. With a hood. Okay?"

Claire beamed a smile at Hank. "Mom said you might come by last night. Glad you waited. Gawd, I love breakfast sandwiches."

"Unfortunately, I'm not somebody you can set your watch by," he said, chuckling.

"You didn't miss anything. Me and Mom and Gram made pizza and watched *Fried Green Tomatoes* for about the eighty-sixth time."

"Hey, I happen to like that movie. It figures, dispatch nabbed me just as I was leaving the cop shop to come here."

"For what?" Claire asked.

He glanced at Zoey and grimaced. Reading it as a cue for a topic change, she said, "Let the poor guy drink his coffee, will you? Besides, your ride will be here in a little bit."

The diversion worked splendidly. Her daughter demurred a full five seconds before asking, "You don't get a day off very often, do you?"

"It seems that way, sometimes." His hand hovered above her hash brown patty. "I'm overworked, underpaid and seriously underfed."

"Yeah, but I'm a growing child." Moving the patty to the opposite side of the place mat, she broke it in half, then devoured it, as though its nutritional value didn't teeter between nil and not much. "What would you say if I told you I was thinking about becoming a cop? Or maybe a lawyer."

Zoey almost choked. An architect was Claire's last-stated metier, with graphic designer a close second. When did cop ascend from three-letter obscenity to potential career? If Claire was jerking Hank's chain, she had the appearance of sincerity down pat.

"When I was a kid," she said, "I wanted to be a veterinarian like Grandpa, except biology's my worst subject and I nearly puked when we had to dissect a baby pig."

"I'd rather you didn't go over to the dark side," Hank said, "meaning law school. Since you're eating breakfast, I'll leave the other at saying law enforcement's not a job for the weak of stomach."

"Yeah. Car wrecks and d.b.'s and stuff."

Zoey frowned. "D.b.'s?"

"Dead bodies," they answered in unison. Claire went on, "But you get used to it after a while, right?"

"Nope." Hank ambled to the counter for the coffee carafe and refilled his and Zoey's mugs. "The day I do is the day I'm done."

Claire chewed that, as well as the rest of her food. "Can I ask you one more thing?"

Hank's nod confirmed her right to ask him anything was equal to his right to not answer.

"See, I don't want to, you know, like, focus on being a cop, then find out I can't, because—well, Mom probably told you already—I got arrested for shoplifting in K.C. and I'm wondering if it's true that people with criminal records are SOL for applying to the police academy."

Zoey stared at the girl who bore an uncanny resemblance to her daughter. Her voice was identical. Ditto her mannerisms and habit of speaking in paragraphs when nervous or excited. Except if Zoey didn't know better, she'd swear a Claire Jones clone had hatched from a pod during the night.

Two car horn taps sounded outside in the driveway. "There's Bella Donna. Up and at 'em."

"She'll keep a minute." Hank pushed his coffee cup aside and leaned closer to Claire. "This is the first I've heard of any trouble with the law, sugar, and it means the world to me that you told me yourself.

"As for a juvie arrest, well, your mom doesn't even know this, but when I was fifteen, I got collared for stealing a car and joyriding. That makes you and me even. Keep the score tied and nobody can stop you from being anything you want."

The horn honked again, longer, insistently.

"Gotta go." Claire jumped up, hesitated, then planted a smooch on Hank's cheek. Running to grab her coat and notebook from the couch, she hollered over her shoulder, "Bye, Mom, love you, tell Grandpa I love him, too," and slammed the door behind her.

Zoey sat motionless, wishing she could push a button for an instant replay of what had just transpired, yet certain she still wouldn't believe it.

"Yo. Earth to Zoey."

"Funny you should say that. The kid who just blew out the door was definitely a Martian."

"Why? 'Cause she thinks she wants to be a cop?" He chuckled. "This one's feeling ten feet tall and impressed to his toenails by her guts. Again. No hypotheticals for her. Just lay it out straight."

"Yeah. That's what has me worried." Frowning, she took a sip of coffee. "Immaturity with random outbreaks of good behavior, I can handle. Maturity with random outbreaks of snide, I'm not ready for."

"Maybe not, but you can't fault her for inheriting the France backbone. There's worse things than being as strong and stubborn as her mother and grandmother."

"And if she goes wacko someday, we can blame that on Daddy's side of the gene pool." Zoey propped her chin on her hand. "Mom's, too, depending on your perspective."

Hank balled the paper wrapper Bob attempted to filch from the table. "I'll bite. What happened last night, besides pizza and a chick flick?"

"That was a smoke screen, so Claire couldn't pester us about the meeting with Schlomo. Abridged version, he wants Daddy to plead diminished capacity. Daddy probably told him to go—ahem—screw himself. Schlomo asked me and Mom to persuade him, in official statements, to cooperate. She did. I refused."

Hank shifted. "I'm not sure I ought to be privy to this."

"Why not? We'll all know the result in…" A look at the clock torched the food she'd eaten. "Five lousy, freakin' hours."

She went on, "Schlomo made it sound as if 'diminished capacity' was legalspeak for 'abracadabra' and Daddy might be home by suppertime. He played Mom and I detest him for it, but I couldn't argue. Honestly, I can't decide whether to hope Daddy wasn't swayed, or hope he was."

Hank's thumb traced the embossed image of Snoopy and Woodstock on his coffee mug. If ever the twist and churn of mental gears were visible on a man's face, they were on his.

"What do you know that you're not telling me?"

Presently, he said, "That I'm pretty well fresh out of leads and too damned tired to recognize one if it jumped up in front of me."

Continuing to memorize the mug's design rather than meet Zoey's gaze, he said, "I finally connected with Marlowe's sisters, Renee and Tammy. They've been living together since Tammy split with her husband after Christmas. I had the pleasure of telling them their little brother was dead and buried."

Zoey gasped. "They didn't know?"

He shook his head. "Sad, but true—not to mention common—that nobody gets down and dirtier than a family feuding over money." A snort, then, "Sibling rivalry and spite disguised as money is nearer the truth. Stir in the repercussions from the fire and 'estranged' shines a rose-colored light on the aftermath."

Zoey skimmed back her hair into a tumbleweed ponytail. "God, I feel so sorry for them. And for you, for being the one to tell them. Especially on the phone."

"Not my favorite part of the job. Which is gonna kill me, sure, if I don't catch a shower and a few z's."

He stood, stretched, grimaced and growled like an arthritic lion. "By the by, Trudy's mother put the kibosh to talking to her, until they're home from the lake. I couldn't argue with her, any more than you could with Vesta."

"How about Andrew?"

"That, I intend to mull after a nap." He motioned for her to fill the arms held out to her, and she did. "Him being sicker than a dog didn't abet the interview. He didn't duck anything, though, or hedge."

Zoey tipped back her head, saying, "Whatever happens this afternoon, happens. The arraignment isn't the end of the world, or the end of the investigation."

He looked away, but not fast enough to hide the torment she'd seen in his eyes, time and again. He was hiding something from her. She was sure of it. Something about her father. Or had Hank lied? Said Charlie denied killing Marlowe, when in truth he'd confessed? The Hank she knew wouldn't do that. But Detective Westlake?

"There couldn't be a worse time to tell you," he said, his voice husky and strained, "but the scared, selfish kid inside me says this second chance may also be my last. I love you, darlin'. I always have. No matter what might happen today, or tomorrow, any and every day for the rest of my life, I will always love you."

He kissed her desperately, crushing her body to his, as though he could somehow join them together and protect her from harm.

Moments later, he was gone, leaving her reeling. Leaving her to again whisper into a whirling, empty space, "I love you, too, Hank. I always have. Always will."

Force of will propelled Zoey upward, raising her head from the dampened pillow, pushing her off the bed and onto her feet. It led her down the hall to the bathroom, stripped her naked, nagged her into a scalding hot shower.

The water coursing down her face, cleansing the tears from her scratchy, swollen eyes, didn't revive her as much as it reminded her that clocks and calendars make no allowances for heartache, confusion and fear.

Hank loved her. She should be overjoyed, at least the part of her that had secretly wished to hear those words for as long as she could remember. How could they ring so sweet and true and echo like the bleakest, blackest omen?

"Trust?" she sneered, tilling drops of shampoo into a fragrant, frothy veil. "What's he hiding behind mine? He can't take and take and not give, except in bits and pieces and then only on demand."

Segregating anger from the emotional tumult was liberating. Marvelously comprehensible, clarifying, purposeful. Ignoring the phone—the third call she'd received since Hank left—she took the first suit she touched from the closet. Undergarments, blouse, shoes—all chosen at a glance. Makeup by rote. Hairstyling courtesy of a blowdryer, round brush and Mother Nature.

After letting out the dogs, she replenished their water dish, noting the answering machine's message light wasn't blinking. Whoever had called hadn't wanted her very badly, either.

After congratulating Bob and Fred for being

good boys and warning them that panty-hose shredding was not a treat-earning activity, she donned her coat and grabbed her shoulder bag. Then the phone stopped her in midstride.

The psychic hum that insists a call is important yields a telemarketer at the other end about two times out of three. Giving in, regardless of the odds, is the human frailty upon which that industry was founded.

"I'm glad I caught you," Vesta said. "Mr. Schlomo just phoned from the hospital. The arraignment has been postponed until Tuesday."

Zoey gripped the receiver. "Why? Has something happened to Daddy?"

"Oh, no, sweetheart, he's all right. Steaming like a teakettle about the delay, I'm told, but fine otherwise. The judge's brother passed away last night, so everything has to be rescheduled."

Whatever happens, happens. The gift of time was also a millstone.

"I'm sorry, Mom. This means another four days of waiting."

"Yes, well, I was thinking, if there isn't anything else you need to do, maybe we could have lunch together."

"I'd love to. Anywhere you want to go, my treat."

"Wonderful! I'll be there in a few minutes."

"Hey—hang on a sec. I have to call Darla to tell her she doesn't need to pick up Claire and Laura at school. Want me to ask if she can work you in this afternoon?"

"Lord, yes. I look like the wreck of the Hesperus."

The reference, one of Vesta's favorites, was repeated to Darla.

"What's a Hesperus?"

"The name of a schooner in a Longfellow poem. One of the lines is, 'And he saw her hair, like the brown sea-weed, on the billows fall and rise.'"

"A boat with hair?"

"I'll explain later," Zoey said. "I have to lose this suit, hose and heels before Mom gets here."

Dressing down to navy slacks, a turtleneck under a gray V-necked sweater and lace-up boots, she remembered the "my treat" promise and checked her billfold. Six dollars and coins indicated a swing by the He Just Left for her paycheck, then by the bank to cash it.

As she gathered her coat and shoulder bag from the bed, another phone call stopped her in her tracks. "Hello?"

"My car...it's not in the lot. It's been stolen."

"Settle down, Mom—"

"Settle down? Didn't you hear me? Somebody's stolen my car. In broad daylight."

Thinking she'd mistaken where she'd parked, as she had earlier that week, Zoey asked, "Have you called the police?"

"I am as soon as we hang up."

"No, no, just wait till I get there, okay? I'm on my way."

A misty medley of snow, freezing rain and sleet was falling as she drove across town. Traffic was medium-light for a midday Friday. Restaurants with delivery service prospered during cold, slushy lunch hours when people were reluctant to go out, or hoped to clear their desks early and head home.

At the hospital, Zoey cruised the lot's aisles, figuring she'd spot the sedan, then pick up Vesta and take her to it. Uncertainty crept in the farther the search ranged from the main entrance. Her mother was an early riser and such birds nabbed the choicest parking places. Wheeling around, she muttered, "Pay attention this time. It's here. You were just looking left and passed it on the right."

Ten minutes later, she was at the pay phone in the hospital lobby punching in Hank's cell phone number.

"Westlake."

"It's Zoey. I know this isn't your thing, but you're the only cop I know. I'm at the hospital. Mom's car has vanished from the lot. We think it's been stolen."

"You're sure it isn't there. It's easy to—"

"Positive. I circled three times, including the employee's section."

"Is she okay?"

"Reasonably. You're aware the arraignment was canceled?"

"I just heard." A three-second pause, then, "Instead of hanging around there, go on home. I'll meet you at your house."

Wincing, Zoey said, "I dunno—"

The line went dead. "Control freak," she snarled into the mouthpiece.

On the way, Vesta nattered incessantly about crime running rampant, Blytheville's transformation from a peaceful town to a city of hoodlums, and the fact that the world in general was going to hell in a handbasket.

"Of course, that car's been giving me fits all week. Maybe I ought to count my blessings, it being insured and all, but if you ask me, I think somebody monkeyed with it at the impound lot. It wouldn't surprise me if that hippie-looking fella in charge decided he'd..."

A sound like abacus beads clacking together inside Zoey's head reduced Vesta's voice and the windshield wipers' thumps to white noise.

Wednesday, the car wasn't where her mother swore she'd parked it. Yesterday, at Schlomo's office, she'd complained about refilling it for the second time that week—except she'd used Zoey's car Monday and part of Tuesday. Today, it goes missing?

"...wouldn't be the least bit surprised—"

"Do you still keep a spare key in a magnetic holder under the front fender?"

"A wha—? Oh—well, yes. Charlie's forever locking his keys in the car and locksmiths cost the moon."

Zoey clenched her teeth to keep from wrenching the steering wheel in half. Detention, my ass. As she turned the corner onto Crocker Avenue, a crimson aura haloed everything, including the unmarked police car at the curb.

"Goodness, Hank's already here," Vesta said. "Of all people, he should know better than to drive so fast. Especially in this kind of weather."

Once inside, she hastened to the kitchen to brew a pot of coffee "to chase away the chill."

"Yeah, right," Zoey muttered, halting in the living room. "Like I'm not on the verge of melt-down." She looked at Hank. "I'm slower on the uptake, Detective Joyride, but I think I know why we're here and not at the hospital."

"Claire."

"Yep. Helluva leap from stealing flip-flops to your grandmother's Ford. It helps, though, when an ignition key is stuck to the fender well."

"Before we rush to judgment, how about if you give the school a call, while I keep Vesta company in the kitchen?"

Confirmation that Claire Jones had not attended classes since Tuesday was Zoey's in two minutes, tops. "How about Laura Peters? Has she been absent as well?"

"I'm sorry, Mrs. Jones. That information is not available to anyone other than Laura's parents or someone they've authorized."

Meaning, yes indeedy, Laura had ditched, too.

"One more thing," she said. "Understand, I'm not shifting any blame onto you, but I do wish you'd contacted me when the absences began."

"We did—or attempted to. Several times, according to the log. No one answered."

"No one—" Zoey blew out a sigh. "I have an answering machine. Is there a rule against leaving a message?"

"We'd rather speak to parents directly, but we quite often leave messages. Might I suggest checking your machine? Perhaps it isn't working properly."

Calling the Peters's home took precedence.

Bella Donna Sewell was astounded at the idea of Laura skipping school, much less being a party to grand theft auto. She reluctantly agreed to find out and call Zoey back.

Hank appeared in the bedroom doorway, coffee mug in hand, which he handed to her. "How's it going?" he asked, as she took a sip of the scalding black brew.

"Claire's been AWOL since Tuesday. I'm waiting to hear whether Laura Peters has been riding shotgun."

"On the way over, I spoke with the traffic division. No accident reports involving a car matching the description."

"That's a relief." Sleet scoured the windowpanes like windblown sand. "So far, anyway."

"Vesta's pretty upset. She divined why you asked about the spare key before the coffee finished perking."

Zoey massaged her brow. "Why, Hank? Why'd she do this? For attention? Some kind of screwball revenge against the system because of her grandfather? Or me? Or you? Or...what?"

The phone rang, startling her. Hot coffee sloshed into her lap. Biting back curses, she felt the sting dissipate when Bella Donna said, "Laura hasn't been at school since Tuesday, either."

Zoey derived no satisfaction from being right.

"It's my fault," the housekeeper went on. "I should have been suspicious about dropping them at the hospital to visit Doctor France before your mother took them on to school. I just thought it was so sweet of the girls to do that."

It would have been, Zoey agreed, if my father were allowed visitors. The hospital wasn't that far from the school. After returning the car, they must have walked or run the distance; hence, the detention excuse for not quite making it in time for the final bell.

That explained the disappearing backpack. Claire had stowed it in her locker so she wouldn't have to run with it on. She couldn't retrieve it, for fear a teacher would see her in the virtually empty hall after school.

The creativity and complexity of the pre-spring break was further revealed when Bella Donna reported their phones' ringers were always switched off while Laura's brothers were napping, but that the voice mail function had also been disabled.

Zoey looked at Hank. "I have a feeling my answering machine is disconnected from the phone line."

Bella Donna said, "Those little scamps thought of everything, didn't they?"

Nouns more colorful than *scamps* burst in Zoey's mind. "They don't know we're on to them, so I'm going to the hospital and wait for them to sneak back with the car."

"Is there anything we can do?" Bella Donna asked.

"Not at the moment. If I think of something, I'll let you know."

She almost collided with Hank and Vesta in the

hallway. "The line from the phone to the machine was unplugged." A muscle in his jaw spasmed. "Claire had no way of knowing the arraignment was postponed, did she?"

Zoey and Vesta exchanged glances. Vesta said, "Do you think that's why she took my car? So she could go?"

"No, no, this started Wednesday morning." Realizing what Hank's question implied, Zoey felt the blood drain from her face. "Wherever she went today, she intended to bring back the car before Mom left for the courthouse."

"That's my guess."

Suddenly, playing hooky seemed as trivial as swiping cookies from a jar. What had she been doing for two and a half days? In February, no less.

Too cold to hang out at a park, or anywhere outdoors. Everybody knew the mall's security guards were unofficial truant officers. From personal experience, Zoey knew that two teenagers loitering on a school day didn't attract as much attention as they thought, but they felt as if flashing neon arrows pointed at them everywhere they went.

That damned backpack nagged at Zoey. No, not the backpack. The notebook Claire constantly lugged, as though it were surgically attached. Whether she had had it when she left for school that morning, Zoey couldn't recall.

Whirling, she opened Claire's bedroom door. The untidy space smelled of perfume, a murky goldfish bowl, dirty clothes and moldering food.

"What are you looking for?" Vesta asked.

"Her Trapper Keeper, specifically. Otherwise, anything and everything that might tell us where she's been all week." Zoey assigned herself the closet. Her mother started pawing through dresser drawers. Hank looked through piles on the floor, then moved to the bed.

Had it not been stashed in a corner under a mound of stuffed animals, the portable tape recorder Zoey found wouldn't have aroused her curiosity. Its unlabeled cassette was stopped at midspool.

Zoey pressed the play key. "Drugs. Buy low, sell high." Over a TV laugh track in the background, Darla's muffled voice and her throaty chuckle were clearly audible.

"A drug deal gone sour is a fast way to get dead, too."

"Yeah," Darla said, "but…Joe Donny was a nice guy. Not that his radio wasn't short a few frequencies, but drugs?"

Vesta turned. "What in heaven's name…?"

"Wednesday afternoon. Darla and I were talking at the kitchen table. Claire had the TV up so loud, she couldn't eavesdrop."

Trembling as though palsied, Zoey looked at Hank. "It was a ruse. She left the Trapper Keeper on the table when she got a snack. The tape recorder was zipped up inside."

He laid a stack of photocopies beside her. "I found these under the bed. Explains why the papers in Thelma Thomason's file were out of order."

"Oh, dear God."

Moving closer, he showed her a credit card receipt charged to Thena Peters. Pages and pages of printouts from so-called Internet detective sites. A sheaf of genealogical material, telephone numbers, reprinted obituaries.

The fear in Hank's eyes nearly stopped Zoey's heart. Claire and Laura hadn't just been chasing a murderer.

They'd found him

20

Seventy-four percent of abducted children later found murdered were killed within the first few hours of the kidnapping. The statistic droned in Hank's head. Pedophiles accounted for most of those tragedies. That possibility, remote though it was, couldn't be ruled out in the Claire Jones/Laura Peters disappearance.

Forty-five minutes ago, Central Point of Contact had relayed by fax a Missouri AMBER alert activation. Local television, radio and cable broadcasts were sounding the Emergency Alert System's eight-second, ascending octave that crescendoed with a drumbeat.

Radio stations interrupted regular programming with Claire's and Laura's physical descriptions, the make, model, color and license plate number of Vesta's car, and a hotline number. That information crawled continuously across the bottom of countless television screens.

Thousands of pairs of eyes were now aiding the search launched by municipal, county, state and federal law enforcement agencies. Would the next reported sighting be another false lead? Would it initiate a rescue? Or would it be the shattering end to every parent's worst nightmare?

Time raced and stood still.

The unmarked car's wiper blades smeared frozen and fluid precipitation across the windshield, blurring and distorting the outside world like a hallucinogenic high. It was just past midafternoon, but many oncoming vehicles' headlights were on. Too soon, the hazy false twilight would fade to darkness, further diminishing visibility. The thick, sodden air would muffle sound, skew its direction.

Hank looked at Zoey, arms hugged tight to her chest, her face as pale and rigid as porcelain. Shivering, despite the hot, dry air blasting from the heater vents.

She should be home with Vesta, Darla and her uncle Al. Should be waiting for the phone to ring, a knock at the door. Protocol, procedure, good judgment, even compassion dictated a degree of separation from the search.

Save locking her in a jail cell, though, she was along for the duration. His only choices were having her in his car, or dealing with her riding the back bumper in hers.

They both were struggling to climb up from the bottom of an emotional well. A radio signal emitting from the global positioning chip embedded in Laura Peters's cell phone had pinpointed an address east of town. Tearing Code 3 to the location, they had converged with police and emergency medical units…on a FedEx drop box. It was stationed, of all places, outside a convenience store.

"We'll find them," Hank said.

"I know." A hand reached out, seeking his. Her head continued to pivot, her gaze constantly scanning left to right. "Soon."

His fingers closed over hers, the coldness of her skin impervious to his touch. "The techs will process that phone and the box's handle for prints. Whoever chucked it in there may have outfoxed himself."

A mathematical improbability wasn't the same as a lie. Excluding Laura's and, likely, Claire's prints without comparisons to go by would be difficult. Identifying any others, virtually impossible. Latents seldom triggered an apprehension. They confirmed involvement in a crime, after the fact.

The log of incoming and outgoing calls might provide a clue, though. The perp wouldn't be the first to forget that wireless communications don't dissipate into the ozone.

Hank's hand moved from Zoey's to answer his own cell phone, lying beside him on the seat.

Chichester said, "Got a weird one for you, Loot. An Ace Hardware store employee just called the hotline saying the girls bought a leaf rake, a shovel and a package of paper lunch sacks this morning."

"What time?"

"Right at nine o'clock. They were waiting outside in the car when the store opened. He's pretty sure they were alone. At least, he didn't see anybody else in the vehicle."

"That's all they bought?"

"Yep, and they paid cash. Two crisp, new twenties. I contacted the officer at the Peters house. Mrs. Peters's ATM card wasn't in her wallet. She checked with the bank. A fifty-dollar withdrawal from a kiosk two blocks from the hardware store was made at 8:47 a.m."

"Is that the only one?" Hank asked.

"So far. The bank flagged the account. They'll notify us if there's any more activity."

Hank repeated the gist of the call to Zoey but didn't mention the paper bags. Their purpose was clear to him. Claire's interest in law enforcement included a short course in basic evidence collection.

"A rake and a shovel?" Zoey said. "What on earth for? I mean, to dig with, obviously, but for what? Where? Ye gods, the ground's been frozen for months."

"Damned if I know." Hank braked for a traffic light. The time of the transactions piqued his interest. "If they meant to have Vesta's car back to the hospital by noon—earlier, to be on the safe side—they had a specific dig site in mind. A place unlikely to be observed or arouse suspicion."

Zoey groaned. "Which could be anywhere in the whole freakin' county."

"Yeah, but the timing narrows it some. They were at the store at nine. Let's allow fifteen minutes to find what they wanted, pay the clerk and hit the street.

"Claire's smart. She didn't know the arraignment was postponed. If I were her, I'd've planned to return that car by 11:30. She'd assume Charlie would be transported to the hearing well before 1:00 p.m., and that Vesta would leave then, too."

"Yes, but that's still a two-hour-and-fifteen-minute window." Tensing, Zoey peered at a medium-blue sedan approaching an intersection—a two-door Dodge, not a four-door Ford.

Sifting haystacks for a needle would be easier on the nerves. Isolating a particular blue car from the veritable thousands suddenly rating notice was maddening—and exhausting. Each sighting spiked adrenaline, the effect cumulative and infuriating.

They were again moving with traffic. Hank's mind and senses compartmentalized, balanced essential tasks: maintain vigilance, monitor the radio, interpret new information, avoid a collision or keelhauling a jaywalker.

"Let's knock the window down to two hours, flat," he said. "Claire wasn't burning asphalt. She'd be extra careful. Stay below the speed limit, yield to yellow lights instead of bulling through."

"What if she did? We can guess and by-golly that time frame till we're hoarse." Frustration rived her voice. "We still don't know where they went and sure as hell don't know where they are now."

A tear trickled from the corner of her eye. It hurt to see the glisten zigzag down her cheek, but Hank said nothing, willed himself not to touch her. She needed the release. The illusion of privacy to let go a trifle.

Teenagers and vehicles didn't vanish into thin air. It just seemed that way, with scant specifics and those several hours old.

Investigations always worked in reverse. The analogy to piecing together a puzzle was valid, but more akin to a crossword than a jigsawed photo of puppies wrestling in a basket.

Searching Claire's and Laura's bedrooms and

lockers at school proved a wash. So had questioning classmates, teachers, the school's librarian and the public library's staff.

The nature of their disappearance was unique. Elements of runaway, lost child and child abduction added myriad complications.

In most instances, lost or abducted children left point A bound for point B, but never arrived. The facts established a geographical starting point and a time factor, and concentrated potential witnesses.

Claire's and Laura's apparently secret agenda negated that. Point A was the hospital, onward to the ATM, then the hardware store. Point B was known solely to them. Where they ventured from there, if they did, when, in what direction, and whether in Vesta's car, a presumed abductor's, or on foot, was as yet impossible to determine.

Hank was mentally triangulating the section of Blytheville within a presumed twenty- to thirty-minute drive time of the hospital when Zoey asked, "Can I borrow your truck?"

He glanced sideways. "My truck? Why?"

"Your apartment's closer than my place. Otherwise, I'd go there to get my car." The heater's fan was switched to low speed, the temperature toggle adjusted downward. "Going with you back to the police station is... Look, there's nothing for me to do there, except get in the way."

"Zoey..."

"Please?" Then, "Okay, fine. Forget it. I'll call a cab to take me home."

Hank's cell phone rang. In the same instant, dispatch announced on the radio channel dedicated to the AMBER alert, "BOL vehicle located. Airport, long-term lot, Aisle 5, center. Vehicle unoccupied."

Accelerating, kicking on the siren, dashboard and grill lights, Hank grabbed for the cell phone. As expected, it was Chichester.

"I'm already en route," Hank said. "Who's at the scene?"

"Airport security. A patrol unit's three minutes out."

"See ya there." Hank dropped the cell phone and keyed the radio's microphone. "This is David 10-57. Inform the en route to the airport to glove up and pop the BOL vehicle's trunk. Otherwise, do not touch. Clear."

"10-4, David 10-57. Clear."

"Also, contact Search and Rescue's K-9 unit to meet us that location, ASAP. David 10-57, clear and out."

Rehooking the mic, he said, "Appears your cab ride'll have to wait."

"That can't be Mom's car. I don't think Claire knows Blytheville has an airport, much less where it is."

A guttural cry wrenched from her throat. "She didn't drive it there, did she? Oh, God, the trunk. You told them to—"

"It's a precaution." His grip tightened on the steering wheel. "Harsh as this sounds, you wanted to be in the middle of this and I let it happen. I can't pull punches and do my level best to find your daughter, too."

Paradise should have a special corner for citizens who gave right-of-way to emergency vehicles. Veering between Samaritans and the oblivious, he gunned a left turn onto the four-laned Airport Drive.

Above the engine roar and screaming siren, Zoey said, "Thank you. I needed harsh. This isn't about me. Panic won't bring Claire and Laura home."

Hank's gut twisted. "I didn't mean—"

"Yes, you did. Now shut up and drive."

An airport security guard manually raised the cross arm barring access to the parking lot. The group milling around the sedan's gaping trunk lid gave Hank reason to breathe again. They wouldn't be talking and gesturing casually if the bodies of two murdered girls were inside.

Zoey promised she'd stay in the car, before he parked alongside a three-wheeled Cushman used during security sweeps of the airport's perimeter. The cart's dingy plastic weather shields obscured her view of the scene.

Staring at the paint cans, trays, cardboard cartons, tackle box, tote bags and typical junk crammed inside Vesta's trunk, Hank was simultaneously relieved and alarmed.

"What do you think, Loot?"

"They didn't hop a plane, that's for damn sure. Doubtful our perp did, either. Airport and shopping mall lots are prime real estate for ditching a hot car."

"Good news is, there's no blood visible inside. Since she's met Claire Jones, Sergeant Ash is reviewing the videotapes." He pointed at a security camera mounted on a light standard. "Between that one, the one at the parking gate and the ones scanning the entrances and exits, we ought to get the bastard's mug shot somewhere."

Hank turned up his collar against the biting wind and ice pellets funneling down his neck. "We're not gonna have a full court press, this time."

Lonnie nodded. "We pulled too many units off the street to that fuckin' FedEx box. Now that you're here, me and the security dude'll canvass skycaps and cabbies."

"The tow truck's en route?"

"Yeah." Lonnie jerked a thumb at the approaching Search and Rescue van. "Good luck. Whatever that is."

Twenty minutes later, Hank trudged back to his car, barely containing the impulse to hammer the roof with his fists.

He'd delayed jimmying open Vesta's car doors to preserve any scent contained inside. Unlaundered garments worn by Claire and Laura had been sealed in plastic bags and distributed to primary members of the search team. Search and Rescue's scent dog was given a T-shirt of Laura's, since Claire routinely occupied her grandmother's car.

As expected, the dog indicated Laura's presence in the front passenger side, but not the back seat, floorboard or trunk. Nor Claire's. That showed their abductor hadn't restrained them, and transported them elsewhere in Vesta's car.

Which rendered the absence of blood, interior scuff marks and signs of a struggle or captivity meaningless. They'd exited the car of their own volition, taken the tools and package of lunch sacks with them and not returned to it.

To no avail, Hank searched the interior for a parking lot ticket. One of the other officers finally ascertained the time the car passed through the gate by checking the security tapes. At 3:32 p.m., the driver held a gloved hand beside his face, obscuring it from the camera lens, as he took the ticket from the machine.

Numerous frames showed his progress across the lot, into the terminal and out the adjacent doors into a designated smoking area. Medium height and build, sunglasses, sock hat, gloves, dark-colored scarf wrapped bandit-style, ski parka, slacks, wingtip shoes. The perp was aware of eyes in the sky and had disguised himself accordingly.

The minute the tow truck delivered Vesta's car to the cop shop, the crime lab would tear it apart with tweezers, inside and out. Unless the abductor had autographed a sun visor, though, forensic evidence might someday convict him but wouldn't identify him.

Summoning what remained of his ability to spin a litany of negatives into positives for Zoey's sake, Hank slid into the seat beside her. Keying the ignition, he flashed a Judas smile. "Okay, well, truth be known, most of what we derived from that little exercise is a whole lotta nothing."

"But—"

"Better than our hell-bent trip to the convenience store, though," he went on, refusing to make eye contact. Not with a woman who could see right through to his soul. "We do have a search area."

Zoey swiveled on the seat. Her face expectant, she clutched the sleeve of her coat like an anchor. "Where?"

He tried to temper her excitement. "We don't have a decent description of the man who left the car, yet. But he hailed a cab outside the terminal's secondary entrance. The driver took him to the Residence Inn."

"A motel?" Her head wagged. She appeared baffled by the news.

Hank's cell phone intervened. They were overdue for a break. He prayed this was it, then brought the handset to his ear.

Lonnie said, "So much for hunches. Andrew Kelly's assistant said he drag-assed himself to the board meeting this morning but was so sick that the prez sent him home."

Despite the intro, Hank's heart skipped a beat.

"The assistant finagled a three o'clock doctor's appointment for him. He's still at the Galloway Clinic, awaiting X-ray results. The chatty Cathy receptionist says the doc suspects a sinus infection's turned into pneumonia."

"You're sure he was there at three?" Hank asked.

"Patients have to sign in on arrival, Boss. His John Hancock's on the sheet at 2:55 p.m."

Hank cursed silently for allowing himself to dress a banker of medium height and build and above-average intelligence in a ski parka, hat, sunglasses and gloves.

"I thought I had a suspect," he told Zoey. "Chichester just disavowed that notion. As for the motel, the cabbie dropped his fare at the rear block of rooms, not the entrance. The manager and a couple of uniforms are knocking on doors, but nobody thinks the suspect was a guest."

"An out-of-towner doesn't make much sense," Zoey agreed. "But who notices a guy getting out of a taxi at a motel?"

"Exactly. There's a chance an accomplice picked him up, but that's doubtful. If he isn't working solo, why take a cab from the airport?"

"Then he left the motel on foot. Question is, how far did he walk? And where?"

No, Hank thought. That presumed the perp was holding Claire and Laura Peters hostage. Searchers would fan out from that location, but Zoey was too smart to focus her attention on the suspect for very long.

Sooner or later, she'd realize the real question was what happened to the girls before the perp disposed of Vesta's car at the airport?

Judging by the effort the abductor had made to conceal his identity and whereabouts, there was only one logical conclusion a cop, or the mother of an abducted child, could draw.

21

Zoey sat with her eyes closed, her hands folded in her lap, trying to wrap her mind around the idea that her daughter was dead. That the man who'd crushed Joe Donny Marlowe's skull with a hammer had murdered Claire and Laura Peters, then dumped their broken bodies, like vermin snared by a baited trap.

Between bursts of static, voices from the police radio dispensed hotline callers' tips, responding officers' disaffirmations, the ever-changing locations of roving patrol cruisers.

Hank hadn't spoken for several minutes. What really could he say? Lend false hope to boost her spirits, until the probable became fact? Offer condolences and comfort, as though words could give either?

Except shouldn't a mother know her child was gone from her forever? Feel a rent widen to a chasm, whether she admitted its existence or buried it deep within?

Fourteen years ago, in spite of the doctor's learned opinion and negative lab tests, Zoey had been certain she was pregnant. Weeks had passed before she'd tested positive. Not until Claire was born six-and-a-half months later and undeniably full-term did the obstetrician admit Zoey had been right all along.

Life. Death. There had to be more to each than the physical. Without proof—undeniable, indisputable—if she could even think a sentence containing her child's name and the word *dead*, as unemotionally as a network newscaster, she must be a monster.

The sensation of floating, swaying, rocking on air was marvelous, as if she were bundled in a cocoon impervious to presumptions and probabilities and premature grieving.

Her shoulder struck something hard. The jolt of pain startled her.

"Zoey." Hank's voice hurt her ears, forced her eyes wide open.

The car was streaking along a narrow road, the headlights carving a tunnel in the darkness. Flanking trees reached down their branches like gnarled, icy fingers.

Her stomach mimicked the bubble light's revolutions, the grill lamps strobing the slushy pavement, the whirling beams from the vehicles behind them careening off the side mirror.

Heels digging into the floorboard, Zoey gripped the shoulder harness, the swaying, rocking motion now pushing a bilious, acrid taste up her throat and into her mouth.

Hank glanced at her, his face greenish and ugly in the dashboard's ambient light. "A hotline caller—a highway department salt-truck driver—

reported that a black SUV pulled out in front of him from Riverbend Park."

Struggling to comprehend, Zoey nodded to indicate she'd heard and was listening.

"He wasn't sure of the time. Between two and three, give or take. Didn't think much of it till he got back to the maintenance shed and saw the AMBER alert on TV."

During warm months, Riverbend Park was a hundred-acre slice of paradise for picnickers, swimmers, canoeists and, after sundown, party-hearty teenagers and college kids. In winter, it was a desolate, forbidding place with rusty log chains strung across its access roads and the river hibernating under a thin skin of ice.

Hank went on, "Your dad thought he saw a dark-colored SUV parked outside the Jiffy Stop Sunday night, then said it might have been a Dumpster. A Dumpster made sense, since there's one in the lot."

If you'd only believed him... Zoey stopped herself. Visually searching for a specific, medium-blue sedan was one thing. An SUV that might be anything from black to cobalt to deep maroon? Impossible.

Hank keyed the microphone. "Chichester, go north toward the river. Ash, you go west. Dunleavy, also west, but along the river. I'll take east, then swing back westerly on the river side."

His eyes flicked to the rearview mirror. He switched the radio's dial. "This is David 10-57. Where the fuck's that ambulance?"

A pause, then "10-30, David—"

"Screw my language, Terry. Answer me. "

"Ambulance en route. ETA, two minutes. Clear."

"Tell 'em to wait by the pavilion. Clear and out."

Muttering under his breath, he tossed the microphone on the seat.

The chain barring the park's main entrance was down. Zoey steeled herself for the sharp, sloping turn. Hank lowered the side windows, then yanked up the spotlight bolted beside the windshield.

Slowing the car to a crawl, he reduced the radio's volume. "Listen and look. Hear anything, see anything, say so. Don't hesitate."

Pulse pounding in her ears, Zoey unhitched the seat belt to crane her head out the window. Frigid air thick with frozen mist glazed her face. Pea gravel strewn with acorns and twigs crunched under the slow-rolling tires. She tented a hand under her nose to divert the vapor streaming from her mouth.

From behind them, a siren wailed, then halted. The ambulance. *Please, God, don't let it be too late.*

The spotlight's beam strafed trash barrels. Pierced shadows and brushy thickets. Washed across picnic tables bolted to concrete slabs. Split around tree trunks and boxy barbecue pits.

Signs on metal posts prohibited littering, alcohol consumption, skateboarding, fireworks, unleashed dogs. Not child abductors, or murderers.

Intermittently, Hank keyed the PA system. "Claire. Laura. It's the police." In the distance, their names echoed back from the west, the north, the river valley.

Panic slithered up Zoey's chest, hampering her breathing. *For God's sake, why don't you answer them? You're here. I know you are. I can feel it.*

The laborious, winding track dropped gradually toward the river, a greenish-white slash beyond the trees.

Following a bend in the path, Hank steered left, the beam scouring the bank.

Zoey blinked. Swiped the moisture from her lashes. Squinted into the darkness encroaching on the park's wire fence line. "Stop. Back up. Shine the light there." Pointing frantically, she shouted. "No, no, over there."

"Sweet Jesus." Hank flipped on the siren to summon the ambulance and search vehicles.

Zoey ran for a dilapidated picnic table. A side plank atop the bench seat had deflected the light, rendering a mounded object beneath the table almost invisible. For the merest instant, as the beam retreated, she spied a yellowish glint.

Wrenching the board away with her bare hands, she dove over the seat, sinking her fingers in Laura's stiff blond hair, then Claire's auburn waves. They were curled in fetal positions, as though fast asleep. "You're all right. Everything's gonna be all right. Wake up, please, please, you've gotta wake up."

Hands gripped the back of Zoey's coat, her jeans, lifting her up and away from the table. "No, no, lemme go. It's Claire, it's Claire—"

Staggering backward, Hank fell to one knee, taking Zoey down with him. Bear-hugging her to his chest, he panted, "Hypothermia. Can't touch her. Rips the tissue under the skin. Movin' her too fast could stop her heart."

Pummeling his arms with her fists, she shrieked, "You son of a bitch, let me go. She's my daughter."

Head pressed tight to hers, his voice gentle but firm, he repeated the same phrases over and over again, adding, "They're alive, baby. We've gotta stay back and let the EMTs take care of them."

Slumping against him, she looked toward the table, where paramedics were lying prone beneath each bench. Shadow figures squatted nearby, holding Maglites, carefully slicing the nylon rope binding the girls' wrists and ankles together. Another ratcheted a crowbar under the table's base, tearing it free of the anchor bolts.

Dunleavy and Lonnie Chichester hoisted it, then cast it aside as though it were weightless. Kneeling over the girls, Eve Ash and one EMT blew warm air into Claire's and Laura's mouths. The other sprinted back from the ambulance carrying blankets, metallic quilted sheets and backboards. Hank helped Zoey off the damp ground and onto her feet, her hand clenched in his. "They have to take things real slow. Warm them from the inside out. Move them as little as possible."

A second ambulance arrived, plus four police cars. Behind them were news-crew vans bristling with antennae and satellite broadcast equipment. Tiny snowflakes cavorted in the glaring onslaught of headlights.

"Dunleavy," Hank shouted. "Tell those crews to back off. Videotape only, on my orders. No live feeds. We'll debate the First Amendment later."

"Yes, sir."

Chichester motioned for the incoming officers to stay put, then moved beside Zoey and Hank. "The girls are coming around a little. You can see for yourself, ma'am, as soon as they're up on gurneys."

To Hank, he said, "Appears that junk heap of a table saved them. Kept them mostly dry. They were still shivering, too. Not much, but enough to kick up some body heat."

Compelled to ask but terrified of the answer, Zoey asked, "Did he hurt them?"

"It doesn't look like it. We'll know more once they're transported to the E.R."

Hank squeezed Zoey's hand. "If Ms. Jones doesn't mind, I'll leave the best part of this job to you. Telling Laura's folks their daughter's safe and to meet the ambulance at the hospital."

Armed with Zoey's number to notify Vesta as well, Chichester was grinning from ear to ear as he strode to his car for his cell phone.

"You're one helluva guy, Westlake."

Hank looked down at her. His face was grave with fatigue, his skin as gray as weathered stone. The corners of his lips pulled into a wan smile. "Passable fair, at best, as long as the bastard who did this is still on the loose."

"Ms. Jones." A paramedic waved her over. In a low voice, he said, "She's a tough kid. They both are. I think they'll be fine, once their core temperatures are up to normal."

"Can I see her now?"

He nodded. "We'll load Laura into the ambulance first. You're welcome to ride up front with us, if you want."

"Yes. Yes, I do, thank you."

"I'll warn you, she's pretty loopy. If she says anything, don't be frightened if it doesn't make sense or you can't understand her. That's to be expected. In fact, it's a good sign. If her core temp had dropped a few more degrees... Well, thanks be to God, it didn't."

Cautioning Zoey not to touch her, he hastened away to help prepare Laura for transport. Both girls lay on their sides, shivering violently, wrapped in blankets like hooded mummies. Claire's complexion was as translucent as a newborn's, her pupils dilated and mouth bluish.

"Hi...Mom."

Bending down inches from her face, whispering, "I love you so much," seemed horribly inadequate, when Zoey ached to hold her, kiss her, stop the awful tremors racking her body.

"Love, too." Claire sounded as though her cheeks were packed with cotton. "Hank?"

"He's here, sweetheart. He—"

"Hank?"

More loudly, Zoey said, "Yes, baby. Hank's here."

Rocking forward, the blanket shifting, as though she were fighting to shrug it off, she moaned, "Hank, Hank."

He must have heard, for he rushed up behind Zoey. "I'm right here, sugar. You're gonna be—"

"Her dad. My pocket. Here."

Closing the gaping blanket, he said, "Easy, now. We called Laura's—"

"No, pocket. Pock-et."

"Settle down, Claire." The paramedics waved Zoey and Hank back. "Time to take you for a ride."

"No-o-o." Teeth bared and clenched together, she shrieked, "Please, Hank. Take it in my pocket."

"Don't worry, ma'am." The paramedics lifted the gurney, rather than rolling it across the uneven ground. "She's just a little confused."

"I don't think so," Hank said. "Hold up a second."

Unlatching the strap at Claire's hips, he gently peeled back the blankets. "Coat pocket?"

"Uh-huh."

He pulled out a charred scrap of fabric. Tucking back the covers, he resecured the strap. "I've got it. Rest now, okay?"

"Yeah."

Zoey stared after her. "What's so important about a filthy old rag?"

"No tellin'." He glanced over his shoulder, then snuck a kiss. "Better hurry. I'll be along shortly."

The bay doors shut with a double thump. Zoey jogged to the cab and climbed inside. When the EMT closed the side door, the oversized mirror captured Hank's reflection.

One hand was balled into a fist. Eyes narrowed, he seemed to be looking through the ambulance, rather than at it.

Hank welcomed the zing of adrenaline accelerating his heartbeat, dissolving the cobwebs in his brain. There'd be time for recriminations later. Plenty of them.

"Dunleavy, I want a rep from every radio and TV station, front and center. No microphones. No cameras."

Turning, he pointed at Chichester. "Get a uniform to tape this scene, pronto. Twenty feet out from that slab. You give the area a once-over with the Mag."

Lonnie's expression was dubious. Rightfully so. With all the vehicle and foot traffic, if ever there had been any evidence, it was long gone. Come daylight, they'd scour every inch, nonetheless.

"Sergeant Ash." Aware of the approaching reporters, Hank jotted a name in his notebook and ripped out the sheet. "I need a street address, phone, vehicles registered and full description, like, yesterday."

"You got it."

A paunchy, goateed TV reporter sneered, "Who died and made you God, Westlake? You can't—"

"Be quiet and listen, all of you. Time, I don't have. We've got a suspect who snatched two girls and left 'em here to freeze to death. He came within a whisker of succeeding.

"Straight out, I need your help. Obviously, nobody's gonna scoop the competition tonight. The public's right to know can wait awhile. If you stopped the AMBER broadcasts and crawlers, get 'em back on and keep 'em on, till you hear otherwise."

"On whose authority?" a female reporter inquired.

"Mine." He didn't have it. "Anybody already report the victims were found, alive and well?"

Goatee and two others nodded.

"I'd be much obliged if you'd air an update stating the victims' condition is unknown."

Another journalist, a Peter Jennings wannabe, piped up. "Are you using us to trick this...suspect?"

Hank hesitated. "Yes, sir. That's exactly what I'm doing."

Whether they'd cooperate or turn his plea into a sound bite wasn't worth speculation. For certain, they wouldn't slink off with their antennae between their legs. With luck, deploying all units at once from the scene and in different directions would leave them scratching their heads.

"Anything else, Lieutenant?" Dunleavy asked.

"Spread the word that we'll hit the streets together, and watch what goes out on the radio. I'll tell dispatch who's going where by phone."

Dunleavy grinned. "Think it'll work?"

"No, but it'll slow them down some."

Eve Ash returned the sheet torn from his notebook with the information he sought written on the back. While scanning it, Hank recalled the question he'd posed yesterday to Andrew Kelly, as well as the response.

What kind of vehicles do you and your wife drive?

Escalades, Kelly had said. *Paint color, white diamond.*

Would he have lied if Hank had said *own* instead of *drive*? A white Escalade was registered to Andrew and Margery Kelly. Had he also lied about his wife and daughter being out of town and used Marge's car this afternoon?

"Sarge, I've got another little job for you. Track

down the Caddy dealership's owner, shop foreman—anybody you can raise to confirm whether this black SUV registered to Kelly was in for repairs this week, when, for how long and whether they loaned him a white one to drive."

Lonnie, who'd materialized beside him said, "What's up, Loot? Unless there's two Andrew Kellys, the one at the bank was at the doctor's office most of the afternoon."

"Which is why you have a half hour to get your hands on that sign-in sheet with his signature on it. If it's the type most of them use, I'll bet a hundred bucks cash that he wrote over someone else's name in that three p.m. time slot with that fancy fountain pen of his, then took a seat.

"Later, when a nurse or the receptionist noticed him, he said he must have been in the men's room at three, when they called him for the appointment."

Lonnie scrubbed his jaw. "The Residence Inn isn't more'n a few blocks from the Galloway Clinic."

"Explains why he was still waiting for the X rays when you checked up on him, too."

"Yeah, but I'll bet a hundred back at ya that without a search warrant, they're gonna scream doctor-patient privilege."

"We don't have probable cause yet, much less that kind of time. Just tell them it'd be a crying shame if the media got wind of them protecting a murderer and child abductor."

Dunleavy pulled the final assignment—interviewing the highway department salt-truck driver and showing him photos of every late-model SUV on the market.

"After," Hank added, "you and I swap vehicles."

"Bait and switch?"

"You got it." His gaze flicked to the news vans, which hadn't budged an inch. "You're a mite shorter than me and not near as devil-dog handsome, but switch off the dashlights and you just might pass."

The eight-unit motorcade left the park like a starter's flag had dropped at Daytona. Dunleavy was in the lead, then Chichester and patrol units without special assignments at the rear. Light bars and academy-trained drivers were terrific advantages. Any reporter dumb enough to pass the trailing officers cruising at the speed limit would star in a justifiable traffic stop.

Hank kept the cell phone hot all the way to town and then some. Dispatch was informed of units' out-of-service status and their locations, and of the switcheroo. The E.R. confirmed Claire Jones and Laura Peters's arrival. Both were responding well to warm water submersion treatment.

Energy flagging, the mosquito whine in his ears a reminder of how long it had been since he'd seen a pillow, let alone buried his face in one, he wheeled into a fast-food drive-thru lane and ordered coffee and a sack of fries.

"You must be new," the girl at the pay window teased. "The police can have anything they want here, no charge."

Ones in bona fide patrol cars, anyway, Hank thought. *If I'm wrong about Kelly and the chief busts me down to traffic division, I'll save a fortune on bad food and worse coffee.*

This afternoon's aborted hunch had to play out. If he was wrong, there was no doubt that Andrew Kelly, his boss and the Bank of Blytheville's board of directors would file suit against Hank and the department.

All he had was a brave, half-frozen teenager's ramblings no sane judge would accept as a witness statement, and a torn piece of fabric stained with what looked like blood.

22

The warm water flowing from the faucet onto Zoey's hands felt wonderful. The hospital restroom's tiled walls and floor magnified her sigh like an echo chamber.

The doctors said Claire and Laura might be hypersensitive to cold for the rest of their lives. A small thing—infinitesimal. They could have lost their toes, their fingers, their ears to frostbite.

Another miracle, second to finding them alive at all.

Feeling a clutching sensation in her chest and tears welling up in her eyes, she bent and splashed water on her face. For all she'd been through, much of it as yet unknown, Claire hadn't cried. Not once. When she did, they'd cry together. In the meantime, she'd be strong for Vesta. Cope the old-fashioned way. The only way her mother knew how.

As for her father, he'd required sedation when the game show he'd been watching had been interrupted by the AMBER alert and Claire's and Laura's photos had filled the television screen.

Nobody had thought to warn the hospital. Vesta had even expressed relief to Darla and Al that

Charlie was isolated from the world and blissfully unaware that the granddaughter he adored had been abducted.

Later, when he awoke from the first dose of morphine, the nurses and his doctors swore the girls had been found and that they were just three floors below him, being treated in the E.R. He didn't believe them. They'd switched on the TV to prove it, realizing too late that the stations were still broadcasting the alert via a crawler at the bottom of the screen.

Zoey shut off the water and moved to a paper towel dispenser to blot her face and hands. Lifting her hair, she massaged her nape with the coarse, damp sheet.

The door swung open. Gasping, she tottered backward, her nerves too frayed and brittle to absorb the slightest jolt. Tailbone colliding with a sink basin, she yelped. Then she recognized Laura's mother. "Thena," she said with a bizarre little laugh. "Ye gods, you must think I'm an idiot for bouncing off the ceiling like that."

"Your mother said you were in here." Scarlet blotches flared on Thena Peters's cheeks. Her mouth twisted into a vicious sneer. "From the very start, my husband tried to tell me that daughter of yours was nothing but trouble. Did I listen? Oh, no. I thought Laura would be good for her. Can you believe that?"

She advanced a step. "I felt sorry for Claire. New girl at school. No father. Mother tending bar till all hours at that sleazy dive downtown."

"That's enough, Thena." Chin jutted, Zoey

pulled back her shoulders, hoping to halt the quaver in her voice. "I know you're upset. You have a right to be—"

"A right to be? That's rich, coming from you. Laura never got into any trouble—*none*—until she started hanging out with Claire. What is that? A coincidence?"

Another step. "Lying. Cutting school. Stealing cars, money. God knows what else your kid's talked her into doing. Are you too stupid to understand that my daughter almost died tonight, because of that smart-mouthed little slut? Even a goddamn cocktail waitress ought to be able to comprehend that."

Pinned against the sink, Zoey yelled, "Stop it. Back off. I mean it."

"Oh, yeah? What're you going to do? Hit me in the head with a hammer?" Moving to the door, she clenched the handle, a retching sound tearing from her throat. "You tell Claire not to call my house and not to ever, ever come near my daughter again. If she does, she'll be keeping her grandfather company in jail."

The hiss of the door's pneumatic hinge followed by the dull thud of its edge settling into the jamb, reverberated in the quiet room.

Knees buckling, Zoey crumpled onto the cold, hard floor, buried her face in her hands and sobbed.

Hank eased off the accelerator for the turn into the half-circle asphalt drive at 5650 Buena Vista Lane. Close behind him were Chichester's unmarked, another attached to the crimes against persons unit and two patrol units.

Small spotlights hidden in the coiffed shrubbery softly washed the two-story house's block stone and rose-brick facade. Towering lancet windows continued the geometric theme, as did the shape of the double front doors' leaded glass inserts. A soaring portico brought to mind Monticello, as engineered by NASA.

A quarter-mil, easy, Hank estimated. Three-acre lot abutting the golf course not included.

The house was dark, other than the chandelier burning in the foyer and a crack of light shining through a second-floor window's drapes. Warrants in hand, Hank gave the uniforms time to jog around to the back of the house, then joined Lonnie on the herringbone-brick sidewalk.

Nodding at the headlights creeping down the street toward them, Lonnie said, "Now there's a surprise. Walter Cronkite could've followed us on foot if you'd taken it a tad slower on the way over here."

Hank moved to the door and thumbed the bell. "Don't begrudge them, kid. Keeping that alert on the air bought us a couple of extra hours."

"Think he'd have rabbited, if he knew the girls were okay?"

Motion swam beyond the opaque glass. Hank's gut tightened. "He snatched 'em, didn't he?"

Coachlights flooded the entry. Chichester's hand went to the service weapon holstered under his jacket.

The door on the left opened. Andrew Kelly was

dressed in deep-green silk pajamas. The robe over them was unsashed. His feet were bare, his hair sweat-dampened and disheveled. Cupped in his fingers was a crystal brandy snifter.

"I can't say I wasn't expecting you, Hank." A stiff smile appeared on his ashen face. "Come in, gentlemen."

Hank displayed the tri-folded papers. "One's a search warrant for the house and grounds. You're under arrest on two counts of kidnapping, child endangerment and charges related to the abduction of Claire Jones and Laura Peters."

The resignation on Kelly's face gave way to a curious look.

"Don't worry." Hank said. "We'll get to the second-degree murder by and by."

"Like about a minute after you're booked and your prints match up with the ones off the Jiffy Stop's back door," Lonnie said.

Ignoring Chichester, Kelly waved toward an adjacent room. "Let's take this discussion to the library. As I'm sure you know, I'm not a well man."

Hank's glance halted Lonnie's protest. Kelly submitted to being frisked for a weapon, then they followed him into a small, wood-paneled room lined with bookcases. Face now flushed and sweating vigorously, Kelly took a wing chair, Hank its mate and Lonnie the leather love seat.

Once Mirandized, Kelly waived his right to an attorney. His wry chuckle triggered a wracking cough. "You must not have had time to delve into my financial position. If you had, you'd realize I don't have the money for counsel."

He sipped from the glass, then eyed Hank. "I believe you could say the fat lady is singing."

"How much of that have you had?" Hank asked, indicating the brandy.

"Oh, I'm not impaired, if that's what you're asking. I'm in perfect control of my faculties. More so, I assure you, than I was Sunday night or this morning."

Lonnie hastily laid a tape recorder on the table between them. "That sounds like a confession to me."

Kelly stared off into the middle distance. "It was an accident. I despised Joe Donny, yes. He was truly one of the most stupid, fawning people I've ever had the displeasure to know."

"You argued over the money from Thomason's estate?"

"No. For months, I'd encouraged him to let me invest his share for him." He sighed. "I would have, too…"

"After you paid down your debts with it," Hank said.

"Of course. I suppose you'll know soon enough, I've been moving a few dollars from other accounts to stay afloat, until such time as I can reimburse them."

"As in, embezzlement?" Chichester said.

"It would have been repaid. To the penny. Eventually, Joe Donny's investment would have been to his advantage, as well."

The surreality of a drawing room mystery's final act had Hank's nerves jangling. Sure, arresting a perp of Kelly's social standing was a first. Bar rats, gangbangers, domestics and fatal shaken-baby syndrome were the norm. He just couldn't quite shake the sense of being manipulated.

"When the idiot told me the money was spent…gone…that he'd bought a ridiculously expensive ring for that trashy girlfriend of his and a tacky little tract house…"

Kelly's raspy voice trailed off, as though words were incapable of expressing his disgust. "Well, I was outraged, to say the least. Of all the stupid, frivolous— I honestly don't recall hitting him. The hammer seemed to fly through the air into my hand.

"The next thing I knew, he was on the floor, bleeding, and—obviously, I must have panicked. I vaguely remember running, getting away, then I was in my car and so sick to my stomach, I had to pull over and vomit."

He grimaced, his head shaking. "Horrible. Horrible."

Hank and Lonnie's eyes met. Which was horrible? The brutality of the murder, or being reduced to pitching his cookies in the bushes somewhere?

No question, remorse had taken a toll. Kelly's illness wasn't psychosomatic, but he wasn't a cold-blooded killer, either. Guilt ate at a body like acid, gnawing away from the inside out.

"What would have happened, if I'd come to you afterward?" he said. "Confessed to it then?"

"Hard to say, Andrew. A good lawyer might have plea-bargained down to involuntary manslaughter. Considering your standing in the community—"

"I'd have been ruined. My reputation, my wife, my daughter… We'd have lost everything. Good

God, Marge has never worked a day in her life. Can you imagine what this would do to Tiffany?"

His pupils blazed in the lamplight, like a photograph with an overbright flash attachment. "The audition I told you about in my office? Tiffany called a while ago. She got the walk-on, in that movie. She was so excited, she was talking gibberish."

"Lieutenant…"

Hank started. Detective Stan Hamilton, of the crimes against persons unit, stood in the doorway. In one gloved hand were the charred remains of a shirt's button placket. The other gripped a leaf rake, the price tag dangling from a plastic tie looped through the tines.

"My partner found the rake in the garage. The cloth came from the backyard, where it butts up to the golf course's out-of-bounds. Looks to me like somebody set a match to a brush pile."

"Good work," Hank said. "Sift those ashes and bag and tag everything you turn up."

Lips pressed together, Kelly stared down at his bare feet, resting crossed at the ankles on the patterned area rug. His shoulders shuddered as though he were crying, but his eyes were dry.

Chills, Hank supposed, from the pneumonia.

"Where'd you clean up, after you attacked Joe Donny?" Hank asked.

No response.

"You couldn't come home with blood all over you and your clothes. What if your wife or your daughter saw you come in?"

Silence.

"Me, I keep a couple of ties and a fresh shirt or

two at the office. Handy, in case I need to change and don't have time to swing by my apartment."

Leaning forward, elbows on his knees, Hank went on, "I'm guessing you do the same. Simple enough, to punch in the security code at the bank and slip in the private entrance. Nothing unusual for you to work late, go back to the office after dinner. I've passed by and seen your office windows lit up at night a hundred times."

Kelly remained motionless, but his gaze shifted to Hank.

"See, the difference between a cop and banker is, cops being low-rent, sport coat and dark pants kind of guys, we can get by in an emergency with a clean shirt. I figure a fastidious young exec like you keeps an entire suit in reserve. Spill coffee down the front of you, a glob of blue cheese dressing at lunch, and buddy, you're SOL. Can't do meetings wearing the jacket to one suit and trousers to another."

Chichester, picking up the need to double-team, said, "Once you were all spiffy again, you couldn't leave that bloody mess of clothes for the janitor. You're too smart to give cutting yourself shaving a shot as an excuse, but..."

He sucked his teeth. "Brain matter stuck to a man's shirt is just awful damned hard to explain, sometimes."

"Tiffany did see you, though, didn't she?" Hank said.

"Whatever you wore when you left to go to the Jiffy Stop, she saw you out back, burning a brush pile in a shiny, clean suit."

"Not something you see every day," Chichester taunted. "Enough to leave a kid wondering out loud about, clear into the next day at school."

"It wasn't Tiffany's fault. Claire Jones and the Peters girl are so far outside her circle of friends, they're invisible. How could she have known they were eavesdropping on her in the cafeteria?"

Now he was crying, tears rolling down his fevered skin, streaking the front of his robe. "When I came home from the office, they were digging in the yard. Said they'd snooped around yesterday. Promised me they wouldn't tell, but I knew they would. I knew they'd tell. The redheaded one came at me with the rake... I—I just couldn't bring myself to...hurt them. It'd be like killing my own daughter."

Images of Claire and Laura lying with their wrists and ankles bound and shackled to a picnic table—their arms and legs rigid from the cold, their faces bluish—scrolled through Hank's mind. With them came blind fury, a urge to strike back so powerful he barely contained it.

"No problem leaving them to freeze to death, though. Real fuckin' compassionate of you, Kelly."

"But there was no other way. No painless way. I thought they'd just go to sleep and then..."

"You'd be home free," Chichester finished for him. "France could take the fall for Joe Donny, 'cause what the hell. His heart's gonna kill him sooner or later, anyhow."

Hank stood. "I don't know about you, Lon, but I've heard about all of this I can handle for now."

Kelly looked from one to the other, his expression as vapid as if their discussion had centered on the weather.

"You're taking me to jail?"

"Yep. That's the next step on the dance card." Lonnie picked up the tape recorder. "Give our stomachs a chance to settle."

Kelly rose from the chair, summoning what dignity he seemed to think he had left. Gathering his robe around him, he said, "May I go upstairs to dress first?"

Chichester deferred to Hank. Ordinarily, he'd refuse, but the man was ill and the outside temperature was below freezing. Bastard might catch his death.

"Go with him. Don't let him out of your sight. Cuff him as soon as he's got his clothes on."

Kelly smiled. "I'll never hurt anyone else again. You have my word on that."

Hank waited in the foyer, hands shoved in his overcoat's pockets. Here and there on the lawn, the glow of tiny red lights was distorted by the door's thick glass. He couldn't hear voices but knew reporters, video cameras, live microphones and rubberneckers were assembled for the perp walk.

He could spare Kelly the humiliation. Order a cruiser to drive around back and escort him out that way. Confession or not, he was innocent until proven guilty in a court of law.

Maybe Hank's personal bias was again clouding his judgment, but too many people had suffered because Andrew Kelly hungered for a lifestyle— at least the illusion of it—he couldn't afford.

Joe Donny Marlowe. Charlie and Vesta France.

Claire. Laura Peters. Laura's family. Zoey. Marge and Tiffany Kelly. Marlowe's sisters. Trudy King.

I'll never hurt anyone else again. You have my word on that.

Hank spun around. Taking the steps three at a time, he was midway up the curving staircase when Lonnie screamed his name.

Kelly was sprawled on his back on the bed. Blood splattered the wall, streaks inching steadily downward. The crystal brandy snifter lay broken on the floor, shards glittered on the nightstand.

Blood pulsed between the fingertips Lonnie pressed to the gaping slash at Kelly's neck. "I was watching him. I swear to Jesus. He just sat down to put on his shoes."

The banker died at 10:39 p.m.

Name, Andrew Stephen Kelly. Five-eleven. A hundred-and-seventy-five pounds. Brown hair and eyes. In police custody at time of death on multiple charges.

Graduate, University of Missouri, B.A., M.B.A. Vice president, Bank of Blytheville. Board member, Blytheville Chamber of Commerce, Jaycees, Glen Oaks Country Club.

Survivors include his wife of fourteen years, Margery Theime Kelly, and beloved daughter, Tiffany Leigh.

He was thirty-four years old.

23

A few hours ago, the sun rising over the golf course had been a pretty sight. Not like it would be in April, mind you, when the bushes and trees were leafing out and the grass was greening, instead of straw yellow.

The wind had shifted to the south, pushing up warm air from the Gulf. The sun toasting it a mite as it traveled across Texas and Oklahoma was dissolving ice fangs clinging to power lines, fences and eaves.

Temperatures in the upper forties were predicted. A chill twenty-eight that night, then mid-fifties, maybe an even sixty, come midday Sunday.

That was Missouri for you. Cold enough to kill one day, warm enough to have folks thinking tomato plants and float trips the next.

Hank cocked a hip on Andrew Kelly's deck rail. Down below, numbered yellow markers dotted a blackened area shaped like a lion's paw on the lawn. Shuddering, he crossed his arms at his chest.

The French doors behind him opened. Lonnie stepped out carrying two go-cups of coffee. Steam curled out the holes in their lids.

"Where'd you get those?"

"Eve Ash stopped by on her way to work. She thought we could use some liquid breakfast."

"Nice of her."

"Sure was." Lonnie peeled off the lid and blew at the steam. "A cinnamon danish would've been, too."

Hank rolled his eyes. "Everybody about ready to call it a night? And a day."

"It's been both, that's for sure." Finding the chairs shrouded in canvas covers, he joined Hank at the railing. "If I hadn't fucked up—"

"Don't even go there. Kelly's mind was made up before we ever rang the bell. Just a matter of when and how."

They sat quietly for a moment, recriminating themselves, then Lonnie said, "Look, whether I did or I didn't, it isn't right for you to catch a three-day administrative leave, too. You were downstairs—nowhere near the bedroom—when Kelly cracked that glass on the nightstand. I couldn't stop him from three feet away."

Hank swiveled around and planted his feet on the weathered planks. "I was the ranking officer. My call to let him go up there. My responsibility, him coming back down in a body bag."

He sighed and set the cup down on the rail. It was the good stuff—fresh ground, a gourmet blend. Sinful to waste on a mouth that tasted like the bottom of a cesspool.

"From the get-go, this case has been one for the record book. Mistakes, volume A through Z." He looked at Lonnie. "All of them mine, kid. Not yours."

"Now who's beating himself up? If you mean Doc France, he looked a hundred-percent good for it, until what? Wednesday afternoon? Even after you questioned him, it was about eighty-five."

"Uh-uh. Two and two made five for me, almost from the start. I overcompensated on the personal angle. Tried so hard to be objective, I leaned too far the other way."

Shoulda. Woulda. Coulda. The guilt triplets.

Shoulda checked the vehicles registered to Andrew Kelly, before the interview at his office. At the latest, immediately afterward.

Woulda realized, had he been on his toes, that money was the key. Badly as Kelly needed it, he'd have been a fool to join in the lawsuit Marlowe's sisters filed against Thelma Thomason's estate. If they'd prevailed, he'd have received a quarter of the proceeds. If they lost, they lost. Either way, he saved a share of the attorney's fees and didn't risk alienating cousin Joe Donny.

Coulda listened to that suspicious voice in his head, that wondered why Andrew Kelly, big dog bank executive, would let Trudy King pay for his cousin's casket.

"What I'll never forgive myself for," he said, "was feeling hinky about Kelly and still missing every arrow pointing straight at him, after Claire and Laura disappeared."

"Arrows? Aw, c'mon, Loot. We didn't have jack-diddly to go on. Albert friggin' Einstein couldn't have divined a rake plus a shovel equals a killer burning evidence in his backyard."

Hank's chuckle held no trace of humor. "Remember the airport video? Tell me, who wears a ski parka with a pair of wool trousers and wing-tip shoes?"

Lonnie's brows met at the bridge of his nose.

"Granted, I caught the proximity of the motel where the taxi dropped Kelly to the Galloway Clinic, but not the clinic's proximity to Glen Oaks golf course. An easy walk home, even for a sick man."

"I threw you off there," Lonnie argued. "I checked his appointment time, not what time he actually went in to see the doctor."

"That little ruse with the sign-in sheet knocked a hole in my theory, when it should've reinforced it. Kelly's smart. A perp ducking every security camera at the airport and the taxi to a motel should have tipped me that we weren't dealing with a moron."

"Monday morning quarterbacking." Lonnie pushed off the railing. "Win, lose, or draw, it's never about the plays you made. Just the ones that fell short."

Hank watered the shrubbery with his coffee, then crushed the cup in his fist. Falling short almost cost Zoey's daughter and her best friend their lives.

The physical damage would heal. Warm baths, intravenous fluids, sleep and some home-cooked meals wouldn't cure the psychological trauma of being face-to-face with a murderer, being taken hostage and the enduring slow torture all alone in the middle of nowhere.

"Hey. You ready to saddle up?" Lonnie had moved to the doorway. By his tone and expression, it wasn't the first time he'd asked.

Administrative leave notwithstanding, there remained a few *i*'s in need of dots. Reconnoitering the house, they ensured all exits were sealed and secured and no ghouls had presumed the yellow crime scene tape wasn't intended for them.

The red seals Lonnie affixed to the front doors usually carried more clout. For reasons Hank couldn't comprehend, tampering with those was as rare as folks razoring a Do Not Remove Under Penalty of Law tag from their mattresses.

As Hank rounded his vehicle, Stan Hamilton shouted, "We're hitting the Waffle House for breakfast, if you're interested."

Lonnie grinned. Hank motioned *maybe next time*.

"Since you're not up for the real thing, there's something I think maybe you ought to chew on," Lonnie said.

Lord save me from Socrates Chichester, Hank thought. "Okay. Lay it on me."

"Well, it's not exactly absolution for either one of us, but…what if Charlie France hadn't decided to hold up the Jiffy Stop Sunday night?"

Lonnie turned to walk to his car. "Just food for thought, boss. Just food for thought."

"Ms. Jones," a voice whispered.

Zoey looked up from the book she wasn't reading. Chichester smiled, crooked a finger, then stepped back from the doorway. She sensed he'd been standing there a minute or two before he spoke.

As guardian angels went, Hank's burly young sidekick was more the Mel Brooks movie kind than garden-variety. Zoey would take him over central casting, any day.

Claire was sleeping soundly in her crate, as she'd dubbed the hospital bed with the upraised side rails. With her hair fanned on the pillow, and the healthy pink tinge returning to her cheeks, she looked almost normal.

If, Zoey thought, *you ignored the gauze wraps on her ears, hands and toes.* Frostnip, the nurses called it, as opposed to frostbite. How the girls had avoided the latter, no one could explain.

"I'm glad you're here, Sergeant." Zoey quickly surveyed the corridor for Hank. "Saying 'thank you' in person isn't nearly enough, but at the moment, it's all I can do. Just don't give me that 'I was only doing my job,' line, okay?"

"Yes, ma'am." He took a jumbo chocolate bar from his pocket. "Laura Peters and your daughter aren't much past the Jell-O and broth stage, yet, but being girls and all…"

Zoey almost cried. She had to swallow hard to stammer another thank-you. "Is, uh, Laura doing all right? I haven't seen her since the girls were in the E.R."

Claire had already asked several times to call Laura's room. Zoey had stalled but couldn't do so forever. How could she tell her that by proving her grandfather's innocence—foolhardy and dangerous a project as that had been—she'd lost her best friend?

His head cocked, as people's do when a comment doesn't jibe yet they're reluctant to press. "She's pretty well conked out, too. Sleep is the best thing for them, I guess."

"No insult intended, but you look like you could use a couple of days' worth yourself."

"Planning on it," Lonnie said. "Chowing down at an all-you-can-eat breakfast place this morning just about had me falling over in my plate."

He shifted his weight. "You heard about Andrew Kelly."

She nodded. Her heart went out to his daughter and wife, but she couldn't summon a ounce of sympathy for him. From what she'd been told, his character flaws and her ex-husband's were frighteningly similar. It was strange to feel something akin to gratitude that Stuart had chosen to run from his mistakes and his family.

"I understand he confessed to everything," she said.

"Yes, ma'am."

She hesitated, loath to appear critical, but she had no one else to ask. For reasons she couldn't fathom, Hank had not responded to any messages she'd left on his home and cell phone's voice mail.

"Without a doubt, this is a time when I should be counting the blessings I have, but—"

"You want to know why there's a guard still posted outside your father's room."

"Yes. I do." Glancing sideways, as though she could see through the wall to her daughter's bed, she went on, "Claire and my mother and I haven't seen him for almost a week. Darla Quinn took Mom home to rest a while ago, but she won't—not really—until our family's all together again. Even if there's a couple of hospital floors between us."

Chichester patted her arm, then squeezed it gently. "That's why I came by. It's unfair as all hell, and me and Westlake are meeting later with the prosecuting attorney, but the fact remains the homicide and robbery charges haven't gone away."

Zoey stared at him, trying to summon the energy to rant, rave or even express hatred of the court system in its entirety and the prosecutor in particular.

"We're on your side, ma'am. You can quote me on that, to whoever you care to. Me and the lieutenant are on administrative leave, but—"

"On what?"

He grimaced. "Standard operating procedure. Westlake'll have my gonads for saying anything, but Kelly being in our custody when he committed suicide means we're relieved of duty, pending a review board look-see."

A truly lousy way to treat two cops who had saved two kids' lives and arrested a murderer, child abductor and embezzler. Another chamber of her heart ached to know why, if Hank was off-duty, he hadn't returned her calls.

He'd checked Claire's condition by phone numerous times. The nurses had informed her of that.

As if reading her mind, Chichester said, "To be honest, I've never heard Loot talk like he did Saturday morning. Said he was responsible for Kelly abducting those girls and the suicide. I thought he was just getting it out of his system, but with the suspension on top of it..."

Advising her not to worry, Lonnie said if Hank didn't crawl from his cave by tomorrow, he'd kick down the door, personally.

Zoey raked back her hair. "This insanity isn't ever going to end, is it?"

"Yes, ma'am, it will. I promise."

"Yeah. After my father's trial for robbing four convenience stores."

24

Sunday, it was. The very name ordained the sunlight streaming through the hospital's fourth-floor window. As she perched on the ledge, the sun's warmth on Zoey's back felt like celestial amnesty after a prolonged literal and figurative absence. Yeah, okay, it had beamed yesterday, too, but for several reasons it had seemed more mocking than comforting.

Chief among them was the prosecuting attorney's stalwart refusal to drop the homicide charge against her father. A mere two hours ago, he'd dispatched an acolyte to apologize for the delay. From a legal standpoint, she'd explained, Andrew Kelly's confession wasn't worth much more than the tape on which it was recorded.

Confessions can be recanted. Accusations of coercion can be leveled against the police. Kelly's ill health, prescription medication, alcohol consumption and subsequent suicide called into question his mental state.

The circumstantial evidence against Charlie France hadn't been chucked in the round file, until after a new investigation—sans Hank Westlake and Lonnie Chichester—had confirmed the statements Andrew Kelly made to the police were true.

Zoey thought, surely, the fact that the prosecutor lived a block from the Kellys and played golf with him every weekend had no bearing on his reluctance to delete homicide from the charges against her father.

Once it was, he'd magnanimously given permission for Charlie to have visitors—family only—from one till three. Upon Charlie's expected release from the hospital tomorrow, he'd be officially on house arrest until Tuesday's arraignment for the convenience store robberies.

Where Hank had disappeared to and why remained a mystery. A huge "Get Well" balloon bouquet had been delivered to Claire's room, along with a dozen roses for Zoey. The message scrawled on the card enclosure read, "I will always love you, Hank."

A declaration, or an allusion to Whitney Houston's ultimate "it's not you, it's me" swan song? Maybe he only wanted what circumstances didn't allow him to have. Zoey told herself she didn't much care.

Since the France's family reunion had begun, Cardiac Care's head nurse, Mrs. Prewitt, had interrupted twice, warning she'd clear the room if Charlie, Vesta, Claire, Zoey and Al didn't put a sock in the noisemaking. What had begun with tears had evolved to a teasefest. Laughter was what they did best and needed most.

"I sure missed you, honey," Charlie told Vesta, when the Enforcer was out of earshot, "but ol'

Prewitt did make things feel a lot more like home around here."

"Did she, now?" Vesta shook a fist at him. "Wait'll I get you home, okay, funny man. You'll be lucky to get a moment's peace."

Al drawled, "He hasn't had one in forty-some years. Why should tomorrow be any different?"

"Dibs on the front seat for the ride home," Claire said, grinning. "I don't like back seats anymore."

Vesta and Zoey exchanged a glance at the reference to the abduction in Kelly's SUV. The more Claire talked, however she spoke of it, the better. Convincing Vesta not to shut down her granddaughter with a "You poor baby" look or an abrupt change of subject would be a challenge.

"Deal," Zoey said. "Except I have dibs on the steering wheel side, pretty much till you're ninety-two."

Claire stuck out her tongue, the ornery glint in her eyes glorious to see.

"I figured Hank'd be here to join the party," Charlie said. "From what I hear, you two've been making cow eyes at each other for days."

"You heard wrong, Dad."

He grunted. "Well, that's a fine howdy-do. I've told folks for years that I didn't raise any stupid children."

Al slapped his thighs and scooted forward in the chair. "I'd better shove off, if I want to get that ramp fixed for Claire's wheelchair before I run out of daylight."

Vesta started. "You can't leave yet, Al." She hastened to add, "I mean, goodness—it's not much past two. There's plenty of time to do that later this afternoon."

Zoey said, "Thanks, Al, but Claire can walk. She needs to, actually. The doctor's advised against marathons for a few days is all."

The circulation in Claire's extremities was normal, but she was still tender in places. Erring on the side of caution was wise. Hypothermia affected the entire body to varying degrees. Now that Claire was eating solid food, another night's stay would confirm that all systems were go.

"Okay, but it's no trouble to do it." Al scratched under an ear, then a spot at his ribs, as though extended hospital visits induced an allergic reaction. "Anything else needin' fixed?"

Zoey hesitated. She'd prefer to speak with him privately, but there was no help for it. "Now that you mention it, there is."

His hand raised. "Girl, I'm a skip and a jump ahead of you. The Help Wanted sign went up in the window yesterday. We'll call this week's check severance pay."

Relief felt like a spin on a merry-go-round. A wee-hour conversation with a nurse about Claire's computerized detective work had led to a tip that the hospital's tech-services manager didn't plan to return to work after her maternity leave.

The job didn't exactly zing Zoey's heartstrings. Returning to Cubicle-Land and its stresses made her temples throb in advance, but the hours were civilized, the salary reasonable and the respectability commensurate with both. Not that she was going corporate again for the Thena Peterses

of the world. They could take their self-righteous-
ness and stick it up their collective derrieres.

She was doing it for her daughter, who deserved
a mother, not the sleep-deprived breadwinner she
passed in the hallway before school, who tried and
failed to make up for lost time on Sundays.

Vesta gasped. "Oh, Al. Giving Zoey last week
off with pay was generous, but this one, too?
That's wonderful. *You're* wonderful."

He winked. "Stingy as you are with compliments, I oughta copy that down and make you
sign it."

"Hey, Gram," Claire said, and indicated her
grandfather's droopy eyes.

Vesta frowned and tapped Charlie's wrist.
"Don't nod off, lazybones."

"Ye gods, Mom," Zoey said. "Leave him alone."

"Hush. I didn't sit out in that corridor for days
on end to listen to him snore. He can sleep through
until morning if he cares to, after we're through
visiting."

"I'm kind of tired, too, Gram." Claire feigned a
yawn. "Me and Mom'll come back later and watch
that motorcycle show Grandpa likes."

Charlie grinned. "I'll sweet-talk Prewitt into
rustling you up a can of soda pop."

They all jumped at a rap on the open door. Osbert Schlomo peered in, then recoiled, a bewildered expression on his face. "I must have
misunderstood…forgive me for intruding."

"It's no intrusion at all," Vesta said. "Come on
in and have a seat. I believe you know everyone,
except Charlie's brother, Al."

Zoey's fingernails tapped a riff on the faux marble ledge. Something smelled, and it wasn't the lingering aroma of the poached fish her father had picked at for lunch.

Reluctantly, the attorney availed himself of an empty chair, balanced his briefcase on his knees, then shook hands with Al. "Well, er, I daresay you're as happy as I am at the recent turn of events."

"Yes, indeed. We most assuredly are." Vesta's tone sharpened. "And I appreciate you coming here on such short notice."

Charlie's arms crossed at his chest. "Goldurnit, woman. I knew you were up to something, the way you've fidgeted and watched that dadblasted clock the last half hour. Whatever it is, forget it. I'm worn out from the company and in no mood to listen to that shyster's gums flap."

Claire turned away to hide a snicker. Al coughed into a fist, obviously measuring the distance to the door and the odds of making a break for it. To her father, Zoey telegraphed, *I'm an innocent bystander. This is as much of a surprise to me as it is to you.*

Vesta said, "It's you that's going to do the talking, Charlie. You're going to tell us why you robbed those stores—right here, right now—or you won't have a home to go to, tomorrow."

Never had Zoey seen her mother confront her father about anything. Cajole, nag, guilt-trip, bully a bit, yes, but threaten? Not with so much as a withheld meal. And she wasn't bluffing.

Charlie, bone thin and weak though he was,

thrust out his jaw, his eyes riveted on the wall. "The hell I—"

"Say it to your granddaughter. Tell her that just because she believed in you so much, it almost killed her, you don't owe her an explanation. Or Zoey. Or Al. Or me. Or the lawyer I hired to help you and you've treated like dirt."

She braced her hands on the mattress and forced him to look at her. "The truth, Charlie. I won't ask twice."

Divided loyalties churned Zoey's insides. Her mother's demand was justified. Entrapping her father was cruel. He should have volunteered an explanation. That he hadn't done so indicated a sore lack of intention. And yes, by God, they did deserve to know why.

"For you girls," he whispered. "I did it for you."

"For...but why?"

His lips compressed, as though that ought to be enough for her, for all of them.

"If that's the way you want it." Straightening, Vesta reached for the handle of her purse, a few inches from Zoey.

"Please, don't go." He grabbed her wrist. "I *did*, honey. For you and Zoey and Claire. Being shut up in this room, not seeing you or talking to you...I kept telling myself I had to go through with it."

Vesta eased down beside him, willing to listen, but her patience obviously as ragged as the seams of his hospital gown.

"It wasn't till I saw Claire's picture on TV that I knew what a fool I'd been. So what if the prison doctors gave me a new heart? I'm no good to any of you, locked up."

His voice caught. "Even if I was, I love you all so much that being apart from you again would just break it all to pieces."

Head sinking deeper into the pillow, he strained to refill his lungs, looking to Zoey, then to Claire and back to Vesta, as if incapable of forgiving himself but begging their forgiveness. "I never meant for anybody to get hurt. All I was after was a little more time—a chance to take care of my family, like I promised I would."

Even Osbert Schlomo's eyes glistened with moisture. "I'd have never guessed, but it all makes perfect sense now."

The muscles in Zoey's nape tightened, offended by an outsider's clairvoyance. Her father's voice was wrenching to hear, but the substance was as cryptic as the plot of a TV movie you stumble on partway through.

Conscious of the attention refocusing on him, Schlomo said, "Your cardiologist told you a heart transplant was the only hope, didn't he, Doctor France?"

Charlie nodded.

The charade was over. Her father's constant, sometimes belligerent refusals to discuss his heart condition. Her mother fluctuating between stoicism and defiance. Zoey and Claire pretending that conclusions they'd drawn from their independent research were anything more than guesses.

Schlomo went on, "Never mind the tens of thousands of dollars you would have had to commit to add your name to the candidate list." He clucked his tongue. "Emotional malpractice, in my opinion. If it were litigable, I'd specialize in it."

"Oh, Charlie." Vesta smoothed back his hair and caressed his stubbled cheek. "That's why you robbed those stores? To pay for a heart transplant?"

Laying his hand over hers, he moved it to kiss her palm. "It's crazier than that, hon. Taking the money was to get myself arrested. I'd've pled guilty, they'd have thrown me in the slammer and everything would've been fine. Jailbirds don't have to pay for haircuts, much less whatever kind of medical care they need."

"Christ on a chariot, man." Al slumped back in his chair. "Where in the world did you get a cockamamie notion like that?"

"It happens to be true," Schlomo said. "It's doubtful a judge would deem four unarmed petty larcenies sufficient for a lengthy prison term, but inmates awaiting the death penalty have received organ transplants."

"What?" Zoey shrieked. "That's insane. It's Daddy who's getting the death penalty, just because he can't afford the surgery he needs."

The attorney spread his hands. "Will you allow a defense attorney a hypothetical question?"

"Sure." She chuffed. "Why not?"

"What if John Doe were wrongly convicted of homicide? Your father would have been, had the arraignment been held as scheduled on Friday and he pled guilty, as I assume he intended."

The lawyer scratched his chin. "Although new evidence shows John Doe may be innocent, overturning a conviction can take years and he's been diagnosed with heart failure. Should medical treatment be withheld pending the outcome of the appeal?"

Reeling from the news that her father would have willingly taken the blame for Joe Donny Marlowe's murder, Zoey said, "Excellent argument, counselor. Except I'm not Solomon and Daddy's heart condition isn't hypothetical."

"Neither are those robberies, Mom." Claire buried her face in her gauze-mittened hands. "What's the matter with you? With *all* of you, sitting there like this is all a stupid game? Don't you understand? Grandpa has to go to prison, or he'll die."

Schlomo stood, walked around the bed and knelt beside her. "Not if I can help it, Miss Jones."

"Yeah, right." She raised her head, her cheeks wet with tears. "Like you've done anything, besides take Gram's money and tell her she'd better scrape up some more or find herself another lawyer."

As Schlomo got to his feet, he looked as stricken as his client. He adjusted his tie, said, "The hearing is at two o'clock, Tuesday," and strode out the door.

25

Zoey's finger fell away from the doorbell's button. She regarded the toe of her penny loafer, then raised her eyes to the door. Its brass, question mark-shape handle-and-thumb latch provided more decoration than security. The round dead bolt several inches above it winked like a formidable eye, daring all comers to go ahead, give it a shot.

Looking over her shoulder at the pickup and unmarked sedan in the driveway, she weighed the odds of getting lucky, finding the lock's Achilles' heel with a solid hit from hers.

A part of her didn't care—a large, irrational spoiling-for-a-fight part that said kicking a dent in the door was worth spending the next six weeks hobbling around with a plaster cast up to her shin.

Before common sense could spin her around, prod her down the steps to her car and back to the hospital where she belonged and so clearly should have stayed, her knee levered backward. Her foot connecting squarely upside the door handle was as loud as a battering ram.

Too stunned to feel the impact, she stood there,

staring as it crashed open and slammed against the foyer wall. Just inside was a slack-jawed Hank Westlake, dressed in sweatpants and a T-shirt. He was barefoot, his wet hair spiky and dripping onto a towel around his neck.

"I was in the shower when you rang the bell," he said, looking from the jagged hole in the dry-wall to the woman who'd put it there. "I unlocked the door and hollered for you to come in, then went to grab some clothes."

Stating the obvious, Zoey said, "I guess I didn't hear you." Anger prevailed over remorse. "Kind of like you haven't heard the phone ring the past couple of days."

His features tightened. "Fair enough."

Stepping inside, she closed the door behind her, willing herself not to think of the crumbs of plaster littering the floor as symbolic. "Dad told us why he robbed those stores. He told you days ago, didn't he. When you questioned him at the hospital."

"Yes."

"You wanted to tell me, the other night, but you couldn't. No doubt he swore you to secrecy, but that wasn't the reason. Professional ethics was the biggest one. That it wouldn't change a thing, other than devastate me, was another. Plus, it'd put me in the horrible position of choosing whether to keep it to myself, or compromise you by telling my mother."

She shrugged. "Not to mention the fact that Daddy's scheme and the cause behind it were his to tell us, not yours."

He swiped a rivulet of water from his neck with the towel. The flatness of his voice was that of a condemned man when he answered, "Right on all counts."

Zoey nodded, as though the conclusion hadn't already been reached. "I love you, Hank. I always have, hard as I tried to convince myself it was only a schoolgirl crush."

Hands thrust in her coat pockets, she curled her fingers tight, fighting to control the emotion threatening to engulf her. "You say you love me. How can you—how can I believe you do when you didn't trust me enough to understand the lousy…make that impossible, position you were in?"

"Because bringing the job home with me has wrecked every relationship I've ever had."

"Oh, yeah?" Justified as he might be, it sounded like an excuse. And a pathetic one, at that. "Well, stand by for a news flash, Westlake. There's more than one way to wreck a relationship. A man who runs and hides when the going gets tough tops my list."

He flinched, the allusion to her ex-husband's defection apparently hitting the intended mark. "How many ways are there to fix one?"

"I don't know." She looked into his eyes, wishing she could let herself drown in them. "My best guess is, for some, more ways than they'll ever have use for. For others, there aren't nearly enough."

He pondered a moment. "I guess it's too late for us to start over."

"Nobody can. Not really." Wistfulness laced her smile. "Especially a couple of people who've known each other since eighth grade."

He eased her hands out of her pockets and clasped them. "I happen to think that's a good thing."

"Maybe." Her shoulder hitched. "Probably."

His thumbs rubbing her knuckles sent tiny shock waves radiating up her arms. "You wouldn't be here if you'd given up on me entirely."

True, but hearing him say it, even if not a shred of arrogance propelled it, had her angry all over again. "No, you're the one who gave up. On yourself and me."

Her chin jutted. "Of course, I should have seen it coming, that afternoon in Mom's kitchen after you searched her house. You don't just live by the book. You wrote the damned thing."

He recoiled, bewilderment as plain on his face as the bristles of a three-day-old beard.

"The timing is never going to be perfect for us. At least, not perfect enough for you to start holding me, instead of holding back because everything's not blue skies and rainbows, like you think it should be."

Pulling her hands free, she reached for the doorknob, the metal warmer than the gaze she leveled at Hank. "If you ever decide you want somebody besides Lonnie Chichester for a partner, let me know."

There were no Blytheville P.D. detectives among the group milling outside the hearing room. Spotting George Santini, Zoey bowed her head, like Sisyphus pushing his eternal boulder up the mountain, rather than a mother pushing her daughter's wheelchair along a polished marble corridor.

It had been Claire's idea to use the wheelchair— a ploy to elicit sympathy from the judge. Silly, Zoey supposed, and probably useless, as it was Charlie France scheduled to appear before him, not his granddaughter. But there was no harm in it, either.

Maintenance workers were wrestling a podium from a hand truck onto the floor beneath the rotunda. Thick black cables snaked across the mosaic reproduction of the Missouri state seal. The governor must be due to proclaim something dear to a portion of the town's constituency, such as Garden Club Week.

Santini moved to open the courtroom's door. His friendly smile seemed sincere and wholly out of place for a robbery victim who'd be seated on the prosecution's side of the room.

Zoey hadn't cleared the door when Claire bolted upright and squealed, "Laura!"

She, too, was wheelchair-bound, but swathed from chin to footrests in a fringed wool throw.

Behind her were Thena Peters, her face as rigid as her posture, and an older, stocky woman whose jet-black beehive looked like a wig. Though they'd only exchanged waves from a distance, Zoey recognized Bella Donna Sewell by her hairstyle.

"Excuse us, Ms. Jones," Bella Donna said, "but Thena would like to have a word with you."

"Oh, really." Zoey's glare should have tripped the ceiling's fire extinguishers. "Well, Mrs. Peters, as much as you apparently enjoy ambushing me, now isn't the time."

"I couldn't agree more, but Laura tied a rope to her bed this morning and shinnied down from a second-story window to go live with Claire. When I caught her, she said she'd accuse my husband and me of abuse, if I didn't allow her to remain friends with your daughter."

"I'll do it, too, 'cause that's what it is," Laura said. "Remember that huge psychology report I did last semester? I know exactly what to say to convince the guidance counselor that I'm emotionally abused."

Bella Donna's impish smile suggested a conspiracy was afoot of which her employer was not aware. "I'll promise you, the same as I did Thena, me and Euell will watch those two like hawks from now on."

Noting the girls' attention was riveted on each other, not the chronological adults, Zoey murmured, "I appreciate that, Bella Donna. Laura can come to our house whenever she wants, but I don't allow Claire to go anywhere she isn't welcome."

Thena's lips pursed. She swallowed, as though concessions were golf ball-sized and equally hard-surfaced. "She will be. If Laura thinks so highly of her, there must be good reason."

Compliments didn't come more backhanded, but Zoey bit off a remark to that effect. Teenaged girls were renowned for outgrowing best friendships like designer jeans. If Claire and Laura's endured as Zoey and Darla's had, they'd be truly blessed.

At Zoey's request, Darla wouldn't attend the hearing. It was open to the public, but Charlie had a right to an illusion of privacy. He loved Darla almost as much as he did Zoey, and her presence would embarrass him terribly.

"Can Laura stay here with me? We can take her home later, can't we, Mom?"

The wheedle shouldn't have caught Zoey off-guard, but it did. Her father had no choice but to plead guilty as charged. How he, Vesta, and even Zoey herself would react to whatever sentence the judge rendered was impossible to predict.

"What if I stay, too?" Bella Donna said. "Ms. Jones won't have two kids in wheelchairs to contend with and, if need be, I'll treat Laura to her first cab ride."

Thena wasn't intuitive enough to recognize it, but her housekeeper was offering Zoey support, not ground-traffic control.

She conceded, albeit reluctantly.

Under their own steam, the girls stationed their chairs in the center aisle, in full view of the judge's bench. The epitome of discretion, Bella Donna sat down alongside Laura, leaving the end of the adjacent row for family members and friends.

Vesta hastened into the room, just as the bailiff laid several files on the judge's bench. A stenographer followed and seated herself at a small desk opposite the prosecutor's table. Had a jury been present, her back would have been turned to them.

"Schlomo is how that man drives, for heaven's sake," Vesta whispered. "For a while there, I didn't think we'd make it from his office in time."

A steady stream of people—thirty or more, Zoey estimated—filed into the courtroom. Briefcases distinguished attorneys with cases on the docket from clients, witnesses and interested spectators.

George Santini and three other men sat down on creaky, wooden folding chairs in front of the bar. They didn't appear to be acquainted, but each clasped a sheet of paper like auditioning actors rehearsing their lines.

Zoey asked, "Where's Uncle Al?" at the same instant Vesta asked, "Where's Hank?"

"Al had a delivery to sign for. He'll be here as soon as he can." Vesta's eyes narrowed. "So help me, if you're blaming Hank for any of this, I'll take a switch to you when we get home."

A tearing sensation, like a knife shearing her heart, hadn't lessened since she closed the door to Hank's apartment behind her. "I love you, Mom, but please, just butt out."

Osbert Schlomo preceded his client to the defendant's table. Charlie's stoop was pronounced and his mouth clamped shut. In rhythmic pants, he inhaled oxygen from the tube under his nose. The tank strapped to a wheeled metal cart was now his constant companion.

He didn't look toward his family, but turned one hand palm-side out, his thumb and index finger forming the standard OK sign.

Vesta hiccoughed and pressed a wadded tissue

to her lips. "I'm all right, sweetheart. It's just hard, watching him go through this."

Zoey would have prayed, had she known what to pray for.

"All rise," the bailiff said. "This court is now in session, the honorable Mark A. Elliston presiding."

Zoey hadn't noticed the prosecuting attorney's entrance. Apparently, he hadn't had time to sit down before the bailiff's announcement.

"You may be seated. The first matter before the court, case number 9783-261, the state versus Dr. Charles Herman France."

Elliston opened a file and flipped through several pages. "You're representing the defendant, Mr. Schlomo?"

"Yes, your honor."

The judge droned out each charge, along with the date, time, location of the robbery and amount reported to have been stolen.

"Do you understand the nature and severity of the charges against you, Dr. France?"

A raspy, barely audible "Yes, your honor" hurt like a physical blow. Even from behind, he looked so small and ancient and frail.

"How do you plead?"

Charlie's body sagged, as though he'd sighed so deeply that muscle was collapsing atop bone. "Guilty, Judge. No three ways about it."

Schlomo's arm rose. "Your honor, if I may ask the court's indulgence before the sentence is passed?" He glanced at the prosecutor. "No tricks."

"Only because you couldn't bring the circus in

here with you." The other lawyer shrugged. "I have no objections, as long as it's a brief indulgence."

"Five minutes, Osbert," the judge said.

"Thank you, Judge." Turning, he made a sweeping motion to the four men seated behind him. "These gentlemen are here of their own volition. Each is employed by one of the stores named in the indictment against Dr. France."

A lanky young man in faded blue jeans and a package-creased, long-sleeved shirt peeled himself off the chair. "Name's Michael Vincent, sir. I work second shift at the Pump 'N Go."

The sheet of paper he held trembled violently. "I'm awful nervous, so I've gotta read this, but I swear, I wrote it all by myself."

Elliston waved him on.

Vincent cleared his throat. "The other day, when the detectives showed me Doc France's picture, I didn't want to tell them it was him that robbed the store. Why, you ask? 'Cause he's a fine man and real good veterinarian and I thought for all the kindness he's shown people over the years, if he needed money that bad, folks ought to just up and give him however much he needed to get by on, 'cause it ain't like he hasn't done the same for plenty of them, plenty of times."

The next man, Jimmy Chang of Chang's Market, admitted he'd cost his father more money in an hour, horsing around in the store, than Charlie France had taken from the cash register. Since the police assured them the money would be returned,

Jimmy's father hoped the judge would consider it a loan instead of a robbery.

Before Santini and the other clerk could speak, the judge motioned for them to keep their seats. "I admire your willingness to forgive and forget, but—"

"Pardon me, Judge Elliston," Schlomo said, "but I believe two minutes and, er, thirty-seven seconds remain of the five you allowed."

The judge consulted his watch. "And counting, Osbert."

The attorney's explanation of his client's motive for the robberies was delivered with such power, eloquence and passion, the courtroom was silent for several seconds beyond his deadline.

Judge Elliston's gaze surveyed the defendant, the oxygen tank beside his chair, the teenaged girls seated in wheelchairs in the aisle behind the bar. "Is that true, Doctor France?"

He nodded. "Yes, sir."

The prosecuting attorney said, "May I approach the bench?"

"No need, counselor. Dr. France has already entered a guilty plea. We both know I can't dismiss the charges against him."

He leaned forward on his elbows. "What I can do, Dr. France, is sentence you to serve one year in the state penitentiary for each count, with the terms to run concurrently."

Schlomo's fist hammered the table. "That is the most ridiculous—"

"Which I hereby suspend in lieu of unsupervised probation for a term of four years."

Cheers erupted throughout the courtroom.

Claire, Zoey and Vesta clasped hands, their emotions fluctuating wildly between joy and grief. It was a victory, yes, but a Pyrrhic one. Charlie wouldn't be escorted to the city jail to await his transfer to prison.

He was coming home with them...to die.

Schlomo practically leapt the bar, landing in front of Claire. "Please, Miss Jones, may your grandfather borrow your wheelchair for a moment? There's no time to explain, but if you'll follow us from the courtroom, you'll see why, in just a moment."

Before Zoey and Vesta could protest, much less demand an explanation, Schlomo had evicted Claire and was pushing a bewildered Charlie up the aisle, the oxygen tank zipping along like a sidecar.

Two bystanders, in danger of being smashed against the oak double doors, pushed them open, then shielded themselves behind them.

Print and TV reporters, still photographers and videocam operators surrounded the podium Zoey had attributed to a gubernatorial announcement. Osbert swung the wheelchair around beside it, then raised both arms, his fingers signaling V's for victory.

"What in the hell does he think he's doing?" Zoey said, starting toward the spectacle.

Into the microphone, he said, "Mrs. France, if you'll join us, please, I have the most wonderful surprise for you and your husband."

"A press conference?" Claire said. I *told* you he was a creep. Don't do it, Gram."

Whether Vesta didn't hear her or chose to ignore

the advice, she marched forward. By her expression, another France might be arrested for murder any second.

Schlomo laughed. "I do apologize for keeping this a secret, but I couldn't be certain how Judge Elliston might rule."

Adopting a pose common to any benefactor of a charitable organization, he said, "First, allow me to present you with this cashier's check in the amount of ten thousand dollars. It represents the first—and dare I say, last—full refund of a client's retainer in the history of my law firm."

Vesta stammered, "Refund? You mean, you're giving back our money?"

"Every penny of it, Mrs. France."

Zoey and Claire looked at each other, their mouths agape.

"Charlie, did you hear that?" Wrapping her arms around his neck, Vesta burst into tears. "He gave us back the money I paid him."

"Oh, that's just the beginning," Schlomo said. From a shelf inside the podium, he pulled out a yard-wide roll of laminated paper. Unfurling it, he held it lengthwise, high enough for camera range.

Claire read, "'Pay to the order of Charles H. France, the sum of…' Oh. My. God." She grabbed Zoey, almost pulling her to the floor. "It's for two hundred thousand dollars, Mom. Grandpa isn't gonna die. That's enough for a heart transplant."

Schlomo said, "Thanks to generous pledges our office's principals and staff members solicited from dozens of local businesses, we are delighted to present Dr. and Mrs. France with this check to underwrite the organ transplant procedure he so desperately needs, as well as much of his post-operative care."

The old courthouse's foot-thick walls appeared to shudder as pandemonium reigned for what seemed like an hour. It was Charlie himself who gestured for silence. "I got something to say and I don't have much voice to say it with."

A beaming Schlomo unclipped a microphone from a stand and handed it to him.

Dabbing his tearing eyes with his coat sleeve, Charlie took a deep breath, then looked at Zoey and Claire. "This is the kindest thing I reckon a town, much less a bunch of lawyers, has ever done for a broken-down old cow doctor. Believe me when I tell you, I appreciate it more than I could ever say. I just hope y'all can understand why I can't accept it."

"Charlie! What are you—"

"I'm sorry, Vesta, but I can't. I won't."

He appealed to his daughter and granddaughter. "I've had the best life, got the most loving family any man could ever hope for, whether it ends ten minutes from now, or ten weeks, or ten months."

He paused for breath, then continued. "One of the nurses' aides at the hospital told me about a five-year-old boy named Simon McCreary that was born with a bum ticker like mine. Nothing in this world would make me happier than to give that little fella the chance to grow up and marry the only woman he's ever loved and have a daughter and granddaughter as beautiful as mine."

A voice behind Zoey murmured, "If you'll have him, that's all this man will ever need to be happy, too."

Tears spilling down her cheeks, she turned with the certainty of a woman who'd sensed his presence, before Hank had made it known. "If there'll ever be a worse time to tell me that, I can't imagine when it would be."

He wrapped one arm around her and the other around Claire, pulling them close. Burying his face in their hair, he said, "Fool that I've been, if the two of you will have me, I promise, I'll never let you down, never let you go, again."

"Well, I don't know about you, but I happen to think that's a good thing."

"Maybe." She shrugged. "Probably."

Hank took her hands in his. His thumbs rubbed her knuckles, sending tiny shock waves radiating up her arms.

An adult rendering of a seventeen-year-old boy's grin crawled across his face. "I'd feel a whole lot better if I knew in advance what you'd say, but there's something I've just gotta ask you, darlin'."

Zoey pulled back slightly, as wary as she was curious. "Okay."

"Well, seeing as how you don't appear to have given up on me, entirely…" The grin widened. "Want to go bowling tonight?"

Head tipped back, she laughed up at the rotunda dome's gilt-edged clouds, rainbows and winged roly-poly cherubs.

"Deal."

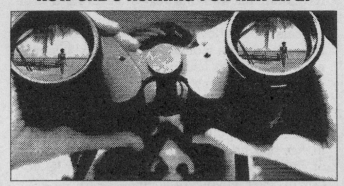

SUZANN LEDBETTER

66848	NORTH OF CLEVER	___ $5.99 U.S.	___ $6.99 CAN.
66797	SOUTH OF SANITY	___ $5.99 U.S.	___ $6.99 CAN.
66687	IN HOT PURSUIT	___ $6.50 U.S.	___ $7.99 CAN.
66597	EAST OF PECULIAR	___ $5.99 U.S.	___ $6.99 CAN.

(limited quantities available)

TOTAL AMOUNT	$_____
POSTAGE & HANDLING	$_____
($1.00 for one book; 50¢ for each additional)	
APPLICABLE TAXES*	$_____
TOTAL PAYABLE	$_____

(check or money order—please do not send cash)

To order, complete this form and send it, along with a check or money order for the total above, payable to MIRA Books, to: **In the U.S.:** 3010 Walden Avenue, P.O. Box 9077, Buffalo, NY 14269-9077; **In Canada:** P.O. Box 636, Fort Erie, Ontario L2A 5X3.

Name:_____
Address:_____ City:_____
State/Prov.:_____ Zip/Postal Code:_____
Account Number (if applicable):_____
075 CSAS

*New York residents remit applicable sales taxes.
Canadian residents remit applicable GST and provincial taxes.

MIRA®

www.MIRABooks.com

MSL0904BL